BLOOD

&

WATER

Edited by
Hayden Trenholm

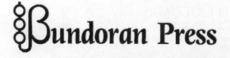

Cover Design: Virginia O'Dine

Printed in Canada
Published by Bundoran Press Publishing House
www.bundoranpress.com

Library and Archives Canada Cataloguing in Publication

Trenholm, Hayden, 1955-
   Blood and water / Hayden Trenholm.
ISBN 978-0-9877352-3-2
I. Title.
PS8589.R483B56 2012 C813'.54 C2012-903167-4

Bundoran Press gratefully acknowledges the support of the Province of British Columbia through the British Columbia Arts Council.

COPYRIGHT ACKNOWLEDGEMENTS

Contents

BLOOD & WATER
AN INTRODUCTION

Imagine standing at the mouth of the Colorado River where it enters the Gulf of California, just across the US-Mexico border. Instead of a rushing river, you see a trickling stream. Science Fiction? Not at all. Like many major rivers in America, the waters from the Colorado are fully allocated—for agriculture, industry, recreation and human consumption—taken up and used long before the river reaches its ocean outlet.

The Colorado, feeding the dry south-western states, is particularly dramatic in this regard. In fact, more water is allocated than the basin produces most years—especially in the last decade—and only careful management of interstate agreements and international treaties have kept all users satisfied. But, as we all know, you can't change the laws of physics. Travel to Lake Mead, one of the artificial lakes created by dams on the Colorado, and you can see for yourself what warmer, dryer weather has wrought. Water levels rise and fall with the seasons and from year-to-year, but the general trend for the last fifty years has been down. You only need to stand on one of the old piers, now extending into open air, and look down on the lake far below, to take the measure of that trend.

Artificial lakes aren't the only ones affected by human demands and changing climates. The Great Lakes, collectively the largest body of fresh water in the world, are at record low levels, as well. Meanwhile, glaciers in the Rocky Mountains that feed the hungry taps of California and supply water throughout the west are shrinking. Those in Jasper National Park, west of Edmonton, used to extend down to the highway; now, it's a fair hike across glacial till to reach their lowest extent.

Fights over water have seldom erupted in a shooting war in North America, but it came close on the Alberta-Montana border as far back as 1909 and occasional violence over water between neighbours in Texas (where water rights go to those who can grab them) are not unknown. But the world has already seen at least one war—that in Darfur—where water and who gets to use it was a major aspect of the conflict. Even as I write this introduction, there are threats of military conflict over water in the Kashmir, a new element in the long-running dispute between India and Pakistan.

Of course, conflicts over resources are as old as human history. 'Blood' diamonds financed the conflict in Ivory Coast and the long, bloody civil war in the Congo was mostly about who got to control, and profit from, its vast mineral wealth. Despite rhetoric about freedom and religion, at least some of the strife in the Middle East has its roots in fights over the region's oil wealth.

Climate change, along with continued population expansion and changes to the world economic order, adds a significant new factor to the equation. We can live without diamonds and gold, we can even find alternatives to oil, but water, food, land, and air are irreplaceable. Major conflicts over those will be driven by desperation and fear beyond any we've seen before. Look at the riots in Indonesia and other countries when food prices rose as a result of redirecting palm oil, corn or rice to energy production. Yet, the United States and Canada continue to pursue a doubtful food-for-fuel subsidy program.

It's not all bleak. Human ingenuity is great and technology may still provide solutions to some resource problems, preventing or limiting conflicts between neighbours. Perhaps the world and its leaders will even come to their senses and find a way to mitigate climate change before the global temperature rises too much for our fragile environment—and even more fragile economy—to handle.

Think it can't happen? Take solace in this. The treaty that divides the water of the River Jordan between Syria, Jordan, Lebanon and Israel has survived more than sixty years of conflict and war. It is, unlike international financial companies, truly too big to fail.

The Stories

When you put out a call for submissions, all you can really do is give a sense of what you're looking for; the rest is up to the writers. I was primarily looking for near-future (next fifty years) science fiction—though I was open to cross-genre and even urban fantasy.

As the guidelines said:

'Blood and Water will gather the stories of the new resource wars that will mark the next fifty years—stories of conflict and cooperation, of hope and despair—all told from a uniquely Canadian perspective. Conflicts with America over Canada's resources, Canadian solutions to global problems or personal narratives of coping with change and conflict could all inspire your stories. Or you could surprise us!'

In the end, there were remarkably few stories where conflict with our neighbours to the south was a central theme. In fact, while breakdowns in social order were a common background element—actual war only appeared in a handful of submissions. Perhaps, that is the 'uniquely Canadian perspective,' we were looking for: every conflict has a resolution, every problem has an answer.

I'm pleased to present an impressive collection of writers—from well established authors to rising Canadian stars to two for whom Blood and Water represent their first fiction sale—representing every region of the country and whose stories are set from coast to coast to coast.

Mostly science fiction, with a sprinkling of the fantastic, Blood and Water presents a mostly bleak future—but also offers hope and even joy. There is great writing here and fabulous stories. I hope you enjoy reading it as much as I did putting it together.

Hayden Trenholm

For further information on resources and the conflicts they may cause, I recommend:

Dry Spring by Chris Wood, Raincoast Books, 2008
Resource Wars by Michael T. Klare. Holt Paperbacks, 2002
The God Species by Mark Lynas, Fourth Estate, 2011
Global Warring by Cleo Paskal, Key Porter Books, 2010

DROWNTOWN

Camille Alexa

Vancouver is a drowned city, and those of us who live here haunt its steel and glass towers like restless ghosts.

At night it's easy to see which towers have squatters. Candles and small fires illuminate randomly punctuated windows of abandoned condominiums and offices, little rectangles of light winking out over the water separating one half-submerged tower from the next. This early in the morning the water is dotted with small rafts, canoes, sailboats— people paddling or rowing or tacking from one square glass island to the next.

The morning sun is glorious, a golden ball cresting the world, casting the mountains into sharp silhouette, burning mist off the water below where I sit cross-legged on the balcony of our drowntown condo, my clean wet hair in a single heavy braid looped over my shoulder drying as I picture what downtown Vancouver must've been like when my mother was a child. Back then, standing on this balcony would've meant looking down eight or ten storeys to the pavement below, to the busy streets of a city thrumming, cars and pedestrians, sirens and streetcars and buses and the pulses of two million people jumping in two million throats to the beat of two million hearts. Not one thousandth that number live here now and those who do are the poorest. Used to be, downtown Vancouver was only for the wealthiest.

Well it's all drowntown now, and the wealthy have moved up the hillside, or into the mountains, keeping ahead of the rising ocean as the polar icemelt gives up its last drops. It's got to stop sometime, though, hasn't it?

Micah pads out through the open glass doors onto the balcony, rubbing sleep from his eyes, looking particularly small this morning, younger than his age. Some days I think he looks so big, the toddler I remember now growing up fast as an eyeblink. Other days he looks so small, too small. Like someone could slip him into a deep pocket and row off with him, or like he could fall between the metal bars of the balcony railing where our raft is moored, splash into the water and disappear from my life forever.

Without speaking, he moves aside the long plait of my hair and curls into my lap, head resting on my shoulder, bony child-knees folded over mine as he toys with the end of my braid. I press my face into his curly hair and breathe his bitter sugar scent. Silent, we watch the sun rise together.

Assessing the little pile of gleanings I've managed to salvage these last couple weeks is discouraging. But it's Market day and I don't have much choice; something here has got to work, got to be worth enough to buy us another month. Things have been so tight lately, I wonder if I should rethink how I've been going about it all, maybe demand chits and set them aside each week like I always say I'm going to, rather than bartering goods directly with neighbours all the time for food, for water cistern repair parts, for other small things that add up so quickly. Did Micah really need that new shirt last week? I thought so at the time, but if it means he has to go without other things… well, I'd rather see him in rags, or in nothing at all. It's warm enough these days, most of the time. Warmer every year.

Packing my raft with barter goods, I take stock again. I'm a scavenger, roaming the uninhabited portions of drowntown towers for stuff people might want. There are several nice-sized mirror shards this month from a bank tower along the old Burrard Street canal. Mirror's pretty common, but there's always a slight street value. These picture frames are nice, and I did find a few salvageable textiles among the water-rotted stuff in a residential tower not far from ours. Hard to tell some days, poking around with your flashlight, wading through pitch dark half-drowned hallways at the waterline in muck up to your hips, what the useful stuff is going to be once it dries out. Textiles are a difficult salvage even on upper floors, on account of the humidity and the damp, and the years of neglect.

The mirror shards, the picture frames, the small pile of carefully cleaned and dried and folded textiles. Five matching high-end plastic shower curtains from one of the old hotels, with pleasing designs and only a few small rends. Some miscellaneous unchipped coffee mugs, cutlery, and two lovely heavy vases in perfect condition. Not much call for those out here, but there's always a few uphill antique dealers shopping the drowntown Market for their Upper North Shore boutiques. My best find this week is the unopened bottle of whiskey, stopper intact, contents uncontaminated. According to the faded label this whiskey was the age I am now about the time I was born. Now it's twice as old as I am, and bound to be worth something to somebody.

One last trip to the rooftop garden to use our latrine and dump the nightsoil into the composter and we're ready to head out. Micah's moving slowly this morning, seeming more tired than usual, though he doesn't say anything. I look away from the dark rings under his eyes, my heart sharply aching like any cramping muscle might.

Micah unmoors the raft from our balcony and we push off. He holds the end of my single braid like he was taught to do as a baby, though he's no baby anymore. It's for comfort more than safety these days, though for the first two years we lived out here I was in constant fear of him falling into the water and told him to hold on to me all the time. I'd have nightmares about him being suddenly gone, in which I'd scour the underwater city, calling his name, bubbles rising from my mouth without sound. Funny that the underwater Vancouver landscape of my nightmares is always the same as in my regular dreams, with people and cars and dogs on leashes all floating and peaceful in a glowing ambient light that softens everything. The Vancouver of my sleeping imagination is like a watery Pompeii, people frozen in space and place going about their everyday activities of eating and working and copulating, glasses of wine on their tables and cats curled on their laps and waterlogged books in their hands as tendrils of their hair and clothing wafts gently around their drowned limbs.

Market is bustling today; Micah and I are later than usual. A few vendors have some lovely plantains, though our rooftop crop is close to fruition. And plantains aren't so great for Micah, of course, though I can certainly trade them for things he can eat.

The cloth merchant is in his stall. He likes my antique textiles, says there's a definite demand for them uphill, says it's in fashion right now to have cocktail dresses made of water-salvaged cloth. Environmentally friendly, or some such. Not sure I fully understand what a cocktail dress looks like, I accept his standard universal barter chits and hand over the folded textiles. I let my fingertips slide across the soft fabric one last time as I pass it to him, imagining a cocktail dress in its faded watery hues.

Drowntown Market is a funny thing, all cobbled together and propped inches above its original site. When Micah and I first came, the Market was on a flat drowntown rooftop perfectly level with the sea. From a distance it looked like the vendors walked on water among their cannonball piles of melons, their cords of wood, their tubs of arable soil hauled from shore to replenish rooftop gardens. In just a few years the water has risen enough so people have built their stalls up on stilts, and fashioned walkways from salvaged planks and metal bars so their prospective clients don't have to stand ankle-deep to haggle for their wares.

One of my regular buyers accepts my mirror shards without enthusiasm, and critically eyes the rends in my plastic shower curtains. I accept her begrudgingly handed over chits and trade one immediately in the next stall for a roasted something on a stick for Micah. Micah's too good; he'd completely crash before he'd tell me he needed to eat. We lounge on our moored raft as he eats with one hand, his other grasping the end of my braid like a baby elephant holding its parent's tail with its trunk. That's us, Micah and me: big elephant and little elephant.

A couple of antique dealers from uphill who often come down with their small dog to trade canned food for fashionable salvage are delighted to take the vases off my hands. I send a secret thank-you to the bank manager who decorated her office with such stupid things two lifetimes ago, and who had the foresight to abandon them in such a conveniently sheltered spot. Disappointingly, the dealers won't take the whiskey. Volatile provincial politics have apparently swung in the restrictive direction again, and fun is out of fashion once more except among the exceedingly rich. There's certainly a market for my antique whiskey in the city, they assure me, fondling the bottle with regret, oohing and ahhing over its peeling paper label. Out here on the water is one thing, but it would be contraband ashore, and more trouble than anyone would want, to be caught in possession of such a controlled substance without legal documentation.

A bitter taste rises in my mouth as I picture someone sipping legal whiskey with all the proper taxes and stamps, wearing a cocktail dress constructed of environmentally friendly drowntown fabric.

My throat tightens as I leave Micah playing with the antiquers' dog and head toward the distiller's stall. As soon as I'm out of sight I fumble the barter chits from my pocket and count. Stomach clenching, teeth clenching, heart sinking, I tell myself it's got to be enough. Surely it is. If we eat only homegrown mushrooms for a week, ignore local warnings against the lead-heavy inlet fish, and don't make a fire, go without new candles or matches… It all depends on what the distiller will give me for the salvaged whiskey.

But he doesn't give me shit.

I plead with him to pay more than he's offering. I beg. He knows why. They all know why, here at the Market. They all know what I buy each month from the vendor who makes his rounds up and down the coast, the specialist, the only person within a hundred miles of drowntown Vancouver willing to accept barter chits for what I must buy.

In the end, the distiller gives me more than he wants to, but less than I need. Before I'm even three stalls away he's putting out thimble-sized cups and a little sign, hand-lettered: *rare antique novelty product, five barter chits per glass.*

I'm adding, adding all my chits in my head. Add them again, as though they'll multiply without any effort on my part. Between two rows of covered Market stalls I see Micah with the uphillers, still playing with their little brown dog. It's only a pot-hound: the animal you get when you toss all the canine DNA in Canada into a single pot and stir. Micah has always wanted a puppy, but I can barely feed two of us.

Don't think about eating. Don't. Just go to the specialist's tent. Ask for credit. Ask for a favour. Ask for mercy. Anything.

He knows me, knows what I've come for as I do every month. Handing over my fistful of chits, I try to still the tremor travelling up my arm.

Not enough, he tells me, thumbing through them. *You know it's not.*

Maybe you can advance me two weeks' worth and I'll pay you back next month, I say. *Or maybe you can make a special trip, come back to Vancouver in two weeks this time rather than four. I'll get more by then. I'll find a way.*

His look tells me his answer. I think I see regret flicker there… or is it disdain? Maybe it's guilt. But overriding it all is hardness. Hardness, and the answer no.

I remember what it's like in the cities. Desperate people clog the alleyways, the doorways, the subways, the walkways. People with no place to go, with nothing to eat. People with nothing to hope for. You harden yourself against it to survive. Harden yourself against it, or get out.

Maybe I've got something else you can use? I say. He startles a little, though surely this isn't the first time he's faced desperation. He lets his glance slide off me, clearly not interested in the obvious; I think his tastes swing the other direction anyway. *This shirt has plenty of wear in it, I say, and begin fumbling with my buttons. If I had shoes I might be ab*le to trade those, but nobody in drowntown wears shoes.

He surprises me with a hand on my wrist. Knowing he doesn't want my shirt, I stop unbuttoning. I'm thinking, my mind churning, wondering what will be worth something to this man, this specialist who has regular customers all the way to Alaska, to California, maybe even to Mexico. What would be unique enough to interest him, and legal, not contraband? Man like him doesn't deal in contraband. My whiskey wouldn't have done him any good: too much risk. That's why I come to him for what I need in the first place; he's legit, and his goods are reliable, and safe, and legally procured, with documented provenance and quality assurance.

He studies me, eyes narrowing to slits. He makes a circular motion with his hand, indicating I should turn around. I do, turn all the way, three-hundred-and-sixty degrees, him scanning me head to toe. Standing under his scrutiny I feel more naked than if I didn't have any clothes on. More naked than without any skin on.

Hair, he says at last. *I'll take all those chits, and your hair. And you can have what you need.*

I open my mouth. Close it. I rarely think about my hair. Even when washing it, even when braiding. I don't think about my hair the way I don't think about the breath in my lungs, or the way my arms swing when I walk.

It's never been cut, I say.

He nods. He knows I'm telling the truth; he's a specialist in exotic goods.

I close my eyes when he saws through the heavy braid, squeeze them shut tight expecting pain to flood my spine starting at my nape where the coldness of his blade bites as though it's my neck he slices and not the thick rope of my hair. Afterward he holds it by its unbound end and studies it, like it's the dangling carcass of a snake longer than Micah is tall. I see bright Vancouver sunlight glinting off its strands from the corner of my eye, but don't look. Instead I gaze out across the water, letting hard light reflecting off a glass tower stab straight into my face until white spots dance across my vision, making my eyes water.

When I do look at him, he's gently wrapping the braid in cloth. He coils the cloth loosely and lowers it into a sack, and turns to find me holding my hand out for his trade. He nods, rummages in a cooler beneath his folding table and hands over the cool white plastic pouch with the blue circle on it like a big blue zero or a rounded open blue mouth with no teeth. It's sealed and stamped, and I trust him, but I still tear the perforated zip-closure with my thumbnail and open the bag, quickly count the month's supply of prefilled insulin syringes inside.

Thank you, I say, my head strangely light, and without waiting for a reply turn and make my way past the distiller's stall, past the heaps of textiles and the stacks of broken mirrors, past the cairns of rooftop-garden melons and tomatoes and strawberries, clutching the bag that will keep Micah alive until next month's Market.

BUBBLES AND BOXES

Julie E. Czerneda

Bubbles and boxes floated past the scanner, hooked nanarms snaring those that reflected red under the laser sweeps, confirming the spec tests. The operation was deceptively familiar, given the scale was so far beyond normality Sara had stopped analogy-hunting long ago.

Scale was irrelevant, she thought, adjusting the gain on her goggles to improve the illusion of depth. They were simply bubbles and boxes on an assembly line. Not very pretty, either; plain better suited them to their function. The nicest ones always seemed to be odd ones, the occasionally irregular shapes that the quality-control nans rightly captured and held for destruction. *Still,* Sara thought, swinging the gymbaled headpiece to follow the death struggles of an elaborate octagon, *it was a shame.* The laser bounced off its stubby strands and floppy corners in unpredictable and changing patterns. A work of almost living art, that took million dollar glasses to appreciate.

Then it was gone, broken into its component strands, twisting ribbons of 80 bases longing for completion, to be rinsed away in the next part of the process. There was the promise, at least, of rebirth.

"If you're finished, Dr. Surghelti," a soft voice breathed into her ear, "you have the usual line-up outside."

Sara closed her eyes before ducking her head from the goggles. It took a moment to prepare her senses for the macro world again. Then she blinked owlishly at her post-doc, Mai Ling. "The 101's?"

Mai Ling's dimples belied her otherwise serious expression. "They didn't like your last question, Doctor. The essay?"

"Show me a first year biotech class that does." Sara waved at the stacks of fresh exam papers turning her desk and those of her grad students into lunar landscapes, cratered by work space and coffee mugs. "At least I don't ask them to mark their own." Out of habit, Sara glanced along the gleaming outer surface of the tube before closing the view port she'd been using. Most of the automatic assembly plant looped through the walls and ceiling, only here dipping to her level like the courteously offered arm of a gentleman octopus, meeting the feeder tubes coming up through the floor.

An assembly plant like no other. Within, girders of DNA were being constructed from raw materials drawn through the feeders. Those girders were joined by nanarms, themselves built of DNA, into whatever structure Sara chose. Today, it was bubbles and boxes, the containment vessels used everywhere to ferry raw materials. Tomorrow it might be more quality-control nans, with their molecular keys and hooks to snatch the unwanted. The results of this self-assembly could only be seen here, through her viewer into the quality-control section, where nanarms destroyed the undesirable.

Sara pushed the massive chrome and black helmet, with its assemblage of jury-rigged wiring and state-of-the-art complexity, upward with a flick of her wrist. It hummed its way into the ceiling cupboard. With her other hand, she poked a loose strand of hair back under its cap.

"They're used to having marks before they leave the room, that's all," Mai Ling considered the towering pile of exams on her own desk. "Maybe next year we could just go with self-marking exams?" she asked wistfully. "I could use more research time. And sleep."

"I never promised you sleep," Sara said with an unrepentant grin. No secret she abhorred the university's enthusiasm for automated grades. *But nothing*, she thought, *told her more about an individual's grasp of concepts than self-expression*. Logical argument, not guesswork, passed students through her classes. Self-marking exams were like the nans: quality control by eliminating the variable—not recognition of excellence.

"Dr. Teig called."

Sara glanced at the lab clock in disbelief. 8:30 AM. *A little early to be one of those days*. "Message?"

"Under the Rock." The weathered concrete lump on Sara's desk was a memento from the anti-biotech riots of the early days, having left a more lasting impression on her office wall than protests had on policy. Sara kept it as a reminder of a time of tumult and disagreement. And for messages from Chuck Teig.

There was a stack of pink slips beneath it. Considering that she'd called Chuck back two days ago, he'd been busy. *What was he after this time?*

A nanarm paused.

There was no question this hesitation was accidental. If any had known to investigate, the culprit might have been identified as a temperature gradient, a miniscule change in local environment, its cause an open door to a hall cooled by a spring breeze, the breeze carried in on the shoulders and chatter of a group of students lingering to talk within the outer doors, preventing them from closing immediately. Still, change occurred. A nanarm paused. And an irregular, beautiful shape, neither box nor bubble, floated past, reflecting new and unimagined colours from the laser, different from all the rest.

Unremarked. And so, uncorrected.

"Yes, Chuck, I've reviewed your latest paper." The flood of messages throughout the day had been a demand for her attention. *Well, he had it.* Unfortunately, formal dinners and discussions with her old friend didn't mix well. Sara lowered her voice in vain hope of keeping him under control. "If I were you, I wouldn't submit it."

"If I were you, I couldn't have done the research," Chuck's answering growl was predictably superior. Self-employed, self-funded, and with enough self-confidence to have alienated more than one scientific community, he had the privilege of independence. And never hesitated to remind her.

Opinionated to a fault, of course. Sara had half-expected Chuck's latest messages to be about his pet peeve: the continuing public release of DNA-based nanotechnology. The nanarms, multi-purpose girders, were the basis of the machinery that sorted and purified vital biological components, from sugars to amines. Linked together, nans formed the molecular bubbles and boxes used to isolate purified substances for transport. Without both, it would have been impossible to develop the GTS, the Global Tubing System.

A system Chuck thoroughly distrusted, making it his mission in life to inform Sara personally about any potential problem he imagined. Why her? Partly because no one else listened to him on the subject, after years of flawless operation.

And partly, Sara admitted, because she'd been the first to release the technology on the 'net, over every one of what she'd taken for his self-interested, profit-centred objections. Models, schematics, procedures—all made public the same night, in hopes of a quick adoption of a worldwide standard, of compatibility. It had worked beyond anyone's wildest dreams.

They'd ended hunger.

The nans made it possible to constantly shift essential nutrients from wherever produced to wherever needed, freed from dependence on weather, climate, or even conventional means of shipping. More than that. It became impossible for any one group to control the flow as dozens, then hundreds, then hundreds of thousands of stations connected to the GTS. The technology had been available to anyone—as a result, the commerce of supply and demand became linked at the level of cities, between marketplaces rather than states. The politics of starvation withered and died.

Despite such fundamental change in their world, despite all signs of a pending golden age, Chuck Teig remained stubbornly skeptical. At least, he'd had the sense to confine his paranoia to her.

Sara sipped her martini and wiggled her toes in too-tight shoes. The Alumni Dinner was her professorial obligation; Chuck was here to accept an award for his company's latest donation. She didn't want the details. Given the success of his last patent, he'd probably funded her own wing for the next decade. A thoroughly obnoxious development, considering she'd outscored him in all their classes.

The dining room could have been any formal setting; its soft ring of fine crystal and murmuring voices the sounds of civilized conversation at any gathering. However, this room was filled with, at a guess, the top 20% of the world's biotech experts, ample testimony to the wisdom of the ULS' founders. A university dedicated to biology had seemed a gamble fifteen years ago, when the forefront of change had been more silicon than carbon. But it had proved visionary. The manipulation of living matter became the hottest field since the quantum computer. Waterloo's University of Life Science, though no longer alone, could boast it remained the best launchpad from which to enter the race.

And one of its biggest winners was preparing to slingshot an olive at her with his spoon. "So why shouldn't I publish?"

Sara made herself smile. "Chuck," she began, then changed her mind. There was an unfamiliar pleading on his normally cherub-like features. His hair distracted her, too. He'd regrown it in a striped pattern this season; fine for Paris but hardly the fashion among the relatively conservative scientists present tonight. To make matters worse, the patches above his ears hadn't taken well, creating a checkerboard look. *He'd probably worn that old baseball cap of his during its early growth,* Sara thought. Biotech was unlikely to ever make hair replacement idiot-proof. "Chuck, the problem isn't the science in your paper—"

"Well, God, that's a relief," he said too loudly. The other four at their table gave automatic shivers before resuming their whispered discussion of the latest affair between the USL President and her staff. "Typos? Told you I'm getting a new secretary."

Sara sighed. "You never could spell," she agreed. "No, Chuck. What troubles me about your paper is its implications."

"Oh." He tossed his napkin into the air with disgust. "That crap." This drew a warning scowl from the Dean at the next table. Chuck saw it in Sara's reaction and turned to scowl back. Sara shrugged helplessly. *They should know Chuck by now.* His donations were the only social link he'd left in this room. "When are you going to step into the real world, Sara-socks?"

She winced at the pet name; another sign Chuck was losing what propriety he possessed. And the main course was only now arriving at the outskirts of the hall. "This isn't the time for a debate—"

"Fine," he said quickly, with a smug look. "Thursday, my place. You've that informatics lab, right? Come after. I still make a mean cocoa."

She knew the others at their table hung on her answer, nothing loath to gossip over her. Then she looked at Chuck and saw the recklessness there, added it to the potential for disaster she saw in his latest work. There really was no option. "10:30 then. Now let me eat my supper in peace."

The new shape was more delicate, its unusual anatomy inclined to split at the edges when jostled by bubble or box. Its then-exposed arms beckoned to the debris of the nans' destructive sorting, an irresistible come-hither, molecular matchmaking of unparalleled potency.

Then, there were two.

"You've gotten better."

Julie E. Czerneda

Chuck poured the last of the cocoa into Sara's cup. "Actually, the cows have," he announced, grinning as she gave the brown liquid a startled second look.

"I hadn't heard. You did it?" At his nod, Sara took another sip, slipping the warm chocolate taste around her tongue. *Perfect.* None of the aftertaste or odd texture that had plagued earlier attempts to biogeneer dairy cows to produce chocolate milk. "Another first for Teig Biotech. My congratulations." Sara didn't bother estimating the return on this particular patent. No doubt it would be a runaway success, especially with the devastation of the cocoa crop in South America. Such a shame they'd used plant retroviruses against the plantations of drug lords and lost so much more than planned. "Solids?"

Chuck pulled out a small foil bag. He ripped off one end with his teeth and poured small brown chips into her waiting palm. "Cookie-ready, Sara-socks. Try'em next time you bake."

Since Chuck knew Sara's culinary skill peaked at reheating packaged dinners, she ignored this, but licked some of the chips from her hand. The background flavour held a distinctive coconut-like tang, but she could find no fault with the chocolate.

"Nicely done. Chocoholics everywhere will bless you." Then she raised a brow at his pleased expression. "Any preliminaries on the economic impacts of increased demand for dairy cows? What about the countries with stockpiles of cocoa beans? Will there be a disruption in milk supplies?"

He wagged one finger under her nose. "Gotcha!" Chuck drew a datacube from his pocket, surreptitiously freeing lint from one edge, and dropped it into Sara's now chocolate-free hand. "Impact studies by nine impeccable experts, a planned two year phase-in to the marketplace combining continued profits for existing stocks with preferential location of biogeneering stations, and my Grandma's recipe for the best cookies on the planet."

Sara held up the cube. "I will check this, Chuck. After what happened to the maple syrup producers—"

Chuck shook his head vehemently, a strand of willful checkerboard hair tumbling over one eye. "Not my fault."

"You sold the patents for biogen maples to Senegal!"

"The marketplace dictates."

Sara rolled her eyes and gave up the argument. Senegal was now covered with two metre-high dwarf, tropical, and year-round productive sugar maple trees, while the maple bush in Ontario, Quebec, Vermont, and Maine was worth more as veneer wood. The only portion of the industry left in its traditional location was the making of cute bottles. Consumers seemed quite happy buying "Made in Senegal" syrup as long as it came with a wood shanty and draft horse on the label.

Sara tossed the cube up and down. "Let's hope this is an improvement, Chuck. That's all I'll say until I read it myself."

With a cheerful nod—nothing seemed to affect Chuck's approach to life for long—he beckoned her to follow him. Sara sighed, straightened her long legs, and unwedged herself from the couch. Her feet had just stopped throbbing.

But this was why she'd agreed to come, after all. Chuck's newest project.

Two became four. Four became eight. Eight became sixteen. Bounced about in the streams, they separated, arms reaching in the laser-lanced darkness. Some were snared and destroyed, only to have their remains snatched up by others.

Then, partial destruction produces incomplete separation. A novel shape appears.

Growth.

Chuck's home was an outgrowth of Teig Biotech's headquarters. In the beginning, he'd lived in his office, rolling out a sleeping bag when biological necessity overcame his creative urges. Once able to afford a house, he'd found traveling back and forth a nuisance and promptly gave it to a grateful, if amazed, nephew. Not that he suffered: his portion of the building included a gamesroom, pool, and ballroom. Sara knew he'd wanted a bowling alley but the vibration would have impacted his research.

Easy to mistake it as the home of a man consumed by his work, Sara thought, knowing the truth. Chuck was having fun. He'd been lucky enough to pick a playground with very large financial rewards. He'd have been as happy still sleeping under his desk at the university.

Well, maybe not, she added honestly to herself. Chuck was happier being his own boss, and so were those around him.

"Through here," he muttered, using his hand on the small of her back to steer Sara from the door she expected towards another.

"Not the main lab?" she protested, and almost bit her tongue. Chuck took insufferable delight in her envy over his newest toys.

"Later. Next left."

They marched down spotless corridors, posters and signs tucked behind glass to permit regular sterilization. Slightly old-fashioned, but Sara approved. Nanarm filters would be in place at every possible cross-contamination point, but that was no reason to neglect the macro safeguards that had permitted the early work to proceed. And kept the early results where they belonged—most of the time.

The corridor branched and Chuck, having kept his hand on her back—a familiarity Sara permitted for the moment—aimed her at the left hallway. They stopped before a security door where he bent forward and spat accurately into the cup offered by the device in the wall. The tiny cup slipped back into its hiding place and they waited for the analysis. "Retina scans' more reliable," Sara pointed out. "And neater."

"Spitting's more fun," he countered, predictably, as the door accepted the taste of its master and opened.

She stepped inside before he could push her, drawn by a bizarre sense of misplacement. "What in hell—?"

"Look familiar?"

The question was rhetorical. Sara stared at a room that was *her* lab, her space, recreated down to the five paper-loaded desks she and her students shared. The papers were blank, but the piles were accurate. It even smelled right.

"If this is your idea of a joke—" she warned, turning to glare at Chuck. Her voice trailed off at his expression. It wasn't the satisfied glee of a prankster; it was the somber look of a man determined to confront something terrible. "What's going on?"

Instead of answering immediately, he strode past her to flatten his hand on the viewport, the duplicate of the one she routinely used to examine the molecular assembly line within the massive downcurl of tube. "Exactly," he said. "What's going on, Sara? Do you know?"

"I know you owe me an explanation, Charles Teig," Sara snapped. Her feet hurt. The taste of cocoa rose up her throat and she regretted ever agreeing to come. "We were here to talk about your work, not mine."

His hand moved in a caressing circle on the metal. "Yet your work is absolutely essential to mine, isn't it, Sara-socks? It always has been. Your tiny machine parts, so perfect and so reliable, are what make all the rest feasible on a global scale. Without DNA-based nanotech, we'd be pumping goo instead of nutrients." Chuck's eyes held hers. "But what about the bigger picture?"

More of the same. Sara wondered about simply leaving, but his effort to reproduce her lab meant something. Chuck, exasperating and full of himself as he was, had never been a fool. "Okay. You tell me. How much bigger than global would you care to go?"

Chuck went down on his heels to pat the series of smaller pipes rising up from the floor to the larger tube. "Where do these come from?"

Sara shoved papers aside on what would be her desk and hitched herself into her favourite thinking position, one knee hugged to her chest as she peered at Chuck. "Locally? That's the regional feeder line, K567 to be exact, given the university uses the same one. Bigger picture? Substation Omaha for the carbos, Sarnia for the fatty acids, and aminos from a dozen or so others. Purines and pyrimidines swap seasonally between Winnipeg and Mexico."

Chuck remained crouched like some unlikely cowboy. "Since the fifteenth Atlantic line went active last month, I'd say Spain for the fatty acids and Italy for the purines, but that's an opinion. They're all shipped together via main pumping lines before sorting and re-separation. No one tracks it, do they?"

Is that *where this is going?* "Probably not. Actual starting and end points are irrelevant. The major nutrients are transported based on supply and demand."

"I agree," he said, which surprised her. "But I still say you aren't seeing the bigger picture—and isn't that a switch, considering you're always on my case about consequences?"

Sara looked around this replica of her life's work as if some unknown danger to humanity would make itself plain. Then she laughed. "I'm not into biogen, Chuck. I'm an old-fashioned engineer, building better girders and wheels."

"And what do your girders and wheels think about that?"

For a moment, Sara couldn't think of anything to say. *He can't be serious.* "I'm going to pretend I didn't hear that," she said finally. "In fact, I'm going to pretend you haven't copied my lab," she jumped down from "her" desk, "and I'm going to pretend this whole evening didn't happen. Good night."

With an agility suggesting he did use the exercise equipment litter-ing his gamesroom, Chuck reached the door first, slamming it closed. Sara's heart starting thumping. *Stop it,* she told herself firmly, gazing into the face of this man she thought she knew. "You've either gone crazy or started taking something you shouldn't, old friend," she said as calmly as possible. "Open the door."

Chuck stepped back, spreading his hands wide. "A few more min-utes—with an open mind."

Sara frowned. "Open the door." He did. Though tempted to walk out, she didn't. "Why did you recreate my lab?"

"It's not just your lab, you know," Chuck said. "This is standard format for every primary nanotech producer, wouldn't you agree?"

She nodded warily. "I'd have a hard time getting grants even from Teig Biotech if I couldn't interface with industry."

"DNA is self-assembled as required for whatever application, and any structures that don't match specs are broken down by quality-control nanarms."

"It's not rocket science."

"And they never miss."

"It's not a question of missing. These are bits and pieces of mol-ecules, Chuck, not living things. Gods above and below you know that as well as anyone! If a batch has too many inappropriate configs, we dump it and cook another. Making a good cup of cocoa is harder. What are you driving at?"

"Have a look for yourself."

Despite her firm conviction Chuck had indeed plunged over what-ever deep end existed for prodigies, Sara activated the goggles. She wasn't the least surprised when Chuck came up beside her and a second set eased down from the ceiling. "Can I have those for the lab when we're done?" she asked. "My students are always fighting over the one."

"Look," he urged.

She looked, fighting déjà vu.

Bubbles and boxes floated past. Sara saw nothing unusual at first. Then she spotted something odd out of the corner of her eye. One of the nanarms didn't look right. She focused on it, raised the magnification. The tip, which should have consisted of block-like molecular teeth, was rounded, the blocks merged with a twisted ring.

"See it?" Chuck's voice echoed within the helmet.

Sara thrust away the goggles, angrily blinking away dizziness. "See what? That a nan's contaminated? It happens, Chuck. Any machinery will get gummed up by what passes through it. Just needs cleaning."

He pushed his own headpiece up and seemed to have no trouble adjusting to glare at her. "All I did was modify the ambient temperature in this room by two degrees and what you call 'gumming' occurred over a hundred times more frequently. But that's not what concerns me. Didn't you see what was wrapped around that nanarm? Your precious packing crates have taken on new configurations. We're not talking about gummed machinery. We're talking about novel combinations of DNA."

"So?" Sara glared back. "What's going to happen with 80 base pairs? It takes hundreds to produce a single gene—millions to make even one of your twisted chromosomes!"

"Yes, and I've watched the production of stable chains, hundreds-long, under these conditions. Granted, the intact nans caught them, but—"

"Worry about your own work, Chuck. Your lab is the one playing with living things, not mine."

He slammed his hand down on the tube again. "Which is why we didn't look in here until I saw your latest reports—"

"You saw my reports?" Sara's fists clenched. "Who gave you—"

"I fund your damn lab. Don't you think I see everything you do?" His voice softened. "Sara. No matter what you think of me or Teig Biotech, we both know that's how it works. I've never taken advantage of you." A glint of something wicked in his eyes. "Mind you, when that talented brain of yours comes up with something revolutionary, we'll have to talk…"

Sara refused to be charmed. "I'd call your latest something else. Foolhardy!"

"Oh, that." Chuck shooed an invisible fly. "Clever, yes? Let the little buggers earn their keep for once."

"Is that what you call it? Oh, you couldn't be satisfied to develop a gene-based resistance to acne, could you?" Sara said furiously. "Not flashy enough for Teig Biotech. Let's insert it into mosquito anti-coagulant! What are you thinking? That people will suddenly want to be bitten? It didn't work for the TB cure—"

"Because tuberculosis is endemic to cities, Sara-socks, where they spray for bugs. It would never have worked. Well, maybe if they'd tried lice. But I have a niche market here. Summer camps."

She realized her mouth was gaping and closed it after one word: "What?"

Chuck looked suddenly tired. "Summer camps. Purgatory for adolescents. Kids who have enough to deal with without breaking out in spots. The camps offer the biogen mosquitoes as an added feature. It's going to be big."

"We've an educated population these days, Chuck—don't mistake it for a passive one. They'll see releasing your mosquitoes as tampering with nature."

"That's what we do—"

"And they accept it in the supermarket or in hospitals. They won't around their children."

"Wanna bet? We've already sold out the first generation anti-zit bugs, before making a public announcement." Another flash of what seemed desperation on his face. "Let's forget my work for now. Grant me that I know my stuff, Sara, and who uses it. That's why you're here."

Sara threw up her hands. "I've no idea why I'm here. You never listen—"

Chuck captured her hands and brought them down, gently. She left them in his grip, feeling his thumb stroke the back of her right hand. The last time he'd done that? The night her husband died and Chuck had sat with her on the deck, the two of them staring at the empty lake without seeing it, in the days when they'd been the kind of friends who didn't need words for what mattered.

"Your lab became the pattern for all the others," he said slowly, searching her face. "That's why it's here. That's why I'm studying it. You know I've had doubts about the GT—"

Sara tried to pull her hands free but he wouldn't let go. "Doubts? About ending famine? About improving life around the world?"

His grip tightened, insisting on her attention. "Sara. You know me better than that. Not the result—the process. And who is involved in it. Oh, I expected sabotage, theft, blackmail, but we're too selfish a species. People grew fiercely protective of the GT, even faster than they fought for open access to the 'net. They see the GT as a matter of survival. It is, isn't it? We can't feed ourselves any other way now."

This time, when Sara pulled at her hands, he released them. "The gumming of nanarms at +2C. And our survival. Make the link for me, Chuck, because I don't see it."

"What if novel combinations of DNA occurred in the other streams, like the assorted amines?"

Sara's eyes followed the tubes crisscrossing the ceiling and floor. "They can't—"

"I say they can—if your bubbles and boxes are as prone to re-arrangement in the wide world of tubing as they are in this room. So what happens then?"

"If," Sara began, unconvinced, "perhaps parts of that DNA might—might—bring some amines into sufficiently close proximity that they might—might!—form a small protein. Enough of those? Might gum the works." She scowled at him. "But conditions in the tubes are regulated—and bricks can't turn themselves into houses."

"Yours can. And if enough different small proteins were coded? Might not one or more be enzymes, capable of catalyzing other reactions?" Chuck began to pace. "Think about it. In the tubes themselves: your bubbles and boxes splitting into new combinations of DNA, at the same time releasing their contents. Enzymes catalyzing reactions even as selection by the remaining nanarms, the conditions in the tubes themselves, favour some combinations and enzymes over others?" Chuck stopped for breath, one hand hovering over the nearest tube. "Evolution."

The word crawled down her spine. Sara shrugged away the shiver trying to follow it. "Contamination. We dump it out—"

"Dump it?" With a violence she'd never seen in him before, Chuck swept a desk clear of fake exams and coffee cups. Sara watched the debris settle in random patterns on the floor. But his voice stayed oddly calm. "Where?"

"From here?" She patted "her" desk. "You know perfectly well. Into a secured holding tank for analysis and recycling."

"What about commercial labs, Sara-socks? Labs where otherwise brilliant, careful people view your tech as nothing more than a filtration system with convenient, microscopic packing crates? What about the other end of the spectrum—the thousands of illicit, uninspected connections to the GTS. Did you think of their ability to react to novel DNA patterns when you gave this technology to anyone who could read?"

Sara shook her head, but it wasn't denial. "It's a self-correcting system," she argued. "Users want pure nutrients—it's in their interest to keep the system running at peak efficiency. They'd starve, otherwise—"

"Big picture. You aren't seeing it yet." Chuck planted his hands on either side of where Sara sat, leaning into her face. "People are convinced your bubbles and boxes ensure purity in their nutrient supply—how could they suspect them of being the source of contamination? Evolution, Sara," he breathed, smelling of biogeneered cocoa. "We've provided all the necessary complex organic chemicals for a new primordial soup. Not merely in puddles here or there—the GT will soon rival the Indian Ocean in volume. And no need to wait eons for mutation and recombination. Changing DNA is now part of the system. It's not just what I've shown you here. Your tiny machines and containers will be modified constantly—by individuals who've no conception of the power in those tiny bricks of yours."

Sara felt numb. "What power?"

"You're like the rest—thinking of DNA as a finite material, forgetting its potential," Chuck straightened to his full height. "But that's what I work with every day. The potential, Sara, for life. When, not if, something becomes alive within the system, it's going to be life evolved for that environment, not ours, life adapted to use what we've provided. You might be an engineer in practice, but you're a biologist at heart. You know how quickly a successful lifeform would replicate under those conditions.

"If we are very, very lucky," Chuck continued, "we'll see it coming before the entire GTS is compromised. We'll have time to start piling wheat on trains and rice into ships, time to save most of a population dependent on a technology that won't be ours any longer. But what if we don't?"

Sara discovered her fingers had clenched on Chuck's arms. She didn't want to believe him. She didn't dare refuse the possibility, not with what was at state. "No one will believe you," she said aloud, hearing the words echo between them.

His smile was infinitely sad. "And you had to ask why I brought you here, Sara? You're the person who started it all, the fairy godmother of the GT. You've got that impeccable reputation to risk. I am sorry—"

She shook her head in disbelief that he would even consider her career. "If you are right—in any sense—this must go out immediately.

Give me your data; I'll get my people working on it."

"It's yours." Then Chuck bent and kissed her cheek. It had the chill feel of a farewell. "Let's hope not too late."

Mai Ling took another sip of cold coffee, shuddering as the too-sweet liquid hit her empty stomach. It didn't help shrink her pile of unmarked exams. Barbara and Miguel were hunched over their desks. The final member of their group was using the goggles to watch the nanarms sort bubbles and boxes.

"Hey, Dev, you asleep in there?" Mai Ling called. There was a chorus of sleepy laughter. This wouldn't be the first time one of them had used the goggles to hide a nap.

The sudden shrill of an alarm made the question moot. With a curse, Dev started working the controls. "What's wrong?" she demanded, hurrying with the others to join him at the tube.

"We've got negative pressure on the purine feeder," he said, voice muffled by the goggles. "The autos' were off."

Mai Ling shot a look at the readout, seeing the red band slashing across the schematic. Whatever problem had occurred was remote, at some station ahead of theirs in the GT. "Check for backwash, people. Dr. Surghelti will go ballistic if we've leaked into the mains."

"I initiated the seal manually," Dev assured her. "Think I caught all of it."

"Let's hope," Mai Ling said, starting a log entry.

Filled with precious cargo, bubbles and boxes slide along liquid laneways, shepherded by nanarms, guided to their varied destinations like so many migrating fish. At junctions, microscopic eddies form, slowing traffic in a moment of insignificant mixing and delay—insignificant until that traffic contains something else. Something new. Arms reach out in an irresistible come-hither...

And then there were two.

PHOEBASTRIA

Jennifer Rahn

Kayla flinched at the sound of gunfire just outside the lab. She had deliberately left the window blinds shut this morning, even though sunlight was as rare a commodity as water these days, not wishing to see a repeat of the bloody corpse that had ended up smeared across the glass last week. The gangs had moved their warfare closer to the University, and at times climbed into the abandoned apartment buildings across the dried river bed, spending days on end peering through the lab windows. It made Kayla feel like she was being selected for someone's lunch.

The centrifuge on the bench beside her popped open and sat waiting for Kayla to retrieve its contents. She lifted the small plastic tube from the rotor and stared at the small volume of DNA she had prepared, wondering if she should even bother trying to put her newly constructed gene into her experimental cacti. The newly designed DNA construct should be able to carry the gene for a 'superporin', a molecule she had designed from the original plant version of aquaporin, a water transport protein she hoped would enable a cactus to extract more water from soil. So far, her efforts had failed—the ground water around the University was so polluted that heavy metals were inhibiting the transporter function of the superporin, and the engineered plants consistently died. It didn't help that her last set of experiments had been sabotaged. She was sure of sabotage; things had resumed working after she'd started mislabelling and hiding her key reagents. The time lost while she sorted out the problem was irreplaceable; rumour had it the Department would be deciding this week whom they were going to keep in the program, and failure was not going to help Kayla's review. Of course, the Department denied they were conducting any such review, and the official stance was that *nobody* was going to be *kicked out* of the program.

The comtack band on her wrist beeped, summoning her to the front lobby of the Biological Sciences Building. That was unusual…unless she was going to be sent outside. She couldn't let herself think about it—the way things were going in the University, it was only a matter of time. Taking off her lab coat, she washed her hands, slipped on her jacket and shoved the tube containing her engineered DNA deep into her jeans pocket. There was no way she was going to leave it lying around for the next available saboteur.

Exiting the elevator, she approached the glass doors of the lobby and stared outside at the curtain wall that ran along Saskatchewan Drive: protection from the surrounding gangland. The gate opened briefly, granting admittance to the camouflaged Humvee from CFB Edmonton. The army vehicle stopped, dispatching a single soldier before reversing and kicking up gravel, leaving as though it couldn't wait to be away from the miserable civilian outpost that was the University. The man left behind seemed instantly bored, jogging lazily over to Provost Saunders to receive his assignment. Kayla's heart sank as she saw the four members of the Selection Committee and the Department Head standing next to the Provost. They all flipped studiously through flimsies stacked on their tablets. Academic records *were* being reviewed. Selections *were* being made. A number of other students from the Department had also been summoned, and were directed to stand in pairs at various exits by the doors. Kayla was pointed towards one of these.

Marcus came to stand next to Kayla, looking far too relaxed, like he was actually enjoying himself. He and the Provost exchanged knowing glances that seemed to make both of them even more smug. Kayla's heart sank. Rumours had been swirling for months that the lotteries were staged, but she had hoped for better upon hearing that her name had been drawn for outside duty. Bracing herself to be sent past the wall, she tapped the comtack on her wrist, ensuring that the links to the University server were active and the GPS was functional. She forced herself to believe that everything was upfront, and even if she were being sent outside, she'd still be coming back.

Marcus smirked and Kayla glared at him, resisting the urge to smack the smug off his greasy face. He was probably the one who'd been messing up her lab reagents. The other rumour being whispered through CAB: data collections outside the Wall were being conducted to reduce the University population. Water volumes in the rainwater harvesting tanks could be validated by satellite or remote conductance. Half of the staff sent out to retrieve the same data never came back.

The facility was so rife with politics that her history-buff roommate had compared it to the time of the Borgias of Renaissance Italy, where everyone had a price, even the Popes. If she'd had the heart for it, Kayla could have played the same political games as Marcus, ensuring that her perceived value to the academic community held out a little longer, but she hadn't. It was small comfort to know that despite his scheming and plotting, Marcus was going to go out the same way she was, because in the end the little weasel was no match for heartless Braeden. She viciously hoped Marcus enjoyed his final few weeks of access to cleaner water. Hydro-privilege was revoked as quickly as it was granted.

The soldier gestured at Kayla to follow him and she took a few steps before realising she'd missed witnessing the coin toss. Well, it didn't really matter. They all knew the decision had been made days ago and the coin toss was just for show. She took a deep breath and resisted the urge to turn around and kick Marcus before leaving.

The air felt sunny and warm, yet Kayla's skin was slick with cold sweat as the heavy gate thudded shut behind her. She traipsed after the soldier down into the river valley, stepping carefully over the smooth rocks lining the now dried watershed of the North Saskatchewan, towards the five metre diameter, puncture-proof cylinders that dotted the former riverbed for over a kilometre. The glacier in the Banff region that used to feed the river had long since been sold to an American company by the Alberta Government, and Edmonton was well outside of the Paskapoo aquifer that supplied Red Deer and Calgary. Small supplies of potable water were traded with Red Deer in exchange for Edmonton's military protection and the residual oil reserves, but Calgary wasn't sharing. That was all Edmonton had to offer these days, armed protection, but the same deal couldn't be offered to Saskatchewan, who got much better service from China in exchange for uranium.

The soldier sat slouched on a protruding, broken rock. He held his carbine with one sweaty hand while pulling on the chinstrap of his helmet with the other, grimacing at the heat of the sun. Well, if he was so relaxed, there couldn't be any of the gangs nearby. She squeezed through the narrow space between the last set of holding tanks she had to inspect, tapping on their sides to estimate the contained volumes and pressing on the siphon ports to collect samples. The ID implant in her arm beeped as the University sent back pings authorizing the release of each microlitre of water taken from the tanks. Her hands were shaking as she tried to record the data on her comtack, the stylus continually dropping from her fingers. Small sounds around her made her jumpy: each rustle and change of the wind transformed into imaginary monsters creeping up behind her.

"I'm finished this section," she called out, clambering back up to where the soldier could see her.

"Ready to move on?" He shifted off the rock and started to collect his gear. As he straightened up, a pair of tattooed arms threw a garrotte around the soldier's neck and jerked him off his feet. He lost grip on his gun, and in seconds was down on his back, kicking furiously, swarmed by a crowd of scruffy gang members whose tattered lumberjack vests flapped as they ripped off his chest plate then repeatedly stabbed him until he stopped struggling.

Everything tumbled from her trembling hands to shatter on the rocks at her feet. Kayla wanted to run, but the muscles of her legs spasmed, holding her in place. Where would she run to, anyway? And it wasn't as if she hadn't been expecting this…just some small part of her brain had still been plotting revenge against Marcus.

A powerful, wiry arm snaked around her neck and pulled her close against a muscular chest. A rust-spotted knife blade flashed in front of her face before grazing her neck under her ear.

"Well, now, we've been waiting for you, girly" her captor breathed into her ear. He spun her around and stuck his toothless grin close to her face. His startling green eyes glared at her from under dark brows. A stylized 'WK' White Killaz tattoo crawled up the side of his neck. A second gang member yanked her arm back and shoved her sleeve up, exposing the barcode implant on her wrist. Kayla didn't have time to scream before a sharp blade sliced the implant that encoded her student ID from her skin.

"Sinjay, hold her still. Hope you had your tetanus shot, girly" joked the clumsy surgeon. She gritted her teeth as he tore it away from her synthetic neural net and held up the translucent blue square to the light to examine the embedded white circuitry. A drop of blood fell from its corner. "This one was a graduate student," he finally said. "Too bad.

Class size is small, which means it will be noticed quickly that she's been swapped out."

"Can we still get in to the University?" asked the Killaz still holding her.

"Sure. But it'll be a commando run. Grab what we can then get out. We'd have at least a few hours, maybe a day before they miss her."

Too bad they wouldn't have a clue where to find the water, Kayla thought to herself. The University changed the shunting paths weekly to compensate for raids.

"And what should we do with the rest of this?" Sinjay moved his arm and grabbed her ponytail, giving her head a shake. "Dump it somewhere in the river valley?"

The other Killaz, finished stripping the remains of the soldier, came over, still admiring their blood-stained plunder. "Whyn't we keep her?" asked one of them.

"For what, Jose? 'Nother mouth to feed," said the surgeon.

"But maybe she can fix the still. Maybe we can get some decent water."

The Killaz looked at each other, like they just had the most incredible revelation.

"Can you fix the still?" demanded Sinjay.

Kayla had to lick her lips before she could answer. "What kind is it?" she managed to stammer out.

"An old one. Lots of glass tubes. Says LD500-5 on it." Jose looked at her hopefully.

"Oh, that *is* old." She gently pulled away from Sinjay, and he let her go. "Where are you getting your starting water from?"

"From the Cree and Dene tribes up in Athabasca. They've got that glacier, but they ain't selling that. That goes to the Danes, Ruskies and Yanks. It's the only thing they can trade to maintain control of the north. They also got control of the old tailing ponds from the Cold Lake tar sands, and they'll sell us that."

"You're drinking produced water straight from tailing ponds?" Kayla asked incredulously.

The surgeon Killaz shook his head. "No, I meant, that's all they'd be willing to let us have. You get it, girly? So for now we're scrounging what we can from plants, sometimes we can buy or steal fresh, but we're all fighting and dying over it. There ain't much. But if we could get more, if we could clean up that tailing pond crap, that'd put us ahead of the other gangs."

Kayla's mind raced as she tried to sort out whether or not her skill set could actually save her life. Produced water was the recovered liquid that had been injected into oil reservoirs to force oil to the surface. It would be heavily contaminated with hydrocarbons, heavy metals, and other production chemicals. Twenty years ago, several companies had tried to recover usable water from it through various separation techniques such as centrifugation, filtration and reverse osmosis, but the cost and ineffectiveness of their methods eventually caused the industry to crash. It had been hopeless then, so what could she, a single, inexperienced academic do to solve the problem on her own? She shrugged, resigned to the truth and her fate.

"You know, even if I can get it working, the water is going to be far from pure," she finally said. "Some of the contaminants in the ground water have the same kind of volatility as water. They co-purify with it, so you can't get them out."

"Yeh, we know." One of the Killaz standing in front of her lifted his shirt to show a massive scar across his abdomen. "I got born with my guts hanging out, 'cause my Ma got sold bad water that was supposed to be pure."

Kayla wordlessly lifted her own shirt. This was no time to be embarrassed. The Killaz gawped at her in amazement; not at her pale skin or her breast, but at the heavy web of scars that ran around from just over her kidneys, across her ribs and up to her heart.

"What the hell?! You're not normal?"

She pulled her shirt back down and rearranged her clothes as best she could. "Of course not. We're all drinking some degree of contaminated water around here. So, yeah, I get it."

"But…you're at the University. You guys…got stuff."

She shook her head. "We don't have fresh water."

"But…can't you fix it?"

"You think we get to keep the water we fix?" Kayla laughed sadly. "Why do you think we need to collect rainwater? Even that isn't so fresh. Got sulfur dioxide and nitrogen oxides in it. Any water we do manage to purify gets shipped off who knows where by the government."

"So this ain't worth crap," said the surgeon, still holding her implant. He waved it in her face as if she had cheated him.

"If you're going to use it, I suggest you do it quickly. I was about to get kicked out of my program. Try to raid the main hospital. You can get the best stuff there."

"You're lying. Why would you tell me all this?"

"I'm not lying. And I'm telling you because it doesn't matter. I'm worth as much inside as I am out here. Why else would they send me to check the rain tanks?"

"You had the guard."

"It was the water samples I extracted they were interested in. Not me. Or maybe the guard's bosses wanted him gone too. They were creating reasons to send us out here. No one was really expecting me to return."

The Killaz gave a wheezing laugh, then flipped his hands up and shrugged. "You weren't valued? You got better clothes than me. You been getting better food. You got a dentist." He grinned and poked his tongue through the gaps in his teeth.

Kayla took her jacket off and handed it to him. "Seriously. I had a 50/50 chance of being out here anyway by next week. And I probably still would be handing you this jacket."

A female Killaz shoved Kayla's shoulder. "What else you got? Can you get into these rain tanks?" She had the strange look of someone who had aged faster than normal; her strength, voice, youthful figure and green vinyl jacket belying the wrinkled skin on her face.

Kayla shrugged. "Only if the University authorized it, and they won't. Everything I had of real value was left behind at the University. Wasn't like they were going to let me take it. And now that they've decided they don't need me to run that valuable equipment..." she shrugged again.

"Damn, that's cold," said the surgeon. "Even we don't do each other over like that." The little oblong square in his fingers blipped twice, then went black. All connections between Kayla and the University had just been severed. The surgeon huffed in disbelief before letting the flimsy object flutter to the stones at his feet.

"Oh," was all Kayla said before her legs crumpled underneath her. The rocks hurt her back and elbows where she hit.

"For real?" asked another of the Killaz. He picked up the ID and examined it, but the implant remained dead.

"C'mon, let's go," said Sinjay. "Nothin' here." He and the others began to move away. Kayla felt her fear of the Killaz dissolve into panic at being left alone. Some of the other gangs were rumoured to be cannibals.

"Forget it, Sinjay!" said the woman with the too-old face. "She's not being left here like this. This is what Cantire did to us, when they shoved us out." She knelt and clumsily put an arm around Kayla, who blinked at her in surprise. "We still got kids, you know. They look funny, but we can still make 'em. Some are both a boy and girl at the same time, some are neither. Some have two eyes in one socket. You have to help us, University Lady, before it all stops and all people are gone."

"There's nothing I can do," Kayla protested.

"Look, nobody big cares about any of us. But you and me, we're in this together right now, so we gotta help each other."

"It's not that I don't want to. I have no equipment. Nothing to work with."

The Killaz woman grinned at her. "I know where you can get some. A lot of it."

"What do you know, Chax?" one of her people scoffed.

"I used to hide in this one place as a kid. It's full of science stuff."

"Then how come you've never said?" asked Sinjay.

"'Cuz she don't want to tell you she likes hiding in that shit-hole," said Jose.

Chax tossed her head defiantly. "Wouldn't tell you, 'cos it'd get stolen."

Sinjay made a dismissive gesture and turned away. "There's nothing there. Else you would have sold it."

"I'm gonna show her anyway," said Chax. She grabbed Kayla's hand and dragged her to her feet.

"You stay out of sight, Chax," cautioned the surgeon, before he too turned to leave.

Chax pulled Kayla through the old downtown LRT tunnels, paying tolls to small children squatting in their path. Shadowy figures, invisible until they moved, withdrew along maintenance catwalks and into side passages to let them pass. They scurried through the pedways, sometimes ducking into stairwells to avoid members of the First Nations who were well supplied with automatic weapons. Chax paid a hefty

$1000 for escort through the eastern part of the North Saskatchewan river bed, into Capilano Park. Just inside the tree line, she turned to Kayla and handed her a hammer.

"We gotta make a run for it from here," she explained. "If the dogs come for you, hit 'em across the nose with the hammer." Kayla's legs threatened to lock up at the mention of dogs, but when she looked over her shoulder, she decided that staying in the trees—now that their escort was disappearing—was hardly the safer option. Chax took off like a sprinter. Kayla hesitated a second and then she, too, ran, as she'd never run before. Then the dogs came, overtaking her and rounding in front of her to cut her off. There were a half-dozen, maybe more, but she was too busy swinging the hammer to count the coyote-sized beasts. Steel impacted on flesh, drawing yelps of pain. But she didn't stop, not even when teeth tore at her pant leg and scraped her skin. Chax vaulted over a four-foot-high metal gate, not missing a step. Kayla scrambled after her. Teeth closed on her foot and her shoe tore away when Chax hauled her the rest of the way over by the front of her shirt. The dogs tried to jump the gate, only discouraged by Chax's hammer. Kayla rolled over and groaned in pain, one arm wrapped around her bruised ribs.

"C'mon. We can't stay out here," Chax urged. "I don't even know whose territory that is, but if the dogs are making so much noise, some-one's gonna come looking."

"You used to run that as a kid?" Kayla gasped, struggling for breath.

"Sure." Chax grinned. "That was nothing." She pulled Kayla up again. "Let's get inside. No one goes in there normally because of the smell."

As Kayla limped towards the complex of grey concrete and steel buildings, she caught a whiff of what Chax meant. A few steps closer and the wind changed, allowing the thick stench to hit her full in the face. Kayla retched and put her sleeve over her nose and mouth. "It smells like rotten raw sewage," she choked out, doing her best not to step in anything unidentifiable with her bare foot.

Chax grinned and nodded at her over her shoulder. "Yep. That's what it is. Back in the old days, they used to clean up the water here." She pointed at a sign that read: Gold Bar Wastewater Treatment Plant.

"Really? You think the equipment here is still operational?" Kayla felt her heart speed up at the thought.

Chax shrugged. "If it is, I don't think anyone knows how to use it all. But maybe you do. I always wondered why the University folk never tried to get the army to claim it for them."

"Maybe some parts need replacing that they can't get. Or the tech is so outdated that it wouldn't have been efficient to keep running the plant."

"Maybe," Chax agreed. "I'm hoping you'll see some stuff in there you can use."

The lighting inside the buildings was sporadic. Chax flicked every switch she could find, but only some of the lights worked, casting the long hallways with a dim, yellow glow. Shrouded figures flinched from the light and scuttled from view. Kayla caught at Chax's sleeve.

"There are people here!"

"Don't worry. They're just crazies. C'mon. I'll show you where I used to hide out."

Chax led her through the labyrinth, the smell growing ever stronger and nearly unbearable. Kayla coughed and gagged into her elbow, which she had crooked across her face.

"You'll get used to it," her companion assured her. "Here are some of the labs." She gestured at some broken doors. Kayla stepped through into the spaces lit by weak light streaming through broken windows and ceilings. The equipment was in disarray, but some of it still seemed functional. The computer stations had been dismantled, but much of the scientific equipment had been left behind, after obviously having been looked over and rearranged. At least the crazies hadn't taken it upon themselves to trash the entire place.

"Come see my favourite part," Chax coaxed. "I know you like the science stuff, but you gotta see this. The smell is even worse, but I just love the colours."

Despite herself, Kayla smiled at the implied intrigue. Chax seemed more alive and interested in the world around her than any of the students or faculty at the University, and it was finally easing Kayla's spirit. Maybe being kicked out wasn't so bad–provided all the crazies and cannibals could be avoided. Chax seemed to have managed all right. At least the threatening people around here were upfront about it, unlike her former colleagues. She gamely limped after Chax, curious to see what colours she was referring to.

They entered an enormous room that stretched at least a kilometre from where they stood on a catwalk, which was suspended over several parallel giant troughs of brackish water. The foul liquid lapped serenely against the edges of the troughs, gently agitated by whatever forces now regulated their flow. Kayla thought it smelled like dead people had been pulverized and poured into the water. The air she drew in through her mouth felt thick and like it was leaving deposits on her tongue.

"We have to get closer," said Chax, enthusiastically climbing down to a lower catwalk, and then onto the tops of the concrete walls that made up the troughs. "Look!" she insisted, pointing at the water. Kayla followed, watching her step and making sure she kept her balance as she moved along the wall. She imagined that falling into the water would cause so many infections that death would occur inside of a week. What she saw when she squatted next to Chax made her forget everything else.

"What are they?" she asked in astonishment.

"I don't know. But aren't they pretty?" Thousands of tiny worms, all different colours and glowing slightly with bioluminescence were twisting through the dark liquid, gradually coming into view as they neared the surface, then fading again as they sank.

"These are neat, too." Chax ran along the wall for a distance before kneeling again, and turning to smile at Kayla as she pointed at something attached to the opposing wall of the trough. Kayla crept up to where she was and thought she was looking at an uneven set of pipes that were trickling out water. "It keeps changing," said Chax. "It grows. See how the surface of it is full of holes? Sometimes the worms crawl in there, and if it's dark in here, the whole thing glows."

"Is it...coral?" asked Kayla.

"What's that?" countered Chax.

"It's a kind of water animal, that gets its food by filtering it out of the water...Chax! Look at the water coming out of the top of it. Does it look cleaner?"

Chax looked with an expression of confusion at the pumping creature stuck to the side of the trough. "I suppose. I still wouldn't want to drink it, though."

"But...if the coral were to be set up in sequential chambers, each one continually purifying the water of the previous tank, it might work."

"Looks like it would take a long time to fill up any kind of tank. It's not pumping out that much water."

Kayla took a long look at Chax, her mind racing through

possibilities. She turned and regarded the worms once more. Worms were extremely easy to transfer artificial DNA into. She still had the small plastic tube in her jeans pocket, containing the engineered super-porin gene. Pulling it out, she gazed at it speculatively.

"What's that?" asked Chax.

"Have you ever wanted to be a scientist?" Kayla countered.

Six months had passed since Kayla and Chax had set up shop in the old Gold Bar labs, which remained undisturbed because of the smell. They had adapted the worms and coral to growth in tanks filled with gravel and sand, and managed to isolate worms that carried the superporin gene. Not only were the little creatures able to absorb greater amounts of water, after having evolved in the dank murk of the aban-doned sewage, they easily took to processed water from the Athabasca region.

Kayla watched with satisfaction as she dipped a handful of sand, writhing with her engineered worms into a bucket of processed water, letting the gritty silt dissolve into the muck. The latex glove she wore came away coated in the gunk of the impure water. Her little pets could still swim despite the toxins and glowed prettily as they twisted through the water, swelling into little colourful balloons over several minutes. She fished them out with a straining spoon and transferred them into the gravel base tank in which the strange coral grew. Once taken out of the liquid, the worms shrank again as the water they had collected oozed out of them. Their bodies contracted and squirmed through the sand as the liquid within them reached equilibrium. The water filtered through the grit, into a portion of the tank that was separated by a permeable mesh that only allowed liquid through. The base of the coral grew there, drawing up the water for the next round of purification. Their spouts slowly dripped into another bucket, into which Chax lovingly deposited a second handful of sandy worms.

By the third round of purification, the coral was allowed to drip into one of the plastic bottles the White Killaz had recovered from aban-doned depots. They had filled twenty four of them today. Sinjay took each one over to the jury-rigged chromatography column Kayla had made operational, and tested the water for poisonous impurities. Each time the bottles passed testing–and all of them were passing–he would let out a whoop of joy, give the women his 'thumbs up' dance and let one of the children carry the bottle off for distribution to the Killaz's allies. They had stockpiled enough for themselves, and hoped to expand the growing tanks so that they could supply greater regions of the city.

The old Killaz surgeon strode into the lab, swinging his arms behind himself, looking like the happiest person in the world. Kayla was still a little afraid of him, even though he had not threatened her since their first meeting.

"Hey girly!" he called out cheerily. "Got some good news for you. Guess who got kicked out of the University last week due to…oh what was it now? 'Consistent and colossal failure,' I think is what he said." He turned around and waved at someone in the dark hallway behind him. "C'mon, then! C'mon in here so I can ast girly what she wants to do with you. She gets first say, don't cha know."

Kayla watched in amazement as the Provost of the University crept into the dim light of the lab. His grey hair and beard were bedraggled, his clothing torn, and his shoes were missing. He looked as if he had been hiding in the streets since being let go. She wondered who had become so powerful that they could have ousted this man.

The surgeon laughed himself silly. "Look at him, girly! After having thrown you out, look at him now! Stupid bugger! See what girly's done for us here? She could've saved you all. You shoulda kept her. But now we gots her. What say you, girly? Shall we keep him?"

Kayla opened her mouth to say yes, they should, because she could not bring herself to cause anyone to suffer, not when she was now able to offer so many people relief.

The surgeon's expression hardened and his hand flashed out towards the Provost's neck. The old academic stumbled awkwardly as he fell first on one knee, then to the ground, his hands uselessly trying to hold in the blood squirting from his throat.

"Nope!" declared the surgeon. "He no good to us. Failures don't get kept around here."

He took a step towards Kayla and grinned at her.

"Best remember that, girly. We're not gonna be all nicey nicey to everyone now like you bin thinking. This water is *power*, not freebies. And power is something I'm gonna be needing to keep the Killaz alive. It's a hard, hard world, girly. And you're still livin' it."

HARD WATER

Christine Cornell

Apathy—lethargy—confusion—coma... or was it apathy—shivering—confusion?

Trey wished he could unread the description of how he was going to die. He wasn't even sure if he was simply having trouble remembering or was already at the confusion stage. What he did know was that his fingers weren't hurting anymore and that wasn't good.

Can I be confused, if I'm wondering if I'm confused?

Before Trey could answer himself, another wave broke over his head. Coming up gasping and blinded, he tried not to think about the body heat being sucked from him with each wave.

When he had his breath back, he resumed shouting: "Dad! Dad!" He'd heard nothing from his father or the others since they had gone into the water. Maybe they'd made it into the life raft, although it always seemed like an empty raft was the first thing searchers find. The night, high seas, fog, and rain made it impossible to see, and the lights of the *Dora Marie* had disappeared within minutes of them abandoning her.

How long has it been? How long would their survival suits give them?

"Dad!" Timing the shouts between waves wasn't easy. Trey could tell by his thirst he'd already swallowed more salt water than was healthy. But he was more worried about his father. For the first time in his life, it occurred to him that his dad wasn't a young man.

What was he? fifty-two? three?

Trey tried to reassure himself that his father knew exactly what he was doing. He'd ordered them into their suits as the storm had worsened. In the last moments he'd reminded them to swim hard away from the trawler so they wouldn't be sucked down with her.

Try as he might, Trey couldn't stop replaying those terrible moments.

"Another wave, Tim. Hang on!" Trey's father shouted to Tim out on the deck as another massive black-green wave broke over their bow. Russ issued another mayday on the radio: the deckhand was doing what he could to leave his skipper free at the wheel. The fast-closing ship was ignoring their hails.

"She's almost on top of us!" Trey couldn't hide his panic, although he knew his dad could see the approaching ship on the radar as well as he could.

"Get up on the deck, b'ys." John barked out the order without taking his eyes from the sea ahead. "I still can't see the bitch! Where the hell is she?"

"Dad—"

"Move. Now!"

Russ grabbed Trey by his sleeve and hauled him away. Out on the deck, Trey turned back to look for his father. And there she was. Coming out of the waves and fog. A nightmare wall dwarfing the *Dora Marie*. The biggest fucking tanker Trey had ever seen. Her lights splitting the night.

A sickening crunch and the grinding of metal on metal sounded above the wind, while a shudder ran through the deck beneath their feet.

We're going to die. I'm going to die. For a summer job. That was all. Enough friggin' money to make it through final year. Was that too much to ask?

"So did you have a good term?" Trey's mum was doing her best to keep the conversation afloat.

"Yeah, it was good," said Trey, nodding a couple more times than necessary, then fixed his gaze on his well done roast beef. Trey's mum was a folk artist whose brightly coloured paintings sold well with the summer tourists. During the winter, she painted and Trey's dad took over most of the cooking. The results were mixed.

Trey's dad steered straight for the conversational rocks. "Are you not done yet? Seems like you've been in school forever."

Strange, that's exactly where Trey wished he was right now. If only he could have found a summer job in Halifax, he sure wouldn't be on the Rock now. "Just one more year. It's a four year degree." He'd only been home a day, and already living in a cardboard box next fall was starting to look like a reasonable alternative.

"And what are you going to do with that degree when you're done?"

Why couldn't Dad save his teeth for the beef? He was being a regular bear with a thorn in its paw.

"It'll depend where the jobs are. I might end up working for a TV news show, or newspaper, or even radio."

"Well, those would all be interesting wouldn't they?" Mum's smile was looking a little tight.

But, Dad was on a roll: "I just wonder why Trey isn't working at one of those places this summer."

Trey found himself shooting his mother one of those looks he perfected by the time he was ten: half entreaty, half angry-you-married-this-guy. Unbelievable, one day home and he was a kid again.

"What does it matter? It's nice to have him home for a bit." Before his dad could answer, she tried to swing his attention around to a new heading. "Have you heard anything about Jake's boat?"

Dad bit. "Still no offers. He's asking too much, and no one wants a forty-footer these days. But he's a stubborn old fool—might as well talk to a wall."

"Are we talking about Jake Shortall?" Trey couldn't believe it. Jake had been an icer for as long as Trey could remember.

"Yeah. A boat that size, you just can't make a go of it anymore." Trey's dad shook his head.

"The bergs can't be running out," Trey laughed.

"Not yet, anyway. No, it's these big American tankers. The little guy just can't compete."

"But they must have to stay outside the two hundred mile limit?"

His dad pushed back from the table while Trey's mum cleared and began to serve a partridgeberry pie. "Where have you been, boy? Do you not get any news in Halifax? Technically the Yanks have to respect the limit, but since they cut a deal with Greenland, they go right up iceberg alley to the Davis Strait."

"But that doesn't mean they can ice in our waters!" Trey wasn't even sure why it bugged him.

"Whose gonna stop them? You think our frigates are going to shoot across those bows? It's not the 1990s, and we're not talking some Spanish fishing trawler."

"It worked then, though." Trey had heard the old stories of the collapse of the fish stocks and the fight to protect them till they could recover. And they had. The cod had come back when many had thought they never would. But the boom of the twenties had been followed by the bust of the thirties. Warmer waters devastated the fishery, and men had once again looked to the oil fields of the west or had converted for icing—harvesting the ancient glacial waters of the passing icebergs. Fresh water was the new oil. Could it be only twenty years later even the icers would be out of work?

"It's not like it was when I started icing with your grampie. A man could make a decent living then. But the worse the American dust-bowl's gotten, the more of their tankers we see. They suck up bergs like they're ice cubes."

Trey still couldn't see how you'd get chunks of a berg onto one of those giant tankers, but they were interrupted before he could ask.

One knock on the back door and Tim Wolf let himself into the kitchen.

"Trey! Good to see ya. Didn't know you were back in town. But your timing's perfect." Tim shook Trey's hand.

"So have you come for some of Dora's pie?" asked Trey's dad.

"Well it wasn't to see your mug, John." Tim was in his late thirties and had been part of John's crew for the better part of a dozen years and mate for half that. Tim was always the shortest man on the crew, but his wiry strength was always more than a match for the greenhorns that came and went every couple years.

"So what's this about the boy's timing?"

"It's Mike—"

"Of course it is."

Mike was Tim's brother—a few years younger and about half as smart. Trey'd always suspected his dad only kept Mike on so he wouldn't lose Tim.

"He was heading home from Sheila's last night. Three sheets to the wind. Thinks he tripped over a cat or something. But was likely his own feet. Broke his leg."

Trey's dad gave his son a sardonic smile. "Guess there's a job if you want it."

"Great," Trey tried to sound just as casual.

"'Course the season doesn't end till the end of September. That a problem?"

Trey knew a test when he heard one. "No problem." But it was. Trey wasn't going to screw up his final year just to keep his father happy. Or less grumpy. But he'd burn that bridge when he got to it.

Tim wisely ignored the undercurrents. "Glad that's settled. Now we just need some bergs."

The next morning Trey's dad rousted him at dawn and sent him off to meet Tim at the dock. Trey shivered in his grey hoodie and wondered how he'd forgotten how friggin' cold it could still be in early May. Getting by without his favourite morning coffee stop wasn't going to be easy.

At the top of the long curve of Cove Road that lead down to the town wharf, Trey caught up with Tim.

"How's Mike doing?" Trey asked.

Tim grinned. "Pretty good with the stuff the doc gave him for the pain. Glad I won't be around later, though."

"Too bad he'll miss the season."

"But handy for you when you're needing the work." Tim didn't begrudge Trey the job.

"I don't get that, Tim. Dad's always run crews of five or even six before. What gives?"

"Not now. Not if he's going to make boat payments and pay the crew."

"How the hell can it be that bad?"

Tim shrugged. "Look." He pointed down into the harbour.

Trey froze. "Holy crap."

The beast tied up in the harbour looked to be a converted stern trawler—converted by Jules Verne. A crane arm at the stern was outfitted with a huge auger Trey thought looked more like it should be in a mine somewhere. Tim pointed out the conveyer belt running from the stern ramp to midship.

"That sucker's got to be thirty-five metres."

"Closer to forty. These guys are eating bergs for breakfast."

Trey didn't think he'd ever see a scowl like that on Tim's calm face.

"There's more than one of these things?"

Tim's lip curled at one corner. "Oh, there's more than one. A big tanker might have three or four of these buddies. They chew the bergs up, melt them in their holds, then pump the water straight onto a tanker. These guys can stay with the bergs all summer while the tankers go back and forth to American ports. Wouldn't want all those pretty water fountains in Vegas to go dry. Thirsty bastards."

Trey didn't know what to say. His dad wasn't exactly a sunny person to begin with, but his new touchiness was making sense.

"Dad!"

Trey couldn't give up, although the only answer he'd had was the relentless roar of the wind and waves.

"Dad!

Trey felt himself rising with another wave, and he looked down into the trough to come. For a moment he caught a glimpse of glowing green. Between the waves and the awkwardness of the survival suit there was no point in trying to swim for the object. The best he could do was let the momentum of the wave carry him down into the trough. There it was again. Trey just had time for a lunge and grab before the next wave broke over him.

Still gasping and blinking salt water out of his eyes, Trey began to laugh. He was holding a glow-in-the-dark flashlight his mom had given his dad for Christmas. For as long as Trey could remember each Christmas his mom had found some odd piece of safety equipment for his dad. His dad would grumble, but somehow the waterproof matches, or hand warmers, or crazy flashlight would find their way onto the boat.

It took a couple tries, but Trey managed to get the flashlight loop over one wrist. Fumbling at the switch with uncooperative fingers proved useless, but he was finally able to work it with his knuckle. Between each dunking, he searched for signs of the other two men. The wind was likely drowning out Trey's calls, but the light might help the others to find him. He wondered if he'd ever get to tell his mom he'd found the flashlight.

Trey hugged the flashlight to him and watched the thin beam of light reflect off waves and fog as he searched around him.

There. A shape bobbing on the water. Trey kicked hard, fighting the waves, but lost sight of his target. Desperately panning the flashlight beam, he picked up the dark shape and tried for it again.

Struggling for what seemed like an age, Trey finally closed in. "Dad!"

Trey wanted to believe he'd seen movement.

"Dad!"

By the glow of the flashlight, Trey could make out someone in a survival suit half draped over a chunk of wood. He wasn't moving.

Trey finally got one arm over the wood and the other arm around the man's shoulders. Slowly, as if half asleep, the man turned his face to Trey.

"Dad! Thank God. How are you doing?"

John gave a ghost of a smile. "Trey, you're okay."

Miles off shore, at night, shipwrecked in a storm, developing hypothermia, Trey returned his dad's smile. "I'm fine."

"Others?"

Trey shook his head, then realized his dad's eyes were shut. "I haven't seen them. Can you get yourself further up?"

John slowly shook his head. "Leg's broken."

Trey couldn't help asking, "They saw us, didn't they?"

John nodded slowly, then dropped his head back to the wood.

"Hang on, Dad. Hang on." Trey slid as tight to his dad's side as he could and kept one arm around him. "I'm glad we got to work together." And he meant it.

Trey had expected monotony. He theoretically knew the routine: spot and net the ice, lift it aboard with the deck crane, steam wash the brine off, break up and add to the tanks. Repeat. For months.

Their first two days out, Trey had been assigned to hosing down the ice. Tim and Russ would take out the skiff and net the bergy bit, tow it back to the *Dora Marie*, then Tim would come aboard and operate the crane to lift the ice. Trey would wash it down, then the three of them would use picks and axes to break the ice up for the tanks where it would melt. The entire process was slowed by the smaller crew.

The third day, Trey's dad asked if Russ and Trey were ready to take the skiff out. They jumped at the chance. Russ took over the tiller of the small outboard, while Trey worked Russ's place in the bow. Before long they netted a good size bergy bit—about two metres high and likely six or seven tonnes.

"Ya got her boys?" Tim called from the rail.

"Haul away," answered Russ.

But as the net began to tighten, Tim shouted, "Back off! Back off!"

Russ threw the outboard in reverse, just as the berg began to roll. The mini tsunami that fanned out from the berg lifted the small skiff and threatened to flip her. Trey was knocked to the bottom of the boat. Fortunately, the skiff righted herself, but they'd be bailing for a while.

Trey looked up at the rail and found his father looking down at the pair of them.

Here it comes.

Trey could see his dad draw a deep breath.

"If you ladies are done dancing with that bit, can we get 'er aboard?" He walked off, laughing.

At dinner Trey and Russ took some more ribbing and heard a few hair-raisers. Unpredictable ice meant the job would never be entirely routine.

When Trey and his dad had a minute alone, John had only four words for his son, "Never tell your mum."

John was very still. Trey figured they'd been in the water four or five hours by now. He jostled his father with the arm he kept around him.

"Dad. Say something."

The wind roared.

"Dad?"

His father spoke very slowly, each word an effort, "You might want to try journalism."

Trey laughed. "Got my first story planned."

Trey was still laughing when the helicopter's lights found them.

RABBIT SEASON

Fiona Moore

Ken, crouched at the prow of the low flat boat in the mangrove swamps of upstate New York, saw it first. A flicker of something off-white between the twilight trees, not a bird, not one of the horrible oatmeal-coloured giant squirrels (they'd had to shoot another last night and it had fallen into the camp chirping and twitching; nobody had dared even suggest that they should do the sensible thing and skin it and cook it). An enemy sniper? Despite his lack of field experience, Ken knew better. He crouched lower, willing it to show itself. He knew he should feel afraid, yet the comforting familiarity of the swamps, evoking early childhood memories of riding the poling boats through the tropical Toronto causeways, kept the adrenaline from coursing.

The adrenaline had been coursing the night he ran all the way out to the tundra, the sound of the goretex trouser legs squeaking against each other as they scissored over snowy hills, thick tread boots crunching the Nunavut late-winter snow. He had come out there before, mostly to escape the bigger boys who always seemed to find him, saying *swamp-boy, refugee*, and other things he couldn't repeat to his worn-looking parents, but he had never run so hard as when he had that *thing* after him.

"Storm coming," Al said idly, his right hand on the outboard in the stern, keeping the boat on course as he cradled a pistol with his left.

Captain Manders slowly turned his leathery face, with the remains of a slightly fey handsomeness, and slit his pale eyes meaningfully at the black youth. Al raised an eyebrow at the rebuke.

"Come on, sir, if there were Reds in this neck of the woods we'd know by now," the young man protested. "Just trying to make

53

conversation."

"Trouble can come from anywhere," Manders retorted. Again Ken wondered at the remains of the peculiar accent. The Seaboard States, with their dwindling population, battling their neighbours on one front and the environment on the other, were more than happy to accept volunteers, mercenaries even, from Texas, California, or even Europe, but it was unusual to see one in charge of native-born Seaboarders.

"Ah, you're seeing Reds under the bed again, sir," Al replied. Then again, perhaps Al wasn't a native-born Seaboarder himself. He sounded like one to Ken, but come to think of it he'd never told Ken exactly where he was from.

"Mind the tiller, Private," Manders said with finality, and Al quieted down with a slight pout on his post-adolescent face.

That day he had gone out to the snow-heaps at the edge of the town, where the industrial-scale hydroponic plantations loomed, to be alone, hating the Inuit children with their funny language he could never learn. He missed the hot swamps of his hometown, the threadbare stuffed rabbit he'd lost in the rush out of the South, sinking beneath the waves in the wake of the overcrowded commandeered ferryboat, *never mind, Kennie, you're a big boy now,* brooding, conjuring up armies from the South, from the fierce Red States that kept threatening war with their neighbours, drawing up battle plans with pebbles and discarded bottle bits. Something bigger than him, bigger than the Inuit boys, bigger even than the teachers who kept telling him it was up to him to stop complaining and fit in.

Looking up, he froze. He saw a rabbit, white for winter, hopping along urgently. Behind it was a raven, hopping in front of it was another raven. They were driving it on, herding it, chasing it with their wings every time it tried to break away. He did not think they meant that rabbit well. Ken ran at the grouping, yelling, scattering ravens and rabbit alike, hoping the rabbit would understand later that he'd saved its life.

"Do you see something?" Manders joined Ken in the prow of the boat, moving in that silent way he had.

Ken indicated the jungle. "Not sure if it's an animal or a sniper."

"If it was a sniper, we'd know by now," Manders said. "What did it look like?"

"Just a bit of white, something following the boat through the jungle."

"Keep a lookout," Manders said. "We're due at the Detroit Line by tomorrow night, so I don't want to waste time chasing phantoms. But if it is something, I'd like to know about it."

Ken's parents said it must have been old Nick Fivefingers, the local tramp, in a Hallowe'en mask. The police chief who heard Ken's story put it down to a recent screening of the *Star Wars* prequels and an overactive imagination, and warned his parents gravely against too much General Grievous. But Ken knew what had chased him for three kilometres through the snow, bursting ptarmaganlike out of the drift in a flurry of black and white bones and ragged fur and feathers, bigger than a grownup, bigger than a bear, then running, running before he found himself falling, bright light and rush of stinking air and he was lying on his back in a heap of melted snow with nothing to prove to parents, police chief or worried school guidance counsellor that it had ever been there.

Ken felt that animal being-watched instinct, before he even saw it again, flickering through the trees. A cold shiver started at the top of his scalp, ran down his neck (where his hair had been pulled back in a tight sweat-resistant ponytail; barbers were scarce in the swamplands, and he didn't have the courage to shave his head like Al did, or hack it off raggedly like Manders) and along his shoulders.

"Did you see that, sir?" Al said, before Ken could even open his mouth.

"Yes, I did." Manders shifted position in the boat, adjusting to a kind of down-on-one-knee pose. But for the accent, the semiautomatic shotgun and the combat gear, he might have been Daniel Boone, all stubbly beard and farmer's tan, scouting through the primeval wilderness of America. "Get down, Usagi, last thing we need is another inquiry into the death of an idiot journo."

Ken obeyed, but dug in his bag for his binoculars. He had to see it, to know for sure that it was what he thought it was.

In a way, the spirit or imaginary monster or Nick Fivefingers with too much whiskey incident had some kind of cathartic effect. Although the local children still teased him (particularly Steve Tulugaq, the police chief's son, who knew how to jimmy the lock on his father's filing cabinet), it didn't seem as important any more, and his lack of caring eventually caused them to start leaving him alone. As he began working out, joined the school hockey team and got grades good enough to mark him out as someone who could be asked for revision advice (though fortunately not good enough to mark him out as an incurable nerd), he began getting on with the others. Even if, occasionally, in moments of boredom, he would doodle its bony, beaky, bucktoothed face on random pieces of paper, in school, at university as he drifted through a major in English and journalism followed by an interminable internship at globeandmail.com, and out into the adult world.

A few minutes later, Ken saw it for certain. Just for a minute, but he recognised that bony face, that skinny frame, that could, admittedly, have passed for scrawny old Nick Fivefingers (now long-dead of exposure) albeit in a Hallowe'en mask of a kind the general store never sold.

"Got it!" he hissed.

"Thought I told you to stay down," Manders said absently, holding out a hand for the binoculars. "Hm, yes," he said. "Funny-looking thing, isn't it?"

"Will-o-the-wisp," Al remarked.

"What?" Ken said.

"Will-o-the-wisp," the young man repeated. "Don't you know? A kind of spirit, you see it out in the swamps. It pulls people off course, out into the treacherous parts where you drown."

"Swamp gas," Manders said dismissively.

"Isn't," Ken heard himself saying. "Al's not entirely wrong, Captain."

"Kennie, why?" his mother asked. "You can surely aim higher. The salary's less than *half* what that environment zine was offering you, and you *know* there's no future in online media...."

"I want to go South," Ken had said, resisting anger at her use of the nickname. It wasn't her fault, just too many memories of what had happened when the other kids found out what his mother called him.

56

She was right about the online media— as pads became harder to get, fewer people read the dotcoms— but job security could wait.

"Let him go," his father said. "It's just nostalgia. Misplaced memories of Toronto. When he's done making his macho gesture, and found out there's nothing South but fish and Americans, he'll come back."

"What if he takes a bullet before that happens?" his mother mourned. But Ken's father was wrong. He no longer wanted to go back to Toronto; he knew it would be nothing but swamp now, and he wanted the ethereal green place of his earliest memories to remain inviolate. But something was driving him South, to the place where armies fought over the bare remains of the increasingly-scarce fertile land, and away from that Godforsaken place of snow half the year and dust the other half, of decaying polar ice and ravens and rabbits and diminishing marine life statistics, slightly hysterical assertions that the hydroponic systems and the increasingly-short winters would make Nunavut the agricultural saviour of the world, the last of humanity fading out against the surging ecosystem. He thought, *Better to be eaten by bears than nibbled away by rabbits.*

"You know what it is, then?" Manders asked Ken softly. They could see the strange thing flickering closer to them now.

"Sort of," Ken said. "I've seen something like it before, and other people have seen them too." He dug into the pack at his ankles, pulled out his armoured fieldpad (about thirty years old and an army reject, but still serviceable once reconditioned), and called a file up onto the screen.

Manders took it, scanned it with practised eyes. "So what are they doing?"

Ken had recorded so many interviews with Seaboard soldiers that once-thrilling tales of hand-to-hand combat in the eerie jungles around Lake Michigan, stories of battles in open desert south of Chicago with ageing kerosene-powered tanks, had lost their glamour and so, his mind drifting, he almost missed the crucial detail.

"Hang on," he said. "A weird bony thing?"

The Marine paused, frowned. "Fuck it, I knew you wouldn't believe me."

"No, no, I do," Ken said hastily. "Tell me what you saw."

"Well," the Marine continued, brows beetling further into her scarred face, "it was the strangest thing. Skinny, like a skeleton, only not quite, you know? Like a famine kid, but huge, seven feet tall in this funny mask, kind of beaky, and this outfit like feathery rags. Don't know where it came from, one minute we're shooting at each other over a rise, and the next minute it's standing in the middle of the firing."

"What happened then?"

"Well, we kept shooting, obviously," the Marine said. "And this creature, this thing, just raised its arms and blam. Next thing I knew the two grunts beside me were crispy fried, and same with the Reds on the other side, once I got a look at them. Don't know what saved me, maybe it was cause I was sunk behind the ridge, reloading. The thing was gone, and there's no proof it was ever there. Captain says it's PTSD, and you know, I kind of wonder if he's right."

Ken watched the movements of the creature. He found himself remembering the rabbit, desperate, driven along by the ravens. Unable to understand, to see the bigger picture. The birds now hopping in front, guiding it, now flapping behind it in a burst of wings, chasing it, carefully keeping it in line.

"It's either following us or—"

"Or?" Manders looked up from the fieldpad.

"—it's herding us."

The man outside Ken's studio apartment was polite, probably sixty-something, with thinning short hair and a pleasant smile over a sharp black suit. He introduced himself as Hase, an officer in the Seaboard Intelligence Corps, glancing briefly at the spare white walls with their studentish collection of 1970s movie posters, the Swedish knockoff flatpack furniture, the half-packed rucksack and bedroll.

"I understand you've been asking a lot of soldiers questions about some thing they see on the battlefield," he said.

"Yes," Ken said. "It's my job. This is my press pass." Hiding the memory of stories the other war correspondents told, of people who asked the wrong questions disappearing, maybe turning up later in conveniently untraceable pieces in the war zone. He'd had his share of spat insults, demands to know when Nunavut would stop pretending to be neutral and recognise the Red menace for what it was, barely-polite refusals to his requests for an embedded post, all par for the course for any of the foreigners in Seaboard territory. He told himself this visit was no different, just more official intimidation.

Hase sat heavily down. "Maybe twenty-five years ago, I wouldn't be here, telling you this," he said, without the slightest humour in his voice, "but the war's changed a lot of things. I don't work for the FBI any more, hell, there *is* no FBI anymore—" Ken began to speak, but Hase gestured impatiently, "—the Reds may *call* their intelligence corps the FBI, but it's sure as hell not the one I knew, and the Seaboarders aren't that deluded—so the information I have from back then is mine to keep or give away as I see fit." He activated his pad (Ken noted with slight envy that it was a relatively new Korean import), showed Ken the files.

"Bunnygirl.docx?"

"It's what I call it, the Bunny Girl. Or them. Could be there's more than one; if there's only one, it sure moves around. I first heard about it from soldiers coming back from the war zones. This bony scavenger-bird thing, appearing in the middle of skirmishes, or ghosting along with patrols. Some of 'em think it's Death. They got songs about it."

"And you?"

"Whatever it is, it's not too bright. That's why I call it the Bunny Girl; it seems to just dumbly follow around the troops, like some gal who doesn't know better. But it's pretty deadly if you get it on the wrong day, and not in the way you expect."

"Can you get me closer to it?" Ken asked Al.

Al glanced at Manders for affirmation, and the captain looked at Ken. "You got an idea, Usagi, I'd like you to run it past me."

"It's just…" Ken struggled for the right words, awkward under the military glare. "I think we should call its bluff," he said. "If it's herding us, then the last thing to do is let it."

Manders nodded at Al. "Take us in to shore, Private," he said.

"But what is it, really?" Ken asked.

"I wish I knew," Hase said. He transferred the file to Ken's fieldpad. "I don't know if it's alien, or some weapon built by the people who were here before us—no, I don't subscribe to all that Great American Empire shit, but they did know how to make things we don't—or what.

I don't believe in the supernatural, but who knows, maybe I'm wrong. Whatever. We just think it might be important." He looked Ken in the eye. "You're starting out to the Detroit Line tomorrow, aren't you?"

Ken nodded. His first embedded post. "I'll be meeting a two-man patrol boat at the marina and riding up with them along the Great Lakes. Get some stories from close to the front lines."

Hase sighed. "Yes, that's what you say, but I know you're really going out there looking for that thing. I know you've seen it before."

Ken couldn't resist. "You ever see it yourself?"

Hase nodded slowly. "Once," he said. "Out near O'Hare, around the start of the war. Ran into a militia patrol. My driver was killed; I only got away because it went for the militiamen." He handed Ken a data dot. "This is an app. Download it onto your pad, and when you find it, activate it. There's a lot of money riding on finding those things, finding out where they're from, and tracking them to the source."

"Supposing I say no?"

Hase smiled. "You know how your request for embedding finally came through? Well, there's a condition." He held up another data dot. "This here is another app. Do this thing for us and you've got SIC-mandated carte blanche anywhere you can find Seaboarders or their allies. Don't, and you're going to be back in Iqaluit covering the techno-agricultural beat within the month."

Ken nodded. At least things made more sense now.

The boat bumped the shore. Ken leaped out, surprising even himself with the speed of his movements, chasing the flickering creature through the trees. He heard a crashing sound behind him; Manders and Al, or perhaps just Manders, following. He flung himself at the creature, tangling himself in the ragged, reeking fabric and brought it down.

"Kenichi Usagi," the young private said, looking at Ken's press pass. "What sort of a name is *that*?"

"I don't know," Ken said. "It's Japanese, and I don't speak it." Semi-truth; his father, driven by memories of his own childhood, had enrolled young Ken in Saturday-morning language classes, but they'd been mercifully abandoned along with Toronto, and he saw no reason to translate his name for the kid. "Does it matter?"

"Not much," said the youth. "I'm Private First Class Benjamin.

Benjamin Bunny."

Ken stared. "You're kidding."

"Ignore him," said a tired voice behind him. A worn, leather-skinned man with faded captain's bars on his collar slung a bedroll into the boat. "His name's Al Benjamin, and the only thing remotely rabbit-like about him is his wearisome drive to leave as many offspring behind as he can. Now, Usagi, I don't take passengers and it's a three-day trip under the best of conditions, so journo or no, you alternate between watch and tiller along with us."

"Yes, sir." Stowing his fieldpad in his camera pack, Ken followed.

"What the fuck—" Manders, crashing to a halt behind him, instinctively swinging his shotgun to ready position.

Ken looked back, his arms spread where he'd pulled the furs open on the struggling creature. It looked different up close; hard to tell, now, if it was more like a rabbit or like a bird. "I know," he said. "It's some kind of robot thing. Or cyborg."

"That's insane. Not even the Taiwanese have managed to build—"

"Not the Taiwanese, I don't think," Ken said. "There were theories that it was the old Americans, before the split, or aliens, and I wasn't too sure, but, look, it's human-made, and it's recent, and it's got a purpose." He showed Manders the odd seed-pod cases under its forearms. "I think they're some sort of projectile firing thing. And around its body; hooks for, I don't know, grenades perhaps?"

"A kind of mobile armaments platform," Manders mused, lowering the gun. "That thing in the middle; some kind of power core?"

"I guess," Ken said. "I don't think it's got any actual weapons left, or it'd have used them on me. I think it's just following its programming."

"Its programming being?"

"That's the question," Ken said. Drawn North for some reason, looking for something or someone. The one driving the rabbit on, the other leading the rabbit forward. Something bigger, bigger than him, bigger than his boss, the government, the war even. Something that had been driving him on, even when he didn't realise it. And then he remembered; remembered how, after meeting the thing in the snowdrifts, he'd stopped running from the bullies, started his slow trajectory South. He knew he had to stop being the rabbit now, start being the raven. Stop running away, start chasing. Find what the *something* was. Take control.

Ken reached out, grabbed the apparent power source, pulled and twisted. Manders gasped slightly as he did, half-reaching out as if to prevent him. Ken dug through the flimsy plastic and membranes like a butcher, cutting or ripping out anything that looked like it could store data, contain a programme. Then he stood, pushed the metal, bone and fur thing into the swamp. It fell with a splash, then sank gracefully out of sight, in the water, so much like the waterways of his earliest childhood. His stuffed rabbit falling, falling into the water from the ferryboat, *never mind, Kennie, you're a big boy now*. Al watched straight-faced.

Ken straightened, looked at Manders. "I've got to go South," he said, surprising himself with the sound of conviction in his own voice. "Way South. Mexico, maybe, or further. That's where these things are from, that's where this one was headed." Where the ravens were driving the rabbit. He thought of the app, wondered when he dared activate it. "I've got an official commission from the SIC. I need to find out what they are and why they're here." For Hase, but also for himself. To find out who was capable of building something like the Bunny Girl. To stop running away, start chasing. To find out if, somewhere down South, there was hope. Or death. Either way, childhood's end.

Manders looked in the water for a while, until the last white trace vanished. "Come on, then," the old soldier said, straightening up and shouldering his gun. "We've got another three hours before it'll be time to make camp."

〜

AND NOT A DROP TO DRINK

Stephanie Bedwell-Grime

You could say I found my new job in the want ads. Or through staring out the window instead of reading them.

Summer arrived in Toronto that year on May eleventh. I was sitting in my box-sized kitchen, watching the sun set in a huge crimson ball, and wondering if using the coffee maker could possibly make it hotter.

Queen Street was a sea of black leather and blue denim, broken only by the multi-coloured vests of sidewalk vendors selling silver jewellery. Thanks to an endless line of bumper to bumper rush hour traffic, the air was stifling and yellow with car exhaust. But it was half a degree cooler than inside, so I sat in the wheezing breeze, coffee in one hand, want ads in the other, staring down at the street below.

That's when I saw it.

In spite of the heat, he was wearing a suit of black and yellow corduroy. Bopping to the beat of the Mp3 player I could almost hear from my window, he performed an intricate dance while waiting for the streetcar. I watched, fascinated, wondering how he could possibly move so nimbly with the crotch of his pants hanging down about his knees. He twirled, shimmered. I blinked.

He vanished.

At the streetcar stop lay a pair of black sneakers, the only evidence a person had been standing there.

The streetcar cruised to a stop. People got off, more got on. Someone kicked the shoes into the gutter.

"It's a symptom of withdrawal," said my friend Chloe. "You're missing the structure of your working life. You feel unimportant."

"Work doesn't make you important," I insisted. "What I really miss is my paycheque. And I know what I saw!"

"Perhaps you should do some volunteer work at a hospital or something. Get out, connect with people. This solitude isn't good for you."

"Solitude! This is Queen Street, for God's sake. There isn't solitude here, even at four in the morning."

She looked me up and down, taking in the faded, shapeless t-shirt and leggings that were my hanging out wardrobe. I felt vastly underdressed against her power suit, power haircut, power earrings.

"Honestly, Rox," she said, shaking her head. Thankfully, she didn't say what she was thinking, which was obviously, 'what a loser'.

Toronto's grown to the kind of world-class proportions that missing persons don't make the papers anymore. Makes you feel just a little insecure to think you could just up and disappear and no one would notice, that the sum of your life could be relegated to a file marked "whereabouts unknown".

But the thing bugged me. Okay? And I knew I wasn't crazy, no matter what Chloe thought. I had time on my hands, nothing better to do, and Chloe was safely at work and wouldn't know what I was up to. So, I set off to do "research".

For three days the forecast had called for rain. The evening sky was still brown with haze and not a rain drop in sight. Yonge Street, I decided. Between the drop-in centres, the stereo stores and the X-rated movie houses, all manner of strange things happened on Yonge. If it wasn't an outright riot, probably no one would notice.

I passed Dundas, heading north, feeling increasingly foolish with each block. Night was falling, the sidewalk packed with office workers heading home. I was just about to turn back, when there on the corner of Gerrard, I spied them.

A pair of fuchsia spike heels, abandoned mid-stride, as if the former occupant had vanished before she left the curb.

I looked around. No one even glanced in my direction, so I snagged the heels and kept on going. I turned onto Bloor and headed west towards the trendy shops in Yorkville. Cafes spilled out onto the sidewalk where the beautiful people displayed their perma-tanned bodies like the jewellery in the nearby boutiques.

Coffee and a muffin at an upscale diner were all I could afford, though I would much have preferred wine. I nursed the coffee as long as I could, while the manager told me with pointed glares it was long past time I vacated my seat.

Finally, feeling truly stupid, after all none of the passersby had miraculously disappeared, I gathered up the fuchsia shoes and headed for Yonge Station.

Rush hour commuters poured down the stairs, buffeting me with elbows and briefcases as I rummaged in the pocket of my jeans for a token. I squeezed onto the crowded platform, carried forward by the press of bodies. The doors closed, leaving me to gaze in frustration at the departing train. I sighed, resigned to waiting for the next train. But as I turned away toward the seats against the far wall, a flash of colour drew my eyes downward.

On the edge of the platform was a single, green loafer.

"It's happening all over the city, I tell you." I gestured to the neatly ordered piles of shoes in my tiny living room. "There doesn't seem to be a pattern. It doesn't seem to matter whether they're male, female, rich, poor…" I pointed to the graph I'd been drawing on a scrap of paper. "Five pairs of beat-up running shoes, three pairs of Italian leather pumps…I saw a pair just like this in a boutique on Bloor for a hundred and fifty bucks…loafers, deck shoes, you name it…"

Chloe looked in dismay at the assortment, then back at me with eyes full of pity. "I really wish you'd lay off with this delusion of yours." Exasperated, she turned in a flurry of tasteful couture and strode toward the door.

"Nice to know I can always count on you Chlo—" I said as she beat a hasty retreat down the stairs. Chloe never did like to play on the losing team.

In the orange twilight I watched her walk away along Queen Street, heels clicking along the sidewalk. Perhaps she was right. Maybe I was crazy.

The crowd closed around her. I saw the top of her flame-coloured hair bobbing among them, then…nothing.

"No!" I screamed. Before I knew it, I was down the wrought-iron fire escape and tearing up the sidewalk. People parted to let me pass. Just one more crazy person on Queen Street, I might as well have been invisible.

Before I reached Spadina, I found them. Chloe's tasteful suede pumps, lying abandoned under the sign for a mexican restaurant. Up ahead I saw a glimmer lost in the twilight and scrambled towards it.

Electric shocks rippled the length of my body as I hit the invisible barrier. Then I was falling. Falling into nothing, air beneath my grasping fingers, my feet wind-milling helplessly.

I hit bottom and rolled with the impact, grazing knees and elbows. For several seconds I lay there panting, afraid to move and find out what was broken. Ahead I heard a whisper of cloth, the slap of bare feet against the ground. I opened my eyes.

A column of people marched past me off into the featureless horizon. Tentatively, I got to my feet. No shattered bones screamed at me in agony. Everything seemed to be in one piece.

I was standing, barefoot, on a vast field of clay, cracked and scaled like the back of a snake. In the distance, a tumbleweed rolled forlornly across the barren landscape. A weak red sun bled across the skyline, drenching the world in crimson. It didn't look like anywhere on earth I could name.

It didn't look like anywhere on earth.

The troop moved out, eyes fixed solidly ahead, hands hanging limp at their sides. Apart from their glazed expressions, they were alike in one thing: none of them were wearing shoes. Vagrants in tattered clothing, stock brokers in banker's grey, secretaries, shop keepers, paraded past me into the blistered landscape.

"Wait!" I dashed after them, scanning the faces as I ran along the column. In their midst I caught a glimpse of scarlet hair, a flash of a gold, button earring. "Chloe!"

An arm seized me by the shoulder, hauling me roughly backward. I looked up into golden eyes, framed by raven hair. He had a straight nose and proud, high cheekbones. Yet he looked vaguely otherworldly.

"Trust me," he rasped, "you don't want to go with them."

"Who the hell are you?" Shaking myself from his grip, I debated whether to take a swipe at him. Not a good idea, I decided. Beneath the brown, suede shirt was a well-muscled body. I thought of all the times I'd cancelled aerobics on Chloe, and regretted it.

"Watcher," he said. His voice was deep, synthetic almost, like something out of a bad movie. Then in an approximate imitation of my indignation he said, "Who the hell are you?"

"Roxanne," I said, absently, then mentally kicked myself for telling him. "Where are we?"

"The name of this place would mean nothing to you."

"Yeah? Try me."

He hesitated. "Between the earth and sky."

"What?"

"I told you."

"Listen," I said, desperately trying to get a grasp on the situation. "I don't care who you are, or where we are. My friend's in that group of zombies. All I want to do is get her out of there and get us back home."

"It's not that simple," he said with a blink of those golden, cat's eyes. "Come."

"Why should I?"

"Because it's better than going with them."

"Thanks, but I'll take my chances." I started off after them. He hauled me back.

"Are they all like you?" he asked, exasperated. Up close he was taller than I'd realized.

"Who?"

"Your…kind."

"What *kind* do you think I am?" I asked nervously.

"Human."

"And what kind are you?"

"Watcher," he said. "I have told you that, already."

"You have a name, Watcher?"

"Watcher." He put a hand between my shoulder blades. "Come."

I looked behind me at the herd of people that had almost disappeared from sight. "Wait, what about my friend?"

"We will find her, later."

And when I hesitated, he grabbed me by both shoulders and stared down into my face. "If you go with them they will kill you.

"How do I know you won't?"

"You don't," he said.

I followed him into the wasteland. In the distance, a low mountain range jutted from the withered ground like a fence dividing nothing from nowhere. Obviously, this was Watcher's destination. The cracked earth was about as comfortable as walking on a hot, gravel road, and each breath was like trying to breathe fire. Within the hour, I had slowed to a limping crawl.

"Our shoes," I said, and waited while the Watcher impatiently turned back toward me. "They're back…home, aren't they?" I pictured my ragged sneakers lying on the corner of Queen and Spadina, next to Chloe's power pumps.

He nodded, silhouetted by the sickly sun and the dark spine of the mountain range.

"Why?"

"They can't take anything that's touching the ground."

"Who!"

"The Collectors." He gestured to the desert around us. "Natives of this place."

"What do they want people for?"

"Water," he said simply and continued on into the shadows of the nearby peaks.

"But there's lots of water where I come from," I ran in a limping shuffle to catch up with him. "Hell, we'd probably give it to them. We give it to everybody else."

"Water cannot pass the barrier unless it is contained by organic material."

"Organic material! Those are human beings!"

"Yes," he said. "I know." And turned his back on me and nimbly, began to climb.

"They're breaking people down into their component parts and nobody's doing anything about it!"

"It is my purpose to regulate the elements," Watcher called back, as if that explained everything.

"Wait! I don't understand." For a moment I forgot about the flayed skin on the bottoms of my feet and scrambled up after him.

Climbing proved to be a painful undertaking. Ten steps into my ascent, I collapsed against the rock face, panting. Swallowing thickly, I ran my tongue over chapped lips. The arid air seemed to suck the moisture from everything. I realized suddenly that I was thirsty. Unbearably thirsty.

Watcher dropped from the rise above and landed lithely beside me. He wasn't even out of breath.

"What did you mean, regulate the elements?" I rasped. Even my vocal chords seemed sucked dry.

From a leather sack slung across his shoulders, he produced a canteen. I took it gratefully.

"I am…responsible," Watcher said, "for balancing the dimensions."

"You mean, you *approve* of whoever is snatching people for their supply of drinking water?" I raised the canteen to my lips.

"I ensure no dimension takes more than its share," Watcher said. Amber eyes glared indignantly at me in the shadows. "In all things, there must be balance. That is the nature of the universe."

The water had a stale taste to it, as if it had been distilled. "This isn't…" I choked, suddenly realizing with horror just what I was drinking.

He snatched the canteen from my hands. "I did not give you that to waste."

"What about the human lives going to waste!" I nearly screamed at him.

"There is no known species that does not consume another living thing be it animal or vegetable to preserve its own life. That is not waste, it is the way—"

"Of the universe," I snapped. "You've made that much clear." How can I explain the devastation of finding oneself at the bottom instead of the top of the food chain?

Wincing, I stood on blistered feet, and pointed to the top of the rise. "Is that where they've taken Chloe?"

Watcher nodded. Raven hair tumbled over his shoulders. Impatiently, he flicked it from his face and stowed the canteen in his gear.

"Then I'm going to get her." Grimacing with each step, I hobbled towards the next elevation. Through slitted eyes he watched my painful progress, then sighed and slid a powerful shoulder beneath my arm.

Seemingly unaffected by the extra weight, he hauled me to the summit. The air on the top was cooler, but dry as a frost-free fridge. The feeble sun had vanished, leaving only a hint of magenta on the horizon. Soon the temperature would plummet and I was wearing only a t-shirt. Turning my thoughts to Chloe, I looked down into the basin.

At first I thought the structure in the centre was a steam engine with its tall smoke stacks. Then I noticed the line of people marching blankly toward the funnel-shaped entrance.

Crawling about the basin like a swarm of bugs were gnomish beings with brown, leathery skin. Roughly humanoid in appearance, their limbs were short and thick. Red eyes glowed in the dim light as they urged the procession forward with what looked like slender, black clubs.

"The Collectors?" I whispered.

Watcher nodded.

One by one, the line disappeared into the bowels of the machine. As I watched, a middle-aged man still carrying a briefcase came to his senses. Astounded, he looked around him, then screaming, broke from the ranks. Light lanced from the club of nearest Collector. The businessman yelped like a whipped dog, then collapsed back into a slack-jawed trance.

Steam billowed from the smokestacks. The machine belched. A bundle of sticks was dispensed from the back of the machine, which rolled aimlessly across the basin.

Not tumbleweeds after all.

"Oh God," I whispered, looking away.

"There!" Watcher said suddenly. I followed his arm. Among the silent waiting to be slaughtered was a shock of flame-coloured hair.

"Chloe!" I screamed.

A tawny hand covered my mouth and dragged me backward into the shadows.

"Do you want to take her place?"

I looked up into almond eyes that glinted like a cat's in the darkness and shook my head.

"Then be quiet."

I nodded. Watcher removed his hand.

"We have to get her out of there!"

Watcher held up his hand for silence. "That isn't possible, your friend is one of the Chosen."

"Chosen? What for? To be *juiced* for her vital bodily fluids!"

"She has been *selected*. She is part of the balance. It cannot be upset."

I thought about Chloe, my best friend since grade three. We'd played Barbies together, for God's sake! And, in spite of the ways we'd grown apart in adulthood, I couldn't imagine my life without her.

"What about me," I asked quietly. "Am I supposed to be here?"

Watcher's eyes narrowed. "No…"

"Yet, I'm not scheduled for the juicer?"

"You are under my protection," he said, cautiously, then simply, "No."

"So, if I was to stay, you'd let Chloe go?"

"Roxanne, you would have to remain here," Watcher said, "forever."

I thought of my steamy, cramped apartment, and how I longed to be back there, safe in my bed with only the threat of urban crime to worry me. But, how could I ever rest easy knowing I had the power to stop my childhood friend from being pressed into the human equivalent of orange juice with extra pulp?

"All right," I said finally. "I'll stay."

From his sack, Watcher produced a shallow bowl. Uncorking the canteen, he poured an inch of water into the palm-sized vessel. He waved his hand over the water. It shimmered. Chloe's image appeared in the liquid. Watcher waved his hand again. The water disappeared. I looked down into the basin to where my friend had patiently been awaiting her death.

Chloe had vanished.

Being a Watcher is not for the faint of heart.

I don't know what would happen if someone dared to upset the balance of the universe by finding a way to close the door between dimensions...

But I intend to try.

〰〰

SCRABBLING

Isabella D. Hodson

The heat. It permeates everything. There's no escaping its touch. It's a dry heat here. We're lucky. It's worse in other places.

The skin of my face burns. Sunscreen will do no good. Besides, no one sells it anymore. There's no point. I look up at the sky and see the heat sizzle. It undulates in columns; they'd be almost pretty if we didn't despise them so much.

I look down the mountainside and watch the river below. Far down the slope, a hard climb back up, scrabbling over rocks. I remember when I used to walk this path, back when I worked as a tour guide. Showing these pristine mountains off to people from the world over. Canada's Rocky Mountains: a treasure for the world. Back then, there were buffaloberry bushes all along the path, from the river valley, scattered through the poplar and spruce forest, and up a little ways into the treeline. And kinnikinnick—bearberry—right here where I sit. Right here. Great merry tufts of it, hardy little plant. Tough woody stems knitted into rock, shooting out pinky-white flowers then mealy red berries. Now, everywhere the sun dapples the rock. No berries here anymore. No, not by a long shot.

I watch the river below. Its waters more blue than brown, and leaner. The Athabasca used to run grey and thick, filled to bursting with rock flour, the same silt that hovered in the mountain lakes and painted them turquoise when the sun's rays hit. I told my guests stories about the fur traders, those driven young fools with more than a touch of wild in their heads. Skidding down the river on canoes heavy with furs. Paddling a mad chase, sleeping beneath their overturned boats. The river swollen, its current so quick a man could die in its rapids, crushed between rocks, water like ice. I paddled along this stretch myself, from just south of Jasper to the old pulp mill in Hinton. I was so careful not to fall in; a person would lose the ability to move after three minutes in water that cold. He would shudder, then still.

That was when the glaciers spilled into the rivers. When icefields spanned mountains and a person had to take an aeroplane ride to see their breadth. How the world has changed.

I could be on the coast. It's not far. A few weeks' walk across the Rocky Mountains, through the very same Athabasca Pass that the fur traders took two hundred years ago, after the Peigan people blocked Howse Pass off by force. The traders had to find another route west. Through the pass, down into the valley, and then a long hike through the Pacific side of the Rockies, still lusher than Alberta's drier offering, even after all this time. Funny how the world works, how the needles keep clicking, knitting the unraveled strands together.

I could be there now, in any of the dozens of ecovillages that dot the coast. I tried my hand there once, forty years ago, with the cob houses and pigs, thick vegetable gardens, erosion fences built from old rubber tires. It works, there's no doubting that. A person can live in the mostly-sustainable community, live in his tent or one of the purpose-built buildings, and spend his days toiling, helping the village keep on. He becomes part of the whole, the whole whose parts work together so well.

Or I could be in the city. Any of the cities. Calgary, Vancouver, Kelowna, Victoria, or further afield to the east. They still stand, resilient as ever.

I don't want either. The villages and the cities—they all house people. And people mean politics. Talking about the weather, the latest wave of food stamp recalls, sitting in a circle on the sidewalk and listening to a strummer's song. Humming and swaying to the music. I was never meant for that false reality. Perhaps I am too much of a loner, too independent, but I much prefer the honesty of life in the mountains. It's real here. And I can be alone when I wish; I have only to walk away from my group. Not to stray too far, mind you—that could be dangerous—but far enough that I can find comfort in solitude.

I enjoy the peace of the mountains. It feels more natural to rise and slumber to the calls of the birds, the sound of the wind rustling the aspen leaves, the gurgle of water nearby. Here, a rodent can startle me from my sleep, its tiny body capable of making such a loud, furious rustling. I wake sometimes with my hand grasped around the hilt of my knife, adrenaline pumped through my veins.

It's colder here. Harder. But it's better. There are no people to deal with, no gangs in the streets, no bullies to pull your water bottle from your fingers and steal its contents for themselves. Here there are no mad runners foretelling the end of the world. No crack snorters who've turned away from the desperation to focus on the quick, sure death that comes from being high all of the time, a strong string of hits until the final one, when the heart sings loud and chattering, a drumbeat of blood in the veins before a quick spin and drift into nothingness. Like a toilet flushed.

Nope. Not my order. I know too much to want to take that route.

"Lizbeth?" I start with surprise. I didn't hear her coming; maybe she's learning, getting better at concealing her footfalls. Tesa, short for Teresa, sits beside me. I ruffle her hair and put my arm around her. She's so small. I don't know if it's because we don't give her the nutrition she needs or because children are smaller now, their bodies adapted for a world that has less to provide, not because it wants to but because we've plundered its depths and its pockets are now empty.

We watch over this little girl like gold. She's as precious to us as a photograph, curled at the edges and folded over a thousand times, that finds its home in a breast pocket. Irreplaceable.

"What are you up to, little girl?"

She opens her fist and shows me two yellow mushrooms. "Look what I found!"

I smile at her and she beams with pride, her precious catch staining blue where her tiny hands have bruised it.

"Well done, little rabbit. We'll have those with our meal this evening. Would you like to come and check the snares with me?"

No one eats meat anymore. There's no market. The planet cannot afford the cost. Methane gas, irrigation, the land required to raise the fodder. Too many people, not enough food to feed them all. No one raises cattle or sheep or pigs. Not on a large scale. The ecovillages have pigs and chickens, and some of the richer farmers do, too, but for the most part people eat the fruits, roots, seeds, stems, and, sometimes, flowers of plants. Vegetables, fruit, grain—that's enough. Enough to live on, not too hard to grow. It can be done.

Here in the mountains, beyond the reach of the city or its roving gangs, we eat rabbits sometimes, when we can catch them. Or squirrels.

If we're lucky, a grouse. And, more often than not, a deer.

The deer do well. They always have. An adaptable species, like coyotes. They thrive on the edges. Where forest meets field, mountain meets city. They eat the grasses and shrubs that push through the rooted soil of clear-cuts, and they thrive on the quick growth that follows a forest fire. They taste a heck of a lot better than the grubs we dig up, and the meat of a deer lasts us more than one meal.

The deer knew what was coming long before it hit. People started seeing them in the Northwest Territories in the early 2000s. Traveling north, more north than their ancestral range had ever extended, following the warming trend, munching the grasses that grew for them in new places. The government had to change the hunting regulations to include this new resident. They were a surprise at first, but quickly became a common sight. And other species followed.

I watch Tesa bend to check the wire. She knows better than to touch it. She squats and peers at the circle it makes, just a couple of inches off the ground, perfectly positioned to snare a rabbit's neck as it bolts along its run. She is careful not to leave too much of her scent. She knows that a rabbit won't run where it can smell a trap.

We check the rabbit runs and then the smaller snares set along fallen logs and low-hanging branches by the squirrels' middens. All empty. It's a little disappointing, but at the same time I am relieved that I won't have to help prepare the animal—tug off its skin, beat at its joints with a stone until the feet come off, string out its guts on a rock.

The cities may have food stamps that a person can redeem for precious bounty from the fields, a cargo that the government orders from the farmer. Soldiers stand around the fields, watch that crop grow from seed to fruit. They take their percentage, trade it for other crops or water or stamps. The currencies that have replaced cash.

"Let's gather some camas," I tell Tesa. We wander through the woods and find ourselves out in the open, where the sun hits hard, where I usually sit and watch the river and let my thoughts drift with its course. It's still pretty here, and the camas grows abundantly in the sun. We are careful to distinguish the white camas from the death camas—one small plant can mean the difference between a tasty bulb and a slow, painful death for everyone in our group. We harvest the bulbs, collecting them in our pockets, to stew over the fire this evening, and then we enter the forest again, searching the shade for more fungi, any of the edible mushrooms and truffles we can find. Funny how the forest starts so suddenly. The clearing gives way to shrubs and grasses. Saplings grow in the shade of the bushes, pushing up from thin, hard soil. Moments later, mere steps away, a person finds himself among trees. Poplars here, but soon spruce, pine, and fir. A mixed forest, greens in every shade.

The sun hangs halfway down the sky when we return to camp. Tesa empties her pockets of camas bulbs, mushrooms, and witch's butter, an orange jelly fungus collected off the bark of a rotting log. I drop a polypore into the brewing stew, its hard brittle contours hiding edible flesh and medicines in its tea.

Thank you, honey. Anna, Tesa's mother, holds out her arms and folds her daughter into her embrace. The others walk around the camp, helping out, making themselves useful, or sitting and talking, sharing the passings of the day. There are nine of us. Used to be more. We don't look like much from afar. Nine lost souls, far out in the forest, in the wilds of Jasper National Park. Roaming through government lands—protected areas we have no business being in. But no one really cares now. No one collects tariffs or permits. If they tried, they'd disappear, another body hidden in the woods. There's a different attitude now—people find a way to get what they need to survive. If they've got to enter the wilds and fend for themselves, they do so.

There aren't enough of us to leave a heavy footprint, but there are enough that we make do. We carve out our existence from the world around us—we dig it out of the earth, pluck it from the plants that grow here, hollow it from the trees whose surfaces we carve to make tools, drink it in our tea and chew it between our teeth.

The Athabasca no longer looks anything like it used to. The Athabasca, the Fraser, the North and South Saskatchewan, the Columbia. None of them. They've lost their source. Not a squeak of ice left in the glaciers that fed them. They used to flow so fast and furious, with water cold as ice. They flow slower now, dirtier, warmer. Different fish inhabit their flows now, too. The grayling disappeared, and the dolly vardens. There are still a few trout for the fishermen wily enough to catch them, but no one fishes north of Whitecourt. No one touches the few hardy fish that survive past the former Athabasca townsite, or north through Slave Lake and Fort Mac. People, even the hungry ones, know better than to touch the fish who've swum through the river there, where the water from the old, crack-bottomed tailings ponds leaches into the ground. The tribes gave up on the deer in that forest long ago, too. Even in 2000, if a hunter shot a deer in the Swan Hills, its organs would be one red mass, each piece bleeding into the others so it would be impossible to tell the heart from the kidney. The flesh fell apart in your hands so fast you wondered how the deer survived at all, how its muscles stayed attached to its flimsy bones. Chemical soup. So many rigs in the forest, so many pipes cutting through, so many roads and cutblocks, paths that used to feed the oil and lumber industries of the west. Paths now traveled by people looking for escape.

You still see cars driving the roads. Commuters, travelers, even tourists wanting to write about the mess here, or those who seek better climes, whose mess is bigger than Canada's. People still drive; they just pay a king's ransom for the privilege.

A chickadee cheeps overhead as we collect greens. At this time of year the earth gives to us in abundance. Rhea and I pluck bunchberries from their stems. We pull the clusters of orange berries from the ground; here, there are mats and mats of them. The sun touches this spot; it sneaks through the canopy, and this is where the bunchberries grow. We have a basket for them and another for the other plants we harvest. A few late-season arnicas, clinging tenuously to life even this far past their prime. I dry these upside-down; we'll use the stems, flower, and leaves to grind into an ointment to apply to our skin after a mishap in the woods or a fall when traversing the scree. I find yarrow, too, in the valleys, and store it in my basket for the same purpose. Such an ancient plant—Achilles used it to treat his own soldiers in Greece. We're lucky we haven't destroyed it too.

Rhea abandons the bunchberry patch for a bearberry patch she finds upslope. She plucks the small red berries from underneath the mat of leaves, then takes a few leaves too and pops them into her pocket. She'll smoke them later with Sam, as they sit by our clearing in the evening, as they always do, and give thanks for the day.

"Y'know, I used to tell my kids to watch out for bears when we road-tripped to the mountains. My mom got so worried about us whenever we camped out here. God, those were the days. She made us watch those park ranger presentations—you know the ones they used to do where you got to touch the real bear fur? Man, I wish we still had those. So I take Matty out to Banff when he was six on a special trip for his birthday. I rented a car and everything, wanted him to have this great special memory for the rest of his life, to get in touch with nature, y'know? And I'm telling him, Hey, watch out for bears and don't stray too far from where I'm setting up the tent and he's like, Mom, there's no bears. And I'm like, What do you mean there's no bears? There's black bears and grizzly bears and if you're not careful they'll eat you all up. And he looks at me and says, Mom, there's no bears. Brian's mom told me that and she knows everything. She reads the paper. No more grizzlies in Alberta. No one's seen one in ten years. They're like Bigfoot now. They don't exist." Rhea huffs. "Can you believe it? My own son, my little baby Matty, telling me this. Jeepers. Who the hell would've thought? And here we are collecting these stupid berries that don't even taste good, doing the bear's job. Shitting in the woods. My shit's all red and seedy like a friggin' black bear's."

"I remember when I'd show people bear scat on the trail and tell them what it was. They were so afraid. "

"Afraid of ghosts."

"There are still bears. They're doing just fine despite us."

"Yeah? When's the last time you saw bear scat?"

"I heard a bear just the other day. It was cracking through the woods right next to where I was harvesting mushrooms."

"I bet it was a deer."

"I know my stuff, Rhea."

"Sorry. I just… Man, I'm so tired of this. I wish life would just go back to normal. Why can't things just…be good again? Shit. I sound like my kids."

"It's okay, Rhee. We're doing all right."

"But, like, this is forever. Haven't you thought about that? We're living in the fucking mountains. The *mountains*. And when are we gonna head back, hey? Never. Never! I'm going to have to sleep in a shitty tent for the rest of my life, make love to my husband on the freezing-cold ground, and use a rolled-up sweater as a pillow until my dying day. Fuck me. And don't even get me started on my kids. My poor, poor kids." Rhea starts to sniffle and wipes her eyes. "Shit. Why am I crying? I'm just so *mad*."

"Oh, Rhee. It's gonna be all right. Look at your basket. We're going to eat delicious berries all winter long and be cozy and snug in the snow."

"Lizbeth, if you even get me started on the freezing-cold snow, I *swear…*" A smile pops through Rhea's tears.

"Mmm, bearberries. Been eating them since my good old days of guiding." I toss a handful into my mouth. I tilt my head for a second and peer quizzically at Rhea. "We should do a survey. I wonder what's worse? Bearberries or bunchberries? They're both pretty crappy."

"Buffaloberries win hands-down."

I laugh. "Heck yeah."

It's strange that we came to be this way. In the forest. It's how we started. Living with the land. All of the different nations treaded here. The Cree in the prairies and forest, the Dene and Inuvialuit in the north, the Blackfoot in the south, the Kutenai in the mountains, the Beothuk on the inhospitable shores of Newfoundland and Labrador, the Haida in the foggy islands of the West Coast. The Peigans, Sarcee, Blood. The Huron, the Iroquois. And fifty other nations. The First Peoples. They knew how to do it—burn strips of land so the forest regenerates, travel with the seasons, harvest the fruits and roots and fungi and medicines from the earth. Well before anyone from the outside world made contact in the name of progress, exploration, and a clear route to the spices of India. Then there was exploitation, agriculture, tools, guns, more exploitation, pioneers and villages and later cities and railroads then cars and asphalt. Such a fast, crazy tumult. Did we really need to have so many kids, give ourselves so many mouths to feed? We did at the time. It was natural and right; go forth and procreate. It seems delusional now, with everything stretched so thin. We've bounded ahead in so many ways, but in the process of looking forward, we forgot where we came from. We leapt on a path of flower petals; they didn't stand a chance beneath our weight.

Each and every one of us lived in the city. We drove cars, bought and rented houses, got married in churches and city halls. We grew gardens in our backyards and surfed the internet. And yet, a few mistakes later, here we are. Back where we started, in the woods. But we aren't really where we started; we're worse off. Because we broke our shiny new toy.

There's solace in the forest. Beauty in the trees and sunlight. In the wind that sings through the leaves, the sunrays that dapple the earth. I like living here. Hard, yes, but I feel so much more alive. This is back-country camping that doesn't stop at the end of the trail.

We travel frequently. Four tents, three lean-tos. Anna and Tesa share a beaten-up old Eureka, Rhea and Sam sleep in their fire-orange, two-person The North Face, and Eddie calls a hardy Marmot home. Adam has a camo duck-hunting tent, far too heavy to be practical, and the rest of us build lean-tos and A-frames. Sometimes, if we're in a hurry, we share. I've bunked with Hick. George has slept in my shelter, too, when the rain leaked into his. But we like our space, this little niche we carve out of the woods every time we reach a new place.

We started in Banff and followed the river. Not all together yet; scattered. But there were too many people roving those woods. With Calgary so close by and all those desperate people, it wasn't safe. So we headed north, through the green wilds, rock and trees and lakes, staying as far as we could from the road. We have knives by our sides, and George has his bow, but we need those to survive. We disappear when we can but sometimes people get hurt. No one's out for war here; we just want to live.

Morning. Sam extracts powdered dandelion root from a sack and brews us a coffee. We all drink—something hot to warm our bones after sleep. Anna doles out breakfast into our bowls and we eat in silence, our thoughts tuned to the day ahead. Today we travel, a little further north. This place has been good to us, but it's time to move on. No matter how good it gets, we can't stay. Too much risk. Eddie saw movement on the shore when he fished yesterday. People in the trees. Not soldiers, but another tribe, perhaps, looking for better ground, better purchase. People need things to survive—we might have a nicer blanket, a warmer sweater, medicine, a child in our midst. A man will trade, sell, steal almost anything. We cannot afford to be discovered.

Rhea holds out the sack as Sam stuffs the tent inside. Adam tucks his mess kit into the front pocket of his bag, already packed and ready to go. Tesa hums as she watches her mother put away their sleeping bags. She holds tight to the foam pads she rolled up; the elastic band broke.

Eddie kicks apart the last cooking fire as Adam checks that we all have fresh water. Then we are ready to go.

The sun burns my cheeks as we walk. We head straight for higher ground, upslope through the spruce toward the treeline. The treeline's starting to rise; I can see it. Someone without a practiced eye would not notice the difference, but I see the saplings making their way up. They can do this now, with the heat. It bakes the earth, and grasses shoot out from the rock. These are hardy species—mountain flora. The wildflowers that burst into life for two short weeks, all of their DNA wrapped into the pretty colours, waiting for the bees and mosquitoes and buzzing insects that will sip nectar and unwittingly dust their bodies with pollen. So many means to spread their seed. These flowers sit tight to the ground—closer to the earth, away from the bite of the wind. Compact buds—they give only enough to get back. So much hope tucked away into each flower, the seed gifted with everything it needs to survive where it lands. Its parent can only hope, if it can hope at all.

We trudge through the scree, following a goat path. Adam scans the trees below; he leads the walk, Hick right behind him. George pulls up the rear, his bow strapped to the back of his pack just in case. Sam and Rhea behind Hick, Sam walking so his body wraps his wife. Behind them, Anna and Tesa, with Eddie watching out for the little girl. Then me. I watch their steps, how they walk on the scree. A tricky gait, with plenty of opportunity to sprain ankles and twist knees. My knees ache; I've walked through the mountains all my life, and the rocks take their toll on the body.

A raven flits by overhead, watching our progress. I spot four bighorn sheep above us, blending into rock, visible only because of their movement. A group of ewes. They can live to twenty years old out here; the rams are lucky to reach the age of eight. Too busy bashing heads and roaming far, right where the cougars can pounce on them. Nobody will pay me to tell them about the fireweed at our feet anymore. The avens and moss campion, the lichens that still cling strong to the trees and rocks even with the air quality not quite what it used to be. There are no luxuries like that anymore. No market.

A plane cuts the sky far above; a big, silver span, but from this far away it looks like a toy. I wonder who rides inside of it. People are more careful now; planes are a rare sight in the sky. From up here we can see the valley below us and the mountains beside us. An endless chain of peaks to the north and south, blanketed with green below, rock above. They used to be dusted with snow, just a little, in the summertime, when I worked here. But that hasn't been the case in over a decade; it's too bad, really. They looked so magnificent.

We could allow ourselves to be intimidated by this place, if we chose. Socked in by giant rocks folded together by the earth's crust.

Eddie's pants make a *hush hush* sound as his legs brush against each other. The rubbing nylon, the wind tickling the backs of our necks, and the sound of our steps against the scree. The only sounds we hear. Otherwise, there is only the overwhelming press of silence. We could be entirely alone out here for all we know, the rest of the world blown up in our sleep.

I read a poem once in university, in a class taught by a man who inspired me to love our writers. "The Forsaken." An old poem, not old by world standards, but old enough for Canada. Full of old ideas—the noble savage, the church in the wild. An old Ojibwa woman, weak with age, ripe with life. No longer spry. A grandmother. Too old to stay with her people as they traveled through the lakes and woods. Instead of holding this woman to their breasts, this woman who birthed chiefs and fished food from the water with a line baited with her own flesh, her people forsook her. They left her in the snow until it covered her body and her breath spilled from beneath a blanket of white crystals.

The forsaken woman. Such a familiar story. And yet, she has no regret. No bitterness, no anger. Instead, a quiet resignation. When the deer can no longer keep up with the herd, the herd leaves it behind. This is our pact. If one of our group falters or falls, breaks a leg or injures a spine, the others will go on. We agreed to this. I am intently aware of my age, my failing knees, the arthritis that steals into my fingers on cold mornings. One day, sooner or later, I won't be able to keep my feet moving to the rhythm of my mates. And then, they will move on. I imagine we will say our goodbyes, that Tesa or Anna or soft-hearted Hick might protest, but in the end, we will all agree that this is what we promised. And a person must keep her promise.

It might not be me; Eddie could fall victim to one of the groups of raiders that scout the river shores for fishermen, ready to plunder another man's hard-earned catch. Tesa could fall and break her arm; our bones are brittle without a steady source of calcium. Anything could happen to any one of us, and that would signal the time to part ways. There's no one to blame; it's merely a fact. This is how it is now. We left the cities for the mountains, the people for the trees, and we chose this life. We could go back anytime. George could decide this afternoon that he's had enough of taking the rear, or that he needs to find himself a woman and get her with child, if only to hope for a better future for someone else. He could scrabble down the scree, one step at a time, until he's in the trees and then the valley, then by the river shore. He could travel alone through the mountain passes, following the path of the grizzly bear, heading east into the foothills before they soften and flatten, making way for fields and pasture, before reaching the folds of the city. He could fend off the thieves or join a gang, or find refuge in a safe house. Or he could head west and join a commune, raise pigs and practice permaculture. There is more than one solution to our problem. Yet here we are, following a path in scree, watching the trees for movement, finding safety in numbers. Building fires no bigger than necessary, leaving no prints large enough to scar the land. We leave no trace. This is how it always should have been, but at least it's who we are now. Leave no footfall, no blemish, no impact. Just live.

We travel today, and we could stop this evening. Or we might travel further tomorrow. We will see what the day will bring. There is only this day today; we will worry about tomorrow when it happens. For now, there is just this. Placing one foot in front of the other, walking. Pitching tents and plucking mushrooms. Teasing fish from the water, breaking bone with stone hammers. Simple, necessary tasks. Nothing complicated. A new adventure might lie ahead. A troop of soldiers could find us and bring us back to the city. A pack of wild dogs could choose us as their prey. Or, maybe someone will find a solution and bring everyone back together, knitted into a blanket that spans the earth. But for the time being, for the entire foreseeable future, we live in the now. Make do with what we are given, the bounty and the hardship of the mountains. The beauty and the splendour, the grass and the scree. Snow in winter, heat in summer. Precious moments lived. We take peace in one another, thankful for the company, the help with the burden of survival. And we take solace in the wild. Because no one knows what tomorrow will bring.

BAD BLOOD

Agnes Cadieux

"The bus is here," Tabila called out.

Her mother ran out from the kitchen, down the porch and towards the yellow school bus turning up the lane. She waited by the old beacon light, the one her father painted purple with green dots, just like Samir wanted, and bounced on the balls of her feet as Tabi's little brother shuffled off the bus. Her mother scooped him up into her arms, delivering peck after peck of frantic kisses, and carried him back to the house. She set him down on the stone walkway and went back into the kitchen, humming as she passed Tabi.

"Hey," Sam said, wiping the leftovers of their mother's affection off his face.

"Hi," Tabi said. She picked up her math text off the top step and slid it over so Sam could sit beside her.

"How are you feeling?" she asked.

Sam huffed loudly and collapsed theatrically onto the porch. After a moment he got back up and flicked his eyebrow up. "I feel fine; like I did yesterday and the day before."

"They'll probably ask you to go donate again next week."

"So? I don't have to if I don't want to."

No, he didn't have to, Tabi thought, but she knew he would. She wasn't on the list to receive his blood this time and that was fine, it didn't really matter anymore, anyway. They were leaving town soon and, once they were gone, she wouldn't have to wait in line again. For now, though, she wasn't feeling sick.

Tabi looked out at the front lawn, wild and haphazard beyond the porch. Thickets of crab grass sprang up in tufts, slightly greener than the rest of the yellowing lawn, holding on to their lush majesty while the rest of the vegetation dwindled around them. She could smell the crispness in the air, a sure sign that summer was over. Soon the warmth would fade and the cold would turn biting, then bitter as it always did in the valley. She didn't mind the cold, though, nor did she mind the predicament the world was in. This was her home, and she didn't want to leave. It was selfish, she knew, there were other people to think about, but it didn't prevent her from feeling resentment towards this unusual twist of fate.

"Wanna play hangman?" Sam asked.

"Sorry, I have to get this homework done. Calculus takes me forever, you know?"

"Yeah, sure. See you later?"

"You bet."

Sam stood and shuffled through the front door. Tabila looked down at the equations on her worksheet. She'd only completed two out of six questions but who cared? It wasn't like she was going to live long enough to make it to university.

She heard the grand notes of the church organ long before she saw the bus crawl down their street, the brass speakers atop its roof blaring the latest hymn, broadcast via wifi direct from St. Mark's Pentecostal. A line of people followed after it. They lumbered along, big blue veins webbing across their pale skin, their eyes and nails jaundiced by failing livers. None of them strayed from the line, nor did they look at Tabi as they passed by.

"...God is with you, children. He is merciful and he is loving, and your reward will be great. You do not suffer in vain. God is with you, children..." the speaker blared. It rambled on, but Tabi no longer paid attention. She watched Carmella, their neighbour, follow the bus. She was fourth in the long string of people and carried her daughter, Angelica, in her arms. The girl was slung over Carmella's shoulder. Her little arms hung limp and blood snaked its way down them, dripping to the dusty ground and soaking the bottoms of her pink shorts.

Another One Bites the Dust started playing in Tabi's head and she looked away from the procession, embarrassed and amused all at once. Carmella had knocked on their door last week asking if they knew how to get bumped up in the donation line. She'd said Angelica wasn't herself lately—if they knew what she meant. Her father said he knew, but he didn't know how Carmella could get a priority card. He never told her that Tabi had the next ticket, even though she really didn't need it. She wondered if this was payback for the taunting her mother and father got from the neighbours before the MKB virus struck. *Fuckin' sand niggers*, they'd called them. *Where's your camel?* the school kids would say. Now they all chummed up to her and Samir during lunch like they'd been friends forever—if only to get an advance ticket to her brother's veins.

Sam's condition was rare, Tabi'd learned in biology. Alpha thalassemia of the three-gene malfunction, it was known as. Hemoglobin H disease, the doctors called it. The cells were abnormal, different shapes and sizes and not as robust as normal cells. They were more fragile under the wrong conditions, and lacked the functioning structures found in normal blood cells. It was a mutation seen in people of Mediterranean and Middle East communities, her teacher had said—fucking Arabs to Tabi's classmates—and even so, there was only a one-in-four chance of inheriting it *if* your parents were carriers. But these were the cells which repelled the MKB virus, made the host system inhospitable and thus, saved the unsuspecting victim for an equally terrible fate. Her teacher told them it was the same concept as Sickle Cell disease repelling malaria parasites.

Except malaria was random.

Engineering efforts to create synthetic blood—a cocktail of oxygen carrying granules which lacked the alpha gene the MKB was so fond of—failed. Not because science was incapable, but because nobody ever lived long enough to finish their research. Many of the premature trials ended more horrifically than anything the virus was capable of and in the common good of the people, the government banned any further research. Panic, thought Tabi, it was fear and panic that stopped it, not interest.

The other option was voluntary breeding. Alpha-thal people screwing other alpha-thal people to make more freak children for the sake of human kind. Tabi watched the debates on TV, saw the United Survival Party rattle their sabres in the faces of the Human Rights people. After hours of ongoing name-calling, Tabi agreed with the Humans Rights guys. Why should Sam be forced to have sex with someone he doesn't know or like just to make more sick babies?

Yeah, that's something the United Survival Party always forgot. Sam's cells weren't normal. He wasn't normal. Tabi knew he would probably die early, partly because they bled him almost every two weeks, but also because his circulatory system couldn't keep up with the faulty cells.

Her brother was good about donating, though. Every two weeks they would go in, hook him up to one of those machines and wait while the red stuff pumped out of him into a little baggie. The lucky recipient in the next cubicle would already be hooked up and bled to accommodate Sam's donation—the lease-on-life lottery winner, Tabi called them, though never to their face. Some weeks, when the doctors felt brave enough they'd ask Sam if they could take two bags—he was the god-child of Glen Eagan County, after all—but only when their father wasn't in the room. Tabi wasn't sure what happened to that second bag of blood. Maybe the doctors sold it to the highest bidder, maybe they used it for themselves; whatever they did with it, there was never a second recipient waiting. Right now this whole process was all calm and civil, but Tabi wondered how much longer before things got out of hand? How many more people had to die before someone got desperate enough to tear Sam to shreds, rip him open and drink him up like some modern day vampire?

Tabi watched the procession continue. A trail of bloody footprints stained the cracked pavement. At least this time none of the sick and dying fainted in front of their house. Tabi never liked going to help when one of them fell. The other patrons would paw at her and her dad, scratch at their skin with dirty fingernails like the Saviour Blood pulsed through their veins as well. Some spat at them, speckling her face with bloody spit, saying this virus was *their* fault, while others begged for mercy.

They got what was coming, Tabi thought. Maybe now they would know what it was like to be considered a lesser human.

One of the boys in the procession veered away from the line and started towards their house. Tabi closed her book and got to her knees. She shuffled closer to the door. The boy was Stanley Farrell, one of the seniors from Lancaster Public, the high school from the neighbouring town. He stopped in front of the porch and smiled at Tabi. She grimaced back. Blood trickled from his ears, and the dark blue veins on his face reminded Tabi of a time long ago when Sam got into the magic markers.

"You look good, Tabi," Stan said.

"Thanks," Tabi replied. She glanced at the door again.

"Do you want to go to the prom with me?"

"I can't. I'm not allowed."

"Why not?"

"Because… I can't."

Blood dripped from his hands to the walkway in sharp pats.

"You're not sick," Stan noted.

"Not yet."

"You're lucky Sam's your brother." Stan took a step closer.

"I don't get special privileges."

"Do you know they're thinking of forcing the alphas to donate? They're going to take them away to a distribution centre and keep them tied up so they can be bled when they need to."

"That's a lie."

Stan shook his head. "No, it's not. It was on the news last night. It'll be like fast food, but with blood. We'll drive up to the window and order a transfusion—super sized—and then they'll ask if we want fries with that."

He laughed, coughed, and spat a bloody wad onto the ground. "I'm not going to make it," he said. "I'm too sick to even be on the donation list."

Tabi looked down at her math text book, then back at Stan. He had balled his fists.

"You never get sick, Tabi, nor does your mom or dad."

"We *do* get sick," Tabi said. She had her hand on the doorknob and if Stan took another step she would run inside. The hymn from the bus was just a dull buzz now, but the procession of people continued.

"Yeah whatever, you do." Stan turned and stared back to the procession. "I used to like you," he said without looking at her. "Even after 9/11."

They would never be considered equal, Tabi thought. Not even now.

Stan dragged his feet as he went, and Tabi heard his warning as he stepped off the driveway. Watch your back.

The breeze stirred and rustled the yellowing leaves. The crab grass shivered, but held its ground. Unlike Tabi.

"They hate us even more now," Sam said. Tabi hadn't heard him come to the door, but he stood on the other side of the screen, looking at the people.

"They're just scared," Tabi said.

Sam came out onto the porch and sat beside Tabi's books. "Was Stan telling the truth? Are they going to tie me up and bleed me whenever they want?"

Tabi shook her head, but she didn't know for sure. The United Survival Party had suggested it in one of the debates. They aired schematics of what the distribution centre would look like, said that residence would be voluntary (though strongly recommended. *Strongly* recommended...) without immediate consequences for those who chose not to participate. Tabi always wondered what the long-term consequences were.

"Dad got the syringes," Sam said. "We can leave whenever."

Whenever meant by the cover of night in an RV packed full of medical supplies, gasoline and guns. *Leaving* meant driving up to Webequie in Northern Ontario to a remote conservation area, south of Winisk River Provincial Park. It was cold up there, colder than here, and consisted of lakes, bears and not much else. They could only drive up there by a winter road on the Northern Ontario Resource Trail, and it had to be frozen enough to hold the weight of the RV. It was late October now and although it was warm enough to do homework outside here, her dad said the roads were safe enough to tread up there. Safe *enough* made Tabi nervous, but she tried her best not to show it.

She didn't want to go, it would be lonely up there and the Indians weren't always the nicest people, but if luck was on their side they'd all be dead and Tabi and her family would be safe. She didn't want to go, but understood what would happen if they didn't.

"How long is the trip?" Sam asked her.

"Three days."

"Will we get to stop and pee?"

"Yeah, but you'll have to hurry or a bear might bite your bum," Tabi said.

"Liar," Sam said, giggling. "I don't want to go," he said more soberly.

"Dad says they'll hurt you if we stay here," Tabi said.

"I donate when I can." He was thoughtful for a moment. "What if I donated more?"

"I don't think that'll help."

Sam sighed. He opened Tabi's math text and flipped idly through the pages. "I wish I was normal."

"But we're not."

"No, *you're* normal. I've got weird blood."

"At least people are nice to you."

"It's fake. When they used to tease us about being brown, it was real. Now they're nice because I have something they want. I'm not stupid, you know."

"I never said you were." Tabi thought about what Sam said. What would have happened if history had been different? Would people consider them more equal, instead of judging them on sight like they do now? In truth, how much would Tabi like her friends if she knew what they really thought? Realistically, it didn't matter. People turned face so fast when they learned about Sam and his wonder blood. The same people who whispered in corners of the grocery store were now coming out and shaking their hands, ruffling Sam's hair and putting them up on a pedestal when days earlier they wouldn't stamp them out if they were on fire.

Good for nothin' Pakis...

No, Tabi didn't think it would change anything if she'd known her friends thoughts. The procession had ended, but a handful of people had stayed behind, stood at the end of their driveway, staring at Sam and her. They swayed from side to side, blinking slowly. Some clung to each other for balance.

"They look like zombies," Sam whispered.

"Nah, zombies are green and covered in dirt. They also have superhuman strength. These are just people."

"Dying people."

"Yeah, kiddo, they're dying."

"And we're leaving."

"Yeah." They were leaving. An unusual relief crept up on Tabi.

"So we don't have to watch them die?"

Tabi shook her head. "So we can live."

"What's the point of living if everyone around you is dead?"

"Would you rather stay and watch them die?"

"Wouldn't you?"

Tabi didn't know. What she knew was that humans were no longer at the top of the food chain. Maybe this was the earth's version of a detox—except humans were the shit in this case. They'd gone and pumped too many barrels of sludge in the oceans, too many chemicals into the air. Maybe all the spiders they'd squished caused the virus to emerge—disrupted the balance of things, you know?—like some fucked up real-life comic book. Except this time Spiderman wasn't on their side. It wouldn't be long before MKB mutated to get around whatever defences the alpha-thals possessed, and soon even Sam would be dead.

Tabi watched the last of the onlookers shuffle away. They didn't come up to the house today, but who knew what they'd do tomorrow. Her family had the materials to keep themselves alive, and the smarts to live off the land. She didn't know if their northern hideout would be a safe haven, but it was the only option they had left until humanity discovered a way to outsmart the virus, or made peace with the lonely grave they'd dug for themselves.

"Come on," Tabi said, collecting her books. "I smell supper."

"Woohoo, lasagne!" Sam exclaimed, running into the house.

"Yeah, eat up kid," Tabi said quietly, "You'll be needing it."

She opened the screen door, and stood a moment, eying the bleeding man in the yard before slipping into the house. She only prayed they were able to get out in time.

~~~

WE TAKE CARE OF OUR OWN

Kate Heartfield

She considers leaving the red leather jacket at home. It's too conspicuous, memorable, traceable. The greying Canadian flag sewn onto the sleeve might as well be a flashing light declaring "foodlegger here."

Geri decides she's being paranoid. She *always* wears the red leather jacket. She wouldn't be herself without it. If she gives up the red leather jacket, she might as well give up on everything else she's been holding on to. Calvin. The dairy. She's not going to let anything go without a fight.

Besides, she rationalizes, something *that* conspicuous is as good as a disguise. If she has to go on the run, she'll take it off, and then all the bastards looking for a middle-aged fat chick in a red leather jacket won't find one. They'll find a middle-aged fat chick in a black t-shirt (black is slimming) and they'll be stymied. Or something.

The list of things she doesn't want to forget is disintegrating into questions already. *Passports. Rain gear. Boots. Water. Trail mix. Mindkey? Jacket?*

She rubs her forehead and, for one last time, reads the birthday card Bella sent. So retro, so innocuous a use of snail mail. A letter would have been suspiciously anachronistic, the kind of communication a cabin-in-the-woods gun-rack nut might use. But old ladies still send birthday cards, and no one would bother to open them and read them. Safe as houses, and no encryption necessary. Cousin Bella was always clever.

Geri yanks open the kitchen drawer, grabs the barbecue lighter, holds the flame to the edge of the card, over the sink.

Calvin walks in. Geri looks at her son, and her son looks at the flaming bit of paper in her hands. She's so stunned she doesn't drop the card in the sink until she feels the pain of heat on her skin.

She's almost glad of an excuse to tell him. She's been putting it off. But still, she doesn't know how to begin.

She walks around the counter, yanks the mindkey off his head and turns it off. Then she says, "Sorry. But I have to tell you something in secret, and I didn't want even that much to get through to anyone who might be…out there."

Calvin rubs the top of his ear, where the crescent of moulded plastic usually sits. "Yikes. Paranoid ever?"

"I'm just being careful. Do you remember my cousin Bella? In New York State?"

"Sure," he says, in a way that means he doesn't, but he isn't interested in prolonging the conversation.

Geri spent every summer in New York State when she was a kid, with her cousins, Bella and Rosie. They had lost their father, a Manhattan IT worker, on Sept. 11, 2001—the day Geri was born. One day when Geri was six, she and Bella and Rosie were feuding about something, and her own father took her aside and asked her to be kind to her cousins because they didn't have a dad like she did. Geri was curious. She stayed curious well into her 20s. The first thing she searched for, when people started using EEG networks, was the tweeged memories of those who had been in New York on that horrible day, on her birthday.

Now she's 40, the divorced mother of a teenager who's plugged in 24 hours a day, and she is becoming ever less interested in the contents of other people's brains, other people's messed up stories. She's not trying to figure it all out anymore. She's just doing what has to be done.

"That was a note from Bella." She gestures at the black mess in the sink. "It was…private, so I burned it. She's having a tough time. She and her family. Financially."

"That's rough. Why don't they just move here? The States are a mess."

"They can't move here. Immigration moratorium, remember?"

She remembers an argument with Calvin a few months ago. She said something about the moratorium being a shame, and he shrugged and said Canada couldn't be expected to absorb more hungry people when it can barely feed its own citizens. *Absorb*. Where does he pick these phrases up?

"So, let's send your cousin some money."

She takes a deep breath. "We don't have any to send. Don't worry. We have enough for ourselves. For now. But we just don't have anything to spare."

He frowns. He is, despite her worrying, a good boy, with a good heart. Whenever he's confronted with the fact that other people sometimes suffer, it bothers him. He can't listen to mindkey ads for humanitarian organizations. Most of the time, he shelters himself in a cultivated incuriosity; what he doesn't know can't hurt him. But she figures he'll grow out of that, and the empathy that's so deep in his nature makes her proud.

"Okay," he says. "So do you want to do a fundraiser or something?"

She shakes her head. "I want to do something a little bit crazy. But I need you to trust me. And I need you to promise not to tell anyone. And that means that the second you put this mindkey back on, I need you to put a buffer on it. A big buffer. Like, a minute at least. Can you do that for me? I wouldn't ask if it wasn't really important."

She can almost see his 14-year-old brain working.

"For how long?"

"I don't know. A while. Until it's not going to get us in any trouble. Calvin, it's only a delay. I'm not asking you to unplug or anything. Just to give yourself some time to use your judgment, to delete any blips that get away from you."

He nods. "If it's that important. Okay."

"Okay?"

"Yes, I said okay. So, what's the big secret? What's your crrrrazy plan?"

It's been illegal to export food from Canada for three years. Parliament passed the law shortly after the Great Inflation, the floods and the droughts and the bioenergy spike. Thailand and Vietnam stopped exporting rice first; other countries followed, with more and more foods. Eventually, the dominoes fell and every country put export walls up, supposedly temporary measures to ensure domestic food supplies. The government assured Canadians they'd be fine. There would be shortages of some foods, less variety, but no one would have to worry about going hungry. The same warming that was creating the droughts and floods elsewhere was lengthening Canada's growing season. Canada would be fine. And it would maintain its donations to the World Food Program; Canada had always been a generous nation.

But first and foremost, Canada would take care of its own. No exports out; no immigrants in. Just for a little while.

Then it finally occurred to the terrorists, who have always been a little slow on the uptake, to attack the food system.

The Americans kept exporting for longer than almost anyone else. But after the rinderpest attack, there was nothing they could do but shut their borders. Rinderpest. Most Americans had never heard of the word a couple of years ago. Even farmers didn't know, at the time, what was making their cattle sick. It had been declared eradicated in 2011, nearly three decades before the attack. But then a paranoid conspiracy theorist with a god complex got his hands on a lab sample and infected cattle across the U.S. more or less simultaneously. It wiped out the meat and milk supply in the U.S., which was already contending with a drought.

In Canada, politicians stopped describing the export restrictions as "temporary" and the government put in price controls. That's when the line-ups started appearing at the stores. The price caps bought the government some votes but did nothing to encourage adequate supply to meet the demand.

But as bad as things are in Canada, they're worse in the States.

So Geri's New York cousins found themselves, again, the victims of global circumstance. And Bella sent a birthday card to her Canadian cheese-making cousin, asking her, in the most coded way she could, whether she knows any foodleggers.

She doesn't.

She knows *of* them, of course. It's a fairly common crime these days. The risks are big but so are the rewards. Americans will pay 10 times the Canadian Dairy Commission price, easily. A grilled cheese sandwich, in certain Manhattan parties, is the 2041 equivalent of bathtub gin. No one can blame Canadian food producers for taking advantage of that, and looking out for themselves.

Once the wage and price controls came in, dairy was one of the first sectors the government capped—after all, the bureaucracy and the price-fixing infrastructure was already there from decades of supply management, when the government had tried to keep the number of farmers low and the price high.

Now the price is artificially low, but the number of farmers is still low, too, because who would bother getting into a price-capped business?

Cheese is more profitable than milk, but not profitable enough to make up for the rising costs of everything else. Geri's artisan cheese business, the business her father created, will go further into debt this year.

Meanwhile, there is a big hungry market south of the border, where there are no price controls. And whether the business makes a profit or not, she has to draw a big enough income to feed Calvin.

And clothe him. And pay his tuition. But she'll deal with that problem when they get to it. If they get to it. Some days, she hardly dares to hope Calvin will do something with his life other than sit and stare at the wall while the lights on his mindkey flash red and green.

To her, communicating through EEG is still something a person does consciously for set lengths of time, an activity, like eating or reading or taking a shower. To Calvin's generation, it's like breathing. His mindkey isn't an implant, but it might as well be. It's part of his autonomic nervous system.

"Don't you care about privacy?" she asked him once, uncomfortably aware that she sounded like her parents.

Calvin shrugged. "I don't have anything to hide."

"At least turn on the seven-second buffer, for god's sake. What if you think something, I don't know, embarrassing? Or horribly offensive?"

"People know the difference between tweegs and blips, Mom. Everybody's brain blips all the time. It's just noise. Nobody pays attention. Anyway, you tweeg. What's the big deal?"

She can't explain what the big deal is. Or why she finds it so creepy that Calvin and his friends are so unsuspicious of authority. By this age, shouldn't they be trading websites claiming things about black helicopters or faked Mars landings? Shouldn't they at least be carving anarchist symbols into their shoes? She has always thought all that bullshit was a necessary phase of teenagehood. Kids these days seem to have an unnatural trust of power. Not that it matters, because they soon won't have any civil rights left to give up. The government won't have to go to the trouble to get a warrant to search their brains; it'll just have to set up a software robot to monitor their feeds for keywords. Probably, it already has.

Her son has a Canadian flag on his wall and a photograph of the prime minister. Not a dead kitschy prime minister, like Joe Clark or someone. The current prime minister. It is about as uncool as anything she can imagine, but he doesn't seem to be an uncool kid. He has friends. He's even dating already. Maybe the prime minister photo is so uncool, it's cool. Maybe it's ironic.

Or maybe not, and her son just has pride in his country and admires its current government. The notion strikes her as vaguely fascist in a 14-year-old, although Calvin is hardly the thuggish sort.

She wonders whether she is the worst mother in the world for deciding to take Calvin with her, for making him an accomplice. She doesn't deserve to have him in her life. But she can't bring herself to leave him with a neighbour or a friend, not after she almost lost him a couple of years ago. She tells herself that her decision has nothing to do with the fact that she wants his help and company and that having a kid in the truck might make the border guards less suspicious.

Besides, she keeps telling herself, she's probably doing the right thing, ethically, even if she does plan to make a profit from it. Enlightened self-interest.

Calvin disagrees.

"If we have extra cheese," he says doggedly, "why don't we just give it to poor people here in Canada?"

"It isn't extra. We need to sell it, one way or another. We can't afford to give it away. I wish we could, honey, but we can't. But if we sell it in the States, we'll be doing some good that we couldn't do here. The Americans need food more than we do. And with some of the extra money we get for it, we can help Bella. She's family, Calvin, okay? In bad times like this, it's even more important that family sticks together. Besides, she's going to help us sell the cheese, so it's only right."

"You just want to make money."

"Well, there's nothing wrong with making money."

"There's something wrong with breaking the law."

"Listen. There's the law and there's, I don't know, rules. Regulations. Like the law against murder is a law, but the rules against exporting cheese are just the government trying to cover its butt."

"The government doesn't have a butt, Mom." Smiling.

"You know what I mean. They don't want a food riot on their hands. They saw what happened in Washington and Miami and they don't want the same thing to happen here. But they're not actually fixing the problem. They're just making it look like they're doing something. They don't care that people in the States are suffering way worse than us, or that it would help Canadians make more food if they were allowed to sell for even close to what the Americans will pay. The rules are stupid and they're hurting people. We have a right to take care of ourselves. Does that make sense?"

"No."

"You mean it doesn't make sense for producers to look after their own interests? Who else is going to?"

"No. I mean what you're saying doesn't make sense. You can't just decide you're only going to obey the laws you agree with. And I think it's only right that the government is trying to put Canadians first."

Put Canadians first. Jesus Christ, he's a walking talking point. She wants to tell him, "Look, we're Canadians, the dairy's a Canadian business, and the government screwed us over. They betrayed us. They're destroying everything your grandfather worked for. They're telling us we're doing god's work but we can't sell our cheese for what it's worth. We've got to be martyrs to the cause. Screw them. They'll kill our business if we let them. They have no idea how to get out of this mess. They haven't got a goddamned clue."

But she doesn't trust herself to not get so angry she'll regret letting him see it. She has been very careful not to get angry around Calvin since he returned to her, two years ago, delivered to her doorstep by a police officer whose face she can't recall. She was almost crazy by then, after three weeks of not knowing where Calvin was. She's still terrified, every day, that he'll run away again, go find his dad again. So she just stops talking.

Calvin never says he agrees with her plan. But he starts to help her with it anyway, so she figures that's that. He helps Geri go over the spreadsheets to make it look like they haven't produced as much as they have. None of the dairy's employees keep track of production; none are involved in the bookkeeping, so Geri isn't worried about any awkward questions.

And it is Calvin who comes up with the plan for how to hide the cheese in the pickup truck. Geri planned to build a false back or bottom to the bed, although she had no idea how. Calvin suggests they put the big camper shell on the back and fill it with tackle boxes, suitcases, sleeping bags, tent bags, big garbage bags. All the bags and boxes are full of cheese, but it looks just a like truck packed for a camping trip. And anyone who goes nosing into a bag or box will find a layer of musty camping equipment she dug out of the garage, feeling slightly guilty it's been so long since she and Calvin used it for real. Inside the garbage bag, there's a sleeping bag—and inside that is the cheese.

It looks absolutely innocent, just messy enough to be real. They can't carry a lot, but it's enough to make the trip worth the risk. Maybe. And if it works, they'll do it again in a couple of months. Nothing unusual about a middle-aged woman and her son going camping in the Catskills. She just hopes the border guards—the Canadian border guards; the Americans hardly bother keeping people and food out—don't have good noses.

She checks the charge on the truck's battery. Enough to get her past the border before they'll have to make a stop. That is, if Calvin doesn't decide he needs to pee half an hour out.

The morning they leave, she reads a news article with her powdery Canadian coffee-substitute drink. It's about the RCMP cracking down on foodleggers. The article is sentimental; it makes much of the RCMP's origins in fighting the whiskey traders more than a century ago. She doesn't read it to the end.

They are about an hour down the road when Calvin switches the music off on his mindkey and says, out of the blue, "One of my teachers says foodleggers are traitors."

She lets her knuckles tighten on the steering wheel, forces herself to take some time before she responds. The truck has autodrive but she never uses it. She learned to drive in 2017 the old-fashioned way. The really old-fashioned way, on a 10-year-old gas engine with a stick shift.

Her dad barking commands, his hissing intake of breath whenever she ground the gears. Her dad taught her many things, and most were things he didn't mean to teach her. Like the tendency to love best those skills, and people, who were hardest won. She enjoys her mastery over this metal monster even if there is no such thing as a manual transmission any more.

She wonders what she is accidentally teaching Calvin.

"Do you think I'm a traitor?" she asks patiently, generously, being the grown-up, trying to pretend it's a teachable moment.

Her peripheral vision catches his shrug. She waits for him to compose an answer. It doesn't come. So she takes her eyes off the road long enough to glance at his face. He wears the calculating, absent look of a person communicating by EEG.

"Shut that thing off, Calvin," she says, annoyed that he could say something so hurtful without it bothering him even a little, that he could drop that conversational bomb and walk away whistling.

"It's just…"

"Shut it off! Jesus, Calvin, of all times…"

She trails off, looking in the rear-view mirror. How long has that OPP car been behind her?

"Mom, relax. I'm just—"

"Shh. Do me a favour and don't talk and for god's sake don't tweeg and just sit there for a minute, okay? Can you do that? Just sit. Just give me a second here."

The police car is a few car-lengths behind. It stays there for two minutes. Geri keeps an eye on the clock, keeps making sure the cruise is set to exactly one kilometre under the limit. Then it comes, like she willed it to happen. The lights come on. No siren; in fact, the world goes quiet.

She considers making a run for it. She can feel the muscles in her calf extend, the satisfying complete circuit of foot-pedal-floor, the engine balking for less than a second before it yanks them down the highway. She imagines veering off into a dusty field road, losing the cops. Abandoning the truck with its incriminating cargo and getting lost in the woods. Hiding with Calvin. Peeling off her bright red jacket and stuffing it under a bush. Blending in to the background.

She imagines all this for about five seconds, before she lifts her foot off the gas and flips on her right turn signal.

"Shit," she whispers as she brings the car onto the shoulder and brakes. Then, louder, "What did you tweeg? C'mon, Calvin, what did you say on that thing?"

"I said where I was and where I was going. Because –"

"Because you think I'm a traitor," she says, her jaw tight. "So you're turning me in. Because you think your dad will get custody. I get it."

The cop is there at the window. Calvin takes a noisy breath in, preparing to say something, but she holds her index finger up, sharply, like she's training a puppy. *Quiet.*

She presses the button that rolls down the window. Even she, with her eccentric insistence on driving her own car, usually controls things like windows, temperature and sound system with her mindkey. But she decided, in the end, to leave hers at home.

The officer is a short woman with red hair. She's burly, or maybe everyone looks that way in a uniform. She asks for Geri's licence and registration, scans it.

Here it comes.

"Do you have a renewal for your plate?"

Geri looks dumbly at her, unable to process the question.

"I'm…"

"Your plate. Do you have a sticker for it? In the car, or at home? The one you've got back there is last year's."

"Oh. Um. No. I don't think I… I must have renewed, I'm just having trouble remembering what I did with the sticker…"

The cop smiles. "Crazy that we still use stickers, eh? In this day and age. But I am going to need to see a proof of renewal."

Calvin is rummaging in the glove compartment, which is stuffed with junk, including the piece of paper that carries Bella's address. Geri just couldn't bear to not have it written down somewhere, and paper seemed safest. She disguised it by adding a couple of ones to the beginning of the street number, and there is no name, no city, no state, no country. All the same, it's the end of a thread that connects her trip to a destination in the United States, a destination that is not a campground.

It's proof.

She realizes all this in about three seconds, as long as it takes for the police officer to say, "Young man, stop what you're doing there."

Calvin draws out his hand with a scrap of paper in it. But it's not Geri's address. It's a renewal sticker.

"I put this in here a few months ago," he says. "Sorry. I forgot about it."

Geri waits, watching the police car go, her turn signal still clicking. She turns to Calvin. "Tell me what you tweeged. Maybe there are more coming."

He scowls. "I just said I'm on the highway headed for New York because I'm going camping with my mom. And I allowed GPS. I wasn't going to but then I realized I always check in my location and if I took a trip and didn't mention it or check in, that would look weird. Suspicious."

She stares at him for a long time.

"So you're not turning us in?"

He shakes his head, still frowning.

"But maybe you let a blip out. Accidentally. About why, about what we're doing."

He shakes his head again. "I'm not an idiot, Mom."

She presses her fingers around her eye sockets, pressing back the tears. "Okay. I'm sorry I snapped. I was scared. So does this mean you're okay with all this?"

He doesn't say anything for a moment, looks out the window. Finally he says, "No. I still think it's wrong."

"Then why are you helping me?"

He turns to look at her. "I don't know. Isn't family supposed to stick together? That's what you always say."

"That is what I always say."

She flips the turn signal over to left, curls her fingers around the steering wheel.

"Okay," she says. "Let's make the decisions together from now on. Deal?"

He nods.

"So. First decision. Which way?"

THE PARABLE OF THE CLOWN

Derek Künsken

Mohamed thought he'd come close to solving his clown farting problem on the same day that the Vice-President from the big multinational came to Grand Prairie. Mohamed had founded the company Clownvironmental based on a technique that could extract clowns from boreal forest without clear-cutting. It left pristine forests, but was not as profitable. Worse, the methane from clown farts interfered with his fogging compound.

The Vice-President was accompanied from his jet by Charlie, an aide to the Minister of Natural Resources, who ceremoniously took pains to explain that he wasn't really there, but that if he had been, he would have let everyone know how delighted the Minister was with the Vice-President's visit and Mohamed's chemical breakthrough.

Mohamed brought the Vice-President and the Ministerial staffer into the complex of trailers that formed the field headquarters of Clownvironmental. Lai Hanlin, a Chinese immigrant, Mohamed's number two man and his best friend, joined them. The sound of clown horns in the northern boreal forest penetrated the thin windows.

The Vice-President had several billion dollars and the unenviable task of cornering a market, reinvigorating a paradigm and leveraging innovation. He wanted to invest in clowns, perhaps positioning his investment to be the one that weaned the US from its dependence on Middle Eastern clowns. Mohamed knew very little of geo-politics, nor had he ever reinvigorated a paradigm, but he'd often dreamed of getting rich ethically. He very much wanted a big investment, but he couldn't see how he could scale up operations to the tune of billions. When the Vice-President and Ministerial staffer had left, Mohamed turned to Hanlin.

"How are we going to do this?"

"Even if we partnered with every company in Alberta, we'd barely have enough labour," Hanlin said.

"We're not partnering with every company in Alberta."

"You can buy the ones you don't want to partner with," Hanlin said.

"She'd never sell."

"Sometimes people have to."

It was true. This was business after all.

"Look into it," Mohamed said.

Mohamed's mediation session with Sarah had been delayed several times. Mohamed didn't trust Sarah to hand him a coffee without burning him, but the judge would not proceed with the hearing until they had seen the mediator.

Two months ago, Sarah's lawyer had found a way to freeze the assets of Clownvironmental. It had only lasted a week, but it had strengthened Mohamed's intellectual property suit against Sarah's company, although the gathering of evidence dragged. That was only the latest strike by her racist lawyer, who had also reported him to Border Services, even though Mohamed was a third generation Canadian and had grown up in Calgary. It had taken a day to get that sorted out. Mohamed's lawyer offered to sue Border Services for harassment, but Mohamed didn't see the point.

Sarah was in the waiting room, legs crossed, head down, typing away at a pad. Mohamed sat across from her. She didn't look up and he felt the old angry jealousy. They'd loved each other for real, in the kind of magnetic way that made for the fiercest of emotional knife fights. He had not forgotten any of the reasons he'd loved her, but the reasons had deflated and discoloured, like a balloon animal left overnight. Her pale, flawless skin had pinkened since he'd arrived. Her cheeks did that when her temper was building a head of steam. He didn't look away. She did angry well and he wanted to let the mediator see what a looney-toon she was.

The mediator was a kindly woman of about fifty who spoke in soft, metronomic cadences. At first, Mohamed got the sense she could be trusted, but after a very short time, he and Sarah were interrupting her.

"There is nothing to mediate!" he said. "Everything we have accumulated, I paid for by sacrificing my own interests. Sarah can't keep two dollars in her pocket for ten minutes!"

"That's a lie!" Sarah said in her thick Irish accent. "My income covered not only all our fun activities and a car, but financed more than a few of his patents that were based on my ideas!"

"Those were my ideas alone!" Mohamed yelled.

"There wasn't a thing you came up with that wasn't inspired by something I was doing!"

It took some time for the mediator to make herself heard.

"As you are both working professionals, it is very likely that the judge will just split everything evenly, in which case, you will have spent a lot of your assets on lawyers for nothing. Despite a great deal of obvious emotion, an even settlement now would save you both tens of thousands of dollars and free up resources in the court system."

"I have a case," he said. "I have no interest in rewarding her bad choices twice."

"You were my only bad choice," Sarah said. She rose. Mohamed rose. The mediator rose. "My lawyer informed me that if there is no common ground, the attempt at mediation is simply pro forma. It's now out of the way."

Sarah glided from the office, leaving the aching smell of lavender with a hint of cotton candy.

"You see?" he said.

Mohamed reinforced his line of sixty workers with thirty new guys. Some he'd tempted with higher wages from companies as far away as Quebec and Labrador. Some were straight out of trade school and green. Some knew nothing at all and were being yelled at by supervisors who had better things to yell at. This was shaping up to be a mess.

The fog machines were set up about two hundred feet into the trees, while big collection trucks were idling at the ends of logging roads, speakers quiet. Within the trees, guys in ones and twos held big hoop frames covered with brightly-coloured paper. The hoops had been angled with GPS to channel the drive towards the trucks. Hanlin was beside Mohamed with three laptops fanned before of him, waiting for the boards to go green. Charlie, the tightly-wound ministerial staffer, was making another non-visit.

"You're scaling up," Charlie said.

"Everywhere," Mohamed said. "I've got three more crews fifteen kilometres north and my lawyer is about to buy me controlling stakes in SunClown and Circus Husky."

"The Minister is delighted," Charlie said with a smile. "Actually, the Minister is very worried. You don't have the volume to meet the investor needs. I've done some research, not myself, you see, but someone has. They'd love to invest here in Alberta, but the multinational is taking a good look at other jurisdictions, especially Nigeria. We've thrown in some major tax concessions to sweeten the deal."

"So?"

Charlie's earnest nonchalance faltered. "You're doing a great job of scaling up, but that's actually terrible. MegaClown is also scaling up."

"What is Sarah's company doing?" Mohamed asked. "MegaClown can't scale up, because she's entirely dependent on giant machinery that takes three years to build."

"MegaClown got a loan to order five more big cullers," Charlie said, "and she bought two used ones from Russia. They'll be here in twelve weeks, with maybe another six weeks for retrofitting."

"What?"

"Yes, isn't it great?" Charlie said. "We've given her forestry and clown licences similar to yours, but that's not going to be enough for investors either."

"How can you let her do that?" Mohamed demanded. "She's going to clear cut the province at that rate! It will take twenty-five, maybe thirty years, before anything she touches is capable of supporting clowns again."

"The province gets the forestry royalties too," Charlie said, "and China is buying up not only every clown we can give them, but all the lumber too."

"She can't deliver the clowns, even with the machines. There aren't enough qualified workers to extract all those clowns. If Megaclown didn't have its licence, I could absorb their workers and make a real run at the investment."

"The Minister is sympathetic to your labour problems," Charlie said. "The Government is going to churn out job offers for foreign workers. We're talking thousands of experienced clown extraction workers from Venezuela, Brazil, Russia."

"Whoa," Mohamed said.

"But our chances double or triple if you and MegaClown work together. Your early research on combined techniques is promising."

"Take away her licenses, I'll buy up her stock. I can run her equipment. She can't run mine."

Charlie pursed his lips, looking more like a university student than usual. "The Minister prefers that the companies sort things out."

"The Minister controls the licenses," Mohamed said.

"Intervention can't make companies work together," Charlie said bleakly.

Mohamed shrugged. "I'm going to have to get back to this test."

"Let me know if you ever need any help with your immigration problems," Charlie said. "You're a very valuable addition to Canada."

"I was born here!"

Charlie frowned. "Sorry. Maybe I was thinking of Sarah."

Mohamed read the reports in his field trailer. His new test fogging chemical reduced clown flatulence by twenty-two percent, but the scale of the clown extraction stretched the crew resources and the new hands. At two points, clowns leaked through the lines, cart-wheeling around the trucks and honking down the logging roads.

These were small leaks and the foremen moved the lines to stop further leaks. Some of the escaping clowns would complete the circle of life, capering up dry river beds in pairs, leaving little yellow Volkswagons in secluded areas, where, a few years later, twenty-eight clowns would emerge to the spring sounds of circus music.

Coal and steel were the gold of the nineteenth century, and oil the black gold of the twentieth. Clowns were the polka-dot gold of the twenty-first, a renewable resource flowing from forests to cities and countries around the world, reusing gags that were old a hundred years ago, but still funny now.

The trailer was packed with equipment and amenities for living in the field, so they'd had no place to put a big map. Hanlin had found some linoleum flooring with the map of the world on it. They'd put clown-face stickers on all the major spawning forests, and marked the clown consumption in every country with plastic stickers of circus tents. Supply. Markets. A big web, with Alberta possibly emerging as a major player. Filling the world's needs.

In the beginning, Sarah and Mohamed had only fought over clowns. The young lovers, Sarah, a temporary foreign worker fleeing the economic morass of Ireland, and Mohamed, the rising inventor who'd cut his teeth in the nascent clown extraction industry, had very different ideas of feeding the needs of the world. If she'd been a dentist or he a teacher, they'd still be married. Who knows best can be a short struggle if one really does know more than the other. The worst of fights are between twins who never learn to give up, or those unfortunate lovers who are experts in the same field.

The trick in fogging clowns out of their spawning areas was controlling the rate of extraction. Too few clowns wasted manpower. Too many and it could take weeks to round them all up, if ever. And a few weeks of panicking through northern Alberta forests wasn't good for clowns; they scuffed their shoes, their rubber noses came unstuck, their baggy pants ripped and faded. Worn out clowns just weren't funny.

Sometimes, Mohamed tired of the struggle to make a company happen, when everyone was chasing the same customers, and resources. Companies fought over skilled workers. Over provincial licenses. Over shipping schedules. Over clowns. When he was really tired, he thought about chucking it, moving to somewhere else in the food chain, finding a nice, cozy monopoly. How much capital would it take to build a clown refining school? Canada was going to be an exporter of natural resources as long as clowns had to be piped to Texas for refining. The Canadian dollar was just funny money, like Venezuela, or any of the members of the Organization of Clown Exporting Countries. No matter how good Mohamed's company got, no matter how big he got, in the end he was just extracting a natural resource and shipping it elsewhere. Much movement, but most of it in cartwheels.

Long lines of trucks jammed with clowns drove to the railway spur, while the night crew came to replace the day crew, setting up trucks with tall light booms four kilometres deeper down the logging roads. Barrels of fogging compound were driven closer. To attract the clowns, speakers were set up to play circus music and strings of lights were shaped into words like 'funhouse' and 'big top.'

He was getting tired, and turned for more coffee, when his lawyer called. Not only had Mohamed's offers to buy out Trapeze Parts and Supplies fallen through, but they had closed a deal with MegaClown. Sarah got their equipment and twenty-five experienced workers. Wonderful.

"There's something else," the lawyer said.

"It gets better?"

The lawyer explained that it looked like Sarah was getting a common work friend to testify in the divorce hearing that Mohamed spent most of his time working on experiments for patents that went nowhere.

"What? How would they know?"

"Doesn't matter," the lawyer said. "They're set to testify and this will strengthen her intellectual property case, unless you've got some similar witness."

Mohamed groaned. He could do something similar, but it would take more time and money. Weeks. Months more of lawyers on both sides, charging by the hour. Maybe it would just be easier to give up. At least if this was over, he'd have some closure and something left to build with. He said this.

"I'm sympathetic," the lawyer said. "Sometimes you have to start over. Maybe Sarah is starting over. I saw her the other night in Fort McMurray. Looked like she was on a date. Good for her, right?"

Mohamed's blood boiled and froze at the same time. He was so angry with her, but he missed her too. The thought of her sitting down for drinks with some guy ate at his insides.

"Start preparing the defense for whatever she's throwing," he said in a monotone. Then, he threw the phone.

"Damnit!" he said.

"What's up, boss?"

Hanlin approached, from Asia to Italy on the great floor-map. The Trapeze deal suddenly seemed the much smaller of the two pieces of news.

"Sarah just bought Trapeze Parts and Supplies."

Hanlin ooohed. "Why do you think they went with her offer?"

"I don't know," Mohamed grumbled.

"Maybe because she's prettier?"

Mohamed glared at him and stepped across the Atlantic, surprised at the heat in his stomach. Hanlin put up his hands. "Bad joke, boss."

Bad joke. Sarah was a beauty. Mohamed was not. It was a bite at an old sore spot.

"I don't know if we can still make it," Mohamed said. "Alberta might not be big enough for the two of us."

Hanlin nodded sagely. Mohamed struggled for words, frozen in France. Sarah always won in their marriage because he loved her more. He'd given in, often when he shouldn't have. He'd created this situation. But this was his time now. He was right this time. Mohamed crossed the Rubicon to whisper to Hanlin.

"Can you find someone, one of our workers, to take a job with MegaClown, to start messing up their operations?"

Hanlin didn't seem surprised at all. Mohamed had never dreamed that he himself could sink this low, but he hadn't expected the absence of judgement in Hanlin's eyes.

"Well? Can you find someone?"

"I could probably do it myself," Hanlin said.

"No, you couldn't. Sarah knows you. Knows you work for me."

"Yeah, but two weeks ago, she started paying me to sabotage you."

"What? You're sabotaging me? She's sabotaging me?"

"No, no, of course not," Hanlin said. "I figured I'd take the money and do nothing."

"Why didn't you tell me?"

"I didn't want to make you suspicious."

Mohamed's hands floated between them for a long moment, as if they, not he, were contemplating the best way to grip Hanlin's neck. Then Mohamed threw them in the air, and shrieked.

"Goddamnit!"

He punched the pre-fab walls of the trailer, shooting pains up his wrist.

Mohamed leaned close to his friend. "So you want to be a double agent?" he said.

His twisting stomach hardened into iron at the thought of Sarah turning friends against him to support her side of the divorce.

After a week of playing double agent, Hanlin had not managed to get to MegaClown's critical equipment.

"Sarah is too suspicious," Hanlin said. "She has everybody checking on everybody else, like she expects espionage."

"Maybe we see the world we create," Mohamed said. "She must be up to something."

"How am I going to get in deep enough to do anything useful?"

Mohamed's mind was on a parallel track. Charlie had called last night. The Minister was becoming impatient. The Vice-President was cooling to Alberta. The Nigerians had sweetened the prospect of investment there by throwing some kind of unclaimed inheritance into the deal.

"I need a knock-out punch," Mohamed said.

He called the ministerial staffer back that night, and proposed a bidders' summit, a combined demonstration where the Minister and the Vice-President could compare the companies. The possibility of billions of dollars of investment attracted politicians the way cotton candy drew clowns.

The Ministry of Natural Resources had rapidly constructed a warm and roughly furnished lookout on ground high enough to overlook a broad, forested valley bisected by a wide logging road. MegaClown was set up on the west side of the road, and Clownvironmental on the east side. Each had rows of laptops and communications equipment. The caterer circulated with espressos and mini-croissants.

The RCMP had barricaded the road into the test area, to prevent the environmental protesters Mohamed had quietly tipped off from getting close. Hardier militants forged paths into the thick forest with signs like "Clear-Cutting Sells Out Our Future," "The Alberta Clown-Sands are an International Embarrassment," and "Clown Farts are Killing the Earth."

The noise of the activists reached even the lookout, and the Minister made the best face he could to the Vice-President. He then spoke quietly to Mohamed and Sarah.

"This investment is ours to lose," the Minister said. "Alberta needs one big clown extraction company to make this bid work. Compromise."

"I appreciate that, Mister Minister, but I just don't believe in the extraction practices of MegaClown," Mohamed said. "They're not sustainable and they're the reason the protesters are out there." He didn't expect him to agree. This was the Minister who had pulled Canada out of the Coney Island Protocol on Big Tent Gas.

"Clowns make the world go round," Sarah said, "unless we want to go back to the dark ages. Clownvironmental's technique simply can't be scaled up to make a real run at the bid."

The Minister frowned. "Ours to lose," he muttered.

Sarah was invited to introduce MegaClown. She presented impressive numbers, only partly cooked with optimistic assumptions. Listening to her speak took him back to their days together. Breathtaking, inspiring, frightening, intimidating and occasionally bruising.

She worked like she loved and lived. Although she'd not known in advance that the protesters would be in the distance, she acknowledged them, but also that the evidence for clownthropogenic climate change was questionable.

Mohamed's presentation took a different tone. He played a recording of a long, slow clown fart, the silent but deadly Pan's flute leading the world to environmental disaster. He got smiles from the VP and Minister, but Sarah frowned. There had been a time when he'd made her laugh. The world needed clowns.

Mohamed admitted Sarah was right. Circuses powered everything that made the world modern. Clowns enabled travel, communications, the density of cities and the feeding of the world's population. The noise of the protesters grew as he spoke, sometimes distracting, as he'd intended. The traditional methods of clown extraction had not only their obvious contribution to global warming through big tent gases, but the clear-cutting destroyed clown habitats on the scale of decades, turning a renewable resource into a non-renewable one. The protesters outside would pressure Governments and industry unless more sustainability was injected into the industry. Climate change was more than just hot air. People expected more. Mohamed's company was partnering with start-ups who were developing anti-emission clown pants to scrub clown farts. Prototypes were in testing now. The pants were just as funny, but cut big tent gasses by ninety percent. The world was willing to pay more for a clown whose farts didn't smell.

He showed how to scale the fogging process up, in terms of manpower, equipment and exploited land, to meet investment needs. Now his projections were optimistic and Sarah's frown tightened, but he had not padded his profit margins much. They were still far lower than traditional extraction methods, but very profitable nonetheless. If he ignored Sarah's glare, he could be almost giddy with the conviction in his voice. The VP and the Minister looked impressed.

"Laying it on a little thick, aren't you?" Sarah whispered as everyone moved to watch the demonstrations.

"Only because you laid it on too thin."

"Businesses make big profits or they go out of business," Sarah said. "When I've got the investment, maybe I'll call you for parts sometimes."

Sarah was on her side of the lookout before he could answer. She was quick with words and life. The nagging guilt he felt about having sabotaged her operation dissipated like clown gas, the smell sticking only in memory, in a world with the temperature slightly raised.

The demonstration surged ahead.

To the west of the logging road, Sarah's giant machines waded into the forest, saws whirring at ground level. Grapplers pulled falling trees onto huge racks, the impact shaking tree-hidden clowns into trapeze nets beneath, before the trees were rolled into other saws and then onto great flatbed trucks that began hauling away enough lumber to build subdivisions. The sound and violence of the clear-cutting flushed ground-based clowns out in a panic, where they were attracted by coloured barrels and lassoed like poorly-placed rodeo clowns. Sarah had deployed her equipment well; only stray clowns made it to the logging road where their cavorting barely slowed the big trucks.

To the east of the logging road, the hoses laid earlier in the day by Mohamed's teams began fogging the boreal forest. Great white clouds billowed around the tree trunks and rose. Blotches of colour trembled behind trees, then somersaulted or cart-wheeled out of the fog, making for the coloured paper and bright lights around the trucks.

Far more clowns emerged than he expected. Even those on unicycles, who usually signaled the tail of a movement, were out early. Was the new fogging compound really working that well? He turned up the microphones set on the hoses. Sure enough, over the patter of giant red shoes on the underbrush, the unmistakable patterns of stampeding clown flatulence. And despite the methane, the effect of the fog was holding. What a time to hit success. In front of investors, in competition with Sarah.

He looked Sarah's way. She was tense, fingers on a microphone headset, lips pursed to give an order. Her cheeks were flushed and a lock of brown hair fell from behind her ear. In times past, he would have put it back in place and she would have smiled.

"Get it up! Get it up!" Sarah yelled into her microphone.

Mohamed snapped his eyes back onto the valley. Sarah's lines were breaking. Clowns were getting through. Lots. Leading others through. His heart lifted. This was it. A real clown spill. Hundreds of clowns capering and miming and making balloon dogs, running away in oversized red shoes. Sarah's men were well-trained. They reformed the line with emergency cables, but the line wavered again as hundreds of clowns ran for the leaders instead of towards the trucks. Clowns stuck together. They were funniest in gaggles.

And yet, in this sudden triumph, guilt twisted at how Sarah must be feeling. There was no way to win without crushing her, and despite everything, he didn't want that.

"Boss, we got a line going red!" one of his techs said.

Red? It hadn't even gone yellow.

A truck, the big one, designed to hold most of the clowns and bring them to the pumping station, had broken open along one wall. Clowns were spilling out. The truck was good for three hundred clowns and it looked to have been half full.

How? It was regularly inspected. No amount of metal fatigue or corrosion could have done that since the last inspection.

He narrowed his eyes, making fists out of his hands.

She sabotaged me.

The Vice-President and the Minister were retreating, likely to make it to the RCMP roadblock before the leading edge of the clown spill. All of the escaped clowns were miming up the logging road. At the roadblock, they might divert, but at this size, the crowd of them might form an impromptu circus act and no one without a painted face would be able to get through for days.

Charlie stood between Sarah and Mohamed. He seemed heartbroken. "Your companies could have been so beautiful together," he said with a trembling voice. Teary-eyed, he fled after the Minister.

〰

BLUE TRAIN

Derryl Murphy

An explosion shattered the silence, and after a moment Andy saw a plume of smoke and dust rise up from behind a distant hill. "Anyone else supposed to be out prospecting in this area?"

"Negative," said his quad. "I'm attempting to patch into a network satellite, see if I can get a fix on what's over there."

Andy collapsed his sleeping bag and stuffed it into a saddlebag, took a last swig of strong Indian tea, then hopped onto the quad, battered cup still in hand. "To hell with the network. So many birds going down, that could take hours before you get an idea what's happening."

"What's over there is using explosives. If you insist on going to look, then I would ask that you please leave me behind. My sense of self-preservation has certainly not been depleted by your rough treatment."

"Shut up," said Andy, flipping open the control panel and tapping at a gauge. "Your battery is still at forty- five percent, so we'll run electric and leave the fuel for later. Quieter that way." He thumbed a button and turned the throttle, and the quad jumped forward with a rising hum.

"That hill will likely leave my battery at less than twenty percent, Andy."

"And the sun is already out. Start recharging and stop worrying."

They drove across the dry creek bed, the quad steering them to the part of the opposite bank that looked easiest to mount. From there it was a steady ride up the hill, tacking back and forth to avoid tipping over, Andy leaning hard uphill each time to help with balance. As they neared the crest, there was another explosion, much louder this time.

Andy let the throttle snap back to off, and the quad slid to a stop on a small plateau near the top, parked beneath a sickly stand of aspen. He reached back and grabbed his old binoculars, then jumped off and

115

hurried up the hill.

He dropped to his belly at the top and, using a bush as cover, snuck a look. "Fuck," he whispered. "Last thing I wanted to see out here."

Less than fifty metres away just past the bottom of the hill sat a sniffer, settled down in a low crouch on all six legs. In front of its battered metal and ceramic body was a large gash in the earth. A look with the binoculars confirmed what the sniffer was looking for; moisture was beginning to pool, flowing from the water table that Andy had been scouting.

He crawled backwards down the hill until he was sure he would be out of sight of the device, and then stood and skidded the rest of the way down to the quad. "Find a network yet?" he asked.

"Nothing," replied his machine. "What's over there?"

"A sniffer. It found the water."

There was a pause. Then, "That isn't good. Without a network we can't register this find. Anything on the side or top of the sniffer to tell you to whom it belongs?"

"I didn't stay around long enough to really look. Figured I'd come down first and see if there was a way we could beat it to the punch."

"Go back up and look, first, see if you can make out any markings on the side. Come back down and tell me what you see, and I'll cross-reference that and then we'll know what sort of chance we stand to save this claim."

Andy nodded, turned and ran back up the hill. The sniffer was still sitting in place, which might have been a good sign, but might not have been one as well. It could have been using this time to recharge some batteries, or it could have been in contact with its own network. If the second was true, then it had access to much better resources than Andy, and besides already registering this claim would be able to cause Andy no end of trouble if he tried anything.

Some of the ID on the side of the sniffer was illegible, scorched by previous blasts or worn away by time and weather. He was able to make out a string of six letters and numbers, though, as well as what looked like a faded picture of a star riding above what looked like a bear, only with something wrong with it.

He was about to sneak back down out of sight when a glint of sunlight in the distance caught his eye. Leaning back down on his elbows, he maxed out the mag on his binoculars and focused in on a giant gleaming silver snake, riding on large wheels and coming slowly his way.

"Oh, shit."

Back down the hill, then, faster than the last time. He almost fell as he tried to stop by the quad, but he managed to grab the bag rack on the back, almost ripping his arm out of its socket in the process.

"What is it?" asked the machine. "Why the rush?"

Andy climbed on and throttled the quad up, driving downhill as fast as he dared. He was too busy concentrating on not tumbling over that he didn't answer.

"My battery is only at twenty-five percent, Andy," warned the quad. "If you don't switch over to fuel soon, we won't be going anywhere and I won't even be around to talk to you."

"Whiner," said Andy. The quad was silent, likely pouting in response.

They finally came to a stop after climbing and descending one more hill. Andy got off the quad and paced for a moment before finally sitting on the ground in front of the machine.

"There's a pipeline coming. Maybe two klicks away at the outside."

"Already? There's something wrong with that sort of speed. What were you able to read on the side of the sniffer?"

"A bunch of the numbers or letters were pretty much erased. I was able to get 7Q6-CA-6, as well as a picture of a star sitting above a bear that looked like it had a tumor on its back."

"Ah," said the quad. "That certainly explains a lot, as well as opening up some new questions."

Looking up at where the sun had managed to crawl in the past ten minutes, Andy opened his pouch and pulled out a small pot of sunscreen and started smearing it on his face. "Tell me just what it explains," he said, wiping an extra-thick layer across his nose.

"American," answered the machine. "Judging by your description of the seal, I'd say the animal was probably a grizzly bear, so this would have come up from California."

Andy stopped, cocked an eyebrow back at the quad. "Grizzly bear? What the hell's that?" But before he could get an answer, another thought occurred to him. "And there's no fucking way that can be an American sniffer and pipeline! Shit, nobody even pays attention to where the border is anymore, but we sure as hell aren't so close that the two of those would crawl all this way for water! Especially from, from…" He snapped his fingers, trying to remember.

"California. And you're right, Andy, they wouldn't crawl all this way. Likely a pumping station has been set up, in Montana or in Idaho Free State to get it over the Rockies, or even on our side of the border."

"Well shit," whispered Andy. "Couldn't be our side. Enough gunfire over water rights on either side of the border without bringing it an international flavour."

"Most states are now cooperating, Andy," replied the quad. "It is equally difficult for all of them these days."

"Hmph. No network yet?"

"Nothing. I begin to wonder if any incoming signals are being deliberately blocked or scrambled."

Andy sat back down on the quad. "Why would that be?"

"It is a good chance they aren't allowed to be here. Unlikely that they have signed any sort of agreement with the feds, but that's the only way they should be allowed to get an extraction deal."

Andy laughed. "I don't see the feds sticking their noses in anything out here anymore."

"A signal, Andy! Wait one moment," said the quad. Andy stood silent, nervously rubbing his fingers on his palms while he waited.

"That wasn't the network. The pipeline is almost in place, and was broadcasting its claim. Says it has permission of the Blue Train to be here."

"Son of a bitch!" Andy kicked at a rock, sent it caroming off one of the quad's tires and into some squat bushes nearby. "Who the fuck do those provincial assholes think they are, giving permission for something like this? They pull up stakes and head out for no one knows the fuck where, and next thing you know they're cutting deals they aren't allowed to cut to give away our water. My water."

"The message repeated twice and then went dead. Still no access. I'm now fairly sure that I'm being blocked from getting at it."

"Fine." Andy started rummaging through the field equipment box that sat strapped to the back of the quad.

"What are you looking for?"

"Gonna take care of this myself," he answered. "I don't give a shit if it's the Blue Train or not, and I sure as hell don't care about the Americans." Andy pulled out three chunks of explosive and detonators, slipped them into two different vest pockets, then pulled his old rifle out of its holster and shouldered it.

"You can't be serious," said the quad. "You have no idea what will come down on your head if you get caught. When you get caught. At the very least, you lose any chance you have to claim this water."

"Doesn't matter. I want you to be ready to broadcast this location to the network as soon as that block is dropped. Tell everyone there's a new lake been found." He dug out an extra box of bullets, tucked it into a pants pocket.

"A lake? Andy, I don't know what you are talking about, but any call like that will bring in prospectors from miles and miles around. Probably bring in ordinary folk, too, if they're stupid enough to still be living out on the land." The machine paused for a second. "And it occurs to me that if the Blues signed a deal to give up water rights, they might be bold enough to sign a deal to try and circumvent fed jurisdiction with extradition."

"There you go with the feds again. Look, the Blues don't run this province anymore; they gave up that right when they packed up and headed out on that goddamn Train of theirs."

"But they are still the nominal power in these parts, since no one sees any sign of the feds at all these days. And back to the topic at hand, all American and former American states have the death penalty for anyone who sabotages their water supplies. The feds historically wouldn't ship anyone south if they face hanging or the firing squad, but based on philosophy the Blue Train may not feel so concerned for their own nominal citizens."

Andy shrugged. "Still my fucking water. If I'm going to give it up, everyone gets it. Took years of looking through charts and maps and infrareds we cheated from those birds in orbit to find a spot where the table had come back up. And I'm not gonna lose it to some mechanical pirates from another country."

The machine made a sound like a sigh. "Very well. You can't do this alone, then." A small dark green metal box spit out of the side of the quad and landed on the ground. "That's my beacon. I've tied it to a…" The machine paused, made a sound eerily like a shudder. "To a deadman's switch I've just programmed. I can set it off if need be, but if I become incapacitated while following you around like a fool, it will start to broadcast a signal. It gives the approximate coordinates for this magical new lake of yours."

"You don't have to do this, you know," Andy told the quad. "I'm sure I can figure out some way of getting to them."

"Unlikely. The sniffer won't be expecting anyone, but it also won't just let you walk up and attach some plastic explosives to it, and those bullets won't do anything but ricochet off its body and maybe bounce back to put a big ugly hole in you."

"So what do you propose?"

"Leave your gun. How steep do you think that hill is leading down to the sniffer?"

"Fairly steep. No way you can ride straight down there. You'd tip and roll, likely squash me flat."

"Exactly what I thought," said the quad. "But what if I went around the side of the hill with my engine roaring? Do you think you could do a decent tuck and roll?"

Andy scratched his beard, picturing the process. "Not too many trees in the way, or big rocks. It'll hurt, but I think I could do it without too much pain. But I'm gonna be dizzy as hell when I get to the bottom."

"Good point. I keep forgetting that the limits on humans just don't seem to end."

"But I see where you're going with this," said Andy, "and I think I see a way around it. Just trust me on it, and do your level best to divert the sniffer's attention. Give me thirty seconds after I wave at you from the top, all right? I don't know how well I can time this."

"Climb aboard then," replied the quad. "I'll take you to the bottom of the hill. But don't you start until you know I'm in place."

The quad brought him back to the hill, then headed off to the east, leaving Andy to lean hard and run up the slope as best as he could. Just short of the top he pulled out one chunk of explosive and inserted a detonator into it, held on to it tight. Then he double-checked his pocket to make sure that the remote for the detonator was still there.

Finally, he peeked over the edge and down the hill. The sniffer was still sitting in place, and the pipeline was now set up by the hole the sniffer had made. It was drilling deeper, braces having dropped down to keep its front wheels from moving anywhere. Already he could hear the motors as the powerful miniature pumps inside the pipeline started pulling the water up from underground.

He stood and waved to the quad, took a deep breath, then dove headfirst over the top of the hill, hanging tight to the explosives and the detonator. The first roll on the rocky soil knocked the breath right back out of him, a big whoosh of air that he could feel but not hear; the only sounds he could make out were the rustling of his clothes and the thumps and bumps and cracks as his body and head hit dirt and rocks and dried branches. He tried to keep his eyes closed, but they kept opening on their own, giving him a stomach-churning view of harsh blue sky swiftly followed by baked brown earth, and then repeated again and again.

And then he hit a small bump and went spinning into the air, rolled to a stop face up on the ground, hot sun trying to burn its way through his eyelids. He stayed still, feeling every muscle in his body trying to twitch, feeling the agony of the bruises, but thankfully not finding anything that felt like a broken bone.

Andy could hear the sniffer walking towards him now as he played dead, steady thumps reverberating through the ground and into his skull with background accompaniment from the pipeline as it pulled his precious water from the below. He had kept a tight grip on the explosive and the detonator, kept his fists closed as the American machine approached.

There was a loud roar off in the distance and then a shuffling as the sniffer shifted itself to view the quad. Andy opened his eyes and saw that it was turned the other way now, about three metres from him, and he rolled quickly to his knees and then jumped up, with two quick steps getting to the sniffer and slapping the explosive charge onto its body and then turning and running as fast as his dizzy state would allow.

One quick look behind showed that it had turned and was following him; too close to set off the charge, really, but if he waited any longer it would be closer still, or would catch him and then put in a call for help. He thumbed the trigger button.

There was a loud bang and then a sort of double-*whumpf*, and Andy was thrown to the ground. Something slammed into his back, once again knocking the wind out of him, and immediately after he felt something slice through his forearm. The heat on his back was fierce, even worse than the sun at noon.

Rolling onto his back, Andy held up his arm and had a look at the damage; nothing too serious, more of a scratch than anything, he decided. A small cloud of smoke hung in the still air and some of the scrub was on fire now, but the flames were small and already burning themselves down.

He sat up, put his hands to his ears to try and block out the ringing that started there, and watched as the quad rolled up to him. There were some muffled sounds coming from it, but nothing he could make out.

"Shit, I guess that thing still had some explosives inside it," he said. His voice sounded muffled, like he was talking with his mouth full of cloth.

More sounds from the quad. He waved his arms and shook his head, winced and put a hand to his forehead. "Can't hear a damn thing, quad. The explosion must've done something to my ears." He looked over to the pipeline, which appeared to be undamaged. "You getting through to the network now? Roll backwards a bit if yes." The machine rolled backwards. "Sending out the message I wanted you to?"

It stayed still.

Andy reached forward and grabbed a handlebar, pulled himself up and leaned heavily on the quad. "Well why the fuck not?" He yawned, felt a popping in his ears. "Sounds like…" He grinned. "Good. Hearing's coming back. Now, why the fuck not?"

"Climb on me and I'll show you," said the quad, still sounding distant.

"In a minute." Andy reached into his pocket, pulled out the other two chunks of explosive and detonators, and started running for the pipeline. He heard the quad rev up and start following him.

There was a good point about fifteen metres away from the snout and drill of the pipeline, sitting just back of another set of giant wheels. He got there and bent over, trying to catch his breath and feeling all of the new pains from the past few minutes. When he looked back up, the quad was back beside him.

"I'm sending out the message now, but I'm not happy about it," it said. "You need to hurry and do this, though. I've got something to show you and then we have to get out of here."

"Right." Andy reached up, but the pipeline was still well beyond his hand. He tried jumping, but couldn't get much height with all of his muscle aches. He turned to the quad. "Come here, closer."

The machine moved to a place under the pipeline, and Andy climbed up and stood on the seat. Reaching high and standing on his toes, he was able to stick the charge to the battered gray metal pipe. He squatted down and grabbed the handlebar, told the quad to move another metre down the line, then he stood up and attached the other explosive, just in case. In the distance, the pipeline marched on through a gap in the low hills that surrounded them. A perfect place for a lake.

"Okay," he said, sitting down and grabbing a handle with one hand, pulling the detonator out of his pocket with the other. "Show me what you think I need to see, and let's get this done with."

The quad gunned its engine and they tore back up the hill Andy had just rolled down. Halfway up he yelled "Stop!" and then turned and pressed the button. Two simultaneous blasts pierced the air, chunks of metal flying high into the sky, and then a great gout of water began to spew forth from the pipeline, spilling out onto the parched earth. More water than Andy had ever seen, and all of it pouring free.

He tapped the side of the quad's fuel tank. "Show me."

The engine roared to life again, and soon they were at the top of the hill. Andy sat for a second, mouth hanging open, watching what approached from the west, and then dismounted and stood beside the quad.

"Haven't seen that in twenty years, maybe more." His voice was almost a whisper. "How long do you figure we have?"

"Less than an hour, I would guess. Can't outrun it, though. It got a fix on us as soon as I found my way back onto the network."

In the distance, towering above the tallest trees this parched land had to offer, the Blue Train was coming. Too distant to hear, its visage wavered in the hot air, a mirage one moment, more solid the next.

Andy shrugged, suddenly aware that the fight had finally left him. "We'll stay here, then. Wouldn't want to leave my lake without seeing how it turns out, anyway."

He sat painfully on the ground and leaned against a tire. Sometimes Andy would turn his head and watch as the Blue Train continued its approach, growing ever-larger and more foreboding by the minute, but more often he sat and watched the water pour forth, already a good-sized pond, arcing out and then splashing down from the wrecked pipeline like some mythical fountain, sunlight reflecting brilliantly off the water, mesmerizing in its unfamiliarity. Soil was stirring up underneath, giving most of the pond a dark and muddy look, but now Andy could see that in the centre, at its deepest, it was starting to reflect the pure stark blue of the sky.

Eventually a deep rumble began to overtake the sound of the dancing waters, something Andy felt in his bones and teeth before he could really hear, but becoming more audible with each moment. Finally he had no choice but to turn and watch the Blue Train, remembering that when it was present there was nothing that could overwhelm it.

There were eight cars now; the last time he'd seen it there were only five, rushing past in the distance and still large enough to blot out the mountains that had sat behind it, a train without tracks built to carry a government and its people when the capital city had—metaphorically, at least—collapsed in on itself. Twenty years ago it had still carried that new sheen, sparkling and shining in the harsh light of the day, metal gleaming in a way that was both uplifting and vaguely threatening.

Today there was nothing vague about the feeling. The Train was huge, menacing, almost angry-looking. Any polish it had once carried had been lost to the elements and the years, and now, even from this distance Andy could see the rust and grease and soot that pockmarked its surface, the rusted-out holes that ran along the bottom.

"It looks nothing like the pictures I see over the network," said the quad.

Andy shook his head, trying to force away the fear he felt in the pit of his stomach. "I guess we all change, don't we? Maybe not on the inside, but sure as hell do on the outside."

The Train began to slow down now, hissing and screeching with angry blasts of steam as it broke its way through small stands of quivering aspen and dipped and rose over smaller hills. Dry earth split and cracked beneath its wheels, small boulders shattered under its weight, and as it finally came to a complete stop a blast of extra-hot air sent a wave of dry soil across Andy and the quad. It shuddered and roared for a few seconds, and then with one last string of noisy farts, the engine fell silent.

For minutes the only sounds were the gurgling of the slowly growing lake and the squeaks, moans and hisses of the Blue Train as it settled. Andy just sat on the ground, watching and waiting, wiping grit from his eyes, nervously drumming his fingers and chewing on his lip.

Although the Train had come to rest at the bottom of the hill where Andy was, its peak was almost equal to that of the hill. The engine was larger than the other cars, over eighty metres long, and its wheels, dozens of them, each stood three times his height. Every wheel had a flaw of some sort, and some were so badly worn down that they didn't even touch down to the ground, were held up by the others to spin fruitlessly in the air. Deadfall stuck out at odd angles from various holes, and there was even the rotting corpse of a deer impaled on a stray piece of rusting metal.

The car behind the engine was only a bit smaller, dozens of rows of windows reaching from bottom to top. From some windows Andy could see faces peering briefly out before hiding back in the shadows, the mysteries of their lives and tasks intact for the moment.

A loud squeal interrupted the silence, and a door opened at the bottom of the first car, metal grinding against metal. Two men, tiny figures dwarfed by the Train, jumped to the ground and then pulled out two slats of rust and white metal, laid them down to be a ramp. There was an echoing growl from inside the car, and then a real automobile exited from the darkness, descended to the ground and started up the hill.

"What is it?" asked Andy.

"A Jeep," answered the quad.

Andy stood and held his hand over his eyes to keep the sun out. A real Jeep, driving up the hill toward him. Two miracles in one day. He looked down at the quad, wondering if he should try to make a break for it now, knowing as the thought touched his mind that he wouldn't get halfway down the hill. He steeled himself and continued to watch its approach.

The driver gave the accelerator an extra touch as it crested the hill, and then spun the wheel and brought the jeep to rest beside them. Two men carrying guns immediately jumped out, muzzles pointing at the ground but with their threat clearly implied. Then the driver also climber out, running around to the other side and opening the door for his last passenger, standing back as that man stepped to the ground.

The first three men were all dressed in gray and brown camo, but this last man wore the uniform of the Blues, gray pants with only one or two small patches, a similar jacket, a light blue shirt and a red tie. His hair was also gray, perfectly combed, and he was freshly shaved. His teeth were white and even; his smile never wavered, seemed to be pasted on his face. For a few seconds he stood and watched the lake, then turned and looked at Andy. "It is a beautiful sight, isn't it?"

Andy blinked. He hadn't expected polite conversation, even if this man was a politician. "The lake? Yeah, it is. Never seen anything like it."

The Blue seemed to find this amusing. His smile grew even more, and he glanced back at his driver and the two men with guns, who also smiled. "Then perhaps you should find your way further north some day. There are still some small streams there, and even ponds that have not gone stagnant. And yes, a nice lake or two."

Andy shrugged. "I've heard stories. I'm also told that high in the mountains there are still some crystal-clear lakes and streams, and even some animals to be found. Not as if that does either of us any good."

"Yes. Sadly, the Train won't let us take our government into the mountains," said the Blue. "Too big. Pacifica claims that land now, you know, and holds back what water they can."

"Then why give this water up to the Americans? If you can't get any of that water that used to belong to us, then why not take advantage of the water that we do find here?"

"Oh, we wrote off this area long ago. Most of the south. Since the Exodus boarded the Train we've concentrated on our resources north of the Dry Zone."

"You've given over the south half of the province," said the quad.

The Blue's smile faltered for a fraction of a second, but a blink of his eyes seemed to reset it. "Ah, his machine speaks. I keep forgetting that before the Train departed we still allowed intelligent machines." He looked back to Andy. "Your device is correct. We have ceded territory over to our friends to the south, in exchange for some future, ah, considerations." He smiled, as if at a secret joke. "So now we will wait until our friends can muster a replacement pipeline, as well as officers to take you south for your trial and likely execution. I think we will have plenty of room on a lower level of a rear car, and I'm sure that your ATV will have parts we can use."

"You have no jurisdiction," replied the quad.

Now the man frowned. "I didn't come here to argue with a machine," he said. "The feds have no business here anymore, no longer even poke their heads west of Lake Winnipeg. And as the Deputy Minister of External Affairs, it is my job to make sure things run smoothly between those of us on the Train and those governments outside that we still have dealings with."

There was a buzzing sound then, a droning that started at a higher pitch and got lower as it became louder. With a sudden screaming roar two more quads jumped over the far edge of the hill, they and their riders coming to a stop behind Andy.

"Son of a bitch," whispered one, pulling his goggles off. His eyes were tearing up. "It really is a lake."

His companion was grinning wildly. "And the Blue Train, too. Almost two miracles in one spot. Like maybe a whole new life is gonna start, right here."

The Blue looked panicked by this suggestion. He lifted his arms to wave off the thought, but then there were more distant engine sounds, coming from all directions. Andy turned in a circle, counted at least a dozen quads riding over distant hills on their way. "The network tells me at least three hundred patched into our announcement, Andy," said his quad. "Some of them are two or three days away, but they're all headed here."

Andy looked at the two newcomers; he didn't recognize either one, but there had always been too many prospectors. He reached down and picked up a couple of large rocks and dropped them into a saddlebag, then sat on the quad, smiling. "Well?" he said to the two of them. "What are we waiting for? Let's send out a few invitations."

The quad gunned its engine and jumped around the Jeep before the Blue could order his men to do anything, the other two following close behind. They raced down the hill, whooping and hollering. By the time they were at the bottom, water was coming through a small notch between two hills, spilling out and pooling underneath the wheels of the second Train car. A new stream beginning its life here, not letting anything get in its way.

Andy grabbed one of the rocks, flung it high and watched it bounce off a window of the first car. Faces started to appear, and some doors opened a crack. "A lake!" he screamed. The other two joined the chorus. "Water! Here for all of us!"

They splashed across the stream, and he hurled the second rock high, yelled more of the same. Now people were coming out, a few wearing Blue uniforms, but most just dressed as ordinary citizens. Some, judging by their age, who had maybe never been out of the Blue Train in their entire lives. At first they were silent as they stepped out, speechless at a sight many of them had only ever heard about. But then, almost as one, they were all yelling, some crying tears of joy, and right away more took over from Andy and the others, beseeching their fellow residents to come out.

Andy stopped the quad and watched as they splashed through the stream, mothers dipping infants into the flowing water, children kicking and splashing, one man in uniform even stripping off his coat and tie and rolling in it. More quads arrived, adding their steady buzz to the cacophony of joyful shouts and laughter, hundreds of people all out and together, under the burning sun, in one spot and sharing a purpose.

Andy gunned the quad, steered past a knot of old women who were crying and hugging each other, raced back up the hill to where the Blue stood by his Jeep. The driver and gunmen were no longer there. He looked down the hill, saw that some people were now making their way upstream, and finding the amazing source of the water. "You can still lock me away," he said, "and get all those people back in the Train to go find some ponds that aren't too stagnant. But it will have to wait a little while." He patted the quad. "Keep broadcasting."

"Oh, I am," said the machine. "So are a few of the others, including two that still have working network cameras. We're causing quite the sensation."

"Good to know." Andy jumped from the quad and ran back down the hill, this time making sure he didn't lose his balance until he was right at the edge of the water. He knew before he got wet that nothing would ever feel this good again.

≈

THE COW'S IN THE MEADOW, THE BLOOD'S IN THE CORN

M. L. D. Curelas

A dense black cloud of flies buzzed over the carcass. A magpie cawed a warning to the insects, hopping across its claim as it peeled strips of flesh from the body. As it left one area unprotected the flies descended, feasting until the magpie returned to chase them away. The dance would continue until a larger predator discovered the free meal.

Laura would have laughed at the intricate game played by the flies and bird if she hadn't seen the same display on four other cows this morning. She'd lost close to thirty cows in three weeks. She swept her flat-brimmed hat off and swiped at the bugs and bird, shrieking her own harsh threat. The magpie fluttered to a spot about a metre away and cocked its head at her, bright black eyes watching her with a fixed interest that would have given her the creeps if it had been human.

She knelt beside the cow and examined the wound at the neck. Straight and clean: a knife. "God dammit," she said. Laura removed her phone bud from her ear and snapped pictures of the wound, the cow, and the tattoo in the cow's ear. She'd have to identify the animal through her stud books. With an absent wave of her hat, she scattered the reforming cloud of flies and stared at the cow in grim silence for a few minutes before rising.

Laura activated the black phone bud and pushed it back into her ear. "Hey, Greg," she said in response to the gruff voice that greeted her. "I've got five cows that I need you to salvage."

She flapped at the flies again. "No, not for human consumption. The zoo again, if they'll take them."

Plopping the hat back on her head, Laura shooed away another wave of flies with her hands. "Right, thanks, Greg, see you in a few." Laura ended the call and took a couple more photos of the cow and the spray of blood discolouring the prairie grass. She jabbed a hot pink flag into the ground next to the corpse and returned to the barn.

The herd knew something was wrong; no doubt they could smell their slain sisters. The cows milled in the paddock, lowing nervously. They weren't eating. Laura cursed again. She didn't need the cows upset with breeding season coming up; they wouldn't catch. She frowned, wiping a sweaty palm on her jeans. She'd have to increase security around the bull barn. Her livelihood depended on Highland Laddie, her champion bull.

Murmuring a stream of soothing nonsense to the cows, Laura broke out a bale of pea hay and scattered it among the troughs. It didn't have a lot of nutritional value, but the cows loved it, and they deserved a treat with all the trauma of the past few weeks and the constant stench of blood hanging over the pasture.

The crunch of gravel announced Greg's arrival. Laura met him at the pasture gate. She unlocked it and pushed it open and Greg's old-fashioned pick-up truck—it ran on diesel rather than the new corn ethanol fuel—drove into the field, the refrigerated compartment rigged to the bed swaying as the truck jounced over bumps and dips in the ground.

She waited for him at the gate, staring at the wide blue expanse of sky above, and mulled over who hated her so much that they'd kill cows. The corn farmers topped the list, but there were a few competitors who might feel threatened by her business. When the truck returned, Laura opened the gate again, closing and locking it after Greg had gone through.

Greg rolled down his window. "You sure you don't want this for yourself?"

Laura shook her head. "My freezer's full. Do you think the zoo will take them?"

"They took the others, and I don't see why they'd turn these down. Lions gotta eat every day too." Greg peeled off his cap, wiped his glistening forehead with his forearm, and smashed the cap back onto his head. "Laura, girl, you need more people watching your cattle at night, or you're gonna lose 'em all."

Laura's chin lifted. Asking for a punch, her father would have joked. "I don't have enough people, Greg. Everyone wants to get into corn."

"Your daddy would want me to help you out." He drummed his fingers on the steering wheel. Laura's eyes were drawn to the thick, gnarled knuckles. Greg was too old to babysit cows during the wee hours of the night.

"Look, Greg, there's no need—"

"Hush." Greg popped open his glove compartment and rummaged in it for several seconds. "Aha!" He leaned out his window and waved a small rectangle of paper at her.

Laura took it from him, rubbing a thumb over the soft, textured paper. She hadn't seen a physical business card in years. The ink had faded; she had to squint to make out the words. "MacDougall Security?"

"Yep. Give 'em a call." Greg tweaked the bill of his cap, put the truck in gear, and drove off. Laura watched until he had turned onto the main road, then went back into the barn.

Laura flipped the card over and over before abruptly coming to a decision. It took a few minutes to arrange for Charles, one of the ranch hands, to come down to the cow barn. While she waited for him, Laura went into her office and booted up her stud book. Responding to voice prompts, the computer accessed her phone's data and downloaded the photos. It found results almost immediately and displayed the matches for her approval. Laura sighed and recorded the date and cause of death of the cows, and how the bodies had been disposed. The computer chimed when it finished updating the cows' records.

"Save and shut down," Laura said, pushing out of her chair. She didn't wait for the computer's confirmation beep.

Charles stood at the corral in the main barn, bare arms propped on the beams, watching the cows dig for the remaining wisps of pea hay. Rivulets of sweat carved trenches on his dust-streaked face. The large ceiling fan spun at its highest speed, but did little to cool the barn's interior.

Laura gave Charles instructions for cleaning the bloodstained pasture grass and the cows' care for the day.

Charles nodded, pushing the brim of his hat up onto the crown of his head. "The cows will be fine, Laura. You go on into town."

A yellow-brown haze crowned Calgary, making the city one brown splotch from the ground to the sky. Even the Bow River, sluggish and dull these days, looked more like a ribbon of mud than of water. Laura wrinkled her nose. The blistering hot summer wasn't kind to Calgary; winter, with its thick blankets of snow, hid the city's flaws—the tall slabs of tenement buildings which had sprouted up to curb the city's sprawl, the shabby houses of the eastern quadrants.

The dashboard computer accessed maps of the city and programmed a route through the maze of one way streets of the downtown core. Poverty had not breached this part of Calgary. Sleek skyscrapers brushed the sky with brassy arrogance. The logos on the buildings may have changed, but the people within them hadn't. Fuel was fuel, whether it was ethanol or oil, and there was money to be made.

In defiance of the heat outside, the receptionist of MacDougall Security wore a long-sleeved blouse and a chocolate brown wool skirt that complemented the peach and aqua decor. She arched her eyebrows at Laura. "Do you have an appointment?"

"No." Laura refused to look down at her plain cotton shirt and jeans. "I was in town and decided to stop by. Is Mr MacDougall available? He was recommended by a friend of mine."

The woman sniffed. "I'll see, but don't be surprised if he's not. Mr MacDougall is terribly busy."

"I'll wait, thanks." Laura sat on one of the plush, peach-coloured chairs, and picked up a reading tablet. Current issues of several magazines were loaded onto the device and Laura hummed as she scrolled through the list. Beneath her feet she could feel the thrum of air conditioning working at full blast.

Laura knew what the answer was before the receptionist opened her mouth; her heels had a sullen click. "Mr MacDougall can see you now."

"Thanks." Laura set down the tablet.

He waited for her inside the open door of his office. "Laura Lochlin? Greg called me earlier today, said you might drop by. I'm Archie MacDougall."

Tall, with raven black hair, tanned skin, and sky blue eyes, Archie MacDougall looked nothing like what she expected. Laura blinked, aware that she had been gawking at him. "Sorry," she said, "I was under the impression that you were a friend of Greg's." She took the hand he proffered and gave it a moderate squeeze, noting the lack of calluses.

Archie laughed. "He's an old friend of my dad. I've known him since I was a kid. Here, have a seat." He perched on the edge of his desk as she sat in the red leather chair. After a couple moments of silence, he said, "Greg mentioned trouble with your cows?"

Laura nodded. "Someone has killed twenty-seven of them in the past few weeks."

Archie whistled. "Any idea who?"

"Sort of," she said, "I have a lot of land and I don't use it to grow corn. I've had dozens of offers since I took over the ranch after my father died. Someone's trying to take my home and ruin my business."

"Pardon me for asking, but wouldn't corn be more profitable than cows?" His tone implied: *wouldn't corn be safer?*

Laura shrugged. "You'd think so, but with the shift in the corn market, there's a demand for cow products. For beef, sure, and I'd be lying if I said that most of my income didn't come from supplying high-end restaurants. But there're also medical uses for cow organs. And now…well, there isn't enough corn-based food for humans, let alone for grain fed cows, not since the U.S. started concentrating on ethanol production. That's why the Ontario beef market went under— they couldn't finish their cattle on corn grain." She leaned forward, eyes sparkling. "I have Sussex cows, able to survive drought, but they can also withstand the cold. They're just about perfect for the climate we have now in Calgary. Plus, they don't need fancy grain to produce good quality beef."

"OK, so you raise cattle instead of growing corn, and someone is killing your cows to intimidate you into selling the land. Or drive you out of business if they can eliminate enough of your herd." Archie cocked his head. "Does that about sum it up?" When she nodded again, he said, "What security do you have now? Cameras? Retina-scanners on the barns and fences? Voice recognition locks?"

Laura worried her bottom lip, taking a perverse pleasure in the slight sting of pain. "Nothing."

"Nothing?" Archie glared at her. "Not even a dog?"

Her eyes widened. Pets, even working pets, were expensive, a luxury. In addition to affecting corn grain production, the U.S. diversion of corn from food to fuel had impacted domestic pet food. Often used as filler for cheaper brands, the disappearance of corn had put a lot of the pet food manufacturers out of business. People with dogs and cats had to invest in organic vegetarian brands or the all-meat brands; those companies had jacked up the prices of their product. Dog and cat populations in animal shelters had ballooned as the number of abandoned pets soared.

"I have an arrangement with my butcher to send all the unused meat and bones to the Humane Society." Laura smiled. "In a way, I have dozens of dogs, but none of them live with me."

Archie muttered something and stood up, crossing to the other side of his desk. He slid open a panel, revealing a tablet which he then proceeded to manipulate, scrolling, typing, and pressing. After a few minutes, he swivelled the tablet around and showed her the screen. "It won't be cheap, and you may lose more cows, but I think we can catch the bastard."

"With that thing?" Laura's eyebrows shot up in surprise. "Are you serious?"

"Completely."

Laura braked, careful to bring the truck to a smooth halt so she wouldn't jolt the box beside her. It was a simple cardboard container, with a lid that folded into a handle and holes punched along the top, much like what pet stores used. Archie had said that the box was cam-ouflage, meant to fool people.

Laura grabbed the handle and slid out of the truck, kicking the door shut. The barn was empty. Charles, she knew, would be out in the pasture with the cows while they grazed, and would guide them back to the barn at dusk.

Once the box rested on the desk in her office, Laura wiped damp palms on her jeans. Holding her breath, she peeled away the flaps of the box like it was an artichoke.

Within sat the mech cat, silent and motionless. Beneath the ma-chine was an instruction booklet and a slim white cable. Laura pulled the booklet out from under the mech cat and flipped through the pages.

"This had better work," Laura said. She straightened her shoulders, cleared her throat and said in a clear, slow voice, "Kitty. Wake."

The mech cat whirred. Eyes opened and ears twitched. Kitty stretched, first leaning back to work out the kinks in its front legs, then putting its weight on its front paws while it shook first one hind leg, then the other. Its tail pointed straight up. Only after the ritual was completed did the mech cat look at Laura. "Miaow."

Laura's hand hovered above the cat's head. Gulping, she gave the cat a nervous pat on the head. Beneath the realistic gray tabby fur,

Laura felt the vibration of gears and motors. It was abnormally warm. It was close to being real, but just alien enough that her arms erupted in goose flesh.

Her mouth scrunching with an unvoiced "ew", Laura yanked her hand away with a shudder. "Good Kitty." Luckily, it would respond to vocal commands; there wasn't a need for her to touch the thing.

The mech cat purred. If she listened closely, Laura could detect the faintest of burrs in the sound, what she knew to be a hint of the mechanical workings of the device, but what anybody else would assume to be just a throaty purr. Archie had been right. The thing was worth every penny she had spent on it. There wasn't a question in Laura's mind that it would trick people, especially the fiends that kept killing her cattle. The mech cat would have more than enough time and opportunity for its visual, audio, and infrared sensors to record every movement of the villains.

Laura spent hours testing the mech cat's various security protocols, the clarity and efficacy of the sensors, and programming commands. Kitty did not have wireless capability for security purposes, but the company had included the cable to compensate. Laura linked Kitty with her stud registry computer, which had extensive maps of her property, and programmed a route for the mech cat to patrol at night.

When dusk fell, Laura put Kitty outside. "Patrol, Kitty."

"Miaow." Kitty strolled into the pasture with the languid confidence of a queen surveying her domain. Laura would have sworn it was a real cat.

Laura met Kitty at the barn before dawn. The mech cat purred and rose up on its hind legs, attempting to bump its head into Laura's palm for a pat. Laura flinched and stuffed her hands into her pockets. "Report, Kitty."

Kitty mewed and a flap of fur sagged away from its neck, revealing a data port. Laura grumbled as she hooked the mech cat up to the computer, her fingers fumbling with the unfamiliar cable. The upload was completed in a few seconds; the stud book displayed the mech cat's report. Zip, zero, zilch.

The barn door creaked. "Laura?" Charles called.

Laura yanked the cable out of the mech cat, tossed it under the desk, then bent over and pushed the skin flap back into place. "In my office!"

"Morning, Laura. What... is that a *cat*?"

Laura's fingers twitched. Gritting her teeth, she gave Kitty a nervous stroke along the neck, making sure the panel was closed. "Good Kitty." At the magic words, the mech cat mewed, stretched a hind leg and hunched over its spine to lick its nether regions.

Laura straightened. "Yeah. A cat." She ran her tongue over dry, cracked lips. She hated lying. "It gets a little lonely, working in here all day, so I thought a pet would be nice."

"Sure." Charles scratched his head. "Aren't pets awfully dear though?"

"I own a ranch, Charles." Laura forced a laugh. "I'm not lacking meat, especially now."

"Oh." Charles eyed the mech cat with distaste. "Well, I was wondering if Highland Laddie should be brought down today. It's getting a little late in the season."

An icy tingle swept up Laura's back. Risking Highland Laddie, was this what the cow killer had been waiting for? The locks on the cow pasture and barns hadn't been a problem for whoever the villain was. She glanced down at Kitty. She did have the mech cat and all the hands would continue to watch the cattle at night. She gave an abrupt nod. "Yeah, let's move him down today and reacquaint him with the girls."

Shrill yowls woke Laura up. A fleeting glance at the clock told her it was nearly four in the morning—she'd only been asleep for an hour. Laura yanked on yesterday's jeans and socks and rammed her feet into boots. As she stumbled out of her bedroom, she jammed her phone bud into her ear.

Laura ran to the front door, grabbing the rifle that she'd placed there earlier, when her guard shift at the barn had ended. Kitty joined her and both jumped over the porch steps and sped towards the barn. Laura could see a strange truck parked by the building and she increased her pace. Kitty raced ahead, body stretched low over the ground, tabby fur blending into the gray shadows of approaching dawn.

Two men hunched over the lock on the barn door. With a shriek, Kitty launched itself at the nearest man, back claws sinking into the meat of his shoulder while its front claws raked his face. Screaming, Kitty's victim clutched at the mech cat and stumbled in a lopsided circle. The other man swore, dancing out of the way of his blinded partner, and flapped his arms at the mech cat. Kitty hissed and swiped at an arm, ears pressed flat against its head.

Laura skidded to a halt and raised her rifle, sliding the safety off. "Kitty, light!"

Eerie green light flooded the night. Even though she'd been expecting it, Laura flinched at the sight of Kitty's glowing orbs. The uninjured man shouted, one hand sketching a cross in the air.

"Kitty, come," Laura said. The mech cat detached its claws, hopped off its victim, and sauntered to Laura, its tail lashing the air. Kitty butted its head against Laura's knees before sitting at her feet, directing its green shafts of light at the two men.

The injured man lowered his hands from his face and Laura hissed. Charles. Keys glittered in the gravel at his feet. No wonder it had been so easy for the cow killers; they'd had inside help.

Laura kept the rifle pointed at them as she activated her ear bud and called the RCMP. She recognized the other man now, Hal Reynolds, one of the corn farmers who had tried to buy her land several times. Neither man spoke as she talked to the dispatcher.

"I hope you got something on these guys, Kitty," she said.

"Miaow." Kitty's mouth unhinged, giving the feline features a crocodile look.

"What the hell is that?" Charles asked, an edge of hysteria to his voice.

The faint hiss of white noise came from the mech cat, and then Charles' voice again, thinner and tinny.

"...brought the bull down today on *my* say-so. He won't be no problem, he's pretty tame."

Hal Reynolds' voice next: "Be a bigger mess, though."

Both men laughed, the guffaws sounding like squawking crows through the mech cat's speakers.

"Thanks, Kitty. Sound off." Laura's hands clenched around the rifle, her knuckles showed white. "Why did you do this?"

"*Why?* You're wasting good land on cattle, that's why." Reynolds spat in the dirt.

A sour smile curled her mouth. "At least I'm feeding people. Your damned corn is feeding American cars, fattening up fuel barons." Laura flicked her eyes to Charles. "Where are the others?" Her gut tightened, waiting for his answer. Had she been betrayed by all of her men?

The bloody stripes on Charles' face made him look fierce. "I sent them to bed. Said it was almost light, nothing would happen." He shrugged.

Tension eased from Laura's shoulders. "Fine."

Headlight beams bounced down the drive. Laura kept the rifle trained on the two men until the Mounties had climbed out of their trucks and taken over. She levered the safety back on and excused herself. Then she ran to the barn.

The padlock dangled from the latch. Laura slipped it off and swung the door open, reaching with her right hand for the light switch. Even from the doorway she could pick out Highland Laddie's bulk amidst the cows. The bull lifted his sleek red head and blinked at her, lowing. At his call, the cows raised their heads, brown eyes sleepy and bewildered.

Laura smiled. The bull and the cows were fine. There would be calves next spring, and her herd would continue to thrive. She would keep her home.

Kitty rubbed against the back of her legs, its rough, whirring purr demanding attention. Laura crouched and scratched the cat's ears. "Hey, there, Kitty. We make a pretty good team, don't we?"

The cat's warm body felt good against her cold fingers.

≈

A RASH OF FLOWERS

Ryan McFadden

The smell of antiseptic couldn't mask the stink of the sick and dying. Victoria Liang rolled her suitcase down the pitted floor, trying to keep up with Doctor Singh, director of the Quesnel Institute.

"Your father and I worked closely together developing the Reintegration Centre in Alert Bay, years before he left the Program." Victoria expected him to ask how her father was doing, but he didn't. He motioned to the dining hall. "Dinner is served at precisely 5pm in the faculty hall," he said. "Mingling with the students is discouraged except under controlled conditions such as lectures and seminars."

She tried peering through one of the windows in the corroding metal doors lining the hallway, but Singh didn't slow for her to get a good look inside. She'd been here thirty minutes and had yet to see students. When they'd recruited Victoria from Western University for a teaching contract, they'd shown her pamphlets of an idyllic campus, red-brick towers, and Recombinants excited to be part of The Program. Those pamphlets were hopelessly outdated.

Doctor Singh turned down a corridor.

Victoria gasped and halted. Corpses lay on cots covered with drab blankets. Feet protruded from beneath, some bare, and others wearing scuffed shoes. Several cots had two bodies piled atop each other.

"We're in the middle of an outbreak," Doctor Singh explained. "Genetic disorders travel quickly through the Recombinant community. The young are especially susceptible since the Program hasn't had a chance to strip them of their genetic mapping."

"There's so many," she said. "Should they be out here?"

"This is a 1200-bed facility with 2800 students. We've used every closet and every alcove for the living. Our gymnasium is full of dead, and the crematorium can only process two corpses every hour, as per government guidelines. It's not ideal, but unfortunately, very little here is." Doctor Singh must've seen her hesitation because he said, "There's no danger of a genetic download once they're dead, Miss Liang."

Recombinants were human except they could transmit their genetic material through touch, though Victoria knew it usually took prolonged and intimate contact for transmission.

Victoria rated only a three on the Peckham Genetic chart, meaning she had a low probability of downloading any of their genetic material. Of course, her father had also been a three, and it hadn't helped him when he developed ALS. He claimed he'd developed ALS because of his genetic flaws, rather than a Recombinant's touch. Victoria knew that he was right.

Victoria had to rush to catch Doctor Singh. Five decades of apparent neglect had left Quesnel Institute crumbling. Paint peeled, missing ceiling panels exposed hissing pipes, and the windows were discoloured.

"We follow strict safety protocols. Disregarding those protocols is grounds for immediate dismissal. If a Recombinant touches your skin, you're legally required to report it to Mrs Richardson. We're isolated here, and procedure is what keeps the outbreaks to a minimum."

"It didn't help them," she said.

"Is this going to be an issue with you, Miss Liang?"

"I didn't mean it like that," she said, even though she did. "I meant how common are the outbreaks?"

"It is a difficult situation. They are a very damaged people."

You didn't answer the question, she thought.

Singh showed her to her room, a modest 3x3 metre area with a bed, a desk, and a window. "I trust you'll find your accommodations satisfactory. For your protection, we have a voluntary curfew during the outbreak. We expect everyone to stay to their rooms except for emergencies." He smiled though it didn't put her at ease. "Your first class will be tomorrow at 8am. I'll have a schedule sent up." He excused himself.

She glanced out her third-story window overlooking the brown, nearly lifeless grounds. She'd hoped that the grass would look like it did in the pamphlets, but grass didn't really grow anywhere.

Quesnel Institute had one outbuilding: a squat cinderblock structure, black smoke belching from twin smoke stacks. The *crematorium.*

Since Doctor Singh had never answered her question about the frequency of outbreaks, she wondered if the black smoke ever stopped rising from those stacks. Barbed wire topped the five-metre-tall brick wall that ringed the campus.

Victoria had been recruited from Southern Ontario to assist in the Recombinant Program. She liked to think that it was because of her teaching abilities, but she knew it probably had more to do with her family name. Either way, she had a chance to make a difference here, both for herself and the Recombinants. The Recombinant Genetic Initiative sprung from the food shortages and gene-ripping experiments of the 20s. Rather than genetically alter food, the biotechnology corporations genetically modified humans to extract more calories from less food. Because the process was new, the program was unrolled to a small segment of the population; mostly the poor and the disenfranchised. Problems manifested in the second generation. They developed the ability to pass genetic information by touch. Hereditary diseases became contagious. First-world governments began segregating the Recombinants and administering a mandatory Reintegration Program to strip them of their downloading ability.

Many Recombinants were illiterate, and those that survived the Program faced huge challenges integrating into society. She could help them, and she hoped that the Program could help her.

A year ago, she'd tested positive for ALS. One day soon, she'd develop the disease and it would kill her as horrendously as it had her father. She was young when he died but the memories would never fade. His last weeks were a nightmare. He couldn't chew, couldn't breathe as his body petrified. That was the way she was going to die.

The Program was only open to Recombinant's, but if it could effectively scrub their genes of their downloading ability, couldn't it give her a direction in finding a cure for her ALS disorder? The doctors back home had told her that the Program was too dangerous, but anything was better than waiting for ALS to kill her muscle by muscle.

She watched the black smoke dissipate on the wind. That smoke was all that was left of those people in the hallway. She climbed into bed fully dressed and hugged her pillow. She'd been at Quesnel for less than an hour and she already doubted that the Program could help anyone.

It was night when she opened her eyes. Lights flashed across her window, and she climbed from bed and glanced outside. A three-person crew patrolled the grounds, shining their flashlights into the rooms.

She didn't know how long she'd slept because there was no clock. They had confiscated her personal electronics when she'd arrived, and the data ports were empty holes above her desk. This place was a prison, not a reintegration centre, and she felt like one of the inmates. She fought back tears. She'd heard dark rumours about these centres, but she had believed them to be some self-serving attempt for media play. Something like this couldn't exist in today's society, and especially not in Canada. Then she remembered the bodies in the hallway.

Victoria needed to talk to someone who would reassure her that this was a good place with good people doing an important job. She needed that or she'd go crazy. But who? Doctor Singh? She wasn't sure what to make of him and his abrupt nature. She sensed that he had taken a disliking to her already.

She needed to find a student or a faculty member and she didn't think she could wait until the morning. Her stomach rumbled and she was hungry—she hadn't eaten in over half a day. If anyone stopped her in her search, she'd claim that she was looking for something to eat. She tried the door, half expecting it to be locked from the outside, but it opened, the empty hallway lit with flickering emergency lights.

Victoria padded down the hall and randomly tried doors, but they were locked. The windows in the doors were dark and she couldn't see inside. She stopped at an old-style ceramic water fountain. The water tasted metallic but she drank anyway.

A girl burst into the corridor. She was sobbing and came running toward Victoria, her bare feet slapping against the linoleum.

"Hello?" Victoria said. The girl stumbled, then caught herself. She couldn't have been older than twelve. She looked like she had escaped from a prison camp: rail thin, short hair, and wearing a faded exam gown.

"I don't know you," the girl said breathlessly. "Are you going to turn me in?"

"I don't know anything about turning anyone in. What's your name?"

"Abhilasha, and I'm not sick." She held out her skeletal hands. "See, steady as a rock." She had ligature marks on her wrists. "I didn't start this outbreak but they're using it as an excuse."

"Who's using it as an excuse?"

"Singh said Sandrove is coming to get me. He's seen what I can do at the crematorium, and now he's afraid. You've got to hide me."

"From who?" Victoria said.

An alarm sounded, a shrill screech that echoed through the halls, and the overhead lights snapped on.

"Please." Abhilasha grabbed Victoria's bare wrist. Her grip was strong despite her seeming frailty. "You know what Sandrove will do to me? They'll hurt me just like they did the others. Please help."

"Others? What others?"

Two Facilitators came through the far door. They carried crackling electric batons and wore gold graphite suits to protect against a Recombinant's touch.

Abhilasha ran; two more blocked the other end of the corridor. She frantically pulled at the locked side doors. Victoria resisted the urge to run; they'd come for the girl, not her.

When they surrounded Abhilasha, she lunged at the first man. He sidestepped, then smacked her in the legs with his club. She cried out and tumbled. He jabbed her with the electrodes. She stiffened and he shocked her again. Then the three men were on her. She was so small next to the bulk of the guards. They fastened her hands behind her back with wire ties.

"Did it touch you?" a Facilitator asked Victoria. She remembered the ligature marks on Abhilasha's arms and the corpses in the hallway. They were completely isolated at the Quesnel Institute. The rules and laws that governed civilized society didn't apply here.

"She didn't touch me," she stuttered, hiding her wrist behind her.

Abhilasha cried in pain when they hauled her to her feet.

"You're hurting her!" Victoria yelled. She tried to approach but the man shoved her back. "She's dangerous. And infectious."

The alarms died but Victoria's ears still rang. When Abhilasha pulled meekly against the Facilitators, they zapped her again and she slumped. They dragged her away.

'Please help.' The words bounced around in Victoria's head. Why hadn't she done something to help the girl?

Doctor Singh arrived with unkempt hair and sleep lines etched on his face. He spoke briefly with a Facilitator before approaching her.

"What are you doing out of your room?"

"I was getting water." She absently scratched her wrist where Abhilasha had grabbed it. When she realized what she was doing, she clasped her arms behind her.

"Did she say anything?" Singh asked. Victoria shook her head and he regarded her sceptically. She suspected if she told him the truth that they'd haul her away too.

"I...the alarms started going. Then the men came and hurt her. They didn't need to do that."

"She's very dangerous, Miss Liang. I fear the Institute may've failed her. In her anger, she wants to infect us. She's a very troubled young lady," he spoke as if with heavy sadness, but the way his gaze darted past her, she didn't believe his sincerity.

"I need to go back to my room," she whispered. "I don't feel well."

"Of course, Miss Liang. Quite a first day. Get some sleep. We'll continue our discussion in my office. 9am."

"I have a class," she said.

"I'll take care of it." He squeezed her shoulder. "Tomorrow will go more smoothly. I promise."

A Facilitator escorted her back to her room. She undressed quickly, and climbed under the sheets with the lights still on. She remembered the fear in Abhilasha's expression: *'Sandrove is coming to get me.'* Why would Abhilasha be terrified of a multinational agricultural corporation? Sandrove held the UN license to monitor and distribute the world's seed supply. It was their food patents that helped the world through the food shortages of the 40s, and no wonder they now aggressively protected their investments.

Her wrist tingled and Victoria's breath caught when she looked at it.

A rash had formed where Abhilasha had touched her. It appeared more a standard skin allergy than the silvery white scales indicative of a download site. It usually took more than a touch to infect someone. Still, Victoria couldn't quell her anxiety and she lay curled in the foetal position.

"Just a rash," she said. Maybe if she just told them the truth they'd help her. *Or they'd shock me with electric batons and bind my wrists.*

She scratched the rash. Victoria wouldn't be able to keep it a secret for long if Abhilasha had genetically transferred to her. Once infected, the two genetic codes would fuse, sometimes exhibiting in minor ways such as a change of eye colour, and other times in far more dangerous manners such as genetic diseases that progressed at an alarming rate. Changes would start manifesting within two days.

The lock on her door snapped shut, and she realized that she had just become a prisoner of the Quesnel Institute.

The sound of the door lock disengaging woke her at sunrise. She hadn't slept much, and when she had drifted off, she dreamt of the black smoke belching from the crematorium smoke stacks.

Abhilasha had said that Singh was afraid of something she'd done at the crematorium. Victoria looked out the window, but nothing caught her eye. Perhaps, if the Quesnel Institute wasn't so hideous and Abhilasha hadn't had rope marks on her wrists, Victoria might've been able to convince herself that everything was okay.

What did Abhilasha leave behind at the crematorium? she wondered. She needed to look. Then, after she'd discovered there was nothing there, she could put the incident behind her. *What if I find something?*

Victoria dressed, resisting the urge to look at her wrist. There was no cure for a genetic download. After all, it wasn't a disease but a melding of genetic code. It was claimed that this merging was too extensive for even the Program to reverse.

Victoria ducked into the hallway. She didn't know her way around but she headed in what seemed a proper direction to reach the crematorium. She found an exit but it was chained shut. She hesitated when she reached a set of double doors leading into an adjoining wing but saw no alternative.

The chaos nearly overwhelmed her when she opened the doors. The hallway was littered with debris. Books, pillows, blankets, papers, clothing. The smell of human misery hit her like a wave. She covered her mouth as she fought back the urge to retch. Facilitators were conducting room shakedowns. A group of stunned teenage boys sat against the wall, their faces bloodied.

"What's happening?" she asked the first boy. He glanced at the Facilitator and remained quiet. Two men tore apart their room while a third documented the discoveries on clipboards.

"This area's in lockdown because of the outbreak. You shouldn't be here," a fourth Facilitator said.

"I'm faculty. What are you doing to these boys?"

"Controlling the outbreak."

She gazed on the three boys. They reminded her of Abhilasha with their short hair and gaunt, defeated look.

"This isn't about an outbreak," she said.

"You must be lost. I'll take you to Doctor Singh's office." The Facilitator took her by the elbow. She considered resisting but she knew what these people were capable of if she pushed too hard. He led her through the chaos, and stopped outside a wooden door with a smoked glass window that had Doctor Singh's name on it. He rapped twice before entering.

Doctor Singh wrote frantically in a notebook. Victoria saw no electronic devices or computers in his office. She realized Quesnel eschewed technology not because of a lack of resources, but because paper was easier to control than electrons.

The Facilitator whispered in the Doctor's ear before excusing himself. Singh put down his pen and motioned for her to sit.

"Quite a first day you had," he said, giving her that smile again. "I'd ask how you're settling in, but I'm sure last night was distressing."

"I'm okay," she lied.

"Are you? I'm getting the impression that you're not adjusting well."

"What did you want to talk to me about?" she asked.

He pursed his lips. "It's my duty as director to properly document all incidents. The Ministry routinely sends investigators from Ottawa and, before I can close this case file, I have to ask you some questions. Obviously, I want you to answer truthfully—this could influence future employment opportunities." He opened a file folder and read the first question, as if he didn't know it already by rote. "Did she touch you?"

"I told you she didn't."

"There's no reason to be uptight, Victoria. Even incidental touching? A hug, or a brush of the shoulder?"

"No."

"What was the nature of your conversation? Be specific."

"She told me her name was Abhilasha, and that she wasn't sick."

"What else?"

"That you were blaming her for the outbreak. She wanted me to look at her hands to show me she wasn't sick."

"The naivety of the young. The hands aren't a good indicator of general health. Especially genetic diseases. Abhilasha's—" He mispronounced her name, "been troubled for several months. The Program isn't easy, for them or us. We caught her two days ago trying to climb the crematorium so she could jump over the wall."

The crematorium.

"They hurt her."

"I read the Facilitator's report. He indicated she was spirited and had to be restrained. I've been assured that it's nothing more than a few bumps and bruises. Regardless, she's being tended in the infirmary. Ironically, she'll receive better treatment than the other students. Squeaky wheel and all that."

Like the students you piled in the hallway yesterday?

"I'd like to see her."

"She's been labelled an Aggressive Offender. She needs to be in seclusion while we dial down her psychological responses."

"You're brainwashing her?"

"Miss Liang, these are board-certified psychiatric procedures. She's a danger to herself and to others. The Program is aggressive, and it can be traumatic. All these controls and procedures are here to safeguard the Program. There are harsh realities, but these realities are necessary measures."

"Why is Sandrove coming here?"

His expression darkened. "I wasn't in favour of hiring you, Victoria, but the Board overruled me. I can't help but feel that your attitude is from a misplaced duty to your father's cause."

"I'm here for myself—not to fight for his causes. I'd like to think that if he knew the condition of these Institutes, he would've tried to stop them."

"Be careful, Miss Liang."

"Why is Sandrove coming here?" she asked again, knowing that she was treading on dangerous ground. Completely isolated, this was Doctor Singh's world.

"I'm not explaining policy to you."

"Tell me why a little girl is terrified of Sandrove, and worse, that *you* facilitated the call."

"Sandrove owns this institute. They own all the Residential schools across Canada. They own everyone in The Program, and because of your contract, they own you. So I advise you to stand back before I'm forced to report our conversation. You've only been here a day. You don't understand the complexities of the situation."

"She told me that Sandrove was scared of her. This whole Institute is just smoke and mirrors to hide systematic abuse."

He laughed mirthlessly. "Sandrove is one of the largest companies on the planet. They hold over 2500 patents for the grain that effectively feeds the world. How could they be concerned about a Recombinant from Quesnel? Don't try to find conspiracies where there are none. That girl was sick."

She could see his anger smouldering just beneath the surface. They said nothing for several long moments while the tension mounted.

Finally, Doctor Singh said, "In light of the recent troubles, Quesnel is being temporarily shuttered. Faculty will be transferred, yourself included. Sandrove will be sending a specialized team to help with the transition, as well as quell the outbreak. They'll be conducting campus-wide DNA checks on all students, faculty, and administrators. That includes you, Miss Liang. This is about more than your job now."

Victoria tried to hide her shock. If Abhilasha had downloaded to her, they'd find her genetic baseline had changed from the sample she gave twenty days earlier.

"Are you...threatening me?" she asked.

"Threatening? I was informing you of policy. You assured me that there was no contact, so you have nothing to worry about, do you?" He picked up his pen and opened his notebook. "You can see yourself out."

Victoria left dazed.

Sandrove would bring their state-of-the-art equipment. Victoria looked at her wrist. The rash hadn't faded, but there was a chance she hadn't been infected. *Maybe*. Her life was based on that maybe. They'd check her DNA. What would they do if they found that Victoria Liang no longer existed, but instead she was a composite of Victoria Liang and Abhilasha?

Victoria had a day to escape, because Sandrove was coming to-morrow.

The hours sped by. She kept expecting her door to lock like it did the first night, but Doctor Singh realized the same thing she did—even if she escaped from the campus, she was a city girl and wouldn't last two days in the wilderness. She paced, trying to concoct a plan to escape Sandrove. She would've called for help if she could've discovered a way to communicate with the outside world. *Except who would come?* Could she talk to the other faculty members? *What would she tell them?* She'd never felt so isolated.

She saw a column of rising dust in the distance as she stared out the window.

Sandrove, she realized.

Victoria wanted to scream her frustration. Her gaze drifted to the black smoke, and she wondered if it ever stopped. What had Abhilasha done at the crematorium that had brought Sandrove running? Were they worried what would happen if the truth leaked about this place? That explanation didn't ring true. This was about more than a scandal, and she needed to find out what Abhilasha had done before Sandrove arrived. She had only five minutes if she was lucky.

She'd have to go out the window. She gave it an exploratory pull. She expected it to be nailed shut, but it flew open. Smoky air swirled in the room. A weathered trellis, entwined with desiccated vine, stretched to the ground; she wasn't sure it would hold her weight.

They're coming for me.

She wiggled onto the window ledge, extending her foot onto the trellis. She shifted her weight until she hung eight metres above the ground. Slivers bit at her hands, and her feet scrabbled for purchase, but the trellis held and she climbed down.

Victoria dashed to the crematorium, kicking up clouds of black dust from the ever-present smoke. Inside two furnaces loomed, one glowing red hot, and the other open. Two men, bandanas over their faces, loaded bodies from a trolley. When they could fit no more, they closed the iron doors and flipped a lever on the wall.

A truck horn blared and her breath caught. *Sandrove is here.* She had nowhere to hide; they'd scan her and discover the truth.

She tucked tight to the building, watching the main gates swing open. A long motorcade drove inside. A transport truck led, the trailer emblazoned with a red Sandrove logo superimposed over a field of wheat. A painted slogan said 'We Grow Your Food'. A fleet of white cargo vans stamped with the Sandrove logo followed. They parked haphazardly on the grounds, doors flew open, and crews hastily unloaded computer and medical equipment. They were accompanied by soldiers in black combat gear.

Doctor Singh greeted the only man wearing a suit. While Singh was animated, the Suit nodded while gazing across the campus. Victoria ducked back before she was spotted, and squeezed her eyes shut, willing herself to blend into the wall. They would find her, it was inevitable, but she had to do something.

Victoria opened her eyes and slid further to the back. Maybe she would take her chances at getting over the barbed wire fence and then into the wilderness. She preferred her odds against exposure over Doctor Singh's supervision.

She blinked. At her feet was a flower, and she scoffed at the absurdity of it. Of all the places, how could a flower bloom here? Flowers were rare, and they certainly didn't grow in the wild, let alone at a desolate place like this. Victoria circled further to the back, and gasped.

A patch of knee-high grasses and wild flowers rippled in the wind. She ran her hands over the top of the grass, then plucked one of the flowers and sniffed it. This was what Abhilasha had been hiding and what had brought Sandrove.

Grass and flowers.

A multinational biotechnology company was terrified of grass— grass that grew wild and wasn't one of their patents.

Four black-garbed soldiers, accompanied by Doctor Singh, rounded the building. Victoria had no escape except up the brick wall, an impossible climb. Singh appeared taken aback to see her but recovered quickly. The soldiers carried stun batons, and the fourth wielded a flame thrower.

"Why am I not surprised you're here, Victoria?"

Victoria studied the pattern of the vegetation and suddenly she recognized it. It was as if someone had traced the outline of a body. If Abhilasha were here, and she lay down, the pattern would match her body. During one of her escape attempts, she must've come here, rested right on that spot. Somehow, her genetic code had altered the plants and given them back what Sandrove and the other companies had taken from them—the ability of natural propagation. Sandrove Corp however, wasn't taking any chances with their grip on the grain market, which was why the one man was carrying a flamethrower.

"I don't want to be a part of this," Victoria said.

That smile again, because he must've known that he'd won. First, they'd test her DNA. Once they did that, they'd know she'd been infected, and then she'd belong to the Recombinant Program. *Ligature marks.* She wished that she hadn't wandered out that first night. If she'd only stayed in her room, none of this would be happening. However, once her eyes were opened, there was no shutting them again.

The soldiers came for her. She hadn't planned on resisting, but just like Abhilasha, she lunged when they reached for her. She punched the first man; he backhanded her to the ground. Before she recovered, they jolted her with electricity. Her back arched and her teeth snapped together.

She wanted to tell them that she'd go with them, but they shocked her with another charge. She convulsed, and her vision flashed. Rather than help her stand, they dragged her away. Her fingers left furrows in the dirt as a last ditch effort to save herself. She felt a blast of heat as they torched the wild grasses behind her.

They pulled her into a tent and stripped her naked. Doctor Singh and the Suit watched. She screamed and fought, but they were professionals and easily overpowered her.

"Her wrist," the doctor said. He knew and now the scanner would confirm it.

They brought her to the DNA scanner. A technician fastened the diodes to her skin while a soldier stood nearby. She complied because she didn't want to be electrocuted again. She entered the chamber and closed her eyes. The scanner warbled, emitting a sound comparable to an unbalanced wheel. The scan lasted twenty seconds. She expected them to drag her forward but no one moved.

The technician frowned. "We need to retest her."

"She's been infected?" Singh asked.

"Don't move," the technician instructed as if she was the cause of the initial reading. She stood motionless while the scanner tested her a second time.

"She's clean," the technician said. "I think."

Singh's expression clouded. "This isn't a subjective decision. She's either been infected or she hasn't."

"There's been no download. But the results don't match exactly with her baseline test."

"Then she's been infected."

"You're not listening. No downloads, no genetic fusion. This is different. Her genes have been...scrubbed."

Singh pushed the technician out of the way so he could inspect the results. He read them, then glanced up at her. "What have you done?" he asked through clenched teeth.

"What's the issue?" the Suit asked.

"Miss Liang's baseline test shows the markers for ALS. Those markers are now gone."

Victoria blinked. *Gone?*

"But no download?" the Suit asked.

"No. She's rigged it somehow. There's no way to strip a person's genes. This is impossible."

He thought it was impossible, Victoria realized, because there was no Program, no way to systematically rewrite a person's entire genetic code.

"Our mandate is to control the Quesnel situation," the Suit interjected. "Return her clothes and get her on the bus with the others."

"I know that—"

"This isn't a debate, Doctor. She hasn't been infected. She's our property for another year. Which means she's getting on the bus with the others and you have a year to figure it out." He motioned and the soldiers returned her clothes and escorted her to the bus. Her legs were weak and her vision pulsed but she managed to climb the bus stairs. She was too exhausted to care about her nakedness. The passengers, who she assumed were the other teachers, wouldn't look at her as they clutched their suitcases, perhaps preferring to keep their eyes closed to Sandrove's policies.

Victoria found an empty seat and dressed. Sandrove quickly and methodically dismantled the Quesnel Institute. Victoria leaned back and watched fire crews patrol the grounds, burning all traces of vegetation. Soldiers monitored the long lines of Recombinants waiting to be scanned. Those that failed were yanked screaming to the trailer. Victoria didn't want to dwell too long on the horrors inside.

Someone knocked on the side of their bus and the driver closed the door. The bus pulled away and Victoria gazed back on the Quesnel Institute. Heavy black smoked clouded the sky. She scratched at the rash on her wrist. *Not a download site.* What was it then? Abhilasha had cured her of her ALS, the same way she had cured the flowers and grasses. She had done what the Program was supposed to do: reset the genes back to their natural state.

Abhilasha had said there were others. Did they have that ability too?

Victoria had to survive a year under Sandrove. They'd be watching her, studying her, trying to discover her involvement. They'd probably shadow her once her contract expired too. She'd have to be careful because any missteps and Sandrove, she was certain, would move to silence her legally, financially, or in ways she didn't want to consider.

For the first time in Victoria's life, time was on her side. Thanks to Abhilasha, the ticking time bomb had been removed from her genes, and she wouldn't wake every morning wondering if that was the day her body would start slowly turning to stone.

Victoria wouldn't waste that gift. Abhilasha probably hadn't realized the power she held. *Enough power to change the world*. Even if she had, she probably wouldn't have wanted that power. She was just a girl who presumably wanted to live a normal life. Victoria knew that there would be other Recombinants that had mutated like Abhilasha. She would find them.

I just have to wait a year.

Victoria closed her eyes and imagined she was in a field of wild flowers.

〜〜

THIS IS THE ICE AGE

Claude Lalumière

Distorted cars litter the bridge, quantum ice fractalling outward from their engines, from the circuits of their dashboards. The ice has burst from their chassis, creating random new configurations of ice, technology, and anatomy.

There was no warning. In one moment the world changed: this is the ice age.

On our bicycles, Mark and I zigzag through the permanently stalled traffic. I try not to stare at the damaged bodies. But Mark is too engrossed to notice my queasiness. Too giddy. Goofy, even. For so many reasons, we were right to leave. Already, his face is brighter.

"Hey, Martha... Did you see that couple in the blue SUV?"

I wish I hadn't: ice snaked around their heads, crushing them together.

"Did you see—"

No, I didn't see. I don't look. At least I try not to. Mark copes in his own way; I can't fault him for doing it differently. He never told me how he lost his parents, and I never told him how I lost mine. I should be numb to such sights by now. In the city, they'd become part of the landscape; we'd ignored them. We'd been too cold to notice. Too cold to care. Barely out of the city, and already we're both thawing—at least a little.

I can't bring myself to tell him to stop. So I just pedal faster. I race off the Jacques Cartier Bridge onto the highway, where the number of cars on the road decreases with distance, leaving Montreal behind, heading for...

...For a new world? Maybe. A different world, at least. I just want us to belong somewhere.

People say the whole planet is like this now. But how can they be sure? Nothing works anymore. No television, no telephones, no computers, no radios. There's no way to communicate.

But they must be right. If the rest of the world were still intact, someone would have rescued us by now. The Army. The United States. Someone. Anyone.

"Martha!"

I look back, and Mark is pedalling hard to catch up to me.

I love how the wind lifts his long, dark hair. His smile is like a little boy's. Already, I've forgiven him for being so morbid, for being so wrapped up in his grotesque passion that he couldn't notice my distress.

Since I've known him, Mark has always protected me. Now he's relaxing about that. I like him even more this way.

He catches up to me, and we stop. We gaze at the transmuted cityscape we are leaving behind.

The sunlight's reflection almost blinds me; ice blankets the Island of Montreal. The skyscrapers of the financial district have been transformed into macabre, twisted spires. The tall downtown hotels bulge with ice—the tumorous limbs of a tentacled leviathan. Like a bed of gems, the city catches the sunlight and glows. Even the heat generated by all this light cannot dispel the cold. The air carries an autumn chill, even though it's mid-July. The ice radiates cold. It never melts; it's so hard it can't even break.

The Quantum Cross, the icon of the city's new order, rests atop Mount Royal.

I close my eyes, not yet ready to cry. Eager to forget. But the memories come anyway.

All I did was shut my eyes, and the world took on a new shape.

Sunday afternoon: my sister in the upstairs bathroom, obsessing over her looks; my parents driving out to the airport to meet Grandma. Me: by the living room window, reading a book, curled up in the coziest armchair. I can't remember which book.

Here's what I remember: the sky was radiantly blue, and the sunlight hit the window with a harsh brightness. I had a slight headache. From reading, from the light.

Music: a trance/jungle mix spun in the CD player.

I closed my eyes. The music stopped abruptly. I heard a weird crunching sound. A cool wave washed over me. My eyes snapped open.

The television looked like a cubist mobile of the Milky Way. In place of the stereo, a crystal statue of a lizard demon crowned with looping horns. The lamps were now surrealist bouquets. Pearly spikes punched through the walls, especially near electrical outlets and light switches.

In the distance, screams rose against the background of cold silence.

I shivered.

My sister, Jocelyne, would never meet her boyfriend again. In the upstairs bathroom I found her skull, neck, and chest skewered by the ice sprouting from her hairdryer.

I hurried outside, onto streets lined with transformed buildings, arrayed with wrecked, deformed vehicles. Wires barbed with ice dangled from poles and walls, lay splattered all over. An instant alien landscape transposed onto a familiar urban grid.

I ran. It was all I could do. I ran, trying to escape the affected zone. I ran. And ran.

Until I stumbled on my parents' car. They were smeared on the seat leather, pulverized by the ice.

I looked around. I'd reached the expressway. As far as I could see, there was evidence of the transformation. For the first time I noticed the new shape of the giant electric cross atop Mount Royal: a violent explosion frozen midblast. Towering over the city, the metamorphosed cross kept a vigil over this new world, claiming dominion.

Since that first day, I hadn't ventured outside. How long ago had that been? I was almost out of food. I awoke sporadically. Sometimes I snacked on stale crackers. I'd exhausted the canned goods. Days ago? Weeks?

In this new ice age, the ceaseless hum of automobile traffic had finally been quieted. The sound of airplanes no longer wafted down from above.

The city was silent. Cold and silent. I felt that silence in the hollow of my bones. The cold had seeped into me, had hardened my insides, had slowed the beat of my heart.

I stared out the window at the unchanging landscape and fell asleep again, to dreams of silent jets falling from the sky.

Even in my dreams, I heard him. Yet, I stayed asleep. The sounds of him taking and releasing his breath replaced the silenced engines.

Eventually, I woke, his presence gradually imprinting itself on me. And then I saw him: sitting on the edge of my bed.

He said, "Hi," neither smiling nor frowning. Waiting.

He had long black hair, and he was maybe a year or two older— almost a man. But he had the face of a little boy, and dark eyes so big that I saw deep into him, saw how he'd been hurt by the coldness of the world. Although I had never met him before, I knew him. In that moment I knew him.

"My name is Mark," he said; louder than a whisper, but without inflection.

I rested my head on his thigh. The touch of his callused fingertips against my scalp shot sparks of warmth through my body, began thawing the cold that had settled within me. I filled my lungs with air. The smell of his sweat eased the flow of my blood. I let go of my breath and moaned drowsily. I fell asleep again. No more falling jets. Finally, I rested.

"Quantum ice. Call it *quantum ice*." Daniel coined the term. The expression stuck. We heard it whispered everywhere by Montrealers who roamed their transfigured city like zombies.

Daniel was Mark's brother, but they were so different. Mark was tall and calm. Handsome. Daniel was short and nervous. Funny looking, in a bad way. And loud. Always chattering, listening to himself rhapsodize. His eyes were wild, always darting here and there, unable to focus on anything, or on anyone.

We saw Daniel infrequently. Usually when he wanted to bum food off his brother. Mark wanted him to stay with us, but, to my relief, Daniel resisted the idea. He'd disappear for days, waiting for Mark to fall asleep before he wandered off.

Daniel had his theory about the ice age. A bomb, he thought. A quantum bomb. The project of the rogue R&D department of some corporate weapons manufacturer. He claimed his blogging community used to keep track of things like that. He said reality—physics— had been changed at a fundamental level. Old technologies no longer worked. We needed a new scientific paradigm. Other things might have changed. Our bodies might not work quite the same way anymore. Nature might have changed. The food chain. The air. Gravity.

Daniel was a bit younger than I was; he certainly couldn't have been more than fifteen. He looked like the type who, before the ice age, got beat up on his way home from school. But the ice age had changed him; it had changed everyone. Daniel spoke with the intensity of the insane. A prophet desperate to convert his audience.

He was full of shit. Daniel was as ignorant as the rest of us. Nobody could know the truth. Maybe the ice had really been caused by aliens, or by magic, or… Maybe God had sneezed, or something. Probably, yes, it had been a bomb. Did it really matter? We couldn't bring back the dead. Besides, there was no proof anything beyond electrical technology had been affected. Fractals of quantum ice had erupted from the cores of our machines, from the wires that carried electricity, from the circuits and engines that fed on electric power. It had taken at most a few seconds between when everything stopped working and when the quantum ice appeared and expanded.

The state of the world: this strange new ice age.

Society had broken down. No social workers swooping down on orphaned kids. We had to take care of ourselves now. No more school. I didn't miss it. I didn't miss the jerks staring at my suddenly developed breasts. I didn't miss the other girls thinking I was too bookish and nerdy to be friends with.

Some fears make you flee, others make you stay. Mark said hundreds of thousands of people had already left the city. Many more must have died. At least a million people, we estimated. In hospitals. In cars. In elevators. On escalators. In front of computers. Using appliances. Snapping photos. Shooting videos. Taking food out of the fridge. Carrying a phone in your pocket meant ice bored into your pelvis. The technology that triggered the ice was everywhere.

The corpses, too, were everywhere. The city should have reeked of rot and decay, but the ice preserved what it touched. I ignored the dead. Every day, no matter where we went, Mark and I saw the bodies claimed by the ice, but we never mentioned them.

There were still thousands of survivors who had stayed behind. They wandered the streets, lost, alone, barely aware of each other. The cold seeped into everyone.

Mark kept me warm, but I still hadn't thawed completely. I hadn't even cried yet. The placid coolness of the ice age, that utter absence of emotion, was almost comforting.

Together, Mark and I fought off the encroaching cold.

We played hide-and-seek in deserted malls. The electronics shops were frozen supernovas.

We explored the metro tunnels. The flames of hand-held torches, reflected on blooms of quantum ice, lit our way.

We walked on rooftops, holding hands, the ice-encrusted city spread below us.

At night, Mark spooned me. We went to bed with our clothes on. I took his hand and slipped it under my shirt, holding it tight against my stomach. He nuzzled my hair.

He always woke before me. Always came back with scavenged food.

One day, maybe we'd kiss.

Daniel acquired followers. He changed his name to Danny Quantum and started believing his own hype. It was creepy, the way these lost people gravitated toward him—obeyed him, even. Orphaned kids. Businessmen in suits that had known better days. Middle-aged women with hungry, desperate looks. Cybergeeks bereft of their only lifeline.

Daniel and his followers gathered in the heart of the city, on Mount Royal, below that monstrous thing that had once been a cross. Daniel turned it into the symbol of his new religion. He didn't use the word *religion*, but that's what it was.

Mark brought me to Daniel's sermons. Daniel didn't use the word *sermon*, but that's what they were.

Feel-good catchphrases tinted with Nietzsche. New Age gobbledy-gook rationalized with scientific jargon. Cyberpunk animism. Catholic pomp sprinkled with evangelical alarmism. Eroticized psychobabble. Robert Bly mixed with Timothy Leary.

We'd climbed up some trees on the outer edge of the area where Danny Quantum's rapt disciples sat and listened to the sermon. We heard every word. Daniel knew how to pitch his voice. He was good at this. Too good.

I said, "Don't tell me you believe any of this nonsense." For the first time, it occurred to me that maybe I couldn't trust Mark. The cold seized my heart.

He said, "Of course not. But somebody has to keep an eye on Daniel. Who else is going to look out for him? Especially now." Mark looked away as he spoke.

As far as Mark was aware, his brother was the only person he knew from before who'd survived the ice age—or who hadn't left without a word in the initial panic. That Daniel was scary, that he was dangerous, Mark wasn't ready to acknowledge.

A fractallized airplane blocked the intersection of St-Laurent and Ste-Catherine, its tail propped up by the ice-encrusted building on the corner, the tip of its nose run through the storefront window of a store the ice had altered beyond recognition. Even the force of a plane crash couldn't shatter the quantum ice. Briefly, I wondered if it might have been Grandma's plane.

Someone had painted a likeness of the transmogrified cross on the hull, with the words *The Quantum Cross of the Ice Age* below it. That day, everywhere we went, we noticed fresh graffiti of the Quantum Cross, on the asphalt of the streets, on store windows, on sidewalks, on brick walls, on concrete blocks.

The next day, Mark and I bicycled out to the airport and stared at the planes: massive dinosaurs with limbs of ice, gore, metal, and plastic.

Before going home—neither my old home nor Mark's, but an abandoned townhouse near McGill University whose windows faced away from Mount Royal—Mark wanted to check in on his little brother. These days, Daniel never left the mountain. His acolytes brought food to him. Brought themselves to him.

I complained. "I'm too tired to bicycle all the way up there." More truthfully, I was increasingly queasy around Daniel and his sycophants, and I was eager to collapse in Mark's arms, even though the sun hadn't set.

He insisted.

So we wound our way up the sinuous gravel path, occasionally encountering Daniel's followers. Despite the cold, they wore white T-shirts—no coats, no jackets, no sweaters. On the shirts, in red, were crude drawings in thick dripping lines: bloody effigies of the Quantum Cross.

When we reached the cross itself, where Daniel's congregation assembled, I noticed that they were all dressed this way, no longer individuals but a hive functioning with a single mind. Danny Quantum's.

First I heard the singing. Mark had just beaten me at croquet for the third game in a row. I looked around, and then I spotted them: to the south of the croquet park, twenty or so people walking down the Jacques Cartier Bridge into Montreal.

One of them pointed at us, and the group headed our way. They waved and kept on singing. I thought I recognized the song. Something from the 1960s. The kind of stuff my parents listened to.

Mark waved back. He said, "Hold on to your mallet. If things get rough, swing for the head and knee them in the crotch."

They seemed harmless. Approximately as many men as women. Long hair. Handmade clothes. Artsy-crafty jewellery. A bunch of latter-day hippies. The song wound down when they reached the edge of the park. I noticed a few of them looked more like bikers. I tightened my grip.

Only one of them came up to us. The one who looked more *Saturday Night Fever* than *Hair*.

He said, "Peace."

Mark said, "Hi. Where are you folks from?"

"I'm from New York City. But we're from all over. Vermont. Ottawa. Maine. Sherbrooke."

Mark asked, "So, it's like this everywhere?"

"It's like this everywhere we've been. The whole world has changed. So many tragic deaths." But he made it sound almost cheerful, like a TV ad.

Mark grunted. Something about Saturday Night Fever—his calculating eyes, his used-car salesman voice—made me distrust him immediately.

"Are you two youngsters alone? It's safer to stay in a large group. We're gathering people to form a commune. To survive in this new age. To repopulate. We need children. Strong, healthy children."

His eyes appraised me, lingering on my hips. I tensed my arms, ready to swing. Mark shifted, his body shielding me from Saturday Night Fever's gaze.

"Well, I wish you folks the best. It sounds like a great project."

"You and your friend should join us. We'd be happy to welcome you." He addressed Mark, but his eyes kept straying to my body.

"Thanks, but we're good here. This is home."

Three of the men in the group were big. Wrestler big. No way Mark and I could stop them if they decided to add me to their baby factory by force.

"Are you sure?"

"Yeah. Anyway, we should be on our way. Good luck." Mark took my hand, and we walked away. We held on to our mallets.

Mark slept. He didn't know, but I'd stayed awake through the previous two nights.

His mouth was slightly open, and he was almost snoring. I loved all of his sounds, even the silly ones. I traced his lips with my index finger; it didn't rouse him, but he moaned. It was a delicious noise.

I stared at him all night, scrutinizing every detail of him.

Dawn broke. As Mark stirred, I pretended to sleep.

The night Danny Quantum and his followers started sacrificing cats and dogs, I told Mark, "We have to leave."

I was bundled under three layers of sweaters, but the cold still bit. Even the heat from the fires around the Quantum Cross couldn't keep me warm. I was tempted to lean into Mark, for warmth, for comfort, but I needed to talk to him, and for that I had to stay focused.

"You tired?"

"No. I mean, go away. Off the island. Leave all this behind. Find somewhere else to live. Somewhere far. Somewhere safer."

I wanted him to say, *Yes, I'll go anywhere with you.*

He said, "Who'll protect Daniel? If I go, he'll just get worse. He'll be lost forever."

"Then talk to him. Make him stop this before . . ."

"It's not that easy. Not that simple. He doesn't hear what he doesn't want to. This is his way of coping. We've all lost too much."

"You know where this is heading. Soon, it'll be people being shish-kebabed to satisfy Danny Quantum's megalomania. To feed the hungry bellies of his flock."

I didn't look at Mark. I didn't want his dark eyes to sway me. I stared at the fires burning at the foot of the Quantum Cross. I looked at Daniel, prancing and shouting. Like the maniac that he was.

"I'm leaving tomorrow morning. Getting away from Daniel. Far away. Find somewhere to grow food. Somewhere with fresh water. Head south, maybe."

Could I leave without Mark? I wanted to kiss him. Would I ever? Even after all we'd shared, the cold still held our hearts in its grip.

"Don't, Martha. Don't make me choose." He turned his face away from mine and stared at his brother in the distance. When he continued, his voice was firm—firm enough to sting. "Besides, we've always lived in the city. What do you know about farming, or even about gathering food in the wild?"

"We can learn how to survive." Despite myself, doubt had crept into my voice.

Was I willing to stay and let this drama play out, despite its inevitable horrors? Wherever I would end up away from here, there might be other Saturday Night Fevers or Danny Quantums. Or maybe even worse.

One of Danny's people handed Mark a wooden stick. There was a roasted, skewered cat on it.

I said, "Are you going to eat that?"

He said, "I'll go with you. Anywhere."

The wind on my face, the smell of grass and trees tickling my nose, I race down the deserted road.

Mark is with me. Laughing. I laugh, too.

In the fields there are cows. Horses. Dogs. Sometimes people.

Some of them wave at us, smiling. Some of them shoot at us, warning us away.

We're not ready to stop yet.

♒

STORM

Gerald Brandt

The aurora sliced across the sky in sheets of green and red. It was bright enough to show the rust and dents on the hood of the pickup truck beneath me. The old truck was Grandpa's, or so he said. It stopped working at the same time everything did, before I was born.

The light shimmered, streaking overhead in its never-ending dance. Stronger today, by the looks of it. Another storm was coming, and we'd have to hide in the old mines until it passed. Grandpa said when he was growing up you could see stars. Millions and billions of them. Or so he said. Now there was just the aurora with a few points of light shining through.

"Come on, boy," I called to Apollo, "time to head back. We'll get some stuff from the house. They'll want us hiding in the mines before morning."

Apollo jumped off the roof behind me, adding another dent to the ones already there. Grandpa said his name was an auspicious one, back from when man travelled in space. The thought of men travelling through space and landing on the moon made me laugh. What a stupid idea. I walked beside Apollo and scratched behind his ears. "Come on, space dog. Let's see if we can get some breakfast before we head down."

Grandpa was waiting for us already, standing on the weathered porch of the house. He wound his watch and looked at it as I got closer.

"Where you been, Alexandria?"

"Nowhere." I sighed loud enough for him to hear. He was the only one that called me that. Everyone else just called me Alex.

"Hmmm. Well, get on in here. We got a long day ahead of us."

Usually the first day in the mines was slow. Everyone getting used to the enclosed space and the air that always seemed somehow sour.

Everyone had a job to do, even me. Though I'd graduated from checking the oil in the lanterns to inventorying the food, it was still menial work. There was never much to do when we were down there.

"You ain't said nothing. What's your mind working on?"

"Nothing."

Grandpa looked at me like I'd grown another head.

"You're gonna have to communicate better than that. It's tough to see attitude through a suit."

A suit? I saw Grandpa grin as soon as the realization hit me. I was heading out during the storm.

"You think you're ready?"

"You bet!" My stomach felt like it was doing back flips.

"Good. We ain't got much, but what we got is ours. Don't want no one stealing it while we ride things out."

Grandpa's been going out during storms since I could remember. I guess my Dad went out, too. He died when I was 3, along with my Mom. I don't remember them, and we don't talk about it.

"What about Apollo?"

"The dog will stay inside with the others. We ain't got no protection for him."

The others were, well, the others. There were ten of us, soon to be eleven. Peter and Naomi had joined us about eight months ago, walking down from further north. They fit right in, helping on the farm. Though the real test was spending a week in the mines. We'd all come through that just fine. The crops hadn't though. We had to dig out anything that grew above the ground and throw it out. It was a bad storm, and they soaked up the radiation like there was no tomorrow. The potatoes were fine though. Damn but I hated potatoes.

"This storm looks to be a light one," Grandpa said. "More chance of people coming to take what ain't theirs." He looked at his watch and gave it another quick wind. "Come on, let's get everyone inside. Then we'll suit up and I'll teach you how to survive out here."

Getting everyone ready was easy. They all knew their jobs pretty well. Leaving Apollo wasn't. When we closed the first set of doors behind us, I could still hear him howling. People weren't going to be too happy about that.

I'd never put on a radiation suit before, though I'd seen Grandpa do it once or twice. He walked me through it and then double checked my work. When we were done, he handed me a roll of tape. Aluminum tape he called it. Shiny metal on one side and sticky on the other.

"I used this stuff lots to seal furnace pipes. Worked like a charm. Now we use it out here. You get a hole in your suit, rip off a piece and tape over the hole. Dunno if it works, but I ain't died yet. Close the hole as best you can and put a couple of layers on."

I put the tape in the utility belt that was part of the suit and eyed Grandpa. His suit had a couple of shiny silver strips on the knees. He grabbed the rifle off the table and turned, ready to go.

The wind started before the sun came up, and got stronger as the time passed. The aurora stayed in the sky, looking redder in the early morning light. Grandpa and I headed down the rocky path to the field. He'd built a shed by the trees, out of wood and covered in whatever metal he could find. Hoods from old cars, corrugated iron. He'd tied them together with wire from the house. He never took anything from the old truck.

I'd played in the shed as a kid, setting up a table and having tea with my stuffed bears. I remember Grandpa coming in sometimes, sitting on the dirt floor and sipping from an empty plastic cup, telling me it was the best tea he'd ever had. By noon we'd all be back in the house, under cover from the full sun.

Now there was an old iron safe in the corner, black with faded gold lettering, filled with food and water. He said we could eat and drink in here, as long as we didn't leave the suits off for too long.

Grandpa took off his suit's hood and got some water from the safe. "We'll wait 'til after the first wave before we head out on patrol. Gotta get the timing right, so we're not out during the next wave," he said. "In these light storms, it ain't so bad, but you don't want to take chances. You'd best have some water, too; it's gonna get hot."

I took off my hood and reached for a bottle. Grandpa stared at me. "What?"

"You're a lot like your Ma, you know, when she was your age. Teenage girls are the worst." He reached out and touched my cheek, pulling my head closer until our foreheads touched. "And the best," he whispered.

"I love you, Grandpa."

"I love you, too." He pulled back. "I always wanted to take you south, you know. They say the magnetic shield's still strong enough down there for people to live normal. I'm too old now, but you're not. When it's time, you go south, you hear?"

I just nodded as he turned away. Just like that, the moment was over. I wished we could have stayed and talked forever.

By the time the sun was fully up, the wind had died to nothing. Everything looked normal, until the first burst hit us. I could see arcs of lightning form between the outside of the shed and the ground, and a hum filled the air. It was like the sun itself reached out to touch the shed. I could tell Grandpa wasn't happy.

"That was pretty strong for a first wave, we'd best wait in here for the next one" he said.

I didn't care. It was exhilarating. The air itself was alive and I could feel my hair stand on end.

When the second burst hit us, the shed seemed to glow for a bit. I could see it even in the bright morning sun.

"Damn."

I looked at Grandpa.

"We need to head back. It ain't safe out here. This storm's a lot stronger than I thought it would be. When I open the door, you run for where the trail goes through the trees. That'll protect you from the next wave a bit. Then you book it for the mine. Don't worry 'bout me. I'll be right behind you."

"I'm staying with you."

"You'll do nothin' of the sort, Alexandria. When I open the door, you run."

Grandpa turned away and undid the latch on the door, swinging it wide open. I grabbed his arm and pulled him out with me. He was old, somewhere around 60, I think. He never would tell me. I pulled him about ten steps before he stopped dead.

When I looked at him, he was staring off to the edge of the field, right along the trail to the mine. His face had hardened and he got a mad look in his eye. I turned and dropped his arm. He unslung the rifle from his shoulder.

"When I say run, you run like you never have before. Head straight for the woods and then for the mine."

"I can't leave you."

The men stood on the trail, watching us. Four of them. Even from here, they didn't look too good. Their skin was red and lumpy, wet-looking. Grandpa took a step towards them. He pushed me to the woods. I swayed away and took the step with him.

"Damn you, Alex. Run! This ain't gonna be nothing but trouble."

My stomach clenched. I swallowed hard. He never called me Alex.

He raised the rifle, not quite pointing at them, but not at the ground either. They each reached in to their bags and pulled out a hand gun.

"You don't know what they'll do to you if they catch you. They're like wild animals. Ain't got no sense of decency."

The next wave hit. A wall of lightning moved towards us from the sun. It hit the men first. Their screams pierced through my suit. I heard a couple of bangs before Grandpa pushed me to the ground and fell on top of me. The front of the wave hit. It felt like I'd run into a dozen hornets nests. They were in my suit, buzzing and crawling and trying to get under my skin. The feeling passed after a minute or so, but Grandpa wouldn't let me up. I lifted my head a bit, and saw two of the men stand up. They left everything behind and ran back to where they came from, I guess.

"Grandpa? They're gone. We can head back to the mine."

He didn't answer.

"Grandpa?"

I rolled over, pushing myself with my left arm and leg. Grandpa had always been a heavy guy, but I never had to roll him off me before. I saw the blood before I'd finished.

It only took me a second to decide what to do. There was no point in putting tape over the bullet hole in his suit. I'd seen enough people hurt in the field to know I had to stop the bleeding before I could move him far. I put my hands under his arms and started dragging him back to the shed. It took longer than it took to get out, and I fell to the floor after I shut and latched the door. It was really hot in the suit, and I could feel the sweat pooling in places that just weren't comfortable.

Another wave hit before I could get my breath back. It didn't feel as bad now that I was inside. I just hoped we'd be protected enough.

When the wave passed, I got the knife from my belt and cut the left side of his suit open. There was a lot of blood. I'd like to say I dealt with it and got the job done, but I guess I'm not that strong. I stared at the blood and the air bubble that formed every time he breathed in. Two more waves hit us before I could move again. I blinked the tears away as best I could; I couldn't wipe them with the suit on. I knew if I could keep it together I could patch Grandpa up enough to get one of the others to fix him.

There wasn't much school, except in the early years. When I got older, Grandpa always said 'you first generation kids. This is all you know, not like your parents who were kids before this happened. You don't need no math or physics. You need to know how to survive in this new world.' So I worked in the fields and studied first aid and survival instead of the other stuff, though Grandpa always insisted on reading and writing.

There was a plastic bag and more water in the safe. I took them out and closed the door again, just in case we had to be here longer than I planned, another twenty minutes at the most. I cut away Grandpa's shirt and washed away what blood I could with the water. The bullet hole was surprisingly small. A bubble still formed every time he breathed and I could hear a whistle from the hole. I folded the plastic bag and placed it over the wound.

The only tape I had was the aluminum stuff. I cut off three pieces and taped down the plastic bag. I looked at it, and added a few more pieces, just to be safe. When he breathed in, the plastic was sucked against the hole, sealing it. When he breathed out, the untaped side let air escape. As the next wave hit, I closed Grandpa's suit and taped shut the cut I made.

I couldn't drag him all the way back. I didn't have the strength. Staying here didn't seem to be much of an option. I pulled some metal and wire from the back of the shed, away from the morning sun so we still had some metal between us and it. I used the wire to tie branches to the metal, and I had a makeshift travois. I went back and cut enough boughs to layer the bottom of the travois. I'd seen the lightning and sparks from the metal shed, and I hoped the branches would add a layer of protection for him.

It was tough getting him on the thing. The first time I rolled him on, he ended up face down. I didn't think that was too good, so I had to roll him off and tried lifting instead. When he got better, he'd have to lose some weight.

I waited in the shed for the next wave to be over, and then opened the door and headed out. The problem was the waves weren't really waves anymore, just a swell in the storm. The second I stepped out I could feel the charge in the air. There wasn't any choice though. I had to get Grandpa back.

The hardest part was starting. The branches bit into the ground, digging furrows into the dirt floor of the shed. My feet slipped as the travois caught on the edge of the door and lurched over. Kicking my toes into the softer soil of the field, I pulled and twisted, releasing the travois from the door frame's grip.

It took ten minutes to get to where the two men lay across the path to the mine. They say you look peaceful when you're dead. These guys didn't. One looked like he fell on his gun. He had a hole in his back the size of my fist. The other one looked like someone had twisted his insides and the expression on his face showed it. His lips were pulled back so far he looked part skeleton already. His teeth were all yellow and black. My stomach flipped over and I forced myself to swallow. Throwing up in the suit just wasn't a good idea. I picked up the guns I found, two of them, and the bags they were carrying and put everything on the travois. Grandpa taught me not to waste anything, there wasn't enough as it was.

I bent over and lifted the travois and started moving into the woods. The trail felt better than the open field. The rising sun was off to my left and the trees threw their long warped shadows across the path. The trail wouldn't last long though, in twenty metres I'd be in the open again until I got to the mine.

I heard more than felt the sharp crack against my ankles. My hands slid off the branches. I flew forward a couple of metres. I landed on my front and rolled over as fast as I could.

Two men stood over Grandpa. One picked up the bags. The other one just looked at me. His face drooped on one side, like his skin had melted, making it look like he was leering.

I grabbed a rock and held it tight.

"Looksh like we got a fighter," he lisped

"Just shoot the kid and let's get the damn food."

I almost dropped the rock. My heart pounded in my chest, filling my ears with a pulsing throb.

Leery took a step closer and pointed his gun at me. I stopped breathing. His finger tightened on the trigger and then stopped. His leer grew more pronounced.

"Not jusht a kid. A girl."

The other guy looked up. "You sure?"

"You think I'm an idiot?"

"Fine, we take her with us."

Leery tucked his gun into his waist band and took another step forward.

I was breathing again. Good big gulps of air that must have cleared my mind a bit, because I was mad. I threw the rock. It didn't have much power behind it, but it hit him in the shoulder.

Leery stood there, his hand on his shoulder, a look of shock on his face. I jumped up and bolted for the trees. Ten steps in, I couldn't see them or the trail.

I didn't stop for a breath. I grabbed a couple more rocks. Still bent over, I angled back to the trail, hoping to come out close to Grandpa. By the time I could see them through the trees, I was sure they'd heard every step I took.

"Watch for the girl."

Leery walked back to where I fell, pulling out his gun.

The other guy flipped the travois over with a grunt. The next wave was rushing at us. Even protected by the trees my skin crawled and my hair stood on end. The bare metal travois started to glow blue. Maybe, if I got lucky...

The wave crashed over us and I stood, my arm cocked. I threw as hard as I could. This time, my aim was true. The rock flew over Grandpa, hitting the guy in the gut. He took a step back, his foot catching the edge of the travois. As he fell, he looked me straight in the eyes. I saw the realization form there. Then his eyes closed and he fell onto the bare metal.

It was over almost right away. A bright flash and the smell of burning flesh and hair. It got Leery's attention too. He didn't see me standing inside the trees. He ran back to his partner, and watched. When the wave settled back into a trough, he rolled the charred body off the travois.

I ran straight for him, the second rock in my hand swinging wildly. The impact with Leery's face numbed my arm. I spun right around as his bones gave way, stumbling until I fell into the trees.

I crawled back to Grandpa, not caring if I ripped my suit as I slid along.

I got Grandpa on the travois again, throwing the bags over his legs.

It took a few more minutes before I could stand and lift the handles. I kept looking at Leery, expecting him to stand up and start the fight again. He never did.

I don't remember much after that. I know it took a long time to get the inner door opened to the mine. They must have thought there was a crazy person trying to get in, with all the banging and screaming I did.

Grandpa didn't make it. They told me he was gone before I even got to the mine. He was all I had left. I still cry myself to sleep some nights; still feel his hand on my cheek.

We left the others a couple of weeks ago, Apollo and me. There wasn't enough food left to last the winter anyhow. Everything in the fields had so much radiation it was worthless. The potatoes still seemed good. Then we got an early frost and snow, and I knew there was no point in staying.

We went south. I don't know if Grandpa was right about people living normal lives down there, but it's what he said. I planned on finding out. I wound the old watch on my wrist and moved on.

≈

LITTLE-CANADA

Kevin Cockle

Uncle Jimmy's condo was third in a row of four, across a pothole-indented street from a row of mirror-image townhouses. I pulled into the driveway of his garage; these places were built in the 1980s, when everyone had cars, even history teachers like Jimmy. I came to a stop in front of the warped garage door, and shook my head; the roof of the garage itself had caved in after years of improper drainage. I pursed my lips. It was frankly disgusting that my father's brother could allow things to have gotten this bad.

I got out of the Mercedes, my Clarks crunching on fresh snow, and looked around as I key-clicked the door locked. Across the street, a few doors down, another collapsed garage sheltered a bunch of kids from a knifing wind. They had a fire going in an old steel drum—very picturesque—and were seated around on dilapidated couches and chairs.

I took the Glock-nine out of my belt holster and held it at my side as I crossed the road. Kids just stared at me, looking hard. I stopped in the middle of the street, and held the gun up so they could see it. My way of telling them I had license to carry-and-kill, so stay the fuck away from my car.

Then I went back to the Benz, popped the trunk, and got out the Christmas bags my wife had prepared for Jimmy.

"Don't mind the mess," Jimmy said as he led me through piles of junk. Old newspapers, boxes, actual hard-cover books stacked in haphazard towers. Off the narrow main-floor hallway, a dining room had been cleared of crap; obviously Jimmy had gotten my emails, even though he'd never answered them.

I set my packages down on an old, sturdy oak table I remembered from Christmases past. I smiled, held out my arms while holding my breath; I couldn't bear the odor of the man when we hugged. His body felt skeletal beneath the multiple layers of clothing he was wearing—a good thirty pounds lighter than when I'd seen him last.

"I'll make tea," Jimmy said as he pulled away. I'd seen the buckets full of snow on his front porch, knew that's what he'd be using for drinking water instead of paying for tap. Either that, or he'd been sneaking down to the Bow River to get untreated stuff, if he could find it unfrozen. I shook my head and gave him a pre-paid metre card.

"Use that instead," I said. "And have a shower—there's like a thousand New Dollars on that thing. You still have a shower, don't you?"

Jimmy grinned—a weird composite of friendliness and resentment and irony. You couldn't ever get a straight expression out of the man. "Still got the shower," he acknowledged. "No idea if it still works."

"Well, give it a shot, or this is going to be a short visit."

He nodded, and headed upstairs. I took the Tupperware turkey and other goodies out of one of the bags, and made my way into the kitchen—praying the man still had a working microwave.

Jesus Jimmy, I thought. Pull yourself together.

I get that Jim's discouraged. He's what—65, 66 now? Wife died ten years ago. Humanities department at the U of C closed its doors due to lack of enrollment, and there's Jim with a PhD in history of all things. "Smartest man you will ever know," my dad used to say. Yeah, so smart he spent his whole life getting credentialed in stuff any kid in the world can pull up on his phone now.

Couldn't even teach after that—not with schools only covering grades 1-to-3 before the corporate partnerships kick in. Plenty of people qualified to teach kids the alphabet: PhD's need not apply. Still, you'd think the smartest man in the world could find *something* to do. Far as I knew, Jimmy'd just dug in with his investments and inheritance—plus money Dad used to send him—and watched as his garage roof caved in.

I heard the shower running upstairs and felt relieved. Eating dinner would have been a serious chore with the smell of unwashed Jimmy across the table.

I rummaged through the kitchen drawers, found plates and silverware. I got things together while Jimmy made himself presentable and we met back in the dining room about twenty minutes later.

"Mm. Good," Uncle Jim mumbled around mouthfuls of my wife's turkey. It was good, actually; I nodded in agreement. The turkey aroma mixed with the odor of mildewed books and unwashed clothes. It was cold in the dining room. I kept my coat on while we ate, though Jim seemed used to it.

"War in Brazil," Jim said after a while, eyeing me.

"Oh yeah?" I said. I didn't know; took his word for it. Here we go, I thought.

"Separatist provincials attacking Petro-dyne installations in the deep Amazon, trying to protect the rain-forest. Mercenary units called in from Oklahoma...how can you not know this?"

"Seriously? Jimmy, have you seen the potholes in your street outside? How 'bout your garage? Who gives a crap about Brazil? Sounds like a bunch of pirates. Why don't they just nuke 'em?" Classic Jimmy, wouldn't pay for water, but he still had internet, or was stealing signal from somewhere. He always knew when some Bolivian village was being relocated, or why Nigerian terrorists were blowing up some refinery. Personally, once companies had their own tactical nukes, I figured that was pretty much the last word. Petro-Dyne would just fry the bastards like the bio-agro land-holding firms had smoked the African insurgents, or the shipping combines had melted the Somalis, and bam: problem solved. Statism was a lost cause, and who gave a crap anyway? The rain forest! I thought that had been paved years ago, and here's Jimmy, obsessing over it.

Jimmy chewed his food, sullen. I changed the subject.

"I brought wine," I said.

Jimmy circled his fork in the air as he chewed, the international sign for "let's pop that cork".

"Still follow the Flames?" I asked as I poured a damn good Syrah into Jim's coffee cup. Red with turkey, I know—but Uncle Jim had always been partial to reds. Didn't seem like the time or place to observe wine formality.

"Nah," he grunted. "Crap hockey these days. Too many commercial breaks. No flow."

"I hear you."

"Hey...you still got that—what the hell—that team with the chicks playing football in their underwear?"

I smirked. I was a limited partner in an ownership group for a Vancouver-based bikini football team. Jim knew it was bikinis, not underwear. I could tell he was getting ready to bust my balls, so I played along. "Yes sir, that I do," I said.

"Wow. Your dad would've been proud."

"My dad had season's tickets, Jim."

"You paying those girls yet?"

"Jimmy," I shook my head. He just didn't get it. "I got a corner-back—smokin' little blonde rockstar…she's got over a *million* twitter followers."

"So…does that mean you don't pay these girls?"

"It means she makes six figures on her own, doing endorsement deals that we set up for her. No, we don't pay her to play cornerback. It would be an insult to pay her to play cornerback. We do, however, pay her insurance."

Jimmy pursed his lips, obviously not buying it.

"Any time you want," I pushed on, gesturing with my fork so he'd know I was serious, "I'll fly you out, and we'll watch a game from the owner's box. Hell, we'll watch all the games. You'll be hooked."

"I can get all the porn I want on the internet."

I rolled my eyes. Porn!

That was the way of it. We drank, ate, tried to keep the talk small. You'd think sports would be safe, but it could be a minefield. For instance, Calgary had its own NFL team now, which, as a sports-agent, I followed with intense interest, but I knew better than to mention it. It would just start Jim on one of his American-bashing rants, and frankly, I didn't want to hear it. My wife was from Texas, our kids went to school down there. We lived in Arizona half the year. I couldn't relate to Jimmy's fantasy-Canada—a place that sure as hell didn't exist now, and may not have existed even when Jim thought it had.

We made it through dinner in fits and starts, neither one of us wanting to talk, but in the silences, we could hear the wind whistling outside and it was just too damn eerie. I told Jimmy to sit while I cleared the dishes, then I sat back down at the table with the presents.

Jimmy sort of snorted, looked away.

"What?" I said.

"I'm 66 years old," Jim said, looking up at me with watery eyes. "Presents."

"Whatever, you old bastard. Here." I handed him a good-sized box wrapped in candycane-striped paper with a curly green bow. My wife was all about Christmas, would not hear of me coming up here with

unwrapped gifts.

Jimmy unwrapped it like he didn't want to tear any paper, it looked so nice. Inside was a 1/48 scale model Mitsubishi Ki-46 Japanese command recon plane from WWII. I'd had to order it from Japan; there was nothing like it in the North American retail space.

Jimmy whistled softly and gazed at the picture on the box. He went into professor mode, and I went into little-kid mode—like I used to when he would tell me history stories. "Yeah, the Ki-46. Such a beautiful, beautiful design—like the Spitfire that way. One of the few purpose-built reconnaissance planes from that period.Spectacular performance. It could fly over American positions with impunity until late in the war. Nothing could touch it. Even the Germans had considered building it under license."

"Figured you'd like it." Jimmy loved World War II stuff, had built models of all the great planes, and I remembered thinking how neat they were when I was a kid. But now, I could never understand how he could be so consumed with it, spend so much time studying it. We never even took the World Wars in school. Google World War II, and you need to go ten pages in before you even get any hits, I mean…what a waste of time. But the plane was the right gift. I remembered him talking about the Ki-46 a few times—wishing he could find it. They just didn't have World War II stuff in the stores anymore. Jimmy was a long time turning the box over and over, reading the various descriptions, imagining those long, fluid lines in flight.

"Merry Christmas," I said.

Jim refilled our wine glasses. "I love the Ki-46, boyo," he grinned. "You're a clever kid, bringing me a model."

I shrugged.

"Nothing like giving the old man a project, right? Something to look forward to."

I made a facial expression that was equivalent to a shrug.

"Did you actually bring what I asked for?"

I sipped my wine. "Can we look at something else first?"

"If you insist."

"Yeah, I insist." I went back into the gift bag and brought out a folder with a red and white Maple Leaf design on the cover. I slid that across the table for Jim and watched as he fingered it open.

"Chindia?" He said, raising overgrown eyebrows at me.

"It's easier than ever now," I said, summoning my sales talent. "There's good jobs there, Jim—call centre stuff, legal boiler-plate, you name it. Some sit-down factory stuff you could still do. Transportation to get there is 100% subsidized now, and you get a credit for your transit expense to Vancouver. China's dropped the restriction on capital flows so you can transfer your savings over…it's a breeze. Cost of living is half what it is here; you can get medical again."

"I'll need medical, breathing that soup they use for air."

"Half a million Canadians transferred over last year, Jim. Two million Americans. You don't even have to alter citizenship. People are starting over. It's good over there."

"Two and a half million, low-income, fungible, disenfranchised labour units transferred over, Todd. They're never coming back. Makes for a nice clean, green, law-abiding Head-Office State here though, don't it? I remember as a young man, kids from P.E.I. coming to Alberta to work the oil sands; we never dreamed we'd one day have to move to India to follow the jobs. Thanks, free-trade!"

"Ah, Jesus!"

"Living in Asian work camps like Birkenau on steroids."

"It's not like that."

"It is like that!"

"How would you know?"

"How do you not know?"

"Oh for Christ's sake," I took another belt of wine, taking a moment to let my temper simmer down. Jim and his fucking 'work camps'. Jesus!

"Uncle Jim, you can't stay here. Minimum—I'm talking *minimum* it takes to live in Canada—let alone Calgary—is a 100k a year, and you aren't even close." I paused to let that fact sink in. I didn't remind him that women who played football in their bikinis made more money than history teachers now. "You're alone on this block. Everyone else has gone…they're going to bulldoze this complex! Everyone is doing this, Jim. Jesus, you can get started again! Pick yourself up! You don't have to live like this."

Jimmy smiled at me. He smiled when he was hurt, when he was angry. I wondered if he ever smiled when he was happy.

He looked at the Ki-46, ran a hand over the picture of the plane in flight on the box. "You know, your aunt died upstairs."

Here we go. I nodded; let him continue.

"Cancer. I could've gotten her into the centre, but she said it would break us. She said 'what's the point of curing me if it kills you?' That's really what it comes down to."

I didn't know what to say. I never knew what to say when he got like this.

Jimmy went on, his voice getting husky. "My grandfather, you know...he fought in WWII. Bomber pilot. The whole country put itself on hold, pulled together as one, worked together to defeat fascism at an incredible cost. You know why they made the sacrifices they did?"

I shook my head. "Okay professor—I'll play. Why did your grand-father make superhuman sacrifices to defeat fascism?"

Jimmy leaned in on his elbows. "To create a world where people had intrinsic value, Todd. A value that can't be assigned by the market-place. A value that meant you didn't just learn how to read, but you learned how magnificent it was to read, how majestic—and you didn't have to be a king or a queen to appreciate that. A value that meant you couldn't put people in a concentration camp no matter what the excuse, or how efficient it might be. A value that meant when you got sick, you could see a doctor no questions asked, because being human was enough. That war shaped a world, and you threw it all away."

"Hey..."

"My grandfather never would have flown those planes, if he'd known that you were going to be the beneficiary."

Here we go. "Right. Because I happen to think art is a scam. We've been through this before. Somehow I don't think your grandfather would have given a shit."

Jimmy sat back in his chair, gave me another, different smile. He said: "We waited until Deborah couldn't take the pain anymore. Ran out of opiates. She said she'd had enough."

"Look...I know that was hell..."

"And then I killed her."

I stared at him to see if he was kidding, or fucking with me or what. But Uncle Jimmy wasn't even smiling then, just looking at me hard with those cloudy eyes of his.

"You killed her?" I said.

"Yeah. With these," he held up his hands. Big, knobby, long-fin-gered hands. He could've done it. He'd been a hell of a hockey player in his youth—had the wrists to prove it.

"Well…I don't know what you want me to say to that," I said at last. What else could I say?

"Yeah, I know. My grandfather though? He'd have been shocked. He'd have been absolutely outraged. That's the difference boyo. He damn well would have given a shit."

Look up the phrase "awkward silence" online, and you'll see a picture of me and my uncle Jimmy right then. I stared at the wood-grain on the table. Jimmy stared at me.

"Okay," I said at last. I reached down for the gift bag one last time. "Your grandfather would've been shocked at that, but my dad? He wouldn't have stood for this." I pulled out Jimmy's gift, the one he'd requested three Christmases ago. That was the last time he'd ever returned one of my emails, and then only to say: "Don't come if you don't bring one."

It was an original, certified-authentic, hand-polished, WWII vintage, Luger semi-automatic pistol. Owned by a Waffen SS captain circa 1944. I could smell the machine-oil on it, sense its deadliness as I felt its weight. In its own lethal way, it was as elegant as that Japanese warplane, and I suppose that's why Jimmy had wanted it. I'd ordered it from the same memorabilia dealer in Tokyo that had sourced the model kit for me.

I put it on the table between us. Still couldn't look at him.

"They say the English in the Indian Little-Canadas is great—better than here," I said quietly.

"Thanks Todd," Jimmy said. The edge had gone from his voice. He really was grateful. "Don't think a sixteen hour shift in a call-centre is in the cards for me."

He took up the gun, staring at it the way he'd looked at the Ki-46. I knew the object meant a lot more to him than it ever could mean to me. He knew so much about that stuff.

"This is bullshit," I said, shaking my head.

"I'm already a ghost, boyo. I'm out of tune."

"I don't know what you mean."

"I know. Kind of proves my point."

I nodded. I was done here. I'm sorry dad, I thought. I tried. This was Jimmy's call all the way.

I stood up from the table, put my hands in my coat pockets. "You going to finish the plane?"

Jimmy looked at the Ki-46. "Yeah," he said. "I think I will." He looked up at me, and I just got this sense of relaxation from him. He smiled at me with the first smile of his that I recognized as being just and only what it appeared to be.

I nodded again, and left him to his history.

SPIRIT DANCE

Douglas Smith

In the beginning of things, men were as animals and animals as men.—Cree legend

Vera made a warding sign as I entered the store, my hound Gelert trailing behind me. She pretended to wipe her hands on her faded blue apron, but I caught the dance of her fingers.

"Hello, Vera. It's been a while," I said.

"Yes, yes it has, Mr. Blaidd," she said too quickly, not returning my smile. Turning from where she'd been refilling a food bin, she addressed her husband. "I gotta check something in the back, Ed." Almost running, she slipped behind the long wooden counter and into the storeroom at the rear of the store.

Edward Two Rivers leaned on the counter beside the cash register, a newspaper spread in front of him, his long gray hair spilling onto the pages. He watched her leave then smiled at me.

"Ouch," I said.

"You still spook her," he chuckled.

"Are you going to run and hide too?" I asked, grinning.

The black eyes narrowed, but his smile remained. "Vera's a white woman. My people have told legends of the Heroka for generations, Grey Legs. I grew up with those stories. I've known others of your kind...and I think I still know you, even if it's been...what?"

"Four years," I said.

"Four years since you left Wawa." He took my offered hand in a strong grip.

"Good to see you, Ed," I said.

"You too, Gwyn." Leaning over the counter, he patted Gelert's huge head. "And good to see you as well, you great beast." Gelert's tail wagged furiously, threatening a display of pop cans. Ed looked back to me. "Did you fly in?"

I nodded. "I landed on Deer's Pond, set up camp on the north shore, then we hiked in. Get my email?"

"Yeah. I made you up some supplies and a map to the truck driver's cabin." He nodded toward a small pile of brown paper packages in the corner, wrapped in twine.

"Thanks. What do I owe you?"

"I'll run a tab. You'll be here a while. Not the best homecoming for you, I guess."

"Could be better. Any word of Robert?"

Ed nodded. "I showed your friend's picture around. He was definitely here in Wawa for the funerals, but kept to himself pretty much. Found someone who talked to him, though. She said he left town about two days ago, but he'd be back. Something about unfinished business here."

"Any idea where he went?"

"Just a guess, but I'd say the Muskokas."

"Why?" I asked, puzzled. The Muskokas were a cottage and resort district a two-hour drive north of Toronto, and a good seven hundred kilometres from Wawa.

He held up a finger for an answer and started flipping through the newspaper. Gelert curled beside our supplies. I waited, sifting through the smells of grains and fruit, wood and burlap—and humans. Vera was muttering in the storeroom at the back. I could have made out her words if I had wanted to, but I didn't.

Ed began reading. "'Local logging baron Jonathan Conrad and his bodyguard were found dead early yesterday morning, outside his lodge in the Muskokas.'"

Footsteps outside announced a customer to me before the bell over the door brought Ed's head up from the paper. She looked early twenties, tall and slim with gray green eyes and long dark hair that wasn't sure where it wanted to rest. Flashing a quick smile at Ed, she moved to the shelves of canned goods.

"Morning, Leiddia," Ed said, eyebrows shooting up.

"Morning, Ed," she replied, then looked at me. A familiar aura tinged her outline. She kept looking as I turned back to Ed.

Ed continued reading, his voice lower. "It says Conrad's wife had gone into town for the evening. She found the bodies about two yes-terday morning."

"How'd he die?" I asked.

The woman Ed called Leiddia turned toward Ed, but I could feel her eyes still on me. I didn't look at her.

"They're bringing the coroner up from Toronto. The cops figure some kind of animal attack, judging from the wounds. They say it was big whatever it was." Ed looked up at me. "Maybe a bear."

I swore silently at that last bit of news. "Guess the environmental-ists won't grieve much."

"The parents of those three boys won't," Leiddia said, stepping closer to the counter. "He killed them, even if he didn't drive the truck. Everybody knows he gave the order."

"Got off though," sighed Ed. "So'd the truck driver. Accident, they said. Bad brakes. Conrad got a five-hundred dollar fine for not main-taining his trucks."

I had heard about the truck incident three days ago. Conrad had been chairman for a company that owned the paper mill outside Wawa and several logging operations north of Lake Superior. Recently, the company had faced escalating pressure from local residents, native bands, and environmental groups. Protests centred on the company's clear cutting methods and general contempt for the old growth forest. The confrontation climaxed when a group of students and other pro-testers blockaded the road leading to the current clear cutting target.

The first truck to reach the blockade had backed off, driving fifteen miles back to camp in reverse. Two hours later, the next truck arrived. This one hadn't stopped.

The kids hadn't used logs or fallen trees to block the road. They hadn't piled boulders, or sprinkled the road with tire punctures. They had just stood across it, arms linked, singing.

The truck slammed into them, killing three local students. A female protestor from out-of-town also died.

"Five hundred dollars," said Ed, shaking his head.

"I went to college with one of them," Leiddia said quietly.

I looked at her, confirming my first impression of the familiar aura. "Were you there?"

She shook her head. "My stepfather works in the mill. He wouldn't let me go." She stared at me hard.

Ed cleared his throat. "Uh, Grey Legs, this is Leiddia Barker. Leiddia, this is an old friend, Gwyn Blaidd. Gwyn's the friend of Mr. Arcas I mentioned."

"You know Robert?" she asked.

The door to the store opened before I could reply. A man stood with one foot in the store, hand still on the door. "Leiddia!" he barked, "Hurry up!"

She didn't look at him. "I'm coming," she snapped, thumping some cans on the counter.

As Ed rang up the order, I looked the man over. Late forties, maybe six feet, a paunch and thinning black hair slicked back. Gelert growled at him, and I didn't stop him. I didn't like his smell.

Leiddia paid Ed, took the bag of groceries, and turned to the door. Not waiting for her, the man let the door slam, walked to a beat-up Cutlass parked in front and got in. He had never even looked my way. As Leiddia shifted the bag to her other arm, I stepped past her and opened the door.

"Thanks," she said, stepping through. Hesitating, she looked at the car, then back at me. "Blaidd. That's a strange name."

"It's Welsh."

"Why does Ed call you Grey Legs?"

The car's horn blared. Jumping out of the car, he moved quickly toward us, fists clenched. "Damn it! What're you doing?" he snarled at her, then spun to face me. "Who the hell are you, mister? I…" His voice trailed off.

"Hello, Tom," I said. "Long time."

He swallowed hard. "Gwyn! I didn't know you were back."

I smiled. "I didn't figure our past relationship called for a postcard."

"Uh, yeah. Uh, Leiddia, don't be too long. I gotta get to work." He turned and got back in the Olds, with a glance over his shoulder.

She raised an eyebrow, staring after him. "Never seen anything affect old Tommy like that." She looked me up and down. "Will I see you again?"

"I'm camping by Deer's Pond. North shore," I said.

Smiling a cat-with-the-canary smile, she strolled casually to the car and got in. They drove off, and I went back inside.

"So what do you think of our Leiddia?" Ed asked.

"I think I just passed some kind of test. She's the one who talked to Robert?"

"Yeah. I said an old friend of his was coming into town and wanted to surprise him. That's when she told me about him leaving." He looked puzzled. "Weird her showing up just as you arrive. She's not in town much. You gonna go see her?"

"I'm guessing she'll find me. How does Tom Barker come to be her stepfather?"

Ed grimaced. "She and her mom moved here about two years ago. The mother had some money and a good property, which got Tom interested. Don't know what she saw in him."

"He's still the same?"

"Grade-A asshole? Yeah, plus there's been some incidents with him and her mother. Cops at the house, but she's never laid any charges."

"Physical abuse?"

He nodded. "Vera knows the night nurse at Mercy. The mother's been in a few times, always with a story about some accident around the home. The nurse said it looked more like beatings." Ed looked grim, then thoughtful. "Far as I know, he leaves the girl alone."

"From what I saw," I said, picking up my supplies and moving to the door, "pushing Leiddia too far would be very inadvisable. He might wake something."

Ed's eyes narrowed. "What'd you see in her?"

"She has the Mark," I said quietly. Opening the door, I stepped out into the street after Gelert, not waiting for Ed's reply.

The first frost had come to Wawa early. Gelert and I hiked back through fall colours, crisp air, and no mosquitoes, reaching our campsite overlooking Deer's Pond just before sunset.

That night, spirits of the firelight danced around me through the trees as the rising moon silvered the smooth surface of the water. With Gelert snoring softly beside me, other spirits danced through my thoughts.

I didn't want them to dance. I didn't want them to even exist. But spirits have their own views on these matters, and are very persistent when they feel it's time for a performance. These ghosts went back fifteen years. The prompting for tonight's tango was much more recent.

Dance, spirits.

Three days before, I had been many miles north. That day, I had stood by the heavy wooden railing of the broad stone promenade running the length of Cil y Blaidd, watching a small seaplane shatter the glass of the lake below. Part carved, part hung from a rocky slope of forest, Cil y Blaidd is a sprawling wood and stone structure overlooking a lake in far northern Ontario. The name is Welsh, for Wolf's Lair.

Built to my design years ago as an occasional retreat from civilization, recently it had become my permanent home. Or perhaps it was my act of retreat that had become permanent.

Accessible only by seaplane, Cil y Blaidd is invisible from the air. Those who had built it had been flown in at night, stayed until completion, and then were flown out again at night. I had piloted the plane.

Only three other people knew its location. As I watched the plane taxi to shore, I wondered which of the three it carried.

The plane pulled up to a long dock hidden from above by arching willow branches. A huge male figure emerged and strode along the dock to stone steps carved from the cliff face.

Well, it's not Estelle, I thought, ignoring the resentment this brought even after fifteen years. Too far to see if it was Robert or Michel. My visitor looked up, searching the slope as he climbed. Our eyes met and he raised a meaty hand to remove and wave a cloth cap, revealing a mass of red curls.

"Lo, Mitch," I called down as I waved back, wondering briefly at my feeling of relief. Turning from the railing, I headed through the house to greet Michel Ducharmes, the Red Bull, and current head of the Circle of the Heroka.

Opening huge oaken front doors, I stepped out onto a graveled path as he emerged from the woods trailed by two great stags, their antlers barely missing trees on either side. As Mitch shoved out a hand to me, the stags turned to the forest, lowering their heads toward trailing gray shadows.

"A fitting honour guard," I commented.

"They felt I needed protection from your troops," he replied, jerking a thumb at six timber wolves hovering at the tree edge.

"Garm, Fenrir, take off. He's a friend," I said, addressing the two largest wolves. They glanced briefly at Mitch, then all six padded into the forest.

Inside, he settled his bulk into an oversized chair, taking the proffered Scotch. "You know this lake doesn't show on any map?" he said, downing the drink, "Not even those the Ministry of the Environment makes from satellite photos."

"Maybe the MOE needs better computers," I offered.

He glanced to where my array of computers resided. "Or better security on the systems they do have."

I shrugged, not rising to the bait.

Silence. He cleared his throat, staring out at the lake. "Speaking of security…"

"I hope you didn't fly up here to pitch that at me again," I interrupted. "I'm out. No more. You've plenty of predator class to recruit for your dirty little jobs."

He reddened.

"Besides," I continued, "Robbie runs security in the Circle. I doubt he'd be thrilled about this."

He said nothing, fixing me with the hot angry stare of the challenged bull. When he finally spoke, his voice was level. "Two years ago, Robert became active with an environmental protest group."

"So what? Lots of us are activists. It goes with the territory. I got Stelle into it. We used to try to recruit Robbie."

"Seen Robert lately?" he asked, too casually.

I snorted. "Mitch, I haven't talked to him or Stelle in eight years. What're you driving at? Is this about Robbie?"

He sighed and nodded, suddenly looking very old. I had never thought of him as old before.

"Gwyn," he said quietly, "Our Robert has threatened to kill two men. One is an important man, the type who attracts attention." He'd been looking at the empty glass in his hand. Now he looked up at me. "I need your help, Gwyn. To find Robbie first."

I shut up then and listened as Mitch told of the logging protests, the blockade, the protestors' deaths, and of Robbie's threat to kill Conrad and the truck driver. He talked and pleaded, pleaded and talked.

Finally, he paused. "There's something else," he said, staring out at the lake. "CSIS knows of this. According to our mole, somebody in CSIS is leaking intelligence on the Heroka to an outside party." He looked back to me. "Gwyn, we think someone's resurrected the Tainchel."

Involuntarily, I bared my teeth. Damn it. I questioned him on his source, what evidence he had, how recent was the tip, but he knew he had me. Finally, I'd agreed, because of the Tainchel angle, and because Robbie had been a friend and Mitch still was. That's what I'd told myself at the time. Now, watching the spirits dance in the firelight, I knew I'd done it for someone else.

Dance, spirits, dance.

Estelle and I had been an item for quite a while, back when I ran security in the northeast. For centuries, the Heroka were nothing more than creatures of legend. Security had mostly amounted to making sure things stayed that way. Then came the Tainchel, a covert operation of the federal intelligence agency CSIS, formed as we later learned, with the single goal of tracking down and capturing the Heroka. For scientific purposes.

Tainchel. Old Scottish term: Armed men advancing in a line through a forest to flush out and kill wolves.

We lost quite a few before we caught on. They'd developed specialized scanners from tests on early victims. Subtle differences in alpha wave patterns, infrared readings, and metabolic rates gave us away, even in crowded cities.

Then they got careless, and we became aware. I leaked word about a meeting that the Circle of the Heroka planned for an isolated spot. At the next full moon, of course. I figured they'd expect that.

Twenty of the Tainchel walked into the ambush, armed mostly with tranquilizer rifles. They didn't walk out. They'd encountered the Heroka before, but never predators. Wolves, bears, the big cats, birds of prey. We didn't take prisoners.

After, we contacted Justice and CSIS. I sent a list of the remaining Tainchel agents, present locations, recent activities, and a note saying, "We know who you are. We know where you are. We will kill to protect ourselves. Back off."

They backed off. CSIS disbanded the Tainchel, and an uneasy truce began.

The truce lasted. Estelle and I didn't. She argued against the ambush, the killings. I argued that we fought for our existence. In the end, we just argued.

Robert and I had been friends for years, and through me, he had come to know Estelle. After I exited the scene, the two of them became more than friends. About then, I resigned from the Circle. Robbie replaced me there too.

Dance, spirits. Dance with the beasts of the night.

Growling, Gelert turned toward a dim rustle in the forest. I gave the dog a mental command to lie down again. Stealth was not my intruder's aim. I stood as Leiddia stepped out of the trees, stopping at the edge of the firelight.

She smiled. "Hello again."

"Hi yourself."

"You don't seem surprised," she said as she approached.

"I had the feeling you wanted to tell me something."

"Yep," she said, "You're a wolf."

I tried to remain expressionless. "Excuse me?"

She walked to the opposite side of the fire and sat on the ground, grinning. "Blaidd. I looked it up. It's Welsh for wolf."

"Oh, right. I forgot I'd told you."

I sat again, as Gelert came over to nuzzle her. She took his huge head in both hands, rubbing him behind the ears. "And what's your name?"

I told her, and she made a face. "Gelert was the legendary hound of Prince Llewellyn of Wales," I explained.

"Hmm. So, why does Ed call you Grey Legs?"

I chuckled. "The Ojibwa and the Cree believe using its name will attract a wolf. So they call it Grey Legs, Grey Coat, Golden Tooth, Silent One. Ever since I told him what my name meant, he's called me that, as a joke."

She smiled again. "So he thinks you're a wolf, too."

I grinned back. In the store, I'd been so intent on her aura of the Mark, I'd overlooked how attractive she was. Gelert liked her too, always a good sign.

She stared at me. "You *are* a wolf."

I remained silent.

"What's it like," she asked, "to change, to be that way?"

"You do know, don't you? How?"

"Your friend, Robert. We met during the funerals at the church. Something about me fascinated him. He kept staring at me."

"Can't say I blame him."

"It wasn't that kind of interest, but thanks," she said smiling. "Anyway, I knew he was different too, but I didn't know what it was."

She shifted her gaze to the flames. "He was so upset, so sad. He said he had something to tell me, about me. That something must be added for what was lost. I didn't understand, but I wasn't afraid of him. Somehow, I knew I could trust him."

I smiled. That was Robbie—the size of a grizzly, but women treated him like a big teddy bear.

"At the cemetery after the burials, we walked together. We found a big stone just inside the forest, and sat and talked. Well, he talked. I just listened. He told me of the Heroka, of how you are a race older than man. How you each are linked to an animal species."

I nodded. "We have many names. The Ojibwa called us the Heroka, or Earth Spirits. They believed my people were ancestrally related to different animals, similar to totems. We bear traits and abilities of our totem animal, like keener senses, greater strength." I turned to Gelert. "And we can command those animals."

Without a word from me, Gelert trotted to my tent and emerged holding a cup in his mouth. He dropped it in my hand.

"Coffee?" I asked.

She laughed. "I guess house-training Gelert wasn't a problem. Thanks, just black is fine." She looked serious again. "Robert told me more."

I reached for the coffee pot hanging over the fire. "That we can change into our totem animals."

She nodded.

"You believed him?"

She took the cup from me. "Pretty well had to. He showed me."

I gave a low whistle. "He must have been sure about you."

"He said I had the right to know, that I had the Mark."

"Yes. Yes, you do," I said quietly.

"Then I'm one of you?" She leaned forward quickly, spilling coffee onto the ground.

I shook my head. "No. Not yet anyway. Very few with the Mark ever become one of the Heroka. They need assistance. Didn't Robert explain?"

"He had something to do first, something he owed someone. He was going away but said he'd be back to explain more and help me."

She got up then and walked to me slowly, as if trying not to frighten away an animal that had strayed in from the forest. She sat beside me, her leg brushing against mine, her breath cool and sweet on my face.

I noticed something else.

"Your cheek," I began, reaching out.

She turned away. "He hit me."

"Your stepfather?"

She nodded.

I turned her face back to me with a finger on her chin. "Why?"

She looked down. "He was…touching me. I made him stop."

My hand squeezed her shoulder. "Has he tried this before?"

"No," she said with a sneer. "He's always saved his special attentions for Mom." She leaned against me, her head against my shoulder. "I hate him and I'm scared, Gwyn." Her voice was low but firm. "I wish I had your strength, your powers."

Wrapping my arms around her, I held her for a long time, neither of us speaking. Technically, I had to petition the Circle first, but I was never much on policy. To me, it was her right. I thought of her mom and Tom Barker. I thought of Tom with her.

"You'll have my powers," I said. "I'll give you your birthright."

She sat straight up. "You can do that? How?"

I grinned. "Well, there's the classical method or the modern approach, plus some, uh, variations. In the classical scenario, I shape shift and savagely attack you. Unique microorganisms in my saliva and in oils excreted from my claw tips enter your blood stream through your various wounds, meeting up with some equally unique enzymes that those with the Mark carry. This results in a mutated enzyme that modifies your cell structure. You're then of the Heroka, assuming you survive my attack."

She snuggled close again. "Well, I like where you attack me, but not the various wounds part."

"Chicken. Okay, the modern version then. I make an incision somewhere you don't mind having a scar, and apply a poultice moistened with my blood."

She wrinkled her nose. "Saliva, oils, blood. The Heroka don't practice safe shifting, do they?"

"We're immune to most human viral and bacterial infections, including AIDS. Some Heroka diseases exist, but they're treatable."

"Hoof and mouth disease?"

"Smart ass."

Leiddia laughed then looked thoughtful. "So I need to get certain of your bodily fluids into my bloodstream." She moved to rest her chin on my shoulder. "You mentioned variations?"

I stroked her hair. "They involve, uh, other bodily fluids."

She leaned forward, brushing her lips against mine. "And other methods of application?"

I nodded, pulling her to me into a long kiss. "So," I asked after a while, "which method would the patient prefer?"

"I'll try," she said, between kisses, "the variations."

Several variations later, we were both asleep.

I awoke alone except for Gelert, which wasn't what I'd had in mind. Over breakfast, I pondered whether I felt used.

She was a big girl. She'd known what she was after. She'd gotten it.

Used. I shrugged mentally. Not the first time.

Leaving Gelert to guard the plane, I broke camp and set out immediately for the driver's cabin. I wanted daylight to scout the area, and assure myself that this was not a trap.

Mitch and I had divided Robbie's two targets. Mitch had planned to cover Conrad in Toronto, while I watched the truck driver, since I'd lived here after Stelle and I split. That was our plan four days ago. Somehow, Robbie had known Conrad would be away from Toronto that night at his lodge in the Muskokas, and had killed him there. Once Mitch heard of Conrad's death, he'd head here, but Robbie had a full day on him.

It was up to me.

Sunlight filtered through the canopy of trees, warming the crisp fall day as I followed familiar forest trails. My thoughts kept drifting to Leiddia and last night.

Ed's map was clear, and I made good time, reaching a rise overlooking the cabin by early afternoon. Finding a spot with good cover and a clear view of the building, I watched, listened, and smelt the breeze. I repeated this process at three other locations before I was satisfied.

The driver was there, plus three men with rifles. Conrad's death had not gone unnoticed. I could detect no one else.

My plan was to intercept Robbie on his way to the cabin, away from the attention of the guards. My problem became figuring which route he'd take.

Three sides of the cabin were open field. Approaching undetected required coming in from behind, moving down through trees from the rise where I now stood. Undergrowth choked most routes to the rise. The best path followed a forested ridge, where the forest floor was clear under the roof of trees.

I picked a spot giving a view of both the ridge and the fields surrounding the cabin, and downwind from the ridge path. After a snack of dried beef washed down with warm water, I settled behind a huge fallen tree to watch, wait, and sniff.

One hour. Darkness. Two hours. Moonrise. Four hours. Predators are used to waiting. I spent the time thinking of Leiddia. Her face and body kept shifting into Stelle's.

Midnight. The cry of a screech owl brought my head up. I shivered in the cold. The owl. A symbol of the souls of the dead in Indian myths. Shamans gave owl feathers to the dying to help them pass into the next world.

Just then, I caught a whiff. A minute later, I saw a huge shadow moving steadily along the ridge. For a moment, I thought I saw two shapes. Must have been the light. I watched long enough to guess his route, then moved to an intercept position.

Hidden, I listened. Twigs breaking, leaves rustling. Closer. Footsteps, breathing. I stepped out in front of him.

Startled, he stopped, dropping back into a defensive stance. Suddenly, I became aware of something some distance behind him. Something big and moving fast. And growling.

Shit. He'd brought help.

"Robbie! It's me, Gwyn!" The grizzly closed on me quickly, while I assessed the best tree to scale.

"Callisto! Halt!" Robbie's voice ripped the night. The huge beast rumbled to a stop at his side, snorted in my direction, then settled back on its great haunches.

Robbie was wearing jeans and hiking boots, and a denim jacket over a white T-shirt. He was bigger than I remembered. Reaching out to stroke the grizzly's hump, he looked me over. "Hello, wolf man. Been a long time."

"Too long, Robbie," I said, trying to sound more casual than I felt.

He seemed to think this over, scuffing the ground with a toe. "Come to help me finish?"

I shook my head.

"No. No, I didn't think so," he said sadly, then his face hardened. Pouncing with a speed belying his size, he caught me in the chest with his shoulder, knocking me to the ground. I rolled and sprang to my feet. If he pinned me, it was over. We circled each other.

"Can't we talk?" I gasped, forcing air back into my lungs.

"Talking's done. We talked, we sang," he snarled, "we died. Now they die."

He tried a foot sweep. I backed away. Apparently, he was keeping his teddy out of it. Maybe he wanted a fair fight, which would be like him. Maybe he was worried I might have some reserves too. About then, I was wishing I'd thought of that.

Robert was a grappler, a wrestler. My style was karate—blocks and strikes. Not needing my hands to grasp meant I had an option he didn't. Staying in a left fighting stance, I moved my right hand closer to my body where my left arm hid it.

"You're not a killer, Robbie. Let it be."

Slowly. Concentrate. Keep circling. Gradually I felt it work. Now, I had to use it without killing him.

"Let it be? You mean, leave him to you. Well, he's mine, Gwyn. He dies by my hand, not yours."

I didn't get a chance to reply. He moved in, feinting a high punch, then dropped his shoulder and threw out an arm to circle my waist for a takedown. I sidestepped and blocked the arm, spinning him around and exposing his side. I drove in with my right hand, aiming for the shoulder.

A useless target for a normal strike. But not this strike.

Three inches of claws sank into flesh and muscle. A cheap shot. In tournaments, you must announce or display shifts. This wasn't a tournament.

He roared, spinning free but tearing open the wound. He stepped back groaning, left arm limp, useless. The grizzly growled but stayed put.

"It's over, Robbie," I said softly, shifting my hand back to normal.

He sank to his knees, head bowed. "Damn you…wanted to do it myself…she was mine too…," he muttered, then looked up. "Take me with you. It's not much farther. Let me see you do it." His face went dark. "I want to see him die, Gwyn."

"What the hell are you talking about? Nobody's killing anybody. What's with you? Stelle's going to flip! She hates killing. You're going to break her heart, man." Like I did, I thought.

He stared up at me, the strangest look on his face.

Something must be added for what was lost.

A chill filled my belly.

She was mine too.

"Gwyn," he said. His voice was gentle.

A lot of us are activists. I got Stelle into it.

"Stelle's dead. They killed her…"

A female protestor from out of town also died.

He dropped his head sobbing. I stood there, feeling like the leaves at my feet—brittle, broken, dead.

I got Stelle into it.

Mitch. He'd known, of course, but he needed me to stop Robbie. Isolated and estranged as I was from both Stelle and Robbie, he'd gambled on me not knowing. With one of the Heroka already out for revenge, he knew that if he told me, I'd be racing Robbie to the kill.

Now I did know. So what was I going to do?

Standing there, I realized that I'd always thought Stelle and I would get back together somehow, sometime. I had never stopped loving her, never believed it was over. I shook my head, fighting the anger and the tears. Too much killing, she had said. I knew what she'd say now.

"Come on, Robbie," I said quietly. "Let's go home."

I'll never know who their first target really was. They must have held back after I appeared, hoping we'd kill each other. When we stopped fighting, they stopped waiting.

I had just knelt to help Robbie up, when the bullet caught him in the bad shoulder. He took another in the chest before I pulled him to the ground and threw myself flat. I looked back in the direction of the cabin. A line of figures was moving toward us through the trees. Figures with guns.

The Tainchel.

"How many?" he gasped.

"Too many."

"Those aren't trank guns," he groaned.

"I think they've given themselves a new mandate." They'd be on us in seconds, but I couldn't leave Robbie behind.

"Just... bought you... some time," Robbie gasped. The next second I knew what he meant.

Sixteen hundred pounds of furred fury burst from a thicket. Charging into the nearest group, it grabbed a man in its jaws and threw him against a tree. Rearing up three metres on hind legs, Callisto sent two more spinning through the air with a slashing swipe of her paw.

I watched transfixed. "Run, Gwyn," Robbie said. "You can't save me."

I shook my head. Bodies at her feet, Callisto turned to charge another cluster. More fell before her. The rest were firing at the grizzly but still she attacked. The shooting continued, and she was slowing. Rushing another man, she reared to her full height and fell on her screaming victim. She didn't rise.

Robbie sobbed quietly.

They put more shots into her. Silence followed. No movement. Callisto had made them cautious. She'd bought us time.

Robbie was pale, breathing in rapid gasps. The Indians believed the bear possessed great curative powers. Robbie needed more than legends.

I called out. "Listen to me! I'll make this easy. Get my friend medical help, and I'll surrender." Robbie shook his head violently, prompting a coughing fit.

Nothing.

"No deals," a voice finally replied, "and no prisoners!"

The firing started again, heavier this time. Keeping my head down, I started to concentrate on a shift. It was our last chance. They wanted blood.

Robbie grabbed my arm just as I sensed them. Too late. Something crashed down on my skull, and I slumped forward, stunned. Fighting for control, I managed to turn my head to look behind me.

Two men. Two rifles.

The firing from in front of us stopped. These two had used that sound cover to sneak up behind us. Focusing on my shift had dulled my other senses.

"Silver bullet time, freak," said the closest one. Grinning, he raised his rifle.

With a roar, a gray mass hurtled out of the shadows. Huge jaws closed on the man's neck with a sickening snap. A black blur pulled down the other gunman. Around us, the Tainchel screamed and cursed, dark forms leaping at them from all sides.

My puppy had arrived, and he'd brought friends.

Gelert shoved his face into mine, licking and whining. I could smell blood. Throwing an arm over his great back, I pulled myself up and looked around.

The wolves outnumbered the Tainchel, but the men had guns, and their initial shock was wearing off. The survivors were in a clump, backs to each other, firing outwards. My gray brothers were falling, dying. Dying for me.

I shifted. The Black Wolf came among them.

I came out of it with Gelert nuzzling my face. A dozen wolves clustered around me, wagging their tails or licking wounds. Pain screaming from a dozen places, I rose stiffly but found no major damage.

I remember little after a shift. Walking around, counting the dead, I figured it was just as well. Six wolves, eighteen of the Tainchel. No human survivors. Naked and freezing, my clothes shredded from the shift, I stripped one of the less bloody bodies for garments.

I found him lying against a tree, deathly white, soaked in blood. I knelt beside him. "Robbie?"

His eyes focused on me. "Gwyn…," he whispered, "there's a girl… Leiddia…"

"I know. She's one of us now."

He smiled. "You and I…always finding the same woman." The smile faded. "Stelle…never stopped loving you. Sometimes…I hated you for that. Sorry." His eyes closed.

I swallowed hard. "Robbie, sometimes I hated you for being with her. I'm sorry too."

No reply.

"Robbie?"

I felt for a pulse, but I knew. I could smell it. The Bear was dead. I wondered if he'd heard me.

In a nearby clearing away from the trees, I built a low bier from rocks, piling it with dried branches. I dragged him over and with a great struggle lifted him on top. Beside him, I placed my dead wolven brethren. Callisto, too huge to move, I covered with rocks.

A search of the bodies provided matches. As I returned, a great horned owl lifted up from the bier into the night. A single feather lay on Robbie's chest. I held it for a moment, then tucked it into his shirt.

I lit the wood and stood back as the fire caught quickly, roaring with the rising wind. Turning from the flames and smoke, I stopped, surrounded.

Black bears, wolves, coyotes, foxes, animals of all kinds encircled the pyre. Gelert began a mournful howl, picked up by the wolves. The other animals joined with growls, roars, and snarls.

Howl, beasts of the night. Howl for our fallen. Howl over the bodies of our foes.

I walked away through smoke and mist and trees, Gelert at my side, until we stood looking down at the driver's cabin. The guards pointed up the hill at the glow of the fire.

One task remained. They had killed my woman. They had killed my friend. Gelert growled.

I began to shift. A wolf howled.

No prisoners.

Ed was behind the counter when I came into the store the next afternoon. He looked up but didn't smile. "Made up some supplies for you."

"How'd you know I'd be heading out?"

He said nothing, but pushed the newspaper forward. I read the front page. The bodies had been found already.

"You'd better go, Gwyn."

I looked up. He had turned his back. Taking the supplies, I placed more money than required on the counter.

As I moved to the door, he spoke again, his back still to me. "Tom Barker was at the hospital last night. Cut up real bad. That nurse Vera knows said it looked like he'd fought a wild cat and lost." He turned to look at me. "He's left them. Says he's not going back."

"Probably for the best," I said quietly.

"Yeah. Assuming they can support themselves," he replied, an edge to his voice.

I walked to the door, not looking back.

"Guess there's one more beast in the night now," he said under his breath. I'm not sure if he meant me to hear. As I stepped outside, I felt that Ed was making a warding sign, a sign to keep away the beasts of the night. I hoped I was wrong.

It is night now. I sit in my camp and stare as the spirits dance in my fire. Feel their heat on my body. Feel my body an empty shell, hollow. Wait for the fire spirits to bake it hard. Wait for the animal cry in the night to shatter this shell, crumble it to dust. Listen to the wind that will blow the dust, scatter me, send me away.

Stelle is dead. Robbie is dead. I am dead too. Perhaps I have been dead these past fifteen years.

The wind stirs the ashes, dancing the flames. Gelert raises his mighty head to stare into the darkness. The fire crackles. A branch snaps behind me. I turn to see liquid night flow feline from the trees toward me. It shifts. It changes. Twin emerald fires melt to gray green eyes. Paws become hands. Paws become feet. Ebony fur fades to the pale smoothness of her skin, streams to the black cascade of her hair. Naked, she stands before me, cat-beast of the night now woman again.

I walk to her slowly, as if trying not to frighten away an animal that has strayed in from the forest. Wrapping my coat about her, I stare at her searching for something there to fill this empty shell, and she endures it.

"Then it worked," I finally say.

"It worked," she replies, a sound with the breeze. She touches my cheek, tracing a line with a long sharp nail. "I need a teacher."

"I need," I begin, before my throat strangles the words and the tears flow. "I need much more than that."

She whispers, "I love you," as we lie down by the fire, and I say I love her too. I hope one day we can mean it when we say it, as I fill her emptiness, and she begins to fill mine.

After, I watch her sleep by the dying ember light. Stelle is dead. Robbie is dead. But another of the Heroka lies beside me. The spirits do not dance. For now, it is enough.

≈

THE GREAT DIVIDE

Brent Nichols

"Alan, you just don't understand."

Camille Johnson, director of the Great Divide project, gave a sigh of exasperation, and Alan Rickard matched it with a sigh of his own. *You're right*, he wanted to say, *I bloody well DON'T understand*. With two million Canadians living in refugee camps, how could there possibly be a labour shortage? People could be trained, couldn't they? He bit back the words, though. They wouldn't help.

"You're a brilliant engineer, Alan, but I don't think people management is really your forte." She smiled, patient and sympathetic, and Alan was sourly aware that Camille, who DID have people skills, was managing him.

"I think I'll take a walk," he muttered, and she smiled and nodded, already turning away. The windows behind her looked out over a breathtaking expanse of mountains. The view went on for miles, just trees and ramparts of stone and not a human being in sight, and that, Alan decided, was exactly what he needed.

He shrugged on his coat and laced up his boots. It was warm out, but it was still October, and at this altitude a wise man respected the vagaries of the weather. He stepped out the front doors of the main building, known as the "chalet," which was done up in the faux-Swiss Alpine style ubiquitous in the tourist zones of the Canadian Rockies.

A handful of smokers were clustered outside the doors. Alan nodded to Patel, the engineer, who was deep in conversation with one of the reclamation specialists from Ottawa. Another woman moved to Alan's side as he stopped to zip up his coat.

"Alan, right?"

He nodded. She didn't introduce herself, and he didn't ask. He'd forget her name immediately. He couldn't help it. He always did.

She took a drag on her cigarette and said, "You're one of the Cold Lake team, right? An engineer?"

"Yes." He edged back as she exhaled, trying to keep the smoke off of his clothes.

She stepped closer, oblivious, and held her hand up, displaying the small iron ring that marked her as a Canadian engineer. "Me, too. We have to stick together, right?" She inclined her head toward Patel and said in a lower voice, "Especially with that lot around. It's getting so we're practically outnumbered."

"I grew up in Calgary," Alan told her. "I know what it's like to be a displaced person."

She rolled her eyes. "At least you stayed in your own country."

There was really nothing to say to that, so Alan didn't try. He just turned his back and started walking across the parking lot, grinding his teeth. Give him a design problem, a computer, some pencils, maybe a pad of decent engineering paper, and he was happy. Throw too many people into the mix and he started looking for the nearest exit.

The tension stayed with him as he cleared the parking lot and crossed the highway. He didn't start to relax until he was among the trees. A few stubborn leaves were clinging to the young broadleaf trees that were slowly supplanting the evergreens. Fallen leaves rustled under his feet as Alan hiked. There was no trail, but the trees were widely spaced, offering no obstacle. The ground rose, and he started to pant as he trudged up the mountainside.

At first he just focussed on putting one foot ahead of the other, burning away the stress of the morning in hard exercise. It was beautiful countryside, and he was going to see a lot more of it if the project went ahead.

Alan was intensely proud of the Great Divide project. It was going to change lives. It would be his legacy, a kind of immortality. He could see every technical obstacle and how to overcome it. If it wasn't for the bloody people involved…

He crossed a ridge and started to descend. That put the chalet and the highway out of sight, and Alan looked around, making sure he had his bearings. The Rockies were no place for absent-minded rambling. People died out here.

His stress began to fade under the combination of exercise and a practical occupation for his mind. Looking around at the trees and mountains helped, too. He started to notice squirrels, and the quick rat-a-tat-tat of a woodpecker had him scanning the branches around him. Soon he was smiling and enjoying himself.

He skirted the shores of a new lake, dead pine trees poking above the still water. He began to scan the ground with an engineer's eye, thinking of the challenges that would be involved with getting the water out.

He climbed a gentle slope on the far side of the lake. Somewhere ahead of him, within a few miles, was the continental divide. All the rain that fell on this side would end up eventually in the Pacific Ocean. Until the Great Divide project was finished, that is. All the rain that fell on the other side would nourish the prairies and work its way eventually to Hudson's Bay, the Arctic Ocean, or the Atlantic. Except the rain didn't fall much on the other side these days. The Pacific side got mad storms and record-breaking rainfall, with new lakes appearing every year, while the prairies crumbled away to dust.

He was panting by the time he crested the next ridge. The trees were tall here, and he couldn't see the lay of the land. It was mostly spruce at this altitude. The broadleaf trees hadn't made much headway yet.

Alan bushwhacked for a bit, forcing his way through a tangle of branches, until a trail suddenly opened before him. It was a narrow path, but well-used, the ground hard-packed. A game trail, he assumed. There wouldn't be people up here. He made sure he could recognize the spot again, and set off down the track.

Ten minutes later, Alan got the shock of his life when a figure with a gun stepped into the path in front of him. He stopped short, gaping, at first aware of nothing more than the rifle barrel pointing at his stomach. Slowly he took in more details. It was a young woman, with dark black skin and a fierce look on her face. She held the rifle tucked close to her hip, the barrel unwavering, centred on Alan. A hunter, he supposed, wearing a strange mix of clothing: tattered blue jeans and a grey nylon jacket with some sort of crude vest over top, made of what looked like rabbit fur.

She spoke, a quick jabber in a language he couldn't identify, and he held his hands away from his sides, doing his best to look harmless. "I don't understand. Do you speak English?"

Her scowl deepened in response. He revised his age estimate

downwards. She was a teenager, at the most. She had to be older than she looked, though. What would a kid be doing in the middle of the Rockies with a gun, dressed like Robinson Crusoe?

She jabbered at him some more, and made a gesture with the barrel of the gun.

"Hey, now," he said, "relax. And point the gun somewhere else, would you? It might go off."

She responded with another stream of words, and another gesture with the gun.

"I'm sorry," Alan said, "but I don't understand. Look, if I'm disturbing your hunting, I'll happily go away."

Another scowl, another stream of angry words. She stepped off the trail, and her gesture with the gun was clear. She wanted him to walk past her.

"No, thank you," he said, "I should really be going. I don't care if you're poaching or something. Nothing to do with me, right? I'll just be—"

She took a step toward him, lifting the gun to her shoulder, and her finger moved on the trigger. Alan's hands shot into the air. She jabbed with the gun barrel and he moved where she pointed, stepping past her. She moved onto the trail behind him, gesturing him forward with the gun.

"Marsh," she said.

Marsh? March? Well, her body language was clear enough. She wanted him to walk. He shrugged, kept his hands where she could see them, and walked down the trail.

When he saw the garden, he knew he was in trouble. It was a haphazard thing, rows of withered stalks curving between tree trunks beside the trail. He couldn't identify the plants, but something had been planted and cared for and harvested here. He hadn't stumbled on an annoyed hunter, or a scared poacher. It was a colony of illegals.

The trail ended at a large clearing. There were half a dozen people in sight, all of them the same dark black colour as Alan's captor. A handful of children played near the trees. They froze when they saw him. The adults he could see ranged in age from a boy not much older than the girl with the rifle to a white-haired woman who leaned heavily on a cane as she hobbled closer to have a look at him.

There was one building in the clearing, a long, low-roofed log cabin, and a boy ran to the cabin, shouting, "Jean-Paul! Jean-Paul!"

Everyone started talking at once, and Alan found he was catching a word here and there. It was French, albeit with an accent he had never heard before. Alan had studied French in school, but in Calgary, three thousand kilometres from the Quebec border, French was a subject as abstract as paleontology. He wasn't understanding much.

A crude door on the log cabin swung open and a man stepped out, straightening as he cleared the low doorway. He was powerfully built, about sixty, with steel-coloured hair and a face lined with care and authority. He wore a buckskin jacket over threadbare, patched trousers, but he moved with an unmistakable dignity. The others fell silent, watching him. He was clearly the patriarch of the little colony.

The man strode across the clearing and stood in front of Alan. He was quite tall, and he looked down at Alan with a disturbing mix of sorrow and determination. Alan gulped and decided to make the best of it.

"You must be Jean-Paul. I'm Alan. How do you do?"

Jean-Paul's voice was a bass rumble, his English accented but not hard to understand. "What are you doing here?"

"Well, I was hiking, and this young lady had a gun, and…"

"Are you alone?"

Alan pondered the question, sensing that rather a lot was depending on the answer. "Pretty much," he said, "but lots of people know I'm up here."

Jean-Paul's eyes, flat, brown, and expressionless, stared down into Alan's. Then Jean-Paul said, "Au revoir, Monsieur," and put a hand under his jacket.

Alan felt a strange paralysis seize his limbs as he watched the pistol swing up. He stopped breathing, his world shrinking to the dark and terrible circle that was the muzzle of the pistol. The gun rose, the barrel leveled, the gun was no more than a foot from Alan's chest as he saw Jean-Paul's finger tighten on the trigger, and a voice cut through the silence.

It was a woman's voice, quivering with outrage, delivering a stream of indignant French too rapid for Alan to follow. But Jean-Paul closed his eyes for a moment, and his broad shoulders slumped the tiniest bit. Some parts of the human experience are truly universal, and in spite of the desperate situation, Alan had to suppress a sympathetic grin. He was about to see a marital spat.

Jean-Paul had seemed to carry authority in every inch of his frame, but he was a pale shadow compared to his wife. She marched across the clearing, bristling, and people melted back from her. She stopped beside Jean-Paul, a short, round figure, her head not quite reaching his shoulder, and shook a finger under his nose while she harangued him.

Jean-Paul kept his head high and scowled at her, but there was something in his posture that made Alan think of a small boy trying to look brave in front of his friends. When there was a pause in her tirade he spoke, gesturing with his hands, the pistol waving vaguely in the air.

Her eyes focussed on the gun, and she spoke sharply. It sounded like, "Tuna paw soldat. Two eh, um de wheel." It was gibberish to Alan, but Jean-Paul seemed to sag.

"Ill knee paw de wheel," he said, and let his arms drop. The pistol was pointing at the ground, and Alan lunged forward, shoved Jean-Paul sprawling into his wife, and ran zig-zagging through the clearing.

He heard a bellow of rage from behind him, and he ran at a group of kids near the edge of the clearing, hoping it would make the man hold his fire. Alan cursed himself for his cowardice, deliberately endangering children. The kids scattered an instant before he charged into the trees.

Alan lunged through the forest, hands up to protect his face from branches. He stumbled and reeled: the sick taste of panic in his throat. The Africans knew the area, they outnumbered him. They had all the guns. All he had was a very small head start.

He ran pell-mell, breath sawing in his throat. He sprawled when a branch caught his ankle. People crashed through the trees behind him. He scrambled up and kept running.

His panic was subsiding, held in check by a lifelong habit of analyzing everything he encountered. They couldn't let him go, he saw. They would have to flee or face deportation. Deportation likely meant death, and fleeing deeper into the wilderness wasn't much better. They would have to give up their shelter with winter coming on, and run with children and at least one senior citizen.

The ground rose in front of Alan, and he swerved to one side. His best bet was to circle around, get back down to the chalet. He toyed with the idea of climbing, making it over the continental divide, maybe running downhill all the way back to Calgary. The stitch in his side and the fire in his lungs pushed that thought out of his mind. He would have to evade them quickly or drop in his tracks from exhaustion.

He stumbled onto a trail and turned to follow it, glad to be free of clutching branches. He was making less noise now, and the crash of branches from his pursuers was suddenly shockingly loud. Then the crackling stopped. They had reached the trail, then, and were coming up behind him.

Alan ran for his life. He was no athlete, though, and he was nearly at the end of his strength. He staggered down the path in a drunken parody of a runner's stride. His arms flapped at his sides, his face slack with terror and exhaustion. Pain burned his legs, his lungs, his feet; terror overwhelmed his suffering, made it an inconsequential thing in a corner of his mind.

Jean-Paul's conversation with his wife ran through Alan's mind as he fled. Tuna paw soldat. Two eh, um de wheel. Ill knee paw de wheel.

Tuna paw soldat. Tu n'est pas soldat? You are not a soldier. Two eh, you are. Um de wheel? Homme de wheel? You are a wheel man? What on Earth did that mean? And what he said in reply? Ill knee paw de wheel. Il n'y a pas de wheel. There is no wheel. Alan shook his head. Clearly he was missing something.

The trees grew sparse, and a ridge of rock appeared, perpendicular to the trail. No time to ponder the decision. Alan veered right, scrambling along the ridge, leaving no tracks and making little noise. If he could be out of sight before his pursuers reached the ridge, they might continue on the path and leave him behind.

The trees were getting thinner with every step, though. Alan felt horribly exposed. How long until the Africans reached the point where trail and ridge met, and saw him? Surely he didn't have more than a few seconds.

He came to a fracture in the ridge of rock. A boulder had broken away, leaving a gap deep enough to hide a man. Alan dropped into the opening, sank to a squat, and fought to control his breathing. It wasn't much of a hiding place, but he would be invisible from the trail. If no one came closer, it would be enough.

He listened intently, trying to hear above the hoarse rasp of his breathing, straining his ears for any sound of voices or footsteps. The wind rustled in the trees, and Alan found himself analyzing the wind patterns as an engineer. Was the wind steady enough to make the Great Divide project work?

Then the click of rock on rock drove all long-term concerns from his mind.

A moment earlier he would have sworn he couldn't have controlled his breathing if his life depended on it. Now he found himself taking long, slow, silent breaths. Sweat sprang out on his skin, and he could feel the thump of his heart against his ribs.

Another click, quite faint. Was the source moving farther away, or had a stealthy foot just dislodged a smaller rock this time? Alan rubbed his hands on his pant legs, craning his head around, trying to choose the best direction to run. But cover was sparse in every direction, and he couldn't outrun a bullet.

Movement, in the corner of his eye. He froze, moving only his eyeballs. It was Jean-Paul, fifty or more paces away, just his back and side visible. He was moving away from Alan, his head turning as he scanned the ground ahead of him. Even if he turned around, Alan would be hard to spot.

Silence, broken only by the rustle of the wind and the singing of blood in Alan's ears. He let himself hope, imagined a life measured in years instead of minutes or seconds.

Then boots scuffed across stone, a pebble went bouncing across the ground, and he heard the clear young voice of a girl. Jean-Paul turned, looked toward the trail, and waved.

A moment later Jean-Paul turned away, but now Alan could hear light steps coming along the ridge. There was no way she could miss him. By her voice it was the girl with the rifle. And she was coming his way.

She would shoot him, he realized. He remembered her fierceness, her determination. She would pull the trigger, and he would have a different legacy, another kind of immortality. His face would haunt her for the rest of her life.

The first time he tried to speak he only whispered. He made himself swallow, took a deep breath, and called, "Jean-Paul!"

Jean-Paul whirled, his eyes scanning the rocks, and Alan stood. He heard the girl gasp to his right, and he raised his hands. "Jean-Paul," he said, "I want to be shot by a man, not a child."

Jean-Paul came toward him, the pistol in his hand. Alan could see the girl, motionless, the rifle raised to her shoulder. Jean-Paul shouted at her, a torrent of French, and she shouted back, the gun never moving. Jean-Paul came within a dozen feet of Alan, leveled the pistol at Alan, and spoke sharply to the girl.

Slowly, reluctantly, she lowered the rifle. She slung the weapon over her shoulder and worked her way back to the trail, and Alan watched her go, knowing that his life was measured in her steps. She looked back only once, as she stepped onto the trail. Her eyes met Alan's for a moment, and then she turned and hurried out of sight.

Alan kept his eyes on the place where she had disappeared, the junction of trees and stone and sky. He was surrounded by some of the most beautiful scenery on the planet. He wasn't going to spend his final seconds staring at a scruffy murderer and his gun.

Jean-Paul said gruffly, "Thank you for that."

A sudden rage filled Alan, and he turned to face this man who was taking away so much. The Great Divide project might even fail because of this. The muzzle of the pistol loomed as large as a train tunnel, but he made himself look past it at the stiff, determined man who was going to kill him.

Alan's feet didn't want to move, but fury propelled him. He closed the distance between them one limping footstep at a time. He didn't stop until the muzzle of the gun was touching his chest.

Jean-Paul stared into his eyes, unblinking.

"Go to hell," Alan snarled. "You think you're protecting your people?" He sneered. "You've made her an accomplice to murder. Fifty years from now she'll still have nightmares about this day."

Jean-Paul's face didn't change.

"Go ahead and tell yourself you're just doing your duty," Alan said. "You're not a protector. You're not a soldier. You're a, a wheel man, whatever that is. You're a killer, and that's all you are."

He stared into Jean-Paul's eyes, and the moment stretched out until the tension was more than Alan could bear. He wanted to grab the pistol, put his thumb against the trigger, get it over with already, but Jean-Paul finally blinked, and his eyes dropped. Then the pistol barrel started to sink. In a moment it was pointing at the ground.

There was defeat in Jean-Paul's eyes, a grim awareness of the consequences, but he tucked the gun into a holster under his coat. "C'est vrais," he said. "Je ne suis pas soldat. Je suis un homme de wheel." Then he turned and trudged back the way he had come.

Alan stared into the space where Jean-Paul had stood, feeling tension slowly drain from his body. His legs buckled, and he half-fell to a sitting position on the ground.

Things would be bad for the Africans. Even if he didn't report them, they would flee. They wouldn't be caught. Their pursuers would be on foot, after all. Twenty years ago they would have been rounded up by helicopter, but not now. There was no more oil.

"There is no more oil," Alan murmured, wondering why the phrase seemed important. "Il n'y a pas d'huile."

"Huile!" he said out loud, and the sound of Jean-Paul's departing footsteps halted. Alan hauled himself up, grimacing as his stiff legs protested. *Good thing I didn't try running.* He turned and met Jean-Paul's gaze.

"You're not a wheel man," Alan said. "You're an oil man."

Jean-Paul nodded, and shrugged. "Once," he said. "But the oil is gone. Now, I'm…" He glanced down at himself and shrugged again.

Alan felt himself grin. "You don't have pipeline experience, by any chance?"

Jean-Paul squared his shoulders, and a note of pride crept into his voice. "I helped build the Buffalo Line from Nigeria all the way to Kenya," he said. Then he seemed to deflate. "But that was another life. I have to go."

As he turned, Alan blurted, "But I'm looking for people with pipeline experience!"

Jean-Paul turned, incredulity and disgust on his face. "There's no oil here," he snapped.

"No," said Alan. "But there's water. So damn much water it's forming new lakes and killing trees. Fifteen kilometres from here and two thousand metres up there's the continental divide, and beyond that, there's a wasteland that used to be the breadbasket of Canada." He hobbled forward, feeling his legs tremble with every step.

"I'm from Calgary, Jean-Paul. My city's dying. It's on a river that used to be fed by a glacier. It flowed through Calgary and irrigated thousands of hectares of some of the best farmland in the world. It's all dying now, but it can be saved. We're going to pump water out of these new lakes and dump it into the headwaters of the Bow River."

Alan staggered over to a small boulder, sat down, and started kneading his thigh muscles. "You know," he said, "it's going to take me days to recover from this little misadventure. But I forgive you. We've been scouring the world for people with pipeline experience. You know pipelines, and you know the local geography. You're a Godsend, Jean-Paul."

The big man stared down at him, his dark face impassive, and Alan chuckled at the sheer absurdity of the situation. Adrenalin and stress might have been factors, as well. His dry chuckle wasn't too far removed from hysterical laughter. "Do you want a job, Jean-Paul?" he asked. "You could pretty much set your own terms. I know some people who will sponsor you for citizenship. If they have to sponsor an extra dozen or so people as well, they won't squawk."

It wouldn't be a problem, he knew. There were a few exceptions, like the woman he'd talked to outside the chalet, but for most Canadians, immigration was a thorny, conscience-provoking issue. A country with so much space couldn't keep its doors shut while entire cities sank beneath the ocean. It didn't take much justification to get an immigration claim approved these days.

"Well?" said Alan. "Don't you have anything to say?"

Jean-Paul stared down at him, and the silence stretched out. Then Jean-Paul said, "Are you telling me the truth?"

Alan spread his arms. "Why would I lie? You already let me go." They stared at each other some more, and then Alan added, "There is a condition, though."

Instant suspicion clouded Jean-Paul's face.

"You have to help me down the mountain," Alan said. "I can barely bloody walk."

Jean-Paul came forward then, heaved him easily to his feet, and let Alan hang on his shoulder for support. Together they turned their backs on the continental divide and set off toward civilization.

〰
〰

DIGGING DEEPER

Susan Forest

Dyan's finger stiffened on the worn book as her niece practiced her reading. "Hush, Kiora."

Something scraped gravel outside the open door. An animal? No. Boots? Couldn't be—this early in the morning was no time for Paolo to be back. Disquiet crept into Dyan's gut. Who was there? Cradling Malcolm as he suckled her breast, she darted a glance at her sister, heavy with child, hand halted on the butter churn. A shadow flickered in the patch of August sunshine streaming into their earthen home through the thick, timber-reinforced doorway.

Arilla blanched and jumped rigidly to her feet. "Kiora!" Her voice shrilled in the silence.

Cold gripped Dyan's stomach. Oh, God. Oh, God not—

Men from the city, ring of raucous faces in the wintry night, sneering down at her on the frozen ground, hard fingers prying her apart. Cruel women kicking her ribs, cutting her face. Arilla's husband, Nathan, bleeding as Dyan ran—

"Dyan!" Arilla squealed. She shoved her daughter through the curtained doorway in the plank wall that divided their home in two, and disappeared after her. To save herself.

Dyan gripped Malcolm to her, scanned the earthen room wildly, gut braced, muscles electrified, stumbling back toward the trap that was their back room. Oh, God, where was the club? Where was the—

"Dyan?" It was Paolo—

Paolo? Good God in Heaven—

Relief drained all will from Dyan's limbs and she fumbled to her chair, trembling. Malcolm lost his latch on her nipple and wailed, then comforted himself and sat up. She struggled stupidly to button her blouse.

"Paolo?" Arilla's scowl appeared in the bedroom doorway. "You

212

asshole! What do you think you're—"

Granddad shuffled through the passage, wheezing, lungs bad from the chlorine gas attacks of the water wars. His bent, ragged form filled the small opening, plunging the dim room in shadow. Their home had been dug—and abandoned—by some previous owner, like a horizontal mine passage into the hillside where the slope met Fish Creek's floodplain. It was cool and dark and smelled of earth and mildew, a haven from the heat even in mid-August.

"Granddad?" Arilla hastened to help the frail man to the chair Kiora had abandoned. "Tully? Is he hurt?" Arilla waddled hurriedly to the water barrel to bring him a cup of flat, clay-tasting water.

Choking and red with heat, Granddad nodded once, then shook his head, gratefully accepting the cup.

"Too many questions." Dyan set Malcolm on his feet and taking Granddad's hat, hurried out into the arid yard.

Tully, skinny and sweating in the searing sun—but unharmed—extended one leg while Paolo scraped congealed, cracking mud from his pant legs.

"Water!" Dyan knelt in the dust beside her husband, touching the soft moistness on Tully's trousers, desiccating in the sun. "Finally!"

Paolo scowled, attacking the flaking mud on Tully's other leg with strength born of anger. A strand of his hair pulled loose from the braid at the base of his neck.

"You frightened us." Dyan sat back on her heels. "We thought you were gang punks from the city."

"No," Paolo growled. He threw down his muddy stick and nodded to Arilla's boy, who ducked into the house. He leapt to his feet and kicked the dry earth. "This *fucking* glacial till."

"What happened?" Dyan pulled mud from the discarded stick and scooting forward, scraped clay from her husband's pants.

Paolo looked down at her in disgust from beneath his straw hat. "Shovel broke."

Their shovel.

Their only shovel, that Paolo'd had when she met him, that Paolo'd had to fight for, when waves of immigrants forced their way across the border in the south, looting and burning, forcing the mass exodus that destroyed the city. That Paolo'd used as a weapon to defend her the night of the rape. The night Nathan died.

"The shaft?" Dyan asked, hoping. But she knew better. The curled and chipped bowl of the shovel had been thin and weak for years. They'd continued to use it, even when it rusted and bent. All of them, loathe to return to the city.

"No." The word fell flat and hard into the blistering compound. "The blade." Paolo waved ineffectually at the smooth hardwood pole leaning against the tool shed, black metal collar screwed to one end, with a few centimetres of lacerated steel gleaming in the sun. The broken bowl lay in the dust beside it.

Paolo had said—how many times?—tools. *Always* had to be put away. *Always* had to be cleaned. *Always* had to be cared for, oiled, sharpened. Their lives depended on their tools. He'd harped at Tully— only thirteen, but doing a man's work—for days when he broke the axe handle last fall, even though Granddad pointed out that the axe was old, and at least they could fashion another handle from wood scavenged from the big houses lining the hills above Fish Creek Park.

But a blade—a steel blade—was different.

"How did it happen?" Not that it mattered.

Paolo ground his heel into the sand. "We were down five metres. Five metres! Jesus, Dyan, two metres below the previous level. This whole country's nothing but rocks!"

Rocks. Gravel. This spring, the water in the old well dug into the creek bed failed to rise above half a metre, and each day the level sank. Thursday, they woke to discover the well suddenly dry. Not damp. Dry. Paolo, Granddad and Tully dropped everything to dig it deeper. Surely if there was water anywhere, it would be beneath the creek bed.

Dyan tossed the stick aside and rose to her feet, slipping her hands around her husband's waist. "But you found water!"

"We're almost there, I swear." Paolo held her to him. "I bet if we go back right now, there'll be fifteen centimetres—maybe more—in the bottom." He disengaged himself. "Another metre and we'd have enough to get through the summer. Shit!"

She pulled him back to her, laying her head against his shoulder. The muscles along his spine were rigid with fury.

"I don't know." He let his hands drop to his sides. "Maybe I got too excited, dug too hard—"

"You can't blame yourself."

"Well, who the—" He clamped his mouth closed and pushed

himself from her arms, turning to the house. "I'm going into Calgary."

She blinked, stunned in the oppressive heat.

Calgary.

Paolo ducked through the passageway into the house.

"Wait—"

Inside, Arilla sat at the table, one hand protectively spread across her pregnant belly, the other around Tully, who sipped from Granddad's cup, face lowered and pale with understanding. Feral dread pinched Arilla's cheeks, as Paolo brushed past her into the back room. "He can't go to Calgary." Her words were flat, final.

Anger blazed up in Dyan's chest. They'd had this discussion.

"They'll get him. Just like Nathan last winter." She lifted recriminating eyes to Dyan. "We can't survive—you, me, Granddad, the children—without him. He can't go."

"He's going now?" Kiora caught Malcolm before he could turn his head away, wiping his smeared nose with a rag. "But it'll be the burning hours soon." Her eyes were on Arilla, and on the opening where Paolo had vanished. At ten, the girl was too young to understand the full impact of the shovel's loss, but the set of her shoulders was filled with apprehension.

Granddad wheezed, his thin frame leaned over the table, elbows propping him up. "I could go with him."

Arilla threw her hands in the air. "Shit, Granddad!"

Dyan rested her rump against the sideboard, studying the dirt floor. "Talk sense, Granddad." She glanced at Tully, shrinking nervously into his chair.

Arilla gripped Tully's shoulders. "Don't even think about it."

Dyan rolled her eyes and stalked to the bedroom.

In the thin light that seeped through the curtain, Paolo sat on their bed, his back turned, scratching the steel rod over his flint. The candle on the night stand awaited the shower sparks on the bowl of thistle fluff.

If Paolo went alone, the punks in the city would kill him. She should—

No! Panic curdled her stomach and drenched her in sweat. She put a hand on the dresser to steady herself.

Paolo scraped, scraped, scraped at the flint. Obstinate.

"It's not your fault."

Scrape. "It doesn't matter."

Susan Forest

"Yes, it does!" The blockhead! "Arilla's right, for once. You can't just rush off into Calgary—"

Paolo's fingers, and the rasp of the flint, stilled. "Dyan."

He was punishing himself. That's what he was doing.

Paolo turned, his dark shape barely visible in the dim room. "How much water do we have?"

He knew how much they had. They all knew how much they had. Half a barrel.

"It won't last until tomorrow night."

"We can make a shovel." She knew she was being unreasonable. "We can dig with a flat rock. We can dig with our fingers. You already found water. If it rains—"

"It's not going to rain."

It was not going to rain.

Dyan remembered rain. The sound of its patter on pavement, in puddles. Its surprising, rejuvenating scent. When she was a girl—her birthday was in June, Calgary's rainiest month—how many times had she looked out the window, waiting for friends to dash under umbrellas up the walk from their parents' cars to bring her gifts—a Game Boy or an iPod or a movie pass—as the rain streamed down the windows and bounced in rivulets to the gutters?

Paolo was at her side, arms around her. "Hey." His forehead touched hers. "I'm going to be careful. They won't even know I was there."

"They killed Nathan." Her throat closed, and only his nearness made it possible for her to force the words out. "Do you even know if you can find a shovel in Calgary?" Her voice sounded querulous and high-pitched, even to herself. "Every back yard tool shed, every hardware store, every Canadian Tire closer than Southland Mall—"

"Calgary's a big city." His voice soothed, seduced.

"If only we had neighbours. Someone . . ." She tried to breathe past the tightness in her chest.

Paolo kissed her forehead and she felt stiff in his arms, unyielding.

He sighed and returned to the bed, leaving her bereft. Sitting by the bedside table, he scratched again at the flint, spraying bright sparks into the tinder. The damn tinder!

Scrape, scrape—

The fluff caught, and the tips of the dry twigs. Paolo blew gently— oh, so patient with his candle, so patient with his plan to rescue them

216

all, so unfeeling toward her—

The twigs blossomed into a tiny flame, and Paolo held the candle wick to the heat.

Last winter. They'd tried, then, to replace the shovel. She and Nathan and Paolo.

Eight months. Not enough time to defeat memory. The ragged men—young men, powerful men with flick-sharp knives and hard fingers, harsh laughter, stink and sweat. With rocklike, rasping penises willing to be lubricated by blood. And women. Cruel, desperate women, unshockable women. Ready to kill, that they might live a day longer. An hour longer. The broken surfaces of the city canyons with their dark interiors. Gang territory, and the hard men and harder women knew it intimately.

"Don't go."

Paolo took his carefully mended backpack down from the top shelf. He stood it on the bed, reaching into its empty space without responding.

Rage rose up inside her and she wanted to pound on that impassive back, scratch his skin, make him see. "Don't you love me? Don't you—" She gripped her hair in agony. She was being unreasonable. Pushing him from her, when she wanted to draw him closer. But all she could see, all she could feel, was the house without his smell. The wind, blowing down the valley, without his laughter. Her bed, her skin, her lips without his touch. Malcolm's tears. Arilla and Tully and Grandpa and her, trying to manage the plough. Trying to dig the well...

Paolo straightened, hands in the sack. "Dyan."

She could not speak through her ragged breathing.

He held out a patient arm and she fell into his warmth, his strength. He squeezed her close and kissed her hair. "I don't want to go."

She revelled in the warmth of his body, the strength of his grip. She lifted her face and touched his long dimples where they disappeared into his wiry, gray-sprinkled beard.

"This isn't foolish bravado."

She tried to protest but he put a finger across her lips.

"I can't sit here and die of thirst. Or trudge across the desert, hoping to find a place to live where there is water. Watch you—all—die of thirst, one by one. Malcolm. Granddad. Everyone."

Her throat ached. His body, solid beneath her hands, pressing against her length, was as precious to her as her own.

"I have to," he said.

"I—should—" She brightened to mask the sudden churn of anxiety that swept through her.

He shook his head. Automatic. Forsaking. "No. You're not coming with me."

Relief drenched her, the smothering weight of panic eased. The disburdening was a solid thing, a comfort to cling to. Safety.

She hid her face against his chest in shame.

"Hey."

She shook her head, mute.

"If anything happens. They need you," he whispered into her hair. "Malcolm needs you. Arilla's baby is coming soon. She can't care for everyone. Not even herself. Tully's just a boy." Paolo lifted her face with hands filled with concern and pleading and apprehension. "You're strong. You have to be here."

"*If* anything happens? You bastard!"

"Dyan—"

"They killed Nathan last time we went looting." She pounded his shoulder with a fist. "Look at Arilla—a widow, goddamn it!" She trembled, cold with the image of the windblown horizon, waiting, empty, for his return.

Paolo caught her fist in his hand and cupped the back of her head in the other. He kissed her forehead. He kissed her eyes. He lifted her chin and kissed her mouth.

Oh, God. Was there nothing she could do?

His kisses had not been enough. Time raced, relentlessly robbing her of her future, and Paolo had broken from her. "If I can make good time, find an unlooted store or garage before late afternoon…" He grimaced at the pack, thoughts elsewhere. "They won't expect anyone in the burning hours."

And then he was moving in and out of the room, packing the things he'd need in his sack, while she sat on a chair, watching, remembering moments of joy—lovemaking, laughter, summer nights.

Malcolm toddled into the room and she caught him up, burying her tears in his belly to make him giggle and squirm. Malcolm, their miracle.

She'd been working in the garden, picking peas, the day he was born. A hot day in early July. The peas, green but thin, had to be harvested before they dried on the vine.

Paolo worked, three rows over, stooping in his straw hat. Dyan felt the water trickle down her legs and straightened, catching his eye.

"What?" he'd asked.

She grinned with her secret, massaging the rock-hard muscles of her belly. "I don't think we're going to finish picking the peas today."

He'd frowned in confusion, then reading her face, split into a howl of laughter. He danced through the garden to plant a sloppy kiss on her face and whooped for Arilla to come.

But Malcolm had not been easy. With the breaking of her water, the contractions came on, sudden and strong, but Dyan paced and squatted and lay on the bed deep into the night as her worry grew. Paolo and Arilla took turns massaging her back, and she moaned and breathed through waves of pain broken by waiting for pain. She remembered lying on the bed in the dark, and the candles being lit and Arilla washing her hands to check her perineum.

And the look of fright on her sister's face.

"What?" The fear infected Dyan, infected Paolo.

Arilla licked her lips, her face drawn in the candle light. "It's not a head."

Paolo's gaze, vulnerable, on Arilla's face— "Breech?"

And the word conjured stories. Death.

A thin wail escaped Dyan's throat.

Arilla was no doctor.

Paolo knelt by Dyan's side and took her hand. "Dyan! Look at me. Breech babies are born healthy."

She clamped down on her cry.

"You're going to do this." Ferocious will burned in his eyes. "We're going to help you. I am *not* going to let anything happen to you."

Impossible, hollow promise, but she grasped at it, believed it, drew strength from it. She gripped his hand with the next wave of tightness seizing her belly, her muscles crushing down on the tiny life jammed into the cruel narrowness of her pelvis.

Again.

And then—the sudden, overwhelming necessity to *push*.

"Wait." Arilla's fingers on her perineum.

Susan Forest

"I *have* to push. Now!"

"No—"

The great, overpowering need. The pressure, the pain, the—

"She's tearing." Arilla's voice in the dark.

Paolo squeezed her hand. "I'm here. You can do it."

"He's coming."

And then a breath. Exhaustion. Respite. "He?"

Paolo pushing her hair back, wiping her face, laughing and crying at once. "A boy."

"We're not there yet." Arilla, peering over her, the halo of her face in the candlelight. "Paolo. Put a blanket on the floor. Dyan. Squat."

Gravity. Yes.

Paolo put down the clean bedding and held her hand as she repositioned herself, knelt in front of her, arms around her shoulders. She held him, took deep breaths, readying for the next wave, oxygenating her blood. Could the baby survive being half born, being folded—

And the pain rose again, and the undeniability of the urge—

"You're doing it." Arilla behind her, hands beneath the baby.

A sensation on her thighs—

"He's out—" Arilla's hands pressing on her, fingers pushing on the edges of her vagina. "But not the head—he's stuck! Push, Dyan! Push!"

Oh, God.

She held her breath and leaned forward, pushing—

A sudden expulsion—

A cry—

"Whoa!" Arilla exulted. "He's slippery!"

And Dyan laughed, and Paolo laughed and kissed her, and Malcolm yelled in outrage—

And the baby was in her arms, swaddled in clean sheets, covered in blood and vernix, and she was on the bed holding him, with Paolo beside her—

She wept then, for his life. For his miracle.

She wept now, and released her boy to toddle to Granddad in the other room.

I am not going to let anything happen to you. Paolo's words. His presence, his belief in her. The heat of his conviction. These had saved her. Saved Malcolm. She smiled gratefully up at him through her tears.

Paolo, tightening the strings on his backpack, turned away, grieved frustration on his face.

"No." She went to him. "I'm not stopping you."

He stuffed food into the sack, her words making no dent in his anger. He misunderstood.

She stilled his fingers. "I'm coming *with* you." *Her* promise, *her* presence, *her* belief. For him.

"Dyan, we've—"

"I've decided." She slid her hands around his waist. "I'm not afraid any more. At least—I'm not paralyzed any more."

He frowned with doubt.

"When Malcolm was born. When we struggled with him and he almost died. You said, 'we're going to help you. I'm not going to let anything happen to you.' Do you remember?"

He shook his head faintly. "No."

"You did." She stroked his beard. "Now I'm saying it to you. This thing needs to be done. All right. We plan. We have a strategy. We protect ourselves the best we can." Fierce conviction rose up inside her. "And Heaven help anyone who tries to stop us."

He bit his lip.

"I mean it, Paolo."

He put a fist to his mouth, squeezing back words, face gray in the thin light of the candle. "Dyan…"

She tried to read the source of apprehension in his face.

"You're not the only one who's afraid." He pushed a strand of hair from her eyes with trembling fingers. "I'm afraid. God, I am so afraid."

"Because of what they did to Nathan?"

"That—but—" He tucked the strand behind her ear and gripped the back of her head. "I'm afraid for you. Don't you see? I can't let you go back there. I couldn't—take it. If they were to get their hands on you again—"

"We won't let that happen. And if it does, I will survive it. We will survive it." She placed her fingers over his. "Ever since last winter. The rape. Nathan's death. We've known this day would come. But we did nothing! We've all been paralyzed. By memory. By monsters made enormous from fear."

"I'm *still* afraid. Terrified."

She took his bearded face in her two hands, and it was warm and rough. "We don't have that luxury any more, Paolo." She shook her head gently. "We can't let fear dictate our decisions."

His gaze flicked again to his backpack on the floor, and the pinch returned to his cheeks. "I know."

"We take our best shot. Grandpa stays. He'd only slow us down. Arilla and Tully are still ruled by fright. They'd freeze and need rescuing. You and I, Paolo. We go."

He took a deep breath and let it out slowly.

"Together. Whatever happens."

Surrender crept into his eyes, then, and he gave a slight nod. A hint of a smile touched the corners of his lips.

She touched her forehead to his. "And we are going to succeed. I promise."

～

WATCHING OVER THE HUMAN GARDEN

Jean-Louis Trudel

The sun was setting over the Mediterranean off the coast of the Cinque Terre, staining the entire horizon blood-red. Aboard the train rushing from one tunnel to the next, passengers craned their neck to glimpse the reddened waves. The artist looked out only once, unmoved. Neither mystery nor marvel; somewhere in India, a forest was burning.

In Riomaggiore, the artist left the train and the furnace breath of Italian summer enveloped him with a fiery intensity that sucked the sweat right out of his pores. Temperatures aboard had been cooler, thanks to the graphene panels topping each car and the nanocrystalline solar cells powering the stingy AC. Nothing more was needed; the train was far from crowded.

Hard to remember now the cool air of the Haida Gwaii rainforests. He tried to hang on to his memories of the windy beaches of the Pacific archipelago off Alaska, pounded by the surf and strewn with storm-tossed driftwood. Even though he was back within sight of the sea, half the planet now lay between him and his native isles, so much greener than the sun-blasted hills of Italy.

The train station, too, was almost deserted. Tourists were rarer. Expense wasn't the only factor, even though increasing fuel costs had turned leisure travel into a high-end luxury. Not to mention the cost of the raw materials needed to build a plane or operate a railway. The artist had never even considered a trip to Europe until his work had turned him into an overnight success in China. Yet, if the train station now seemed much too large for the handful of people in sight, it was for an entirely different reason.

As he headed towards the station, he suddenly noticed the person he was meeting hadn't come alone.

He let the other passengers pass him and exit the platform. The old were far more numerous than the young. The demographic bust in Europe and North Africa had choked off the wellsprings of yesterday's flood of tourists, while cost now discouraged most travellers from North America or East Asia.

He shifted mental gears before walking up to his welcoming committee. He needed to think like an entrepreneur, not an artist. Adopting the role of the businessman, however unsavoury, had spared him from being taken in on more than one occasion. And added to his bank account, to boot. Not that he liked playing the part. He was a sculptor, not an actor.

The young man he was expecting to meet was accompanied by a square-jawed person in uniform—a woman, he decided after a moment's hesitation—and a man who seemed to cultivate a nondescript air. Which had to be a performance, too, the artist decided.

"Rufus Boyko," he introduced himself.

"Lieutenant Marzouki," responded the military person in flawless English. "Of the Union Army in the Maghreb."

"And I'm Arthur Huang," said the other, also in English but with a dreadful accent. "Of the Strategic Analysis Agency in Brussels."

"A science fiction writer?" Rufus guessed, wondering if he should consider Huang a fellow artist.

"On occasion."

Rufus turned to the young man caught between the two. He scrutinized him briefly, checking the familiar features one by one: curly black hair, thin moustache, even thinner eyebrows, slightly hooked nose, smooth unlined skin...

"And you must be Paolo della Chiesa, I assume?"

My native guide and porter, he kept himself from adding.

The Italian functionary nodded.

"You look older," he blurted out with youthful frankness.

"It's a crazy old world," Rufus said curtly, leaving much unsaid. More and more now, he felt as old and wounded as the planet. Scarred beyond remedy.

They had spent a lot of time communicating by screen, but flesh always looked different than pixels. Paolo had taken delivery of his carving equipment and stored it in a safe place. At least, he was supposed to have done so. Rufus suddenly recalled that he hadn't received any confirmation of his equipment's arrival. Did the presence of Marzouki and Huang indicate that something had happened to his tools?

"We've been named to your support cell," explained Marzouki, without actually explaining anything.

"Why in the world… What's going on?"

"Didn't you read your mail?"

"On the train? I was taking in the scenery."

"There's a problem. We've gathered a crisis group at the hotel to discuss the situation."

"With whom?"

"Li Chutu will speak for your sponsors."

"In the flesh?" Rufus sputtered, quite amazed. If China's delegate to the World Environment Organization was making the trip from Beijing, the *situation* had to be desperately serious.

"Of course not. He will be represented. And the mayor Enzo Boscaiolo, for the intercommunal council of the Cinque Terre."

"But what is there to discuss?"

It couldn't be a mere technical glitch or even the loss of his equipment. Neither his trusty old oxyacetylene torch, his diamond drill or his waterjet cutter, nor the rest of his equipment, were valuable enough to justify this much official fuss.

"As I understand it, you intended to use the stones of a house that fell into the sea to build your totem pole."

"Not a totem pole, a *gyáa'aang*," he corrected her, using the Haida word. "The first of a series, in fact."

"Well, the owner of the house in question refuses to let you do so."

The hotel was built on the heights overlooking Riomaggiore, overlooked in turn by a row of wind turbines erected on an even higher crest of land. Distance muted the roar of the blades, softening it into a faint buzzing as obstinately nagging as a mosquito's whine. The building was recent and it had been selected for that very reason by Paolo della Chiesa, by special request. Graphene roofing, smart thermostats, locally sourced cuisine; no chance Rufus would forget why he had come to Italy.

If he hadn't come all this way for nothing, in the end.

Rufus was happy with the choice of the Cinque Terre, a protected enclave on the Italian Riviera between Genoa and La Spezia. Olive groves clinging to steep slopes, terraced orchards planted with lemon trees, villages dotting the sea shore, nestled in rocky coves or perched atop bluffs, their old stone buildings preserved with tender loving care, the colours bright in the noontime sun... The Cinque Terre were a symbol of the Old World. Of an entire way of life made to last, and yet now in danger of disappearing forever. Of the European conviction that wanting the future to be just like the past would make it so.

The Haida knew otherwise.

As soon as he was checked in, Rufus headed for the hotel's storage room to have a look at his carving equipment. Everything seemed in working order and everything was accounted for.

He kneeled to caress, almost tenderly, each one of his tools. They were his last link to everything that he had lost over the years and his only means of keeping his lost ones close.

He only straightened when he recognized Paolo's brisk footsteps.

"Everything's in order, whether or not I need them. Thanks."

"You're taking it well."

"Finding solutions to problems is part of an artist's work. We *make* things—they don't make themselves. Few people realize how practical artists can be. Art may be the stuff of dreams, but the stuff of art can be, well, obdurate."

"People too can be stubborn. What will you do with this old woman? You're a celebrity. You can ask for the full weight of Rome and Beijing to bear down upon her. You could just roll over her."

"The difference between things and people is that you can talk to people."

"Do they still believe in democracy in your country?"

"I believe in giving people a chance. Say, where is everybody?"

"They're eating. Come, I'll show you."

The first meeting of the crisis group was scheduled for the late evening, when it would be cooler. Marzouki and Huang had sought shelter in the hotel bar and ordered panini. Rufus didn't join them. He had eaten on the train and they were chattering in a language he couldn't identify, though he supposed it was French. Or perhaps German. As far as he was concerned, it could have been Russian or Algonquin, for all he knew.

He looked inside the restaurant and was immediately greeted by the hotel manager

"We can clear a table for you, if you want."

"I didn't think it would be so full."

Spring was now the end of the high season, as temperatures soared and discouraged most tourists. Which was also why the train had been half-empty.

"Don't mind the crowd. We've had to open the air-conditioned shelter in the basement earlier than usual for the older folks of Riomaggiore. Such a hot spring. But they won't bother you. They're under strict orders not to speak to the customers."

"Of course."

In fact, the restaurant was strangely quiet, with most of the temporary guests muttering softly to unseen correspondents, ignoring even their neighbours at the same table.

Speaking perhaps to personality emulations of dead relations... It was a new app and the new rage in a world where the aged outnumbered the young, one where many acquaintances of the old were no longer counted among the living.

Rufus smiled sadly. Why be surprised that so many rejected science in a ghost-haunted world?

"I suppose this is where breakfast is served."

"Yes, *signor*."

"I'll just wait in the lobby."

He took out his screen and concentrated instead on the headlines of the current news threads, ranked according to the volume of comments. The experimental Indo-Chinese fusion plant in Bhutan had just come online and yielded its first megawatts—commercial fusion was heralded as being just twenty years away. The reconstruction of Venice in the Po River plain was almost complete—the second inauguration of Saint Mark's Basilica was slated for the following month. The market for the DNA of extinct species was reaching new heights—experts feared that it was a bubble on the verge of bursting just like coral farm valuations had collapsed ten years earlier.

He was checking the weather forecast when Mayor Boscaiolo entered the bar. Rufus folded his screen and stuffed it in his shirt pocket. The official was old and thin, almost wiry, his skin browned by the sun like bread crust. Rufus introduced himself again.

"Is that a Haida name?" the mayor asked in carefully enunciated English.

"No."

The artist did not elaborate. Read one way, his name embodied the entire history of European colonization in the Americas. He did not wish to rehash it. He took advantage of the arrival of the Chinese spokesman to turn away from the Italian alderman.

"*Ni hao*," he said to the newcomer, bowing.

He knew little more. On his trip to China, he had been provided with a bevy of interpreters, translators, and assistants. Once upon a time, he would have reveled in his new-found status, but he no longer made art to scratch that particular itch.

"*Buona sera*," replied the other man with a slight smile.

"You shame me."

"I've been in Italy longer than you were in China."

Rufus found out that the representative of Li Chutu was a Chinese scientist working in the Ligurian mountains, who had been pressed into service for the occasion. Zhou Hanqing, as he was called, did not seem to appreciate the honour of serving the Chinese government, but he was wearing the heavy shades that would let Li Chutu see what he saw. Clasped around Zhou's neck, another piece of apparatus would manipulate his vocal chords through direct stimulation of the vagus nerve in order to make him say whatever Li was saying. The prosthesis would lend the scientist the precise intonations of the bureaucrat, if need be by paralyzing segments of the vocal chords.

Lieutenant Marzouki emerged from the bar to show the way to the meeting room. Rufus kept her in the corridor for a moment to have a word in private.

"What I fail to understand is why this *situation* concerns the military in any way."

"Ever since the U.S. default, China has been the Union's main weapons supplier. I'm here to remind the Italian government that without the Union Coast Guard, nobody would be stopping the human contraband that Italy keeps complaining about to Brussels."

"I thought you were in the ground forces."

"Correct. I was on leave in Genoa when I was ordered to cut it short and get here on the double. Still, the migrants from Sub-Saharan Africa that we're stopping along the Maghreb front lines would have to be stopped by the Coast Guard otherwise. So, one way or another, it makes for fewer climate refugees in the port cities of the Union. All I need to do is show up to play my part. Roger is the one who's going to speak for the Union."

"Roger!"

"Of course. The future is a specialty of his, after all."

They joined the others inside the room. Paolo had taken care of the technical set-up. Earbuds linked to simultaneous translation software were available. Rufus only spoke English in addition to the Haida language, but he guessed that most of the meeting would take place in another language. Italian, most probably.

He put on the earbuds. Everybody else did as well and Boscaiolo spoke up.

"It falls to me to chair this meeting as it is taking place on the territory of the Cinque Terre and as it concerns one of its citizens. Such is the express wish of the Union, which places a high value on the completion of this project. Or so I've been made to understand."

The mayor looked meaningfully at Paolo della Chiesa, who had no doubt conveyed Rome's wishes in this matter. Rufus was still listening to the translation in English, coming out of the earbuds with a lag of a few seconds.

"So, what is at issue?" Boscaiolo asked rhetorically. "The signora Guidoni is refusing that the stones of her old house be reused to fashion a work of art. However legitimate, this wish of hers may not be legally enforceable. I've received contradictory legal advice regarding the status of the debris, but one thing is clear. The highest authorities of the Euro-Maghrebi Union support signor Boyko's project. What is less than clear to me, though, is why he chose a house from the Cinque Terre for his art project."

Boscaiolo was scowling as he looked to Rufus. His features betrayed a mix of puzzlement, exasperation, and regret that he had been dragged into their dispute.

"Fate," Rufus answered. "Fate alone. Not that I believe global warming to be just a matter of chance. But it's led to more rain, in the form of shorter, more intense bursts, especially in hotter countries. The end result? Much greater run-off. Where droughts and fires have reduced forest cover, that means instant torrents. Or landslides. Add in the accelerated shore erosion as a consequence of rising seas and harsher weather, and what do you get? Every week, at least one house too close to the shore that is swept away or simply collapses. It seemed important to me that the building material of my first *gyáa'aang* embody what the project is all about. It was statistically certain that, somewhere along the coast, a house would crumble into the sea within a week of my coming to Italy. Instead of choosing a region at random, I let Nature decide. Since we are all in the hands of Gaia."

"And where do you intend to build this totem pole of yours with good Italian stone from the former abode of the signora Guidoni?"

"I don't know yet. I was going to look for a spot. Ideally, it will stand on the shore, so that the images of the *gyáa'aang* will be able to look out to the sea. And the base will be out of reach of the highest tides. For now."

"I thought the goal was to measure sea level rise."

Huang leaned in to intervene.

"Not today, no. Tomorrow."

Rufus realized the writer had been called in to defend the project because he spoke Italian with a fluency that left the translation software struggling to keep up. As he warmed up to the topic, Huang began describing the project with an eloquence Rufus himself would have been hard pressed to match. The artist in him sat back and admired the show Huang was putting on.

"All the shores of Europe are threatened by sea level rise," Huang was saying. "However, the last fifty years have shown that people rapidly get used to transformations of their own environment. Much too rapidly, in fact. The Spanish coast is turning into a desert, the French coast already looks like part of North Africa, and the Italian coast is overgrown with cactus and palm trees. Yet, nobody notices anymore. Some people may wax nostalgic about the winters of long ago, but it's just a conversation starter. The Union wants to create tangible reminders of how things are changing. For the Italian coast, it was decided to raise concrete markers of the sea's relentless rise. And the project presented by Rufus Boyko, of the Haida nation, was selected because it was wholly original while incorporating a specifically Italian historical allusion. The traditional totem poles of Haida Gwaii are carved in wood, but signor Boyko carves in stone. And while the traditional *gyáa'aang* was chiefly devoted to commemorating a clan mythology or important events, these new totem poles will be a warning of things to come. They will remind us of the futures that may still be averted."

Rufus shared a bemused look with Marzouki, who nodded as if to say: "How he talks!" Boscaiolo took it all in, a stunned look on his face, and he gasped for air before coming up with a question.

"What's Italian about these totem poles?"

"Do you know the Roman temple of Serapis in Pozzuoli, near Naples? Its surviving columns still bear the marks of their subsidence below the level of the sea for centuries, due to local variations in land level. Nothing to do with climate change, everything to do with magma fluctuations below ground. The British geologist Charles Lyell made these columns—mostly standing above sea level again in the nineteenth century—into a symbol of the great consequences that may ensue over time from the operation of causes that produce imperceptible changes in the short term. His doctrine influenced, in turn, Charles Darwin when he came up with the theory of evolution. The project of the artist we have among us is intended to emphasize this basic truth in as tangible a manner. The totem poles of the Boyko Project will be raised just above the shore line, as close as possible to current sea level, so that any rise will become immediately visible. The extent of the accumulated changes, within ten years or by the end of the century, will be grasped with a single look. As in Pozzuoli."

"Or like the stelae raised in Japan to commemorate a tsunami, indicate how far inland it had come, and warn later generations of a tsunami's dangers."

The remark by the Chinese representative threw Huang off-balance for a moment. Rufus bit on his tongue to keep himself from protesting. The reference to another reality, far from Italy, might confuse the issue. He also fought a shiver produced by the uncanny impression that he'd just heard Li speak as if he were in the same room. He'd met Li Chutu in person when he'd been to China. The intonation and cadence of the words uttered by Zhou were essentially identical! They brought to mind thoughts of supernatural possession. The technology of speech transmission had improved to an uncanny degree since the last time he'd seen it at work.

"Thank you," Huang said in Italian

"What is the role of the signor Li in this matter, precisely?"

Boscaiolo's question drew out ever more detailed explanations from Huang. The World Environment Organization had elected to support the Union's project. A multi-year contract would cover the building and sculpting of a number of totem poles scattered along the entire Italian seashore, most often near ports, to stand on shoals, rocky beaches or low headlands. The signor Boyko would design each *gyáa'aang*, but delegate the actual carving to assistants.

Rufus had his own reasons for accepting, but it also guaranteed him years of gainful work.

"Given the Union's other priorities, the project needed outside financing. The signor Li agreed to be the go-between who would raise the money from Chinese ethical funds, once they were persuaded to support Rufus Boyko's vision."

Rufus stifled the laughter bubbling up. Huang was carefully avoiding any mention of the real purpose of China's *virtuous* investment funds in doing so. While gaining face by financing a good deed, the Boyko Project would also remind Westerners that they remained above-average emitters of greenhouse gases and so were largely responsible for the sea level rise the totem poles would reveal over the coming years.

In fact, China deserved a prize for sheer gall. Twenty years earlier, its own emissions had raced ahead of those of all Western countries. By concentrating within its own borders most of the world's industrial output, it had inherited the corresponding volume of carbon emissions.

On the verge of becoming a pariah nation, China had struck gold when its biotech companies had developed genetically-modified cyanobacteriae able to convert carbon dioxide into biofuel. Massive volumes were needed, but China already controlled industries that belched carbon dioxide by the tonne: steel refineries, cement factories, plants synthesizing ammonia to make fertilizers and explosives…and coal-burning power plants, of course.

As a manufacturing superpower, China had taken full advantage of the new bacteria. It had to. In order to remain the world's workshop, it needed to brake the rise of oil prices. Container ships couldn't sail on solar power alone, they needed a carbon-rich fuel. And so China had become a massive producer of biofuels.

From the point of view of climate change, the conversion of carbon emissions into hydrocarbons only delayed the addition of carbon dioxide to the planet's atmosphere since the fuel would eventually be burned by ships or planes connecting East Asia's factories to the rest of the world. There was an efficiency gain, but the end result remained the same. The atmosphere's carbon dioxide would increase in the end and temperatures continue to climb. Except that these emissions were no longer originating solely in China and the profits allowed the Chinese to fund art projects in Italy.

The same thoughts must have crossed Boscaiolo's mind, as he uttered a loud sigh before turning to the Roman functionary beside him.

"Signor della Chiesa, do you have anything to add?"

The young man shook his head.

"It's much clearer now," the mayor concluded, still scowling. "I will discuss the situation with the signora Guidoni and we will meet tomorrow to recap."

The mayor rose, took off the earbuds, and left the room without another word. Even less of a happy camper than he'd been initially, Rufus guessed.

Marzouki and Huang left together, the former holding the door for the latter. Rufus was betting that the two of them would end their long day in the same room and the same bed.

Paolo took his leave and the last one left was Zhou Hanqing, taking off the telepresence rig one piece at a time. Without his glasses, the scientist no longer looked like the older Li Chutu.

"So, like me, you're far from home…" began Rufus.

"In my case, it's for work, not pleasure," Zhou retorted, his voice still husky.

The man massaged his throat, as if surprised to hear his own voice coming out of it at all.

"In my case as well," Rufus protested. "I make a living from my art."

"But your art affords you the pleasure of creating new beauties. It's not quite the same for me."

"Isn't there satisfaction too in finding solutions to a problem or staying on the trail of a hot, new idea?"

"True enough, but I'm older than you. I may have exhausted some of the thrills of research."

Rufus stared at him. Zhou's deeply lined skin revealed a life spent outdoors, in the sun, but it wasn't a sure sign of advanced age. His hair was greying slightly, though that too wasn't conclusive.

"How would you know?"

"I looked up your public profile."

Rufus laughed. He kept forgetting that the contract from the World Environment Organization had turned him into a public figure.

"Let me buy you a drink," he said. "If the bar is still open."

Zhou didn't turn him down and Rufus ordered an Italian wine that couldn't be found anymore in North America. Glasses were filled and refilled. The scientist explained that he was working on the biological control of the tropical diseases gaining a foothold north of the Mediterranean. The first inroads of chikungunya dated back to 2007, but malaria, bilharziasis, and trypanosomiasis were now competing to sicken and kill Europeans. Torrential rains and the rewilding of abandoned farms had made it easier for the vector species to take root.

"We've eliminated malaria in China," Zhou bragged. "And not only with artemisin. Parasites always end up adapting. We needed a way to react faster than the parasites. Faster than evolution."

"Is that really possible?"

"We can choose to target the parasite or the vector. If we go for the vector when it's too old to reproduce, it won't be able to pass on any resistance genes. But any hope of a lasting solution is an illusion. Life adapts. Much better to aim for speed and selectivity. Not all mosquitoes or worms are vectors. If we can eliminate the infected ones, the other ones won't matter."

"Is that really possible?" Rufus asked, repeating himself.

"Aptamers are amazing molecules," Zhou almost shouted. "When I was a student, almost nobody paid any attention to them. And yet, they've allowed us to develop a *selective* form of biotechnology. Capable of targeting infected vectors. Capable of inspiring even an unimaginative scientist like me with new and risky ideas."

Rufus poured himself another glass, repeating himself. Which was probably why the bottle was already half-empty. He tried to be encouraging.

"I'm sure you're as creative as any artist I know."

"I'm sure of it, too. Especially when I tell myself that fighting tropical diseases would be simpler if temperatures stopped rising."

"So many things would be simpler if people were willing to consume less energy," Rufus said, thinking of the inhabitants of Haida Gwaii who still remembered how their ancestors had lived from fishing, hunting, gathering, and a bit of gardening.

"Or if there was an easier way to produce the energy we need without burning hydrocarbons."

"We're halfway through the twenty-first century. Too late now to convert all of the world's cars to run on electricity, but…"

"No, it was so much easier to keep on burning hydrocarbons. Electric cars were too expensive." Zhou shrugged. "Too bad for the corals."

"Not that anybody was going to deprive ambulances of the gas they needed. Or racing cars."

"Or tanks."

And so the climate continued to warm, with the attendant consequences. Recurring droughts, the burning of half the rainforests of Australia, the disappearance of many endemic plants and animals from southern Africa, backed into the ocean by the southward shift of climate zones… The same thing had happened in mountain areas. The fauna and flora of the higher reaches had retreated over the years, losing foot by foot the struggle for survival in a warmer world. The last sky islands were increasingly isolated, reduced to occupying the very summits. Soon, the survivors would be forced to fly away or die.

The carved figures of Rufus were meant to remind humanity that Earth too was a sky island whose habitable surface was shrinking as a result of global warming.

"What if it was possible to keep temperatures from rising…" said Zhou, tantalizingly.

"By reducing carbon emissions?"

"At the source."

"But the source is humanity."

"Precisely. In the same way I can target a malaria-infected mosquito, I could target, well, the individuals who are responsible for the greatest amount of greenhouse gases. The ones, for instance, who dine on red meat, since each kilo of beef implies massive emissions. The largest eaters consume so much red meat that the arteries grow inflamed. Selecting an aptamer capable of locking onto the relevant molecules would be child's play."

"Targeting them…to infect them? To eliminate them?"

"Why not?"

"Seriously?"

"The world has gone mad," Zhou said flatly. "With every car, with every coal plant, with every cattle farm, we are digging our grave. And what are people doing? Nothing. If the world is going to be saved, it will be in spite of itself."

Rufus attempted to catch the eye of the scientist, but Zhou had slipped on again the dark shades of the telepresence rig. Unable to guess what the scientist really thought, Rufus tried to needle him.

"Without humanity…"

Zhou pounded the table angrily.

"Without humanity, life on Earth is doomed," he cried out. "Pluricellular organisms appeared half a billion years ago, and they will disappear in another half billion years, when the Sun makes it too hot for them. The unicellular eukaryotes may last a bit longer. And the prokaryotes that go back to the first cooling of the Earth's crust will hang on for an extra billion years. Ironically, life will end because of a lack of carbon dioxide, bringing photosynthesis to a full stop, outside of a few geothermal sources. Undersea volcanic vents, and the like."

"Without humanity."

"Yes. Only humanity can alter the great feedback loops that convert the atmosphere's carbon into sedimentary rock and the carbon from biomass into various fossil forms. Natural gas, oil, kerogen… Only humanity can save life on Earth when the time comes."

"So, you don't really believe mass murder is necessary?"

"I don't think the development of consciousness happened by pure chance. Life is a phenomenon that is bent on its own perpetuation. For a century now, humans have taken up all the available room on Earth, and more, at the expense of other life forms. Humanity and its commensal species weigh more than all of the planet's other animals put together. Over ninety per cent of the planet's vegetation exists in ecosystems we've modified. Earth is our garden, now, and it must continue to be, otherwise life on Earth won't endure. The only question is, signor Boyko, and I want your opinion as an artist: are we any good at gardening?"

Zhou tried to pour himself another glass, but the bottle was empty. He got up and went looking for the *gabinetto*.

Rufus didn't try to keep him. Time to turn in. The encounter had left him confused. He'd learned not to put too much weight on this kind of drunken talk, late into the night. The morning after, it all blew over. The world was off-kilter, everybody knew it, and apocalyptic scenarios came easily to the best minds. Not that it was easy to distinguish sense and nonsense, not when he was firmly in the camp of the artists and visionaries, not when he worked with more elusive realities than most.

After all, he spoke to spirits in order to clothe them in a likeness and let them speak to humans. Both the spirits of the dead and those of the unborn. Did a man such as Zhou hear other spirits when he played with such dark schemes?

And what did this signora Guidoni think of his own schemes?

He found his room on the top floor. In spite of the AC that encouraged visitors to close doors and windows, each bed was surrounded by a drapery of mosquito netting, all the way from ceiling to floor. Now that malaria raged once more north of the Mediterranean, such precautions were a selling point.

Rufus was getting undressed when his screen fluttered in his shirt pocket like a butterfly fighting to free itself from a child's hand. He took it out and unfolded it to read the message.

The signora Cristina Guidoni, of Manarola, wanted to meet him on the corniche.

Rufus was greeted by a grey dawn when he left the hotel in the early morning to walk down to Riomaggiore. A brisk wind was blowing out of the leaden sky. Somewhere in Italy, it had rained and Italians were rejoicing. It wouldn't last. Once the sun came out, the cool morning would be forgotten.

Only a few watersellers were out in the streets, hawking bottles of desalinated seawater as if he were the last tourist of the season. And if midday temperatures stayed as hot as the last few days, he might be.

Cristina Guidoni was an old woman dressed in black. Keeping the faith by sticking to her own traditions, thought Rufus, recognizing a kindred spirit. She waited for him near the entrance to the pedestrian-only corniche snaking its way along the bluffs above the sea, from Riomaggiore to Manarola.

"Will you come with me to Manarola?"

"You speak English!"

"I used to be an English teacher. Well?"

Why had he thought of her as some fisherwoman or peasant's wife?

She stared at him, curiosity flickering in her deep-set eyes. Rufus had been half-afraid he'd have to deal with some demented housewife, but his opponent was just an old woman, stooped, her white hair wrapped in a piece of cloth and her hand clasping an outmoded smartphone. Did she think she could convince him to go elsewhere?

What did she hope for?

The waves pounded the rocky shore with an insistent beat. The cry of seagulls punctuated the drumming: low, muffled, unceasing. For the first time since he had come to the Cinque Terre, Rufus relaxed. The familiar smells and sounds of the surf exorcized all the strangeness he'd been struggling with. The Pacific surf along the shores of Haida Gwaii was not so very different. A bit more powerful, perhaps.

He breathed in the freshly-cleansed sea air.

"My husband liked to take walks along the corniche after a storm, on mornings like this one," Guidoni declared. "He used to say the air was electric, but I've forgotten why."

The old woman was standing by his side, leaning on the balustrade. The tone of her voice was neither plaintive nor accusatory. She was merely stating what had once been a fact, and now was but a memory.

"It's beautiful," Rufus said as he took in the seaside scenery. "I think fate was right to bring me here. My first *gyáa'aang* will stand where it was meant to be."

"Would it be so tragic if you didn't get to build your totem poles?"

The question didn't surprise him. He expected it. Yet, he did not have a ready answer for her.

"Here is what I believe. We've been acting for far too long as if nothing tragic was happening. It's not working. Nature doesn't ask us if dying is tragic or not. Nature kills and gives life. Nature gives life and kills. Period."

"And if you don't build *one* totem pole, right here in Cinque Terre?"

"The sea will rise anyway. I know."

A wave crashed with unexpected force, throwing up spray all the way to the level of the corniche. A seventh wave? Rufus watched the sea retreat below them.

"You're making predictions. Me, I remember when people predicted we'd all be starving by now."

"Some are starving."

Population had increased faster than food production. Desertification in Africa and North America had taken fertile lands out of the picture, while rising temperatures had eroded the benefits some crops drew from rising carbon dioxide levels. Improved infrastructure had reduced the losses once incurred by harvests going from the farmer's fields to the end consumer, but famines ravaged Sub-Saharan Africa nonetheless.

The survivors huddled in the refugee camps of the Maghreb along the Mediterranean coast or swelled the roving militias and gangs that plagued the ever narrower strip of settlements.

"You speak of it as a mere coin toss. If it's just a matter of chance, why should I care?"

"Because there is still a chance something can be done. I came up with this project because I hoped to change things. If, one day, my *totem poles* rise on dry land and our descendants ponder in vain their forgotten purpose, I will have achieved something really great." He shrugged. "On the other hand, you could be right. If temperatures keep rising, the famines in Africa will be just the beginning."

Environmental catastrophes had struck so very quickly that a world population of nine billion now seemed like such a miracle that fear had waned in the parts of the world spared by the worst. The oil peak had been offset by energy savings; the replacement of silicon by graphene yielding a new generation of highly efficient information technologies. But waning fear could give rise to complacency.

"I'm concerned with the here-and-now," she objected. "I won't live to see the end of the world."

"You have to look further."

"Why? My husband worked for years to make our house into a home. I won't claim that all of the stones and debris that fell into the sea bear his mark, but the wreckage does include pieces of wood that he had sawn, planed, and sanded. Dinner plates we used to eat on. And so many more keepsakes of our life together. Signs of our love for one another. Please leave them alone. I beg you."

"Here," Rufus said suddenly.

There was a gap in the railing where an old set of cement stairs went down to the shore. They left the corniche, walked down, and ventured on the rocks dripping with spray. The artist held the hand of the old woman as she followed.

"This is where I wish to raise the first *gyáa'aang*," Rufus explained finally.

"Aren't you afraid the waves will tear down your totem pole? How are you going to keep a pile of stones standing through all the storms to come?"

"The stones will hold together just like the drums of ancient columns. With tongue-and-groove joints. The carved stones will fit together to make up an organic whole, one that will be as solid as a monolithic shaft. One that will stand up to the occasional hurricanes, at least until the sea becomes too uniformly hot for them."

"In the Mediterranean? There have never been any hurricanes here."

"That's what they used to say about the northern Pacific, before one wiped out an entire Haida village, ten years ago."

"Is that why…"

He didn't let her finish, eyes half-closed to imagine the sculpted stone.

"The rough work will be done with a waterjet cutter. The joints will be carved with a diamond drill. And faces will be chiselled into the stones, one by one… There will be a seagull, I think. And the face of Roger Huang as he explained better than I could have how this is going to speak to coming generations. There may also be a bear cub, playful and mischievous. To finish it properly, I'll use a laser to subject the stone to such high heat that the top layer will crackle and fall away, creating a raspy surface not unlike that of hammered bronze."

The old woman refused to look at the spot that Rufus was gazing at as he already imagined the raising of the *gyáa'aang*.

"You're so far from home," she said. "Why did you really want to come here to make your totem poles?"

"To save whatever I can from drowning. I didn't decide to reuse stones already swallowed up by the sea out of mere whim. That choice is intended to have meaning, for the generations to come—and for me as well. Really, it's no secret. You can find out why by looking up my public profile."

"What are you talking about?"

"The death of my only son, Jacob."

This time, the old woman did turn around to look Rufus in the eye. What she read in his face dispelled any doubt she might have conceived. The artist was also a father.

"How did he die?" she asked softly.

"When the earthquake struck Vancouver and Seattle, three years ago, it happened just as the spring floods were cresting. The Fraser River had never been so high. And since part of the city is built on the delta's alluvial fan, the combination of the floods, of sea level rise, and of a tsunami proved fatal, worse than in New Orleans or Bangkok. My

240

son drowned in a plane that was caught on the runway by the surge before it could take off."

"I'm so sorry."

"Me, too."

Rufus took out his screen to snap a picture of the spot he'd just identified, where the base of his future work would fit into the rocks washed by the waves.

"Ever since," he added, "I include the face of my son every time I carve a *gyáa'aang*. My hands know each of his features. Sometimes, I turn him into an eagle floating high above the sea. Sometimes, I turn him into a fish swimming in the sea. But he's always there. Now that he's one of the dead, he can also watch over the living. A *gyáa'aang* is not magical, signora Guidoni, but it can be sacred, even when it is facing the future."

"I understand."

"Do you have a picture of your husband?"

Before answering, the old woman went to stand on the spot Rufus had snapped. She looked away from the artist and gazed out at the sea. A pained whisper escaped her chapped lips.

"Yes, I'll give you his picture. I really do understand. We watched other people, we watched the skies, we watched all around, but we failed to watch the horizon."

The End.

AUTHOR BIOGRAPHIES
(IN ORDER OF APPEARANCE)

Hayden Trenholm is a Parliamentary policy analyst and an award-winning playwright and author. He has twice won the Aurora Award for short fiction and been nominated for Best Novel three times. His novel, *Stealing Home*, was shortlisted for the Sunburst Award. He lives with his wife, Elizabeth, in Ottawa.

Camille Alexa is a dual Canadian/American living in the Pacific Northwest. Her work appears in *Fantasy Magazine, ChiZine, On Spec,* and various anthologies. Her short fiction collection *Push of the Sky* received a starred review in *Publishers Weekly* and was nominated for the Endeavour Award. More information at www.camillealexa.com

Julie E. Czerneda is a best-selling, award-winning author/editor. Her latest novel was *Rift in the Sky* (DAW) and up next will be her first fantasy, *A Turn of Light* (DAW 2013). Julie co-edited *Tesseracts 15: A Case of Quite Curious Tales* with Susan MacGregor. For more, visit www.czerneda.com.

Jennifer Rahn is the author of two dark fantasy novels, *Wicked Initiations* and *The Longevity Thesis*. She has also published short stories in several anthologies, including *Podthology, Strange Worlds, The Wickeds*, and the *Horror Addicts Disaster Relief Anthology*. While not writing, Jennifer researches brain tumours at the U of C.

Christine Cornell lives in Fredericton, New Brunswick. She has published non-fiction and taught Science Fiction and Fantasy courses at the university level but "Hard Water" is her first fiction sale.

Fiona Moore is an expatriate Canadian, living and working in London. She is an industrial anthropologist at Royal Holloway, University of London, with research interests in emerging economies and the social impact of globalization. Recent publications are in *Asimov's, Interzone* and *Dark Horizons*. She is co-owner of a SF audio production company, Magic Bullet Productions.

Stephanie Bedwell-Grime has published eleven novels and more than sixty shorter works. She is a five-time Aurora Award nominee. Stephanie welcomes visitors to her website at www.feralmartian.com

Isabella D. Hodson is originally from Ottawa but currently lives in Penticton, BC. She has published several poems and short stories, the most recent a fantasy story in the 2012 anthology, *Ride the Moon*.

Agnes Cadieux has written over fifty articles on art and culture for various magazines in Ottawa, but her passion will always be science fiction and fantasy. She has previously appeared in the *Aurora Wolf Literary Journal* and Wicked East Press. You can connect with Agnes at: http://writingdancinganddragons.blogspot.ca/

Kate Heartfield is the deputy editorial pages editor at the Ottawa Citizen. Her short fiction has appeared in *The New Quarterly*, the *In Our Own Words* anthology and *The Puritan*.

Derek Künsken lives and works in Ottawa. His fiction has appeared several times in *Asimov's*, as well as in *Beneath Ceaseless Skies*, *Black Gate* and *On Spec*. He is a 2012 Aurora Award nominee in the short fiction category.

Derryl Murphy is a writer, editor and soccer enthusiast, currently living in Saskatchewan. His novel, *Napier's Bones*, was shortlisted for the 2012 Aurora Awards. Other books include *Cast a Cold Eye*, written with William Shunn, and the upcoming collection, *Over the Darkened Landscape*.

M. L. D. Curelas lives in Calgary, Alberta with two humans and three guinea pigs. Her short fiction can be found in the anthologies *Damnation and Dames* and *Tesseracts 14*, and she is the editor of *Ride the Moon*, an anthology of modern moon myths and legends.

Ryan McFadden is an award-winning author from London, Ontario, and co-editor of the *10th Circle Project*, a shared-world project at www.the10thcircle.com. His most recent publications are in *Evolve 2: Stories of the Future Undead, Broken Time Blues*, and *When the Villain Comes Home*. Follow him at ryanmcfadden.com.

Claude Lalumière (lostmyths.net/claude) is author of the collection *Objects of Worship* and the mosaic novella *The Door to Lost Pages*. He's currently working on his eleventh anthology, *Masked Mosaic: Canadian Super Stories* (with co-editor Camille Alexa). He's the co-creator of lostmyths.net and the Fantastic Fiction columnist for *The Montreal Gazette*.

Gerald Brandt is a prairie boy with a penchant for rock climbing, but no affinity for heights. He was a computer programmer for twenty years before leaving to be a stay-at-home dad and focus on his writing. You can find him at www.geraldbrandt.com, as well as on Facebook and Twitter.

Kevin Cockle's stories have appeared in a number of publications, including *On Spec Magazine, Tesseracts 13* and *15, Gaslight Arcanum, Evolve* and most recently *Ride the Moon*. He lives in Calgary, Alberta.

Douglas Smith's stories have appeared in two dozen languages and thirty countries. He has three short story collections, *Chimerascope, Impossibilia*, and the translated *La Danse des Esprits*. A two-time Aurora Award winner, Doug has also been a finalist for the John W. Campbell Award, the Sunburst Award, and the CBC Bookies Award.

Brent Nichols is a technical trainer and reformed stand-up comic currently living in Calgary. In addition to comedy monologues he has written for *Sheherazade*, a computer game from Black Chicken Studios. "The Great Divide" is his first fiction sale.

Susan Forest is a two-time Aurora nominee and winner of the Galaxy Project adjudicated by Robert Silverberg, David Drake and Barry Malzberg. Her stories have appeared in *Analog, Asimov's, OnSpec, AE Science Fiction Review* and *Tesseracts*, and her collection,

Immunity to Strange Tales, is forthcoming from Five Rivers Chapmanry in 2012.

Jean-Louis Trudel is a science fiction writer. He was born in Toronto and now lives in Quebec City, Quebec. He currently teaches part-time at the University of Ottawa. He writes in both French and English, has won several Aurora Awards and the "Grand Prix de la Science-Fiction et du Fantastique québécois."

Fiction by Hayden Trenholm
Available in trade paperback or ebook at
www.bundoranpress.com

Defining Diana
ISBN 978-0-9782052-0-1

"Defining Diana manages to feel true to both its hardboiled
and its futuristic roots. The writing presents an interesting mash-
up of pulp dialogue and well-researched scientific theory. The
novel's characterizations of the SDU's troubled and conflicted
officers is also top notch. Trenholm's solid police procedural, set
in a cyberpunk Calgary, will appeal to mystery and science fiction fans alike."
-- Chadwick Ginter, www.mcnallyrobinson.com

Steel Whispers
ISBN 978-0-9782052-3-2

"A taut, near-future police procedural with a plot as sinewy
as that cyborg snake in Blade Runner. Hayden Trenholm works
the mean streets and millionaires' mansions of mid-21st century
Calgary and comes up with a winner."
-- Matthew Hughes, Author of the Tales of Henghis Hapthorn.

Stealing Home
ISBN 978-0-9782052-5-6

"Hayden Trenholm doesn't just steal home — he knocks the
ball out of the park with this stunning conclusion to one of the
best SF/Crime crossover series ever written. Bravo!"
-- Robert J. Sawyer, Hugo Award-winning author of WAKE